The Referee

by

James Kirvin

Referee (ref'a re'), n. v.-n. 1. a person to whom something is referred for decision or settlement

Published by Hastings Publishing, Inc.

Printed in the United States of America

ISBN 0-9707659-0-8

To Cathryn, my wife and best friend

Prologue

April 2, 1996

Elizabeth Anderson's day began uneventfully. She awoke at the usual time, prepared a simple breakfast, and walked to school to teach her seventh-grade class. She said goodbye to her students at 3:05 P.M., unaware that she would never see them again. She corrected some papers until 4:10 and walked out of her classroom, almost bumping into her fellow teacher, Mary Bartlett.

"Oops! Sorry, Mary."

"Where are you going in such a hurry?" the much older teacher asked.

"I'm meeting an old friend from college for dinner. I don't want to be late."

"An old boyfriend?" Mary asked smiling, not knowing much about Elizabeth.

"No, an old roommate. I haven't seen her since we graduated."

"Have fun," were Mary's parting words.

Elizabeth walked to the restaurant and arrived before her old roommate, Fran. A hostess showed her to a booth where she waited, wondering which one of them had changed the most. She knew it wasn't going to be Fran. While she sat alone, the eyes that had watched her for the previous two weeks continued to observe her every movement. Fran arrived at about 5:20, twenty minutes late, reminding Elizabeth that some people never change. By 7:30 both Elizabeth and Fran were happy to part company. The dinner conversation was strained, as they were both now very different people than they were in college. They left the restaurant each saying what a wonderful time they had, and each convinced that they would never make the promised calls.

Elizabeth started her journey to her apartment on the Upper East Side. It was a warm spring evening, and Elizabeth still felt a glow from the three glasses of wine she enjoyed at dinner. Even if she were completely alert, she would not have noticed she was being followed. She stopped to window-shop at several of the small fashionable shops along the way, and even granted herself the unusual luxury of purchasing a small leather purse that she had seen several weeks before, which was now significantly reduced in price. As she paid the shopkeeper, she smiled, not looking like someone who had less than three hours to live.

Elizabeth walked north on 2nd Avenue to its intersection with 77th Street, where she lived, and turned east. At 9:50 P.M., as she walked past a small alley only a few hundred feet from the safety of her apartment, she was pulled into the darkness and struck with such force that she tumbled over and over, eventually landing in a contorted pile on the hard blacktop. Slightly dazed, and bleeding profusely from her mouth, she tried to scream, but only a muted grunt emerged. As she struggled to stand, a blow to the abdomen drove her back to the pavement. She landed on her chest and felt the excruciating pain as her lungs deflated. She could taste bubbles of blood in her mouth as she desperately gasped for air. Something struck her face, and then her arm, and then her face again. *My God*! she inwardly screamed, *what are they doing to me?*

Elizabeth was in constant motion, none of which was initiated by her. Blow after blow was delivered to her dazed body. She tried to crawl away, but the motions of her severely broken arms and legs were grotesque attempts at best. Still the questions raced through her mind. Who were these people? Why were they beating her? What had she done? What was happening to her? She knew she was dying, and soon began to drift into that twilight area between life and death that at least offers some peace. Pain was felt, but dimmed as the event became more distant. As she started to leave her body, she faintly heard spoken words, but they had no meaning. The last happy thought she had was that it would soon be over, that peace would come and the pain would stop. As her head was pounded into the pavement, Elizabeth left the world, confused, but relieved. Mercifully, the last indignity she would suffer—the violation of her vagina and rectum with multiple loads of semen—occurred only to her body, not her soul.

The lifeless body of Elizabeth Anderson, 1994 New York City Teacher of the Year, was beaten further and thrown into a dumpster in the back of the alley where it lay overnight, a monument to the occasional horrors of humanity.

Chapter 1

Raul Sanchez was a very happy man. He had a good job at the post office and a lovely family. He wasn't that bright, and was easily led, but he provided well for his wife and three children. He lived in a rent-controlled apartment in Greenwich Village and was able to walk to work. His kids went to St. Mary's Catholic School, which was also within walking distance of his apartment. On his way home from work he often stopped at the little Spanish bodega on the corner to pick up chouricos, his one junk food weakness.

Raul loved New York. It was so much better than Puerto Rico. He would sometimes walk with his family for hours, just taking in the sounds, sights, and smells of the city. He felt that the best thing that ever happened to him was his parents moving to New York City twenty-six years before. He visited his grandmother in Puerto Rico when he was sixteen, and that one visit was enough. He had no desire to return. At age thirty-one he was building a very nice life for his family.

It was 3:26 P.M. on May 10, 1996, a beautiful sunny day, and Raul hurried home from his 7:00 A.M. to 3:00 P.M. shift at the post office. There were no jobs of this quality for anyone like him in Puerto Rico. He was proud to be a postal employee, and worked hard to do his best. He planned to stop and get some chouricos and be home before Juanita picked up the kids from school. His paycheck, with a lot of over-time pay, was in his pocket. He planned to surprise Juanita and take the family out for an early dinner. Life was good. Unfortunately, he only had eleven minutes to live. That was all it would take the tall man with the blue eyes to change the Sanchez family forever. The man felt sorry for the kids and Raul's wife, but ultimately that did not matter; Raul was about to die.

As Raul walked into the bodega, he greeted its owner. "Good afternoon, Mr. Mendez," Raul said respectfully.

"Hello, Raul. I just got in some fresh chouricos."

Raul smiled and walked directly to his favorite section of the store to pick out three sausages. There were several other shoppers in line waiting to check out, and he waited his turn. Just as he was about to place his purchases on the counter in front of Mr. Mendez, a tall man wearing grubby clothes ran into the store, pushed in front of Raul, and stuck a gun in Mr. Mendez's face.

"Please give me all the bills in the register!" he demanded in English draped with a heavy Spanish accent. "Hurry up!" he added.

Mr. Mendez opened the cash register drawer and reached for the money. He had been robbed many times before, and he knew exactly what to do. He just wanted the man to leave as quickly as possible, without hurting anyone. As Mr. Mendez pulled the money out of the drawer, the tall Spanish man turned around, looked directly at Raul, and said quite loudly, "What did you say? Mind your own fucking business, man!" The man then shot Raul in the face, and pandemonium broke out in the store as Raul's head exploded, splashing his blood and most of his brain over the customers who were standing behind Raul on line. The man turned back to Mr. Mendez, grabbed the money, and ran out of the store. Raul lay dead on the floor, his right hand still grasping his three sausages.

The police arrived shortly thereafter. Mr. Mendez described what happened as best he could, but he was an elderly man and extremely upset. Patrolman Juan Cortez's report said it all.

"At approximately 3:37 P.M., an unidentified man ran into a grocery store operated by Mr. Julio Mendez. The man produced a gun and demanded money from Mendez, who was working the counter. The perpetrator had pushed in front of the victim, Raul Sanchez, who was standing in line about to pay for his purchases. Mendez was reaching for the money in the cash register when he heard the perpetrator say to Mr. Sanchez, 'What did you say? Mind your own fucking business, man!' Then the gunman shot Sanchez once in the head, grabbed the money, and ran out of the store. No one ran after the killer, who vanished in the busy afternoon crowds. Mendez did not hear what Sanchez said to the gunman, but he felt it must have been something very bad to upset him so much. Until Sanchez said whatever he said to the killer, the tall man seemed calm, almost courteous to Mendez. The store had been robbed six times before, but no one had ever been shot, much less killed. Mendez described the perpetrator as part white and part Spanish. His features were white, but his skin was brown. He was tall, probably about 6'5", as he towered over Mr. Sanchez, who was about 5'8". There were no distinguishing marks. He spoke with a heavy Spanish accent, but used English. His clothes were shabby. Mendez felt he might be a homeless man. No one in the store saw the events much different than Mendez." It was a perfectly accurate report, which really said nothing.

The tall, blue-eyed, brown-skinned man evaporated after the shooting. Within two blocks of the Mendez store he became a tall white man, completely dressed in white, with a stethoscope draped around his neck. He walked in the direction of St. Vincent's Hospital. He was now a resident going in for the evening shift. Of course, if he were stopped he would be able to produce the proper hospital identification, which would show that he was Dr. John Grimes, a second-year surgical resident at St. Vincent's Hospital. No doubt, Dr. Grimes would be quickly sent on his way. The tall, blue-eyed man did not make it to St. Vincent's; he headed to the subway and eventually made it back to his starting point.

If the blue-eyed man could have read the police report, he would be proud of his work. The desired effect was achieved. He did not doubt the outcome for a minute. The last emotional feeling Sanchez would ever have was not fear, but surprise—total surprise. He had no idea what the man with the gun was talking about. Raul Sanchez never opened his mouth to say a word to the tall man, and he died with a puzzled look on what was left of his face.

The detectives who caught the case were Brown and DeSantis. They would not get one lead. They would not expend much energy on a case with no possible solution, and they quickly concluded that this was just another botched burglary—just another one of the hundreds that occurred in Manhattan each year. They told Mrs. Sanchez that her husband was just in the wrong place at the wrong time. No further investigation was contemplated, although it would remain an open case for quite some time. The official department policy under Chief of Detectives Sal DeCicco was that all homicides were open until solved. In reality, some were more open than others.

Chapter 2

Brian Walsh sat quietly in his chair and stared at the portrait of his family on the wall. He was having a problem focusing clearly. He was astonished that he was able to convince Maureen to marry him almost three decades ago. She was so beautiful. He looked at the portrait again and carefully focused on the woman. The portrait was over ten years old but she didn't look much different today. She still had the same deep blue eyes and the shining auburn hair. He loved her more than anyone could ever know.

The Scotch was making him incoherent. His mind was wandering. He looked at his wife and couldn't believe she was causing such trouble in his usually very compartmentalized life. He wasn't sure how much Scotch he had, but lately this was becoming an all too frequent way for him to get to sleep.

God! Look at those kids, he thought. Brian was extremely proud of his three children, but he always gave the credit to Maureen for raising them to be as accomplished as they were. He continued to stare at the portrait and, without thinking, reached down to the lower right side of the chair and flipped the switch. The whole chair began to vibrate as expected, but it probably would have been a good idea to move the glass of Scotch from the armrest before setting the chair in motion. As the glass dumped its contents onto his lap, he instinctively tried to jump up out of the chair, and he almost made it. Unfortunately, when half up, he leaned on the small table adjacent to the chair with too much force and he catapulted himself and the bottle of Scotch onto the floor. As he sat on the floor laughing, he surveyed the scene as only a detective could. The only thing that made him feel uncomfortable was the ice-cold feeling he had between his legs.

Brian again looked up at the portrait and shook his head. He just didn't feel like getting up. What was she doing to him? He wanted to please her more than anything but she was making him crazy. He sat for a while and thought about his choices. In reality, what she was doing was not really bad. It wasn't like she was banging half of Queens or something; and she really was doing it for him, and out of love. *I mean, shit, cops retire all the time*, he thought. He just thought it would never happen to him—at least not this soon.

Brian Michael Walsh was a New York City homicide detective. He wasn't just a homicide detective, but rather, considered by most, both in and out of the department, to be the elite of the elite. The press was particularly fond of him, and he reciprocated by making himself available to them whenever possible. He learned long ago that a friendly press would make his job much easier. He ran a special squad that worked in a world of its own; there were no jurisdictions to worry about, no commanders to answer to, no timetables to keep. He worked out of a precinct in lower Manhattan. The squad got along fairly well with the precinct commander, although he secretly resented having people in his command over which he had no control. The commander once made the almost-career-ending mistake of mentioning this fact to the chief of detectives, and he was visited the next day by the chief of police and a senior member of the police commissioner's staff. Exactly what was said was never made public, but from that time on the commander was, at least publicly, Walsh's greatest fan.

Brian remained on the floor in a daze as the ice between his legs melted. He helped himself to another Scotch. He was thankful that the bottle did not completely empty when it fell on the floor, for he was in no shape to walk over to the cabinet to open another one. He continued to analyze his situation. He had the world by the balls until two months before, when Maureen started this retirement thing. *Sure, at fifty-three I'm no spring chicken*, he said to himself as he wondered exactly what that meant. *What the fuck is a spring chicken anyway?* He was still in great shape, and worked out with the squad at least three times a week when they weren't too busy. The kids were gone. What did she expect him to do with his time? At first he thought she was only kidding, but as time went on he realized she was dead serious. *Bad choice of words for a homicide detective*, he thought.

Maureen was certainly right about the money. He was one of the richest—if not the richest—cops in New York; well, at least one of the richest honest cops. He could spend his money openly, but he never did. Brian was embarrassed about his wealth and led a relatively modest life. Until six years ago he was struggling. He managed to put three kids through college and, with Maureen's frugality, they were able to save $56,000 over a twenty-four-year period. The scholarships the kids got really helped. Now he had to laugh. His stock portfolio was just over $1,326,000 the last time he looked.

Brian thought he was a pretty bright guy, but compared to his oldest child, Maryann, he considered himself an imbecile. He would see her once a week for lunch, and she would start with that Wall Street mumbo jumbo, losing him in a second. She would try to tell him it was no different than detective work, but he wouldn't try to understand—too boring for him; not enough blood and guts, as she would say. She was obviously one of the best at what she did. *Like father, like daughter.* Modesty was never one of Brian's virtues. He called himself a realist. He would always tell it like it was and let the shit hit the fan. If it got on anyone, then so be it; it was meant to be.

In his present state, Brian considered the money a mixed blessing. He reasoned that there was no way Maureen would be after him to retire if that money wasn't there. No fucking way! She was probably right though. *She was always right*, he thought. He had only been shot once in all these years, and maybe his luck was running out. Poor Jim Clancy was killed last year six days before his retirement party, and he could be next. The thought sobered him up a bit. He never really thought about death until Clancy's funeral. It took him months to get over it, but he thought he had; maybe he hadn't.

Brian again looked at the portrait of his family, and decided he would retire. *What the fuck*, he thought, as he drained the last few ounces of Scotch directly from the bottle. *How bad could it be?* There were other things he could do. He would definitely spend more time at the racetrack. Maybe he would train a few horses; he always wanted to do that. He would tell Maureen Saturday night. He would take her to that Spanish restaurant she loved down the Village and tell her there. Spending the rest of his life with her would be all the happiness he would ever need. He just wasn't sure if it was his mind or the Scotch doing the thinking. He slowly got up and made a feeble attempt to straighten up the mess. He looked at Maureen's portrait once more, smiled at his good fortune, and hobbled into the bedroom to curl up next to the real thing. He put his arm around Maureen and glanced at the clock. It read 2:56 A.M. He began to dose off, having no idea that in exactly seven hours and six minutes he would get a phone call that would change his life forever.

Chapter 3

Brian pulled out of the driveway of his house in Bayside, Queens, on the morning of May 29th, wishing he had gone to bed earlier and in better condition. The house was modest, but quite nicely decorated. The Walsh family lived there for almost twenty-two years, and Brian had no desire to leave. It was a great block with great neighbors. He would keep the house forever, no matter how much money his daughter Maryann would make him.

He never liked the trip to Manhattan on the Long Island Expressway, but he had little choice. The older he got, the more he hated it. That would be one great thing about retirement—no more fucking Long Island Expressway. At least he liked his new ride. The family convinced him that he should splurge a little bit in his old age, so he bought a Jaguar. Brian felt the car made the daily trip to work slightly more tolerable. He hoped the novelty of driving such a vehicle would not wear off with time.

He arrived at the precinct at 9:10 A.M. The one concession he made to his celebrity status was that he would come and go as he pleased. To limit the time he would spend on the road during rush hour he would usually come in to work either very early or shortly after nine. Things were pretty slow lately. Yes, there was no shortage of murders in the Big Apple, but no "special events," as Brian liked to call the ones that were turned over to his squad; nothing that couldn't be handled by the usual rotation of homicide detectives. Today the squad would spend most of the day prepping Willie for his testimony next week in the Ambrosia case, the last noteworthy homicide the squad handled.

Brian walked to his office, and three detectives followed him in automatically. If Brian was the best, these guys weren't far behind. In fact, Brian thought Willie was the best he'd ever seen.

"'Morning, boss," said Tommy O'Neal in his usual who-gives-a-shit style.

"How many times have I told you not to call me boss? I hate that name."

"You mean this week?"

"Willie, are you ready for these guys? They're going to try and screw you over as much as they can."

"I'm ready, Brian," Detective Willie Hayes answered.

"You better be. I've seen the A.D.A. in action and he's not that impressive. You'll have to lead him at every opportunity. I don't have to tell you about our friend Rubenstein. He's the biggest mob mouthpiece scumbag around, and he'll do and say anything to get Ambrosia off. Watch the black thing. He will try to get to you any way he can."

"Boss, I'm ready. I'm going to nail this S.O.B, I promise. If he calls me the N-word to my face, I'll call him sir."

"You probably would."

"Then I'll shoot the prick next month."

"You probably would do that too."

"Paulie?" Brian shot in a new direction.

"Yes, boss?"

"Did anything happen last night? It was your day to be the first one in, right?"

"Just a routine night in the big city. Four murders total. Nothing looks like it will come our way though," answered Detective Paulie Lucero.

Just then the door opened and Sergeant Betty O'Leary walked in. Betty was the uniform cop assigned to the squad, and she had been there for nine years. She was the glue that held everything together. There were no hang-ups about doing anything to help the squad; no women's lib bullshit. She was a cop who just happened to be a woman. She took no garbage from anyone outside the squad. Everyone in the department knew who she was and, more importantly, where she worked. You never said no to Sergeant Betty O'Leary. If you fucked with Betty, you fucked with the squad. But even more scary than that, you would have to answer to Captain Thomas O'Leary, who would come down from his station house in the South Bronx to kick your ass from one end of the room to the other. And he didn't care who was watching. You would never say boo to his daughter again. It only had to happen once, and it had.

"Coffee, boys?"

"Thanks, Betty," Brian replied.

She left as fast as she entered. All business. She loved her job and she got things done.

Brian glanced at his watch for no particular reason. It was 10:06 A.M. He was tired from the misadventures of the previous evening. He heard the phone ring, and almost as quickly Betty was back in the room.

"Brian, the chief is on the line."

"The chief? You mean the chief of detectives?"

"How many chiefs do you know?"

What Brian did know was that this was not a social call. The social calls came at night, to his home. This was business.

"Chief DeCicco?" Brian asked as he picked up his line.

"Brian, what's with the Chief DeCicco stuff? Who's listening?"

"No one, Sal."

"Brian, I need to meet with you today. Drop whatever you're doing and meet me at the usual place for lunch. One o'clock. Don't sign out to anyone. Okay?"

"See you then, chief."

"What was that about, boss?"

"Glad to see you're still awake, Paulie, but I don't know. If you are to know, then you will."

The rest of the morning the squad took turns grilling Willie to prepare him for the trial the following week. Brian was hardly listening. He knew Willie would make Rubenstein look like a fool if Rubenstein was stupid enough to go down the wrong path. It was good practice for Tommy and Paulie, though. Brian couldn't get Sal's call out of his mind. He couldn't remember the last time Sal called him at the office. They were great friends and saw each other often, but Sal made it a point to always work through his underlings when it was police business. He didn't want to show any favoritism. *Well, we'll know soon enough*, he thought.

Brian decided he would take a cab to meet Sal since he always had trouble parking at Ryan's, and he didn't want anyone to see his car. He probably shouldn't have gotten a red one.

He arrived at Ryan's at 12:50. Sal, who was never on time for anything, was already sitting at a table. *This can't be good*, Brian thought as he made his way to Sal's table. Ryan's was a great place to eat, and Brian and Sal met there at least once a month for lunch, but it was always arranged the night before, at home. The food was great; the best roast beef sandwiches in any bar in Manhattan.

"Hey, Brian."

"Chief. Am I eating with you today as chief or Sal?"

"Jesus Christ, Brian, I need your help. But first, how's Maureen? She told Marie that she's pushing you to retire. I never said this, but don't do it. You'll be bored to death in a month."

"Tell Maureen that."

"Do I look that stupid?"

"Nobody looks that stupid."

The waiter came and they both ordered roast beef sandwiches and a beer, just like the last one hundred times they ate at Ryan's.

"What's up, Sal?" Brian asked.

"Another murder. But it has really pissed off the wrong people this time. The mayor, who I'm sure I don't have to remind you is up for reelection this November, is all over my ass on this one. He's all over my ass because everyone is all over his ass. You may or may not remember the schoolteacher who was killed about two months ago. It was a brutal murder, with a rape and mutilation."

"I read about it in the papers, and heard the usual station house talk, but I didn't follow it closely," Brian answered.

"In any case, not a fucking lead in two months. Good detectives on the case, but no leads. It turns out she was not only a schoolteacher but a radical in the teachers' union. I think the mayor got every teachers' union member's vote last time, and he wants each vote again. They are not happy with the progress of the investigation, to use their words. Bad enough, right?"

"It could be better."

"Well, it's even worse than that. Turns out that she is also a lesbo. I mean not a closet lesbo, but a full-blown, in your face, radical NOW gang-type lesbo. The mayor, being a liberal, got every fag vote last time, and he wants them again. They call him every fucking day complaining that if she wasn't a lesbian the case would be solved. Guess who he calls every fucking day?"

"Sal, you don't sound that politically correct. You better be careful what you say if you ever want to be mayor."

"Brian, please. Give me a fucking break. When did you become politically correct? You think the mayor really gives a shit? You think he cares about homosexuals, or teachers, or even his own people? It's all about power and getting reelected; that's all he cares about. He makes me sick. He's such a phony. I don't care if he's reelected or not, but I really like this job, and I want to keep it. So guess what, Brian? The mayor wants your squad on this case, and he wants you on it now. I tried to tell him that this is not your usual type of homicide, but he doesn't care. It's now your case. And don't even think about retiring until it's over."

"Who's got it now?"

"Goldberg and Losquadro."

"Christ, Sal, those are top-notch detectives. If they couldn't get anywhere in two months, it may be a bad one."

"It *is* a bad one. You think you're getting the case because it's a good one? It may never be solved, Brian, but you've got to try. I'll have everything sent over tomorrow. Do the best you can. If you can't solve it, no one can, and that will give the mayor his out, and maybe I'll keep my job."

"Of course we'll do it, Sal. I know neither one of us has a choice. You won't believe this, but last night I decided I would tell Maureen this Saturday night that I was going to retire. Maybe I should. This sounds like a fucking disaster about to happen."

"It is a fucking disaster, and it has already happened. When you see the pictures of the teacher, you won't be able to eat for a week. On a brighter note, how's your daughter Maryann? I haven't seen her for a few months."

"When did you see her?"

"Brian, she's handling my stocks. She's making me rich."

"Oh Christ, Sal. *You* get the fucking check!"

Brian took a cab back to the station house, but he didn't go upstairs. He decided to take the afternoon off and ride out to Belmont Racetrack. He had a feeling that there wouldn't be many days off over the next few months. He went directly to the Jaguar and headed out to the track. He called Betty and filled her in on what was coming over tomorrow. She sounded excited. She loved it when they had a big case, and this sounded like a really juicy one.

"Usual setup, boss?" she asked.

"You got it. Set up a meeting for me with the commander, and leave the names of three uniforms you want for the case on my desk. Make the meeting for 7 A.M. sharp. Have some coffee and those little donuts he likes; we want to keep him happy. Tell the squad we'll meet at 7:30 A.M., and call the chief's office and be sure the file is sent over before then. Tell no one else a thing. If you get any calls from a Detective Goldberg or Losquadro, tell them I'll get back to them tomorrow afternoon. Anything I forgot?"

"Doesn't sound like it," she replied.

"And, Betty, forget about your social life for the next few months."

"Thanks a lot."

Betty knew that Brian knew that there was no social life.

Brian called Maureen and made arrangements to meet her at Peter Lugers for dinner at seven. He figured he would be either rich or broke by that time. He loved the horses, and Belmont was his favorite track. It was the end of May, and the Belmont Stakes was the following week. This was a great time for racing, and he thought back to that day in 1973 when he watched Secretariat win the Belmont Stakes by thirty-one lengths. That certainly could never happen again; he felt fortunate to have witnessed it.

He wished he was really going to the track for pleasure. He would no doubt have some fun, but there was someone he had to meet. He hoped he would be there. *Where the hell else would he be?* Brian thought.

May 29th was a beautiful spring day—not a cloud in the sky and about seventy degrees. Brian felt the cool breeze on his neck. Maybe training horses would be fun after retirement. *How bad could it be coming here every day?*

Brian walked to the paddock prior to the fifth race. He just missed the forth because of a minor fender bender on the expressway. The two idiots involved in the accident were arguing, and were probably not too far from fisticuffs. Brian, only half-kidding, thought about shooting them both. He didn't suffer fools well. He looked around for the man, but his eyes were drawn to a beautiful chestnut filly walking into the paddock. Brian glanced at the *Daily Racing Form*. He wanted any excuse to make a bet on the filly. It was a Maiden race and he didn't have far to look—she had the three obligatory workouts, and all three were bullets. She was the third favorite in the morning line, but only because there were two other fillies who had raced before and finished well. He hated to bet on first-time starters, particularly two-year-olds, but in this case he would make an exception. He temporarily forgot about the man as he walked to the window and placed a hundred dollars on the chestnut filly to win. He walked upstairs and watched as the beautiful filly broke from post position five. Unfortunately, she broke seconds after everyone else, and the five-furlong race was over for her before it started. Brian watched as she loped along in last place, twelve lengths behind the front-running filly, and then marveled as she began a furious stretch drive where she closed for third, beaten only two lengths for all the money. He headed back to the paddock to look for the man. *She's going to mature into quite a racemare*, he thought. He would remember her name.

Brian looked around the paddock and slowly walked over to a stooped-over gentleman who looked about seventy but was actually much older. When Brian got to about twelve feet from the old man, a giant of a man moved directly into Brian's path. The man was about four inches taller than Brian and looked like he could snap Brian in half like a twig. Brian and the giant smiled at each other, and the old man turned.

"It's okay, Joey," the old man said. "How are you, Detective Walsh?"

"I was doing well until earlier today, Mr. G."

"Your troubles have brought you to see me?"

"Yes, sir, they have."

Brian and Mr. G. went back a long way. Mr. G. was well-connected. Even though he was retired he knew everything that happened in the city—at least everything mob-related. When Brian was a young cop the mob tried to buy him. He had caught a major mob player, and it looked like the mobster was going away for a long time. The mob tried money, then threats against Brian, and then threats against his family. Mr. G. was from the old school where everything was fair game except a man's family. It also helped that Mr. G. hated the man Brian caught, and Mr. G. was secretly quite happy the asshole was going away for good.

Mr. G. had Brian brought to him one night. He sent two big goons, and they brought Brian to an old warehouse in Queens where Mr. G. was waiting. Mr. G. was going to apologize to Brian for the threats against his family, but Brian didn't know that. Mr. G. sat with two of his bodyguards while the two goons brought Brian into the room. Brian was pushed into the room with a hood over his head and his hands tied behind his back. Detective Brian Michael Walsh thought he was about to die. As Brian's hood was removed, his hand reached into the belt of one of the goons and, in two seconds, with two shots, there were two dead men on the floor. Mr. G.'s two bodyguards jumped up but were too late. Brian had Mr. G. by the throat and had the gun stuck in his ear. To say Mr. G. was not accustomed to this kind of treatment would be a huge under-statement. One of the bodyguards soiled himself, probably not out of fear of Brian, but rather because of what he imagined would happen to him if Mr. G. died on his watch. Then Brian did a strange thing. He looked Mr. G. directly in the eye and said, "We're even now, right?"

Mr. G. looked at the two dead goons, smiled, and said, "We're even."

Brian dropped his gun, turned his back, and started to walk out. As he stepped over the dead bodies he turned to Mr. G. and said, "Get smarter people."

The legend of Detective Brian Michael Walsh had begun. From that night on a mutual respect developed between the two men. They still butted heads from time to time, but there were rules.

"I have just one question you might be able to answer, Mr. G. And if the answer is the one I think it is, you will save me a lot of time and a lot of digging in the wrong areas, if you get my drift."

"Might we be the wrong areas?"

"You get smarter with age, Mr. G."

"No. I took your advice and got smarter people," he smiled. "Go ahead and ask."

They sat down on a bench by the paddock and talked for some time. When they were through, Brian was convinced that the murder of Elizabeth Anderson, radical-lesbian schoolteacher, had absolutely noth-ing to do with the New York mob.

Brian learned a long time ago that any homicide that had no wit-nesses, no leads, and seemingly no solution, must be considered mob-related until proven otherwise. He felt confident that he had just saved the squad endless hours of work that could now be channeled in a more productive direction.

Brian stayed at the track until the last race. He played the sev-enth and eighth big, but he didn't cash a ticket. He blew his last twenty-four bucks on a four-horse trifecta box in the ninth race and won $564.24. He loved the races. They were more fun than that ridiculous stock market that was making him rich.

Brian pulled into Peter Lugers at 6:10 and parked next to Maureen's van. When he walked inside, the headwaiter almost fell over him. It was no secret who Brian was. He didn't go to the restaurant often, but when he did he was noticed. He didn't like the way he was treated since the sensational Jennifer Baker case eight years ago when he became a celebrity, but he knew there was nothing he could do about it. Maureen would always remind him not to believe all his press clippings. He once asked her how many great detectives she thought there were. Her answer, one less than you think, brought him down to earth. He'd be shocked if he knew of the scrapbook she was keeping for the grandchildren.

"Hi, honey. You look great," he said as he seated himself in a chair across from her.

"Let me guess. Hi, honey. I look great. Peter Lugers during the week. Could you be about to tell me something?" Maureen asked.

"Can't a guy take his wife out for a simple dinner without it being 'something'?"

"Brian, be serious. Besides, Sal called. He told me to blame him for whatever you say tonight. So what is it?"

"Maureen, I swear on the kids that I made up my mind to retire. I was going to tell you Saturday. Sal called me today and dumped this case on me, and I mean dumped. He had no choice. It's a bad one, and I have to give it a shot. But I promise that when this one's done, I'm done. I swear. No fucking way I won't retire."

"Brian, watch your mouth! I hate that word."

"Sorry, honey. Just slipped."

Maureen had spent the best part of thirty years trying to get him to stop using the F-word. She finally realized that it was just part of his world. Maybe if she saw what he did she would use it too.

They enjoyed a wonderful meal, after which Brian followed Maureen home to Bayside to a house that had so many great memories, but which now seemed too big for the two of them. After sitting and talking about the kids, they found themselves in each other's arms and were soon in the bedroom where they made passionate love. As they lay in bed they each thought about what the next few months would be like. *Hopefully*, Maureen thought, *this will be the last one*, and she prayed he would get through it unharmed. She worried more and more about that.

She didn't want to be alone. She loved Brian dearly, and with the kids gone she could never survive losing him, no matter how strong she appeared outwardly. Her last thought before she went to sleep was something Brian said to her many years ago when they were skiing in Utah: "Watch the last run, honey. That's the one that gets you."

Chapter 4

Brian walked up the stairs to Commander Timothy Smith's office at precisely 6:55 A.M. the following morning. Brian was always on time for these meetings. Despite the working arrangement that offended the commander, he genuinely liked the Walsh guy, as he called him. They talked for about fifteen minutes, and the commander assured Brian that he would cooperate fully. The three uniforms would be placed under Sergeant O'Leary's supervision immediately.

The meeting with the squad began at 7:30 A.M. Twelve boxes of material had been delivered to the office earlier, and they were already reading the contents. Betty was ready. She must have come in very early. All the files were set up, and the blackboard and corkboard were on the wall. The "War Room" was ready, and that was exactly what was beginning. Brian ran every investigation like a war; and he never lost a war. Maybe it had something to do with Vietnam, but no one knew for sure. But one thing was for sure: you never mentioned Vietnam to Brian Walsh. There was a cop in Brooklyn in the late 70s who made that mistake. Brian and the other cop have Willie to thank for their lives. If not for Willie the cop would probably be dead and Brian would be in jail, or worse. Willie picked Brian off the other cop before too much damage was done, but it was clear to everyone present what was about to happen. Willie, who knew the other cop, spoke to him briefly the way only Willie could, and the altercation never occurred. Willie had a way of making things "unhappen" very quickly.

Willie and Brian had been inseparable since that night. When the squad was formed in the mid-eighties, Brian told the previous chief that if he didn't have Willie there would be no squad, at least not one that

Brian would run. Willie was not politically correct, and the top brass had serious reservations about his being on such a high-profile squad. In the end, the chief needed Brian, so Willie became the compromise. Willie was a cop—not a black cop, just a cop. He didn't play the race game, and that did not make him very popular with the other minorities on the force. They wanted him to be a leader. What he wanted to be was a homicide detective. Several years ago when a prominent black captain came to Willie to straighten him out about the race thing, Willie told him to go and fuck himself with an AIDS dick. Brian thought it was funny at the time, but it almost ended Willie's career. It took Sal and all his power to smooth it over. Willie's explanation to the Review Board—that it was either say that or shoot the big, fat, fucking son-of-a-bitch—didn't help his situation that much. Willie was the happiest Brian had ever seen him about one year later, when the black captain died of a massive heart attack while screwing an underage white hooker on his office couch. So much for the pseudo-moralists of the world.

"Welcome, everyone," Brian began sarcastically. "Yesterday the chief gave us a present: a two-month-old homicide going nowhere. We will make it go somewhere. Twelve boxes of evidence and two really good detectives got nowhere; we must do better."

"Boss, what's going on here?" Tommy asked. "We never take over another detective's case. Everyone will be pissed at us. We'll get no help from anyone and we'll look like assholes. I worked with Goldberg, and he's a great guy. He'll go nuts on me."

"We have no choice, Tommy. It wasn't a request. It's the mayor's call. If you want to visit with him be my guest."

"I hope that fuck loses," Paulie jumped in.

"Is this a black and white thing?" Willie asked.

Everyone laughed. Willie would put a bullet in the mayor, black or not, and take bets on which way he would fall; he hated him so. Willie only liked real people—not phony politicians or low-life attorneys, just real people who did their job. He detested assholes who did nothing, who accomplished nothing, who just pushed paper from one pile to another. Cops did something; they mattered. They changed things for the better. If a cop was dirty, Willie would just as soon shoot the son-of-a-bitch as look at him. Some say he already had.

"Okay, people," Brian continued. "Everyone said their piece? Let's get on with it. Elizabeth Anderson was murdered on April 2nd of this year. She was a New York City schoolteacher who just happened to be a radical lesbian and was very active in the teachers' union. These two groups are all over the mayor, and that's why he has selected us to find her murderers, or be the fall guys, depending on what happens from here on out. People, we ... will ... not ... be anyone's fall guys, so we will get these crazy fucks that killed Anderson.

"I want to know everything about this woman. Who was she? Where did she eat? Where did she go on vacation? Who did she call? Who were her lovers—female and male? Who did she work with? You know the drill. I want to know more about her than I know about myself. Every interview must be repeated. Take nothing for granted except this: no way was this mob-related."

"Thank you, Mr. G.," Paulie yelled.

"Betty will start making the lists. By the way, Betty, you got your three helpers. Be sure you don't try to do it all yourself, but don't let them know more than they have to, okay?"

Tommy had already started to look at some pictures.

"Holy shit, boss. Someone really didn't like this lady. She looks terrible."

Tommy passed the pictures around. The room became spooky quiet. It took a lot to shut up this bunch, but the pictures of the late Elizabeth Anderson did just that. Even Brian was repulsed. Sal was right; it was sickening. After all these years he couldn't figure out how one human being could do this to another. Intellectually he understood, but emotionally he never would. What a fucked-up world. Betty took the pictures and pinned them to the corkboard on the wall. They would be looking at them for a long time. Unfortunately, they didn't look any better from a distance.

"Betty, be sure this room is locked at all times. I don't want any gawkers in here. Change the lock and don't give maintenance a key. We'll keep it clean."

The squad spent the rest of the day and most of the evening organizing the boxes and reading the contents. Goldberg and Losquadro were good, but they did things differently. Goldberg called at 4:01 P.M. Brian took the call and was pleasantly surprised. Detective Goldberg seemed genuinely interested in helping if he could. Brian thanked him, but knew that he would never call. That was one of the rules—no outsiders.

They broke up at about 10:00 P.M., after each was given an assignment for the following day. Paulie would start with Elizabeth Anderson's coworkers at school, and then he would stop by the office she used at the teachers' union. Willie would interview the residents of her apartment building. Finally, Tommy would visit her lesbian organizations. It would take days to get this preliminary work done.

They all smiled as Brian told Tommy, "Remember, Tommy, they are not lesbos, dikes, fags, or whatever. Treat them with respect or the mayor will have your badge." Brian laughed to himself.

"Sorry, boss, I just hate anyone who is getting more pussy than me."

Everyone laughed, including Betty. The war had begun in earnest, and the days would be long and hard. The work would sometimes be boring, and sometimes very depressing, but in the end it would get done. Elizabeth Anderson would be spoken for, and her messengers would be this unusual combination of the best detectives New York City had ever seen. Unfortunately for the detectives, and for Elizabeth Anderson, their opponent was the best anyone had ever seen.

* * * * * * * * *

The next day, Friday May 31, was another beautiful day in Manhattan. Paulie drove to the school where Elizabeth Anderson worked. He thought that a schoolteacher like Anderson was one of the things really wrong with America. He personally couldn't care less what people did in the privacy of their bedroom but, from what he had read so far, this lady was way too open about her lesbianism. What was she telling the kids? My God, she taught seventh grade. He had a kid in sixth grade and one in third. He didn't want a lesbian teaching them; at least not one that went around lecturing about the topic.

Paulie introduced himself to Principal James Erickson. Mr. Erickson seemed a very bright and caring man. He was openly glad that there was new blood on the case, and he was very cooperative. Three hours later Paulie knew a lot about what Erickson thought of Anderson. Although he did not approve of her sexual orientation, and in particular her openness about it, Erickson thought she was the perfect teacher. She worked hard. She never had a problem with any teacher, parent, or student in the eight years she taught at the school. Her students always scored higher than other students did in their grade level. She always stayed late to help any student. She taught summer school, which many of the other teachers simply refused to do. There was never a complaint about her lesbianism from anyone. He pulled her teaching file, which was still available because of the investigation, and it was spotless. Mr. Erickson concluded by saying that if New York City had more teachers like Elizabeth Anderson the education system would not be in its current mess and the world would be a better place.

Paulie could not resist saying, "All this may be true, sir, but at least four people appear to have thought otherwise."

"Four people? What four people?"

Paulie walked out of Erickson's office without answering.

Paulie spent most of the day at the school. He interviewed several other teachers, a janitor, a security guard, and the vice-principal. No one had anything derogatory to say about the late Ms. Anderson. No one knew anything about her personal life. She didn't socialize with any of them except at school functions. She never brought a date, male or female, to any function. They knew nothing about her family. The files Paulie read the day before said that no family was ever located. *Maybe they disowned her*, he thought.

Paulie left the school and went to the teachers' union offices. It was more of the same. Anderson was a dedicated worker with no enemies—no close friends but no enemies.

Paulie wasn't happy, and he hated going back to Brian with nothing new. Maybe this case was going to really be a bad one.

* * * * * * * * * *

Willie wasn't doing much better at Elizabeth Anderson's apartment on the Upper East Side. She lived in a rather small one-bedroom unit and apparently kept to herself—no visitors, no parties, no real friends in the building. She had dinner a few times with Sally Pepper, who lived in apartment 306, and Ms. Pepper only had nice things to say about Anderson. Questioning revealed that Pepper didn't know Anderson at all. She didn't know she was a lesbian until after the murder. Certainly, at least according to two of the male residents who claimed to know definitely, Sally Pepper was not a lesbian.

It was a relatively small apartment building, but it would still take Willie several trips at various times of the day to speak to everyone. The superintendent knew very little about Anderson, except that she was one of the better tippers in the building. To him that meant that she could do no wrong.

Willie would spend all Friday and Saturday at the apartment building and would find out essentially nothing. He was not popular with the late sleepers on Saturday, but one look at Willie and any thought they had about complaining to the department dissipated. He reviewed all the notes in Goldberg's and Losquadro's file and, although he felt his were more complete, he had to admit that they really added nothing.

* * * * * * * * *

Tommy may have had more fun at the Woman's Individual Freedom League than Paulie and Willie had on their assignments, but in reality he got nothing, in every sense of the word. The group was a radical lesbian organization that promoted every woman's right to do what she wanted with, and to, her body. It's hard to argue with that premise when you look at it at face value. In reality, the group was just another liberal organization with political motives. The League helped to get the current mayor elected.

Tommy did enjoy talking to a friend of Anderson's. It appeared that this was the only friend she had. Her name was Barbara Peterson, and she was a beautiful girl in her early thirties. She knew of no one who could do this terrible thing to her friend. Anderson seemed to be her mentor in the League. Peterson denied she had a sexual relationship with Anderson, and she told Tommy that many of the group's members are celibate.

"What a waste," Tommy inadvertently said out loud, bringing the interview to a screeching halt.

* * * * * * * * *

The squad, thankful that Brian gave them some much-needed sleep, met at the office at 10:00 A.M. on Sunday. Brian summarized what they now knew.

"Elizabeth Anderson was a thirty-two-year-old white school-teacher who was also a lesbian. She wasn't a closet lesbian, but rather a very vocal one. She wasn't promiscuous. She may even have been a virgin. She apparently was the perfect teacher, the perfect tenant, and the perfect member of her lesbian organization. Not one person has anything bad to say about her. She was dedicated, almost passionate, about her work and beliefs. She was not having financial problems. There were no lovers, either male or female. She had no family problems. In fact, she has no family. That bothers me people; everyone has some family. There is no record of her changing her name. Her phone records show us nothing. Her credit cards are hardly used. She doesn't appear to go anywhere, or go with anyone. She hasn't had a vacation in eight years. She doesn't own a car. She doesn't do drugs. She's not a hooker. She doesn't even watch cable TV. She reads like crazy, but nothing bizarre. She is fucking perfect! So please somebody tell me why her body was found in a dumpster, beaten to an almost unrecognizable pulp, and raped front and back by at least four guys? Please, somebody tell me, because I have no fucking clue!"

Brian was not happy. It was always better when Brian was happy.

"The DNA doesn't lie, people. Four different guys. It makes me sick. I want these bastards, and I want them soon. I don't give a damn about the mayor wanting them. I want their perverted asses on my wall!"

Willie looked at Brian. He hadn't seen him like this in years. *These guys are toast*, he thought to himself.

Chapter 5

By Friday June 7th the squad had not made any significant progress. Brian was sick of looking at the pictures of Elizabeth Anderson. He saw them everywhere. He began to dream about her, and he knew that was a bad sign. You had to stay emotionally removed from the case. He knew that; he just couldn't convince his gut. He couldn't wait until Saturday, when he planned to take Maureen, Sal, and Marie to the Belmont Stakes. There would be no talk of business at the track. That occurred Thursday when Sal called for an update. The mayor was happy that the squad was on the case, but Brian and Sal were less excited.

"Not every case is a winner," Sal cautioned, trying to console his friend.

They both knew that the longer you go without a lead the more impossible the case becomes—evidence disappears, fingerprints wear off, people forget things, and, most important, the bad guys go away. With the publicity this case had been getting in the press since the squad took over, Brian doubted that the thugs who did this were even in the states. Brian and Sal begged the mayor to keep it quiet, but he clearly had his own agenda. His plan was obvious. He put the best and brightest the department had to offer on the case. It could not be his fault if the butchers who murdered Elizabeth Anderson, one of New York's finest teachers, could not be found.

The three uniforms who were working with Betty were doing a great job, but it was tedious work. One went through every one of Anderson's phone bills for the past three years and matched names with numbers. A second did the same thing with her credit cards, looking for stores she frequented and places she may have met friends. Their efforts were fruitless. No pattern was obvious. The third transcribed the notes of Goldberg and Losquadro, as well as the daily reports of the three squad members. Brian didn't write reports; he kept everything in his head. Writing to him was a total waste of time. He would spend countless hours reading other people's reports, but he did not like to share information.

The remainder of the day was uneventful. Brian planned to take the autopsy report on Anderson home to read again. Maybe he missed something the first two times he read it; he hoped he had. Old Doc Robinson taught him many years ago that there was more information on a dead body than anyone could imagine. *Let's hope so*, he thought, *because there is no information anywhere else*.

Brian stopped to pick up a *Daily Racing Form* for Saturday before driving home. He gave everyone the weekend off. Elizabeth Anderson wasn't going anywhere, and, unfortunately, neither was her investigation.

* * * * * * * * * *

Maureen and Brian had a quiet dinner. He liked to barbecue in the summer. He grilled two steaks and Maureen made the blue cheese sauce he loved. He was in heaven. Brian loved to eat. If he wasn't so active he would weigh three hundred pounds.

"How's the investigation going, honey?" Maureen asked.

"Slow would be a good word. No, wait, reverse would be better."

"How did it get into the press?"

"That was the moron mayor's idea; hang us out to dry to take the pressure off him."

"Well, I have some good news for you. Brian Jr. called today. You are going to be a grandfather in seven months."

"You're kidding."

"No. Jane is feeling great this time. Everything is fine, really. The miscarriage last year was a fluke. Everything is normal."

"Do Maryann and John know?"

"No. They wanted us to know first. Call him after dinner."

"This is great. Really great!"

Brian ate his steak in what seemed like seconds. He couldn't wait to call his son. *This might be a good weekend after all*, he thought.

He called Brian Jr. and they talked for almost an hour. They had a very close relationship even though Brian Jr. now lived in Florida. His son had earned a masters degree in mechanical engineering from the University of Michigan. He achieved it with a full academic scholarship. Brian was very proud of that. He was even more proud, but he could never tell Maureen, that Brian Jr. said the hell with everything and chucked it all. He was now a golf pro in Fort Lauderdale and spent his days golfing and fishing. He met Jane in Florida on a vacation, went back to Michigan to finish his education, and then went back to Florida to Jane. They were married and appear to be living happily ever after.

After talking to his son and daughter-in-law, Brian poured himself a small Scotch, retired to his chair, and started to read the autopsy report on Elizabeth Anderson. It was depressing reading, but had to be done.

It read: Victim is a white female age thirty-two. Age was obtained from document identification, as the condition of the body would not allow confirmation.

"No shit," Brian said out loud. "She has no face."

It continued: Weight 126 pounds. Height 5'6". The autopsy report then divided into body regions.
External:

Skull: Massive damage to skull with multiple lacerations over both parietal and occipital regions. There is a depressed skull fracture in the left parietal region that measures 6 cm. by 6 cm. A second depressed skull fracture is present in the occipital region in the midline. This measures 10 cm. in diameter.

The animals were bashing her head against the ground, Brian thought.

The report continued: Blood is present in both ears, and cerebrospinal fluid is draining from both ears.

Facial region: Multiple lacerations. Nasal bones obviously fractured with significant deviation to the left. Both orbits fractured. Left eye draining vitreous humor. Right eye bulging. Swelling so massive no description possible. See pictures. Jaw fractured. Left ear severely lacerated. Lips massively swollen. Deep laceration at the left corner of the mouth.

Neck: Contusions and lacerations around neck consistent with strangulation attempt. See pictures. Cervical spine obviously fractured and/or dislocated.

Chest: Multiple contusions and fist marks around upper chest and breasts. Virtually no area spared. Multiple small lacerations left chest wall. Obvious multiple rib fractures that can be palpated bilaterally. Possible bite marks right breast. Left breast severely swollen with several small lacerations.

Abdomen: Contusions and signs of blunt trauma over most of the abdomen. Multiple lacerations. See pictures.

Genitalia: Unusually large volume of semen present in vagina and rectum. Semen present in pubic hair, dried.

Upper extremities: Multiple lacerations and obvious fractures. See radiology report below. See pictures.

Lower extremities: Multiple abrasions, lacerations, and fractures. See radiology report below. See pictures.

Every part of the body was photographed, and a detailed description of every wound, including the exact measurement of each laceration, in millimeters, was cataloged and cross-referenced to every picture. Brian could not read it again; it was just too depressing. He skipped to the radiology report.

Radiology: The whole body was x-rayed. The following fractures were noted:

Skull: Depressed fracture left parietal region measuring 2.5 cm. in depth and 6 cm. in diameter. Depressed fracture occipital region measuring 3.2 cm. in depth and 10 cm. in diameter.

Neck: Fracture-dislocation at C2-C3.

Chest: Six rib fractures on the right and four on the left.

Pelvis: Negative for fracture.

Right arm: Fracture right humeral shaft; fracture mid ulna; fracture 3rd, 4th, and 5th metacarpals; multiple open phalangeal fractures.

Left arm: Fracture left humeral shaft, multiple phalangeal fractures.

Right leg: Open fracture mid shaft right femur, fracture patella, fracture lateral malleolus.

Left leg: Fracture patella, fracture lateral malleolus.

Lumbar spine: Compression fracture L1 and L2.

Dorsal spine: Negative for fracture.

Brian stopped reading. He closed his eyes and looked at the pictures, which now lived in his mind. The pathologist who did the autopsy was right to refer to the pictures so often. Words on a page couldn't begin to describe the beating this woman took. But why? If you want to rape a woman why beat her unmercifully? Did the guys just go nuts? Were they out of their minds on crack? There was something very wrong about the whole thing. Brian could feel it. He had never seen a beating like this in his whole career. Even the mob didn't do this; they might dismember you, but they would not leave you lying around to be found so easily. Something was very wrong; all his years in homicide told him so. But what the fuck was it?

He read the whole report three more times, read the *Daily Racing Form* for a few minutes, and then turned in. Maureen was already in bed. Brian had trouble sleeping, as the pictures of the mutilated body of Elizabeth Anderson danced in his head.

Saturday came too quickly. Brian was tired. He used to go days at a time without sleep, but those days were long gone. Perhaps that wise-ass Tommy was right; he was getting too old for this shit. Maureen and Brian had a leisurely breakfast and headed to Belmont Racetrack in the late morning. There would be crowds, but Brian had a box arranged, compliments of the racing secretary who considered Brian one of his friends. Brian let him think so since it did no harm and came in handy on big days like this.

They met Sal and Marie and had a great day. The amazing thing was that their friendship got better with time. Brian and Sal only partnered for six months more years ago than they would like to remember, but they stayed close.

"Listen, Sal," Brian said. "We're about to make a lot of money."

"What's Maryann up to now?"

"Not Maryann, us, right now, on this next race. The Belmont Stakes."

Sal knew nothing about the horses and hated to part with a penny.

"I'm in for $5.00," Sal said.

"What? Are you kidding? Five dollars. You want me to stand on that line for that? Forget it. Give me $150."

"Are you fucking nuts? Marie would kill me."

"Does she know how much you're making in the market?"

"Jesus Christ, Brian, keep quiet. You know how she feels about taking chances. Here's your $150. You better win. What are you doing anyway?"

"We're going to play a trifecta box."

"Explain."

"According to my calculations, only three horses have a chance in this race. We play all three, and if they come in first, second, and third in any order we win big."

"This is the same thing we did last time we were here, and you weren't even close. Not one of them finished one, two, or three, as I remember. Here, take the money."

They sat and watched the post parade as the band played "New York, New York." Brian got goose bumps. He loved New York City. It was where the action was, and God how he loved the action.

"Who am I rooting for?"

"We bet on Skip Away, Editors Note, and My Flag."

"Brian, what are the numbers?"

"10, 6, and 8."

Brian laughed to himself, Sal must have spoken to fifty people he knows in politics and in the department today. He's got to be the only one who is here to see the people, not the horses.

The two close friends and their wives left immediately after the Belmont Stakes, planning to beat the crowd to Peter Lugers. They all climbed into Maureen's van, Sal having sent his assigned driver home early, and Brian drove to the restaurant. Sal was sweating and was having some problems breathing. Brian turned the air conditioner up all the way and began to laugh.

"How did you two big-time gamblers do?" Marie asked.

"Not too bad, honey," was Sal's reply, trying to keep from screaming.

"Maureen and I each chipped in $5.00 and we bet on the girl horse to finish third and she did. We won $13.75 each."

"Great, hon, you get to pay for dinner," Sal said. He was struggling to control his ecstasy. He had $11,425 in his pocket. Cash. No taxes. Everything legal. He simply could not believe it. Now *all* the Walshes were making him money. What a race! When he saw the results posted he thought they won half of the $914 trifecta. He would have been happy with that. Then Brian reminded him that they had it fifty times.

"Fifty fucking times!" the chief of detectives of the largest police force in the United States yelled as he spilled half a cup of beer over the well-dressed lady in the box immediately in front of him.

Brian decided he would definitely train horses after he left the force.

The dinner and company were great. Brian and Maureen got home about 9:30. They were tired but Brian had other things on his mind. This time it was Maureen, not the case. She looked so alluring to him all day. It was hard to believe she would be fifty next year. *No one should look that good at fifty*, he thought. The big hit at the track had him excited, and he shared the spoils with her. He told her not to tell Marie; she knew as much.

They went into the bedroom where they made love. It was particularly exciting, and they changed position several times. Brian was very energetic, and at one time Maureen slowed him down because he was hurting her ever so slightly. They finished and held each other for a few minutes before Maureen began to dose off. Brian turned on his back and briefly thought about what a great day he had. He was starting to fall asleep when it hit him like a charging bull. He jumped up and ran to the den. He grabbed the autopsy report and yelled. "It was right there. I missed it. I fucking missed it! Thank you, Maureen Ann Walsh. Thank you very fucking much!"

Chapter 6

Brian went back to bed but he had trouble sleeping. He woke up for good at 5:28 A.M. There was no sense fighting it; he new he could not wait until Monday. After waking Maureen up and explaining his plans to her, he headed for the squad's office. He was there in no time, pushing the Jaguar faster than ever before. Sunday was the only day to travel on the Long Island Expressway.

He ran up the stairs to the office, unlocked the door, and ran to the pictures, which had been enlarged and were now jumping off the corkboard at him. He stared at the pictures and then he read one small section of the autopsy report over and over. He called the medical examiner's office hoping to find Dr. Susan Blakely, who did Anderson's autopsy. Of course she wasn't there, but the clerk said she was expected in around 10:00 A.M. He would be waiting for her at the morgue.

Dr. Blakely walked into her office at 10:10, looking quite surprised to see the famous Detective Walsh half asleep on her couch. She knew who he was, but she never had the pleasure in person. He looked taller in the newspapers, but was just as tough-looking in real life.

"Good morning, Dr. Blakely. You are Dr. Blakely?"

"Yes, Detective Walsh."

"Please, make it Brian."

"Okay. Glad to meet you, Brian. I'm Susan," she said as she reached out her hand.

"What brings you to the morgue on such a beautiful Sunday morning? They said outside that we had no interesting victims last night, certainly nothing that would warrant your special attention."

"Susan, I need to bounce a few things off you about the

Elizabeth Anderson homicide."

"I expected you long before this."

"Actually, your pictures were so good I felt I was at the autopsy. You are fairly new here, aren't you?"

"Two years. Bounce away."

"I spent the weekend reading the autopsy report, and last night, while I was talking to my wife, something began to disturb me. I came in this morning to look at the autopsy pictures and something puzzles me."

"Which is?"

"Here is a girl who literally has her brains beat out and damn near every bone in her body broken, and not a mark on her ... on her ... vaginal area. The pictures confirm it. I mean four guys ..." and Brian had to bite his tongue because the F-word almost came out, "had relations with her, and there was no vaginal tearing, no rectal tearing, no bruising at all anywhere in her ... her ... personal area. What do you think? How could that be?"

"Thank you for selecting your words so carefully, Brian, but what you're really asking is how this girl could have had the shit fucked out of her and have her vagina and ass not look like it? Am I right, detective?"

"Well, sort of," Brian said somewhat sheepishly.

"Forget it. My father and brother are cops. They talk like that all the time. It actually sounds better that way, because that is exactly what happened. They definitely did not have relations with her. This was a very violent attack by some very sick individuals."

"So what do you think? What's the explanation? Is there one?" Brian asked.

Dr. Blakely looked at the pictures for some time. She hadn't noticed this now very obvious fact and was clearly uncomfortable. But she was a pro and a rising star in the M.E.'s office, and she would take her lumps if she missed something.

"One of the things that could explain the lack of bruising," she began, "would be that she was dead before the rape. Heart's not beating, no bruising. The lack of vaginal and rectal tearing is harder to explain. Maybe she let them and it just got out of hand."

"I think that this was a little more than just getting out of hand, don't you, Susan?"

"Yes, of course. Let me think about this for a while and I will discuss it with the M.E. I'll get back to you."

Brian left the morgue. He was refreshed by the fact that Dr. Blakely would go to the headman and not try to cover up any mistakes. He had already made up his own mind. The rape was an afterthought. That girl was murdered for one and only one reason. Somebody wanted her very, very dead. Maybe they wanted to make an example of her. But who? And why? If it wasn't for Mr. G's information he would consider the mob, but that was out of the question.

He drove back to Bayside. His daughter Maryann was coming to dinner with a new boyfriend. Brian hoped he would be better than the last. How could anyone so beautiful and so bright be such a poor judge of character? The last guy she brought over was married. He had told her he was divorced and was living in the city. Sure, he had an apartment, but he also had a nice home in New Rochelle. The only problem was that the house in New Rochelle came with a wife and two kids. *These Wall Street types have no morals*, Brian thought. He never trusted the guy, and it was easy to check up on him. The public should only know how easy it is for the police to find out even their most intimate secrets. After Brian was sure about his information, it took Willie less than fifteen minutes one night to convince Mr. Wall Street that things would be better for him elsewhere. Brian laughed out loud. He hoped the jerk liked San Francisco. What would he do without Willie? He hoped he never had to find out.

* * * * * * * * *

Maryann drove to her parents' home with her new boyfriend. Well, not really new. They had been dating for about six months. He was an assistant D.A., and she felt her father would like that. His name was Dennis Michael Sweeney, and she knew her father would like that. He was definitely single, and she was sure her father would absolutely love that. Her problem now was not her father, but Dennis. She had neglected to tell Dennis who her father was. She didn't want to scare him off, and everyone knew her father had a reputation of eating assistant D.A.s alive. It wasn't just a reputation; he really scared them to death. Her dad knew more law than most A.D.A.s, and wouldn't waste his time in a courtroom until they presented their whole case to him—literally. It took a lot of extra time but BMW, as the A.D.A.s called him, never was on the losing side of a court battle. Once a suspect of Brian's was indicted, that was it. You better plea bargain or you went up against a 46 and 0 record. Even moronic criminals could figure those odds.

"Dennis?"

"Yes, Maryann."

"I have a little surprise for you. More like a big shock, actually." Dennis tightened his grip on his steering wheel. Attorneys do not like surprises; they abhor big shocks.

"What's wrong?"

"Nothing wrong really. I just want to prepare you for my parents."

"Oh, don't worry, Maryann, I will be fine. We'll get along great," he smiled. "Parents don't scare me, and I'm sure yours are very special."

"That's an understatement," Maryann mumbled to herself before blurting out, "My father is Brian Walsh. *The* Brian Walsh. The detective, Brian Walsh."

If Maryann did not know Dennis was one of the finest physical specimens she had ever seen she would have sworn he was having a heart attack. She never saw one, but it had to look something like this. Dennis was white. You couldn't see where his neck ended and his white shirt began. He was sweating profusely and, worst of all, mumbling. That the mere mention of her father's name could reduce the man she hoped to marry to a blithering idiot she found both humorous and frightening. Thank God there was no one in the left lane because as the road curved to the right, Dennis kept going straight. He was in the extreme left lane before Maryann screamed at him and brought him back to his senses. He pulled over to the right shoulder of the road, got out, and walked into the woods where he relieved himself.

Maryann didn't know whether to laugh or cry. She began to laugh out loud.

"I guess you won't be dumping me any time soon, will you, Dennis?"

Dennis started to laugh as well.

"I guess not. Maybe it might have been better to tell me when I wasn't driving seventy miles an hour on the L.I.E."

"You're starting to look better."

"I think I hear my beeper."

"Nice try, Dennis. You're not wearing a beeper. Let's go. If we're late my father will shoot you ... only kidding."

They drove the rest of the way laughing about the incident. One day they would tell Brian, but certainly not tonight.

The dinner and evening were delightful for all present. Brian seemed to like Dennis, and they had a lot in common. They both hated criminals; they just dealt with them differently. Dennis, for his part, could not believe this was the dreaded BMW everyone talked about. There simply had to be another Detective Brian Walsh. When Maryann and Dennis left, Maureen turned to Brian and asked, "Do you like him?"

"Is he married?"

"Brian, be serious. Do you like him? You better, because he's the one. I know it. He's the one."

"He seems like a nice kid. He reminds me of Johnny. Have you heard from him lately?"

"No. Not since his last undercover assignment. Why don't you call his captain in Chicago and see what's happening?"

"Maureen, you know I can't do that. You know how sensitive he is about making it on his own. That's why he left the NYPD. How do you think he'd feel if he heard his daddy called to check up on him? He's a big boy. He can take care of himself. Don't worry Maureen. Come on, time for bed. Tomorrow the squad goes into overdrive."

Chapter 7

It was Monday June 10, eleven days since the files on Elizabeth Anderson were sent over. *All and all not too bad,* Brian thought to himself as he waited for the other squad members to arrive. He even beat Betty to the office, and that had not happened for quite some time. Of course, he couldn't expect Betty in the office at five in the morning. She rolled in around six, and the boys followed at about seven.

"Maureen finally throw you out, boss?" was Tommy's greeting.

Willie knew instinctively that something was up.

Brian began the daily briefing.

"Okay, people, listen closely. I spent some time yesterday with Dr. Susan Blakely who, those of you who can read know, did the autopsy on Anderson. New theory. She was murdered."

"No shit, boss," Tommy said. "I thought it was a suicide. One of the worst suicides I've ever seen, but still a suicide. I guess that's why you're the boss."

"Tommy, it's a good thing I love you. I'm glad to see your wit is well rested. I hope you body is equally rested, because you won't rest again for quite some time. None of us will. I want you all to go on the assumption that this girl was murdered for a reason. She was not just a random victim who was raped by some nuts or crack heads. This was a planned execution. The extreme violence tells me that the killer really hated her. He brought three of his closest friends to be sure it would be done right. She may have been an example to someone else.

"This changes everything, people. This is our type of crime. Find the motive and you'll have the killer. I don't care what her friends said, what her co-workers said, or what the other lesbians said; this girl had one very bad ass for an enemy.

"Paulie, everyone likes you. I want you to start talking to every homicide detective in town. I want to know if there has been anything like this over the past five years. I doubt it, but ask anyway. Go visit old friends. Take them out to lunch. Whatever it takes to find out, you do.

"Willie and Tommy. You guys bring up any unusual unsolved homicide that occurred over the past two years, no matter how insignificant it might seem. I want to get them all here so Betty and her girls can start matching everything. Somewhere out there is the answer. Any questions?"

"What's the new evidence?" Betty asked.

"It's right there on the wall. We've all been looking at it. Maybe those pictures are so terrifying that we didn't look close enough."

Brian walked over to the board with the life-size enlarged pictures and circled Anderson's genitalia. As Brian turned to Betty, Willie blurted out, "No trauma."

"That's right, no trauma at all," Brian confirmed. "The rape was an afterthought to throw us off. Their first mistake. They should have cut her up, and we would never have known."

Chapter 8

Peter Salvino was a second-generation detective who worked in midtown Manhattan. He had a good clearance rate and he was happy with his partner, Linda Richter, who was a few years older than he was. She was married to a beat cop in Brooklyn, and they had two grown kids. Peter was forty-two and he guessed she was about forty-six, but it was only a guess. She was relatively private. They had worked together for six years and had no plans to change; simply a good working relationship, no fooling around. They never socialized and Peter had met her husband only once. He seemed nice enough, but he obviously wasn't looking for new friends.

What Peter was not happy about, however, was Hui Chang. He met Hui Chang on Friday March 1, 1996. Peter and Linda were called to a porno movie theater in the Times Square section where they met the stabbed-to-death Hui Chang draped over a toilet in a stall with no door. There were no witnesses, and no one appeared to have any idea what happened. Apparently, no one goes to these movie theaters; that's why there are so many of them. It was over three months since his death, and Detectives Salvino and Richter were no closer to solving Chang's murder now than on the night it occurred. Linda had lost interest in the case. She told Peter time and time again that he was wasting his time, and hers, because the case would never be solved, no matter how hard they worked it. They had no motive, no suspects, no witnesses, and no hard evidence other than a knife with no fingerprints. They had other cases pending, which were alive.

The only thing that kept Peter interested was Chang's mother, who was one of the nicest people he had ever met on the job. She ran a small restaurant in Chinatown, and would stop by the station house each week with a huge lunch for the detectives, hoping to get a progress report. Hui was a quiet boy who kept to a small circle of friends. He had an excellent job working for a medical lab. No one could figure out what he was doing in that porno house; he just wasn't the type. At twenty-eight he seemed well on his way to a great life.

The crime looked like a simple robbery gone bad. His wallet, watch, and ring were all taken. Did he resist? He seemed too smart for that. But something set his assailant off. There was only one stab wound. Both Hui's and the assailant's bad luck that it transected the aorta. He died in a few moments. *The assailant couldn't do that again if he were given twenty attempts*, Detective Salvino thought. A simple robbery became a homicide. Bad luck for all. Really bad luck for the Widow Chang, who lost her only child in a filthy toilet, in a filthy movie theater, showing filthy movies.

* * * * * * * * *

It was Thursday June 13th when Paulie visited his old friend Peter Salvino. Paulie had called the day before and Peter told him about the Chang case. Paulie didn't think there would be a connection, but Brian sent him to check it out. Paulie didn't mind, and he looked forward to seeing Peter, who he hadn't seen in years.

"Paulie," Peter yelled as Paulie walked into Mrs. Chang's restaurant. Peter wanted Paulie to meet her to see why the obvious had to be wrong. Peter did not believe for one moment that Hui Chang voluntarily walked into that porno theater.

Paulie sat down and Mrs. Chang served them a meal to end all meals. It probably looked strange to the other customers that these two obviously Italian men were being doted on by Mrs. Chang. The other customers must have thought they were mobsters.

"Peter, tell me everything about your case. Leave out nothing," Paulie began, as he turned on a small tape recorder. Paulie couldn't read his own handwriting, and Brian made him carry the recorder wherever he went.

"Linda...She's my partner. Linda and me are in the station house at about eleven when a call comes in from the porno theater. The call was 11:04 P.M. according to the log. We took the call and were there by 11:21. We were shown in by a John Savage. He was a real lowlife. It turns out he runs the place; he even sleeps there. Paulie, you wouldn't believe how filthy the place was." Peter was going through his notebook carefully. He didn't want to leave anything out, or make a mistake, because he knew Brian Walsh would be listening to his every word.

"Savage took us to a bathroom. I almost threw up, the smell was so horrible. It hadn't been cleaned in God knows how long. In one of the stalls, none of which had doors, there was a body draped over a toilet. He was face down. He looked like he didn't belong there. He was nicely dressed, Chinese, no tattoos, no earrings—just a clean-cut kid. He looked young, but I later found out he was twenty-eight. He had no identification on him—no wallet, no watch, no rings. I could see from the marks on his wrist and left ring finger that he wore both a watch and a ring. They were obviously stolen."

"I knew you would be a great detective some day," Paulie joked. He could see that Peter was taking this too personally.

Peter continued. "Mrs. Chang later told us he had a very expensive Rolex. It was not the big one, but nevertheless still quite expensive. We didn't identify him until late the next day. He had never been fingerprinted and was single. If he wasn't going to his mother's restaurant Saturday for an important meeting it may have been days before anyone reported him missing."

"What was the meeting about?" Paulie asked.

"Nothing significant. His mother was interviewing a new accountant and wanted Hui there. He was all she had. Her husband was killed in a plane crash years ago on a trip back to China. Hui made good money—$51,500 a year."

"What did he do for $51,500?"

"He worked for one of those medical labs; you know, it does blood tests. Your doctor draws your blood in his office and he sends it to the lab."

"What did his boss and other employees say about Hui?"

"He was a great employee. A real hard worker. He was actually a supervisor of some section. I forget exactly what he did, but everyone liked him. No one could put him together with a porno house, particularly a gay porno house. He had no enemies. The investigation was a complete dead end. We looked at everyone in the porno theater, including Savage. No one ever saw Chang there before. Maybe he just ran in to take a leak and some lowlife saw his watch and figured Chang would be an easy score; I just don't know. We're nowhere with this one, Paulie. You got anything that could help me?"

"I wish I did, Peter, but I don't. I frankly don't see any possible connection between our case and yours. I'm going to visit Hui's employer, with your permission, just to keep Brian happy. Hear that, Brian? I'm working my ass off for the mayor." Paulie then turned the tape recorder off, and they talked about old times.

When the two detectives finished they both thanked Mrs. Chang profusely as they left. Peter had already told her many times that he would never close the case until he got the son-of-a-bitch that killed her son.

Paulie drove to West Side Labs where he spoke to Hui Chang's boss, Mr. Joel Weisburg, who confirmed everything Peter told him. The lab was very impressive. Paulie could not tell exactly how big it was, but the directory listed it as covering three floors. *After all*, he thought, *there's a lot a sick people in Manhattan*, and he didn't mean just the "sickos" he saw in his line of work.

As Paulie got up to leave, he thought of Peter's only unanswered question.

"One final question, Mr. Weisburg. Did Mr. Chang have any special duties at the lab?"

"Yes, he was in charge of our sperm bank. It's the largest one in Manhattan and our most successful section. We will miss him. He had a lot of very bright connections, if you know what I mean."

When Paulie left West Side Labs it was late, and he drove straight home to Queens. "Sperm bank. No wonder he made $51,500. Some people would pay anything for a child," he spoke out loud as he drove.

* * * * * * * * *

Willie and Tommy brought thirty-six unsolved homicides to the "War Room." Betty and her girls were overwhelmed, but they all seemed to like the work. They busily cross-referenced numbers, dates, anything they could think of, but nothing matched. When Paulie came in to work the next day, he added the new file, Hui Chang, to the pile. Still nothing fit. Brian was edgy.

Another week passed, and on Friday June 21, just after the morning briefing ended, Monica Berk, one of Betty's uniforms, asked to see her right away. The uniforms were not allowed in the "War Room." Betty returned in a few minutes and asked Brian to allow Monica to show them something she found.

"Let her in, Betty."

"Good morning, Detective Walsh," Monica said somewhat nervously. She saw the pictures on the wall and almost puked. Brian saw this coming, but he was too late. He led her to a chair facing away from the pictures while Tommy brought her a glass of water. She immediately regained her composure and began.

"I was checking the employment records of several of the cases and I noticed that the only time Elizabeth Anderson took any time off was a two-week period in May of last year. She never took any vacation at any other time in eight years. The strange thing is that Hui Chang took those same two weeks off, and he hadn't taken any time off for at least three years, as far as we can tell."

Brian sat still. He had listened to Paulie's tape and dismissed the Chang case. He jumped up and shouted, "How the hell could they be related?"

Monica was taken aback. She thought she screwed up.

"Monica, you did good," Tommy said. "Don't be scared of him. He's really talking to himself when he yells like that."

"Yes, Monica, good work," Brian added. "Thanks a lot. Any more matches?"

"Not yet, Detective Walsh."

"Keep looking. Where there's one there could be more. Thanks again." Monica was dismissed.

Brian stood up. "Well, people, what do you think?"

"Obviously we have to find out where they each were on those dates in May," Paulie said.

"Exactly. Then why are you still here? Tommy, check where Anderson was. Paulie, check Chang. Willie, stay here. I want to go over some things with you. Everyone, be back here tomorrow with answers.

Call if anything pops up."

Tommy and Paulie left. Betty went back to her uniforms.

"Willie, what's going on in that head? I heard you listening to Paulie's tape all day yesterday. Is something bothering you?"

"They are connected, Brian. I don't know why, or even how, but they are definitely connected."

"How? Make your case."

"It's the sperm. The volume and DNA analysis indicate it came from four men, yet there was no trauma to her genital area; we all agree to that. Now we find a guy who works in a sperm bank. I think the sperm was planted and she wasn't raped at all, just like you said the other day. That would account for the lack of bruising and the normal condition of the vagina and rectum. If Chang wasn't killed a month before the girl, he would be our number-one suspect. The only question is why would a killer this smart fail to mutilate her in the one place she needed it most to cover up his crime?"

"Exactly, Willie. Maybe he wanted us to figure it out. Maybe he's testing us, or playing with our minds. That means there will be more. We might have a serial killer."

"I hope not, Brian, I hate those. Once the press gets hold of that we get every weirdo in the city confessing, and the investigation turns to shit."

"I know. Don't tell anyone, not even Tommy and Paulie. They'll figure it out soon enough."

* * * * * * * *

Paulie called his friend Peter Salvino.

"Peter, I may have been wrong about the Chang case. There was a match with ours. A flimsy match, which probably won't turn out to be anything, but a match nevertheless."

"What's the match?"

"I'll tell you in person. Meet me at West Side Labs this morning at eleven. Then set up a visit with Mrs. Chang at one, for lunch. I'm starting to like Chinese food, but don't ever tell my wife or mother I said that or I'm one dead Italian."

"See you at eleven."

Peter and Paulie arrived at West Side Labs at the same time. They were escorted to Mr. Weisburg's office. A woman was present who was introduced as Nora Pendleton, bookkeeper. She had been working on Hui Chang's employment record since 9:30 that morning, shortly after Paulie called.

"I have his records," Ms. Pendleton began. "He was on vacation from May 8 to May 21, 1995. He came back to work on May 22. I checked with the other employees, as you asked, and no one remembers him going anywhere. He simply asked for vacation time without saying anything else."

"Mr. Weisburg," Paulie started, "could you send for the employee who was immediately under Mr. Chang at that time and have him come here now?"

"It's a she," Mr. Weisburg said.

Mr. Weisburg realized that this was not a request and immediately sent for Janet Thompson, who was now running the sperm bank. Introductions were made even though they had all briefly met before.

"Hello again, Detective Salvino and Detective Lucero."

"Mrs. Thompson, you may be able to help us," Paulie said. "It was very unusual for Mr. Chang to take any time away from work. I believe he only had one vacation in three or four years."

"Five," Ms. Pendleton interjected.

"Okay, five. I want you to think very hard. Review all your records. Speak to everyone who was working under, or with, Mr. Chang last year. Speak to anyone who may have stopped working here. Speak to the cleaning service. Speak to everyone."

Paulie was getting his Italian up.

"I want you to tell me when I call you Monday exactly where Hui Chang went on vacation from May 8 to May 21 last year. It is inconceivable to me that someone would go on his first vacation in five years and not tell someone where he was going."

Mr. Weisburg, Ms. Pendleton, and Mrs. Thompson had just had their first look at a working homicide detective. They felt very uneasy. The first time Detective Lucero had visited was not at all like this. Mr. Weisburg made a mental note to add one more line to the employee request-for-vacation slip.

"Nice going, Paulie," Peter said as the two detectives exited the main entrance of West Side Labs. "I thought that old maid Pendleton was going to pass out. Thank God you told Thompson to ask around, not the old maid."

"What's wrong with people today Peter? Nobody seems to know the guy or give a shit about him. He's dead and they go on like nothing happened. No one should die without friends. Let's go see Mrs. Chang. Maybe with a mother that nice he didn't need friends."

"Maybe," Peter said, "he was just happy with his work."

They arrived at Chang's Chinese Restaurant to the same reception as last time. Mrs. Chang was happy to see the two detectives who would catch her son's murderer and prove that he wasn't some pervert that hung out in those places—places her son simply wouldn't go. The detectives agreed with her. They never found one shred of pornography in his apartment. They found plenty of books—books on art, on music, on drama—but no pornography. Peter had spoken to his friends in vice, and they told him they had never seen a pornography addict without the stuff all over his apartment. They usually had pictures, tapes, books, and all kinds of toys all over the place. No, Hui Chang was at that theater for another reason. What was it?

Unfortunately, Mrs. Chang had no idea why her son was not at work last May. She did know that he definitely did not go on vacation out of town.

* * * * * * * * *

The tall man with the blue eyes knew exactly why Hui Chang was in the porno movie theater—he dragged him in. He had been following Chang for two weeks, night and day. He had been in Chang's apartment several times, but Chang never knew. When the tall man with the blue eyes did not want you to know something, you didn't. He had been at West End Labs also, and Chang never knew that either; no one knew. He had never seen Chang until two weeks before his death, but that was all the time it took to plan and carry out Chang's execution. The man knew several things about Chang that no one else knew. The main thing, and it was the one thing that made his execution so easy, was that he was a nightwalker. Every night Chang would leave his apartment at precisely ten and go for a long, vigorous walk. It took him through the Times Square section and then back to his apartment. Every night, like clockwork, rain or shine. He never changed the route. The tall man noticed that his walk took him past a small, sleazy porno theater. The blue-eyed man despised pornography and anyone associated with it. The theater would be a perfect setting. *How ironic for Chang*, he thought. The blue-eyed man spent several nights in the theater checking every square foot. He noticed that the theater was never crowded. This would be the spot. He would make it look like just another fag being robbed. The cops might not even look too hard at this one. Nevertheless, he would be careful. He would use all his skills and training. He would never be caught.

On Friday March 1st the blue-eyed man waited by the movie theater at 10:25 P.M. Chang would walk by at any moment, assuming he started his walk at the usual time.

Unfortunately for Hui Chang, his desire to remain fit continued.

It was raining slightly when the blue-eyed man saw Chang coming. Chang walked right at him. There was a small collision, a gun was produced, and Chang walked with the man into the theater. The blue-eyed man had previously purchased two tickets and now handed them to the old man in the booth. The old man did not look up. He didn't have to. Just two more fags going in to do whatever they do.

The man walked right behind Chang and held a gun firmly in Chang's back. Chang was terrified.

"Relax," the man said, "just a robbery. Do what you are told and you'll be back home shortly."

Chang was slightly relieved. He had nothing of value except his watch, and that was replaceable. He would cooperate. The blue-eyed man had lied. As they walked into the bathroom, the man switched from a gun to a knife, grabbed Chang from behind by the neck with his powerful right hand, and inserted the knife with surgical precision into Chang's back, just to the left of his lumbar spine below the ribs. He then cut back, transecting the abdominal aorta.

Detective Peter Salveno was wrong—the blue-eyed man would hit the aorta twenty out of twenty times.

Chang was dead in a few minutes. There was no struggle. Chang was no match for the man's strong right arm. The man eased Chang's lifeless body onto a toilet seat, leaving the knife in place until most of Chang's blood was loose in his abdominal cavity and he was sure

Chang's heart had stopped pumping. There was very little mess with this technique, and the man did not want blood all over him for he had much work to do that evening. The blue-eyed man removed Chang's wallet, watch, and ring, and then his real target, Chang's keys. He took the three keys and made careful impressions in a box of clay he produced from his pocket. When finished, he placed the keys back in Chang's pants and walked quietly out of the theater. No one saw him. The old man taking tickets was asleep as the man walked by. Good luck for the old man, who would never know how close to death he came.

The tall blue-eyed man walked north for four blocks and threw Chang's watch, ring, and unopened wallet into a sewer. He turned west, walked for two blocks to a store he had visited earlier in the week, and quickly ducked into a small alley that led to the back of the store. After outsmarting the lock and alarm system with minimal effort, he disappeared into the darkness of a back room. *Some locksmith*, he laughed to himself. Eighteen minutes later he left with three shiny new keys, resetting the alarm as he exited into the alley. His next destination was West Side Labs. He hailed a cab several blocks away and had it drop him at a bar six blocks from the lab, covering the remaining distance on foot. *Continue to be careful*, he reminded himself, even though he felt this was a simple operation.

At West Side Labs he had little trouble with the alarm and was shortly inside. He could not believe that an operation as large as the lab did not have a security guard. The blue-eyed man made his way to the sperm bank on the second floor. Using his new keys, he entered the outer lab and cautiously walked to the refrigerated storage area in the back of the lab. He opened the walk-in freezer with the third key and stood in front of the frozen sperm. The man was very careful; he did not want anyone to know he had visited. He removed a special insulated container from the bag he was carrying and surveyed the numerous sperm samples. He didn't care what type he took; he wasn't shopping for a child. He wanted a small sample from four individuals, which wouldn't be missed. *They must pay these donors quite well*, he thought as he looked at the twelve samples from donor XY 36456A12. They won't miss one. In like fashion, he collected three other samples and put the frozen material into his insulated pouch. He was meticulous, and put everything back in place. No one would know he was here. Well, maybe Chang would know if he were to return. "Not likely," the man said out loud.

A few minutes later, the blue-eyed man carefully reset the alarm and slowly emerged from the building. As expected, there were no problems. He then returned to the apartment his organization kept in Manhattan and placed the samples in the special freezer he had previously procured. He poured himself some cognac and sat down at the desk to plan the final steps of his next project—the murder of that fucking, no-good cunt, Elizabeth Anderson. As he spoke those words in his mind, he became enraged. At the same time, a tear rolled ever so slowly down his right cheek. He did not bother to wipe it away; he just sat and stared into nothingness.

Chapter 9

Tommy made an appointment to see Elizabeth Anderson's principal, James Erickson. After two hours with him and some other teachers, Tommy was pissed. No one knew where this girl was last May. He knew the trip to the lesbian group wouldn't help, but he made it anyway. They were not pleased to see him, especially Barbara Peterson. She did speak to him, though. She was smart enough to know she had little choice.

"Ms. Peterson," Tommy began, "let me apologize for the other day. I'm here to help your friend. I'm sure you want us to get the guy who did this and put him away for good so he doesn't do this to anyone else. Maybe he hates lesbians, and this is the start of many more attacks."

Tommy wished he hadn't said that when he saw the look on her face.

"Do you think that's what happened?" Ms. Peterson asked, horrified.

"No. It's a possibility, but we think it was just some psycho and she was just unlucky. Just a random thing, you know—just in the wrong place at the wrong time. Do you know where Elizabeth went last May? She took two weeks off from work while school was still in session. Was there some problem? Something you may not have remembered last time?"

Barbara could not think of anything. She didn't know Elizabeth went away and she was angry that Elizabeth did not tell her. She thought they were close.

Tommy thanked Barbara, and then couldn't resist. She was such a beautiful girl.

"Now, Barbara, please don't take this the wrong way. You have a right to be whatever you want. I respect that. But here's my card. If you ever want to try a guy out please give me a call."

He thought she might hit him, but she laughed and took his card.

What a waste, he thought, this time making sure he kept it to himself.

His day was finished. He was getting tired of bringing Brian bad news every morning. Something would change, and hopefully soon.

* * * * * * * * *

On Tuesday June 25 the next break—if you can call it that—occurred. Brian had just returned from a 9 A.M. meeting with the mayor and the chief of detectives. Sal had warned Brian of the meeting's agenda late Monday night. The mayor was not happy. It was less than five months to the election, and the teachers' union, and every lesbian group in New York, were still hounding him.

"Why don't they all join one group?" the mayor asked. "They're all driving me nuts. What do they think? Do they think that Republican bastard will care more about them than me? They're nuts if they think that."

The mayor was extremely upset. He was rambling.

Brian spoke. "Mr. Mayor, we do have some leads, and we feel confident that a breakthrough will occur soon." Brian was biting his tongue. He hated lying, but he knew he had to do something to calm this guy down. The mayor knew nothing about police work, and at any moment could say anything to the press. Brian would then have to put out the fires, as the press would be on his back within minutes of any statement the mayor would make. It had happened before; it would happen again. Brian thought how nice it would be to have someone with a brain as the mayor of one of the most important cities in the world. He told Sal once that he would make a great mayor. Brian was sure that was Sal's long-range plan. Maybe in four years. It didn't matter if the Democrat asshole or the Republican asshole won the upcoming election; Sal could definitely beat either one in four years.

Little did Brian know that almost as he was speaking the words

"...a breakthrough will occur soon," one was occurring right in his office. Monica Berk was at it again. *She's like a little girl*, Brian thought after her last presentation. Maybe five feet tall, maybe a hundred pounds. Brian liked her. Betty said she was a work machine, and no one could do what she could do with computers.

Brian left the mayor's office with Sal.

"Brian, he's such an jerk. Don't sweat it. He's way behind in the poles so he's going crazy. Fuck him."

"Sal, I want this guy bad."

"You mean guys, don't you?"

"No. I think it was one guy. And it wasn't random. He wanted her dead."

"What about the four sperm samples? What about the DNA?"

"I don't know yet. And there's more. We are working another case that may be connected to this one."

"Brian, don't fucking say it! Don't say it! Don't say the fucking S-word!"

"Sorry, Sal, we might, and I stress *might*, have a serial killer."

Sal was visibly upset. He hated serial killers. He was involved with the Son of Sam and it nearly put him in the nuthouse.

"Brian, keep a lid on this for now. Hopefully you will be wrong. Who else knows?"

"Only Willie."

"He wouldn't even tell me, so for now we're okay. If you need my help, Brian, don't be afraid to call. I was thinking back in the mayor's office that it wouldn't be too bad if he wasn't elected. But if it's a serial, you better get him fast or none of us will get a summer vacation."

* * * * * * * * *

Brian got back to the squad and found Betty and little Monica in the "War Room." Fortunately, Betty had taken the pictures down. Everyone had seen enough of the mutilated Elizabeth Anderson. "What's up?" Brian asked.

"Monica found another match," Betty answered.

Brian was really getting to like Monica.

"Go ahead, Monica," Brian said, smiling.

"I was looking at the bank statements of Elizabeth Anderson to see if we could find some information which would help us find where she went for those two weeks in May of 1995. I couldn't find anything. If she went anywhere, she didn't spend any money, unless it was cash. But there's no record of any cash coming out of her checking or savings account. No ATM withdrawals. No credit card cash advances. Nothing. I also looked at Chang's records, and the same thing. Nothing. Then I noticed a peculiar thing. On May 23rd last year there was a deposit made into Anderson's checking account of $126.20. The only other deposits made were her paycheck, which is the same every other week. This deposit stuck out."

Brian was lost. This was certainly not the revelation he was hoping for.

Betty saw the look on his face. "Keep going, Monica," she said.

"On May 24th of last year the same exact amount was deposited into Chang's checking account. Again, only a one-time entry." Monica starred at Brian Walsh, whose face made a radical change from skepticism to puzzlement.

Brian thought to himself that it had to mean something. But what? It was too bizarre to be a coincidence. Monica did it again. But what did she do?

"Great work, Monica. I really appreciate it. Great work."

"What do you thing it means, Detective Walsh?"

"I'm not sure right now, but it will become clear soon."

Betty and Monica left. Betty was proud of her girl.

* * * * * * * * * *

Brian sat at his desk. It was almost 1:30 P.M. He would call the squad back. They were just doing repeat interviews anyway. They would brainstorm all afternoon, and they would figure it out. If they couldn't, no one could. He had Betty start the beepers humming with that ridiculous sound they made. Brian would never carry a beeper; no fucking way!

Dr. Susan Blakely called at 1:45 P.M.

"Detective Walsh?"

"I thought we got to the Brian stage."

"Sorry. Brian, I have been going over the Anderson case with the M.E. and some path friends. She wasn't raped. It looks like the only reasonable explanation is that someone injected the semen into her vagina and rectum. I guess they were trying to make it look like a rape, a crime of passion, if you will. I fell for it. I feel so stupid."

"It's okay; we all missed it. I've been looking at her picture every day for weeks and missed it. We all did."

"Thanks. Keep me informed, if you can. I'd like to see you get these sickos."

"I will. And I will."

* * * * * * * * *

Tommy, Willie, and Paulie straggled in over the next hour, all from different parts of the city. Willie had been visiting some of Anderson's neighbors, who were getting sick of seeing him around the building. He wasn't particularly fond of yuppies, and was glad to hear the beeper. Tommy was at West Side Labs talking to the maintenance workers. He hoped someone saw something on Chang's desk that they were afraid to admit before. Paulie was at Mrs. Chang's restaurant looking through Hui's belongings, which she stored on the unoccupied third floor of her building. *She must be doing pretty well with the restaurant*, Paulie thought. He hoped so, because she had nothing else left.

Brian spoke, "Monica has come up with another match. To keep it short, both Anderson and Chang made a one-time deposit of $126.20 into their checking accounts the week they returned from their vacations last May. They never made any other deposit similar to that. They never made any deposit that wasn't easily traced, like their paychecks. What it means, I don't know, but I know it means something. Any thoughts?"

"Such a small amount, boss," Paulie said. "Doesn't seem like anything illegal. No drugs or anything."

Tommy and Willie were silent. Brian called Betty in.

"Monica find anything else?" he asked.

"No. Not yet. If there is anything else there, she will find it."

Paulie got a phone call from Janet Thompson at West Side Labs. She sounded very serious when she told him that no one who currently worked, or had recently worked, at the lab had any idea where Hui Chang was on his vacation in May of 1995. Paulie was not surprised.

Then they got some good news. After a long trial, the jury convicted Ambrosia. They sent him upstate for life without parole. Everyone congratulated Willie. He did get that S.O.B. Rubenstein.

The squad went their separate ways around five. Nothing enlightening occurred the remainder of the afternoon. Brian knew they would be thinking about it all night. He was heading home when his daughter Maryann called him on the car phone. Brian hated the car phone, but accepted it as a necessary evil.

"Dad?"

"Hi, Maryann. How's Dennis? Has he recovered from the other night yet?"

"He's fine. But I'm not."

"What is it, honey?" Brian asked alarmed.

Brian was very concerned. Maryann could hear it in his voice. He would do anything to protect her. Anything.

"Nothing serious, dad. I just got called for jury duty, and there's no way I can spend the time. Can you help me?"

Brian was relieved.

"When you go down to the courthouse, and you have to go down, just tell them your father is a cop. That's all you have to say. No one will pick you then for sure. I can't get you out of going down that one time though, honey, but it should only take a few hours, and you should never be bothered again. Ask for Ramona. I forget her last name, but she likes me. Tell her who you are and she'll have you out of there as soon as possible."

"Thanks, dad. Say hi to mom. Love you."

"Love you too."

Brian continued his drive to Bayside. The traffic on the expressway was brutal. He still loved his new car. He was just getting to his exit when he realized that he had to be the stupidest cop that ever lived. They were on jury duty together. Anderson and Chang were on the same jury for two weeks in May of 1995. That explains everything. No trips out of town. No special phone calls. No credit card bills. No discussions with friends or relatives. And those stupid checks—a "thank you" for two, usually wasted, weeks of your life from the benevolent city of New York.

Things were coming together. He couldn't wait until tomorrow. He was going to solve this whole mess. The asshole mayor would be reelected, but Brian didn't care; he would put this killer away forever.

* * * * * * * * * *

June 26th is going to be a great day, Brian thought as he walked into the office. It was 6:30 A.M., and Betty was the only one there. Brian walked over to the blackboard and wrote, in big letters, "Jury Duty." It explained everything. The more he thought about it the previous evening, the more convinced he was that this was the critical step in the investigation. This would bring the man down. Maybe he was one of the other jurors. Brian would find out.

Willie walked in first. He saw the blackboard and saw Brian smiling. Willie started to smile. He tossed Brian a three-by-five index card that had the words "Jury Duty" written on it in Willie's unmistakable handwriting.

"Great minds think alike," Brian said.

Tommy and Paulie weren't far behind, and they too saw the blackboard. They had no cards to toss.

"That's it, boss. You're a genius. What now?" Paulie asked.

"What now?" Brian exclaimed, "I want the name of every person on that jury, whatever the case was. And I want the names today!"

Willie reminded Brian that it wouldn't be that easy. The names of jurors were kept confidential. There was no ready list of jurors for each case. It would take time, and even if they found what trial they were jurors on it would take the presiding judge to open the files.

"You find out what trial they were jurors on and I'll get the judge to open the files," was Brian's answer. "Everyone to the hall of records. Bring Betty and her girls. There must have been fifty or more trials going on at that time. Maybe there wasn't even a verdict. Look at the ones that were plea-bargained down during that time also. It could have been anything. Go, people, go!"

Brian was wrong. There weren't fifty trials going on in Manhattan during those two weeks in May; there were 176. Sure, they were not all trials; most never actually got to trial. The juries are picked, but they often just sit around waiting while the real haggling goes on behind closed doors. The simple fact is that the criminal justice system has neither the money, the manpower, nor the time to bring every criminal to trial. Quick justice. Get the bad guy off the street as soon as possible, for the most time each side will agree to, for the least amount of money the city can spend, and then hope for the best when the psycho gets out in five to ten years even crazier than before. Maybe the city will get lucky and another psycho will kill him in prison.

"This will take weeks," Tommy said to Paulie. "There's got to be a better way."

Betty was already working on a better way. She knew all the bailiffs in the court system, and she thought it would help if she could just narrow the search to a particular courtroom or even a particular building. Trials took place in every courtroom in Manhattan. Betty took off with pictures of Anderson and Chang and began to visit old friends, both hers and her father's.

Two days later Betty had the answer. One of her friends, Sally Gray, recognized the pictures. There was absolutely no doubt in her mind. Sally had spent two days catering to their every need on May 18th and 19th of 1995. They were jurors on a sex crime case. It took four days of waiting and stalling to pick a jury, four days to try the case, and two days to convict Robert Johanson of molesting little Nancy Tailor. Sally remembered it well; after all, who could forget the rape of a little girl.

Betty brought this information to the squad Friday morning June 28. Brian was ecstatic. It was just a little over one month since they got the case. Things were progressing nicely. Then came the really bad news.

Brian knew it would be difficult to convince any judge to identify his jurors. To do so would undermine the whole jury system. If a juror could not rely on anonymity, or if a juror feared for his or her life, no one would be guilty again. Surely the judge would make an exception in this case. Two dead jurors. No judge wants that. That's when Brian got the bad news, presented to him by Tommy.

"Boss, you better sit down."

Brian knew things were going too well.

"What is it, Tommy?"

"The presiding judge on the trial of Robert Johanson was ..."

"Wait, don't say it! I can't believe it! I can't fucking believe it! Go ahead, say it," Brian almost shouted.

Tommy continued, "... The Honorable Morton R. Levy. Detective Brian Michael Walsh's favorite judge." Tommy wanted to laugh out loud but didn't quite have the nerve. He knew that Brian loved him like a son, but occasionally parents have been known to shoot their children.

Willie just groaned. Paulie said nothing. Betty had no idea what just happened, but from the look on Brian's face it couldn't have been good.

Brian had spent three days in jail in 1982, compliments of Judge Levy. Contempt of court was what the judge called it, but Brian knew better. Brian had just made a fool of the judge in court, and when called into chambers with the prosecutor and the judge Brian only made matters worse. The A.D.A. who was trying the case at the time begged Brian to apologize on the way to the judge's chambers, even though Brian was right on a point of law. Brian and the A.D.A. had done their homework. The judge was dead wrong. The judge was going to exclude evidence that was critical to the prosecution. It certainly did not help matters when Brian told the judge that if the rapist-murderer got off the first thing Brian was going to do was give him the judge's daughter's home address. The judge went out of his mind and, just like that, Brian was in jail for three days. Since that day they hated each other to the extent that the chief judge never assigned Levy to any case that Brian's squad handled. After that incident, Brian's star continued to rise while the judge's fell. The judge blamed Brian for everything that happened to him after that, even though it was his own incompetence that led to his high reversal rate.

Now Brian would have to call on Judge Levy. He wasn't looking forward to it, but it had to be done. He owed it to the squad, and to Elizabeth Anderson, to take whatever shit the judge would try to throw at him.

"Betty, call Judge Morton Levy and set up an appointment for me first thing Monday morning. Tell Levy the mayor wants us to meet; maybe that will scare the hell out of him. Call the chief and ask him to call the mayor and let him know about the meeting, just in case Levy has the courage to call him.

"Now, people, let's find out everything about Robert Johanson. Get a transcript of the trial. Interview the detectives on the case. And maybe you guys could come up with something on this case. If it wasn't for Monica and Betty we would still be standing here with our dicks in our hand. Sorry, Betty. Everybody go."

The squad knew he was kidding. He appreciated their work and loved them all. Every once in a while he had to remind them who was boss. Or maybe he was reminding himself. Who knew? Brian would go home to Bayside and maybe go the track on Saturday. He would relax Sunday and call the kids. He would then be ready Monday for what had to be the most humiliating thing he had ever had to do: ask the Honorable Morton R. Levy for a favor. The thought of it made him sick. He would rather go to Levy's office, beat the shit out of the fool, and go back to jail for a month. But that wasn't an option. He needed Levy, and Levy would know it.

* * * * * * * * *

Brian arrived at the office at nine o'clock Monday July 1st and sat down at his desk to finish some paperwork; but he was really just killing time while waiting for his ten o'clock appointment with Judge Levy. He knew he would remember this day for the rest of his life. The squad was also killing time. They all knew that the next move was Levy's. Levy didn't know it yet, but they did. Tommy drove Brian over to the judge's office and they walked into his chambers at 9:45. A beautiful young girl showed them into the waiting room. Brian felt weird. The girl looked just like Maureen did twenty-five or so years ago. It was scary.

The girl returned shortly and ushered Brian into Judge Levy's private office. Brian told Tommy to stay in the waiting room. Tommy didn't mind. The girl did not go unnoticed by him either.

"Good morning, Your Honor."

An icy stare greeted Brian.

"What do you want?"

The judge looks terrible, Brian thought. He hadn't seen him in a few years but he looked like shit. He was only one year older than Brian. Brian hoped he didn't look that bad; surely someone would have told him if he did.

"Your Honor," the words made Brian sick. *Your Honor my ass.* He continued, "we need your help on a very difficult and important case. The mayor, chief of detectives, and I would greatly appreciate any assistance you could give us." Brian thought he should spread the blame around a little.

"What is it?"

"Last year you presided over a case. A man named Robert Johanson was convicted of molesting a child."

"That was a clean case, no error there. I remember it well. The jury had no problem convicting him."

"I know judge. That's not the problem. It's possible that two of the jurors have been murdered. We need you to give permission for the jury file to be opened. We need to see if there is a connection. You are the only one who can give that permission."

"What? Are you crazy? That can never be done. No way. I would never agree to that. Those jurors have a right to privacy. I won't do it."

"But judge, maybe one of them is a murderer, or maybe others on the jury will be killed. You can save lives here, Your Honor. We really need that list. We're stuck without it. The mayor wants it."

"Don't pull that mayor stuff with me. I know the law. I'm the only one who can give you that list, and the answer is no! Not now! Not ever! Now get out of here and don't come back!"

Brian stormed out of Levy's office. He did not stop to collect Tommy, who was talking to the young girl. Tommy jumped up, said good-bye, and followed Brian to the car. Brian was furious.

"Let's go see the chief," he said.

Tommy drove to Police Plaza without saying a word. This was not the time for humor.

Brian presented his problem to Sal, who sat back in his chair and looked up at the ceiling.

"Why did it have to be him? Any other judge would do it. I'll talk to him, and I'll get the mayor to talk to him, but I can't promise anything. Levy may stand on this issue simply because he's never stood for anything in his life. No one takes him seriously, and this may be his chance to get back at everyone."

Sal walked Brian and Tommy to the elevator, consoling his old friend as he walked. It was the beginning of two very frustrating weeks.

Chapter 10

Friday July 12th began exactly like the previous eight workdays. Brian ranted and raved that nobody was able to get him the list of jurors on the Johanson trial either through proper or, if necessary, improper channels. Nobody, including the mayor, the chief of detectives, or even the police commissioner could get Judge Levy to change his mind.

"Can anyone think of anything we've missed here, people?" Brian almost begged. "I know this guy isn't finished yet. Someone else will be dead soon."

"Sorry, boss," Paulie said. "I've reached out to everyone I know who could help us, but the word is out. The judge will crucify anyone who leaks the names. He's being a real prick."

Willie had nothing to say. He wasn't used to failure and he was thinking way too seriously about shooting that fuck Levy.

"Where's Tommy?" Brian asked.

"He's working on something he didn't want to talk about yet, boss. Too preliminary he said. He'll tell you at the party tomorrow," Paulie answered.

"What party?" Brian asked.

Almost before he finished asking the question, he remembered the answer. He would be fifty-four tomorrow. Maureen was having an evening cookout for him, partly to get his mind off the case for a few hours, he remembered her saying. Some close friends and the squad would be there. *It's usually fun*, Brian thought to himself.

"Oh, that party," Brian added.

Betty came into the room with a large cardboard box. For a second Brian's heart almost stopped. Betty had done it. *She got the jury list,* he thought to himself.

"We finally got the transcript of the Robert Johanson trial. Sorry it took so long, boss," Betty said, dashing Brian's hopes for a great day. "I made a copy for everyone."

"I want to know everything about this Johanson guy. And I mean not just what's in the transcript. Interview everyone again. Maybe something will turn up that will point us in the right direction and we can have an answer before Christmas. Willie, you go up to Attica Monday and find out anything you can. Speak to Johanson. Speak to his cell neighbors. Does he have any enemies? Find out about his family. Bring some pictures of Chang and Anderson; I'm sure he'll remember them. Maybe he can tell us about some of the other jurors. You know what to do. Don't take 'no' from anyone up there. The trial lasted only four days, and the jury was out less than two days. He got twenty-five-to-life so he must have looked pretty guilty to them. Today, people, read the transcript and the police reports. I want the arresting cops interviewed ASAP next week. Do it here; I want to talk to some of them myself. I'm going to see the chief. Have a lovely day. See you tomorrow."

Brian drove over to Sal's office. He needed help with Levy. He simply had to have that jury list.

"I'm sorry, Brian," Sal began, "but we can't get him to budge. He won't let anyone have that list. The mayor has been all over him. We've had congressmen call. Nothing. The stupid fuck wants everyone to remember him as a champion of the jurors or some other stupid thing. I don't know what's going on in his mind. That's assuming the son-of-a-bitch has a mind."

"Sal, I'm telling you there are only two possibilities: either someone on the jury killed Anderson and Chang, or someone is going to kill every single member of that jury. Did you hear me, Sal? Every fucking member of the jury. Twelve citizens. Twelve voting citizens. All dead on our watch. Just because some asshole judge doesn't like me. That's really what it's about; nothing else. You get that list or I'm going to send Willie to his house to get it, and I'm not fucking around here, Sal! Get the fucking list!"

Brian stormed out. Sal couldn't remember seeing him that angry in many years. Maybe he really meant it when he said he would send Willie. Maybe that would be a good idea. Nobody really cared about Levy. Sal shook his head. The chief of detectives couldn't think like that.

* * * * * * * * *

Brian slept late Saturday. After all, it was his birthday, he reasoned. In actual fact, he stayed up until 5:00 A.M. reading the transcript of the Johanson trial. He planned to just glance at it, but he found he could not put it down. It was not because the trial was exciting that had him so riveted, but rather that the man was convicted at all. There was not one single solitary piece of evidence presented during the whole trial that Johanson was a sexual deviate, or that he could even remotely be guilty of this particular crime. Brian was sick over this fact. If he were the detective on this case, he would have turned Johanson loose. Now he's at Attica doing twenty-five-to-life. Brian knew how hard it was to undo a conviction like this. And that idiot Levy was the judge. He had to get rid of Levy. It was no longer personal. It was the only right thing to do.

Just as he was thinking about Levy, and thinking about getting up for the day, an early birthday present walked into the bedroom. Maureen had been up for hours. It was now 1:00 P.M. The look in her eyes and the smile on her face told Brian that this could in fact be a very good day. When she opened her robe, Brian made a mental note to send a thank you to *Victoria's Secret* for having a mail-order catalogue. Maureen would never buy an outfit like that in person; no way. The next hour was one of the nicest in his life, and he would remember it for quite some time. He was glad that life did not end at fifty-four.

Guests started arriving at around five for the party. *It'll be fun*, Brian thought as he greeted everyone, taking the obligatory old man jokes in stride. He made an effort not to talk business, as most of the guests were not cops. Maryann and Dennis were still an item, and watching them look at each other reminded Brian of his early days with Maureen. Maureen was probably right; Dennis would be the one. *Maryann could do worse than Dennis*, Brian thought, and he knew the inevitable loss of his daughter to another man would be sooner than he would like. Actually, never would be soon enough.

Brian assumed his usual position behind the grill. Birthday or not, he wouldn't have it any other way.

"Happy Birthday, Brian," Rosa Lucero yelled as she walked over to the grill where Brian was cooking steaks and chicken. "How are you, old man?" She smiled. Rosa loved Brian. He took good care of her man, who took good care of the Lucero family.

"Great," was Brian's answer. "How are the kids, Rosa?"

"Doing great. Keeping me busy."

Brian knew that she and Paulie were probably as happily married as he and Maureen.

"Where's Tommy?" Paulie added. "Rosa and me have a bet on which one of the bimbos he's bringing."

"Leave him alone, you guys," Maureen interrupted. "You're just jealous; right, Rosa? Those days are gone for both of you. At least they better be."

The party brought everyone into the real world of middle America, at least for the time being; not the real world that Brian, his squad, and even Dennis lived—the world of death and human tragedy—but rather the world of laughter that people like Brian made possible for the rest of society. Even Willie, who almost never socialized with anyone since his wife walked out years ago, showed up. Brian was serving food hot off the grill when Betty came over for a steak.

"I set up the meeting with Judge Levy for ten o'clock Monday morning, boss," she told Brian as he placed a nice fillet on her plate.

"What meeting?"

"The meeting with Judge Levy."

"What are you talking about Betty? I never said anything about a meeting with him."

"Tommy called yesterday after you left and said to set up the meeting. I assumed you told him to call, boss. I'm sorry. What should I do? Cancel it?"

"Where is that little ... never mind, Betty. Don't worry. I'll take care of it."

Brian was at the grill talking with Paulie and Willie when Tommy walked in. No one would be collecting bets tonight, for he was not with a bimbo. On his arm was a strikingly beautiful girl who literally turned heads. Paulie was stunned.

"He's got a new one, boss."

"My God, that's Judge Levy's assistant. I saw her there two weeks ago when we went to talk to him. I was talking to the judge while Tommy was talking to her."

"No kidding," was Paulie's answer to the obvious.

Maureen walked over to greet Tommy and his new girlfriend. They talked for a while. Tommy waved to Brian. Brian could wait no longer.

"Paulie, go get lover boy and bring him here alone. Leave the girl with Maureen. She'll understand."

"Happy Birthday, boss," Tommy said as he approached the boys at the grill.

"Don't give me that Happy Birthday shit. What's this about a meeting with Levy that you had Betty set up?"

"Wait, boss. Look at the girl I brought. Isn't she beautiful?"

Brian, Paulie, and Willie all agreed. There was nothing not to agree with. She was gorgeous.

"Gentlemen, you are looking at the eventual Mrs. Tommy O'Neal."

"What? Again? I've heard that before," was Paulie's laughing answer.

"No really. This is it. I've been seeing her for about two weeks. I'm telling you this is it."

Brian smiled. "Fine, God bless, but what about the meeting with Levy?"

"Boss, take a good look at her. Her name is Margaret Brennen. She is perfect, isn't she?"

"Tommy, she's great. We'll all go to the wedding. What about Levy?"

"Well, she's not perfect. She has one small defect, but I'll work on it. She has a slight problem keeping a secret. It seems that ... Boss, you won't pass out or fall onto the grill or anything if I tell you something that will make this the greatest birthday you have ever had, will you?"

"I'll try not to. I will also try not to shoot you if you don't get to the point."

"It's just so fucking unbelievable that I want the moment to be perfect. Listen to this. The judge is married to this very proper lady from Scarsdale. She's the class and the money in the family. Very active in the New York City social scene. Goes to all the charity balls and fund-raisers; you get the picture. Well, the judge is getting a little on the side. Well, no, I take that back; actually a lot on the side. He's banging not one, but two other women. It's so great I can't fucking say it without laughing.

Every Monday night he stays in town and bangs either Rita Diaz or Lucille Manero. Can you believe it? A Puerto Rican and an Italian. His wife would go insane if she found out. He would be out in the street in one minute."

"Margaret told you this? How does she know?"

"He's so stupid, he has her set things up for him. She makes the calls. She makes dinner reservations. He has even had her send them gifts and lie to his wife. She told me everything."

"This is completely reliable information?"

"Boss, I checked it out myself. All the cops on the Riverdale beat know about the little apartment he keeps there. He supposedly stays there Monday night to prepare for the week. I followed him last Monday, and he's not preparing for the week, believe me. He spent the whole night with Manero. She left the apartment at 6:45 the next morning. I don't know where he met Manero, but Diaz was his assistant until about six months ago, when she transferred to Brooklyn. Shortly thereafter Margaret was assigned to him. I had Betty set up a meeting with Levy for you. If I were you, I would ask him three questions: how is Rita Diaz, are Lucille Manero's tits really that big in real life, and, can I have the jury list, Your Honor?"

Paulie, who probably had a few drinks too many, laughed so hard he almost asphyxiated. Willie just smiled. Brian became very pensive. Could he really blackmail a judge? By Monday he would know the answer. What a really great birthday this was.

Monday couldn't come soon enough for Brian. He was like a schoolboy looking forward to seeing Santa Claus. All day Sunday he thought about what he would say to Levy. In the end, he decided he could not improve on Tommy's three questions. He would go see Levy and do whatever it took to get him to release the list of jurors. Lives depended on it. He would not threaten blackmail, but he knew the judge would get the message. Even Levy wasn't that stupid.

* * * * * * * * *

"Good morning people," Brian said cheerfully as he walked into the squad room Monday morning. Tommy, Paulie, and Betty were there.

Willie was already on his way to Attica.

"Nice party, boss," Tommy answered.

"You made it a great party, Tommy," Brian said with a smile.

They all talked briefly about what to say to Levy and then went over the trial transcript.

"It looks like this trial was a major fuck-up," Paulie summed up. "I hope the guy was really guilty some other time, and is a real scumbag, and this was a payback for something else he did, because he sure didn't do this one."

"Let's hope Willie feels that way when he gets back from Attica. It will make us all sleep better. Now get going and get that cop who arrested Johanson in here this week for an interview. If he gives you any shit, get some uniforms and drag him here if you have to. Go people, go. I'm off to see a judge."

Judge Levy looked forward to his meeting with Detective Walsh. He knew he had this hot-shot detective exactly where he wanted him. It was his turn to humiliate Walsh. It was a small step in regaining his dignity after all the humiliation he suffered at Walsh's hands over the years. He would never give in to Walsh's demands. He would rather die.

"Margaret," Judge Levy called out. "I am expecting a Detective Walsh at ten o'clock. Have him wait until half past and then show him in. Tell him I'm on a conference call and can't be disturbed." *That will really get him fuming*, Levy smiled to himself.

Brian arrived at 9:50 and by 10:25 he was fuming, especially since one glance at the phone would tell any moron that the judge was not on any call. His new friend Margaret confirmed what Brian already knew. *No problem*, Brian thought, *five minutes until question time; then let's see who laughs.*

Margaret showed Brian into the judge's private office, and then she was quickly dismissed by Levy.

"What do you want this time, Walsh?"

"Just three quick questions, Your Honor, and then I'll leave if you want."

"Go ahead. But I will never change my mind about giving you those names."

"How is Rita Diaz? Are Lucille Manero's tits really that big in real life? Can I have the jury list?"

Levy froze. He stared at Brian with a very strange look. Not anger; just total disbelief. He then collapsed into his chair and turned white. Brian got him some water, not out of concern but rather out of fear that the son-of-a-bitch was going to die right in front of him, which Brian knew would be very difficult to explain.

Levy got some color back in his face and said, "I'll sign the papers. You'll have them this afternoon. Never, ever come back here, and I expect never to hear about this again. Now please leave."

Brian left, after telling Levy that he would send Paulie to pick up the signed papers at one o'clock. He winked at Margaret as he walked by and walked to his red Jaguar with a new sense of excitement. He won again. Maybe the bastard would retire. After what he let happen to Johanson, he should be shot. Maybe Willie would do it anyway. Brian drove over to tell Sal the good news.

Chapter 11

Willie enjoyed his ride to Attica. He laughed to himself when he realized there weren't many black men who could say that. The countryside was peaceful. He hadn't seen a sunrise with tall country trees in the background in many years. He arrived at Attica State Prison at 10:15 A.M., after having had a nice greasy breakfast at a rest stop on the New York Thruway. He wanted to catch everyone by surprise, so he did not make arrangements ahead of time. Sergeant Robert Jones greeted him. Willie took one look at the size of Sergeant Jones and was very happy to be just visiting.

"Thank you for helping me, sergeant. I know your time is valuable. I've come to interview Robert Johanson on an important matter back in the city." Willie hated to tell anyone more than they needed to know.

"We like to hear about these things ahead of time, Detective Hayes."

"There was no time. My boss called me at home last night and told me to get my ass up here and speak to this guy. I don't argue with my boss, so here I am. Give me a break; let me see him."

"Can't."

"Come on. Don't make me call my boss to call your boss. That will just fuck us all up."

"I mean I can't, not I won't."

"What the fuck are you talking about?"

"He's dead and long buried. He didn't last two months. He got the shit beat out of him at least three times that I know of. He finally hanged himself to get it over with, I guess. Nobody here likes a child molester. Some of the brothers knew the little girl was black, and it was only a matter of time before they got him. They could have done it anytime. I think they wanted him to suffer first. Funny thing, his beating them to it."

"You sure he hanged himself? Nobody did it for him?"

"He was found in his cell, alone, no cell mate. We're not that stupid to put someone in with him. He did it to stop the beatings. He really messed up that little kid, didn't he?"

"Maybe not. He was probably innocent, at least this time. Did anyone come to visit him?"

"Come with me. Let's look at the book. I can't remember anyone."

Willie couldn't believe how complicated everything was becoming.

"Here it is," Sergeant Jones announced as he opened the sign in book. "No visitors while he was alive, but one week after he died two people signed in on the same day: Peter Delaney and Thomas Zimmer. Delaney came at 10:35 A.M. and Zimmer at 12:45 P.M. Obviously they were told he was dead."

"Could we talk to whoever checked them in that day?"

"That would be Mervin Carr; he usually handles the book. I'll call him down."

It took a few minutes for Mervin Carr to reach the conference room. He was even bigger than Jones.

"Mervin, meet Detective Willie Hayes from the big city. He wants to ask you a few questions. It's okay, no problem. Help him out if you can."

Mervin shook Willie's hand, but was clearly unhappy to be present. Jones told Mervin what it was about on the phone, and nobody wanted to talk about Johanson.

"Mr. Carr," Willie began.

"Call me Mervin."

"Okay, Mervin. We were looking at the sign-in book to see if anyone came to visit Robert Johanson. No one came until after he was dead, and then two visitors came the same day. Somewhat unusual. You would think they would be listed as friends or family, and would have been notified about his death, but obviously they weren't, or they would not have come. See what I mean? Take a look at the book and see if you can remember anything about the men. It's very important. Think hard."

Willie had already come to the somewhat obvious conclusion that Mervin was not hired for his brains. After what seemed like forever, but was only a few minutes, Mervin remembered.

"I remember both of them, detective. The first one was an average guy but very nervous. It looked like he didn't want to be here. When I told him Johanson was dead, he asked a lot of questions and became upset, but then he left. He said he was on the jury that sent him up."

"On the jury? Are you sure he said that?"

"Definitely. Ain't never heard of that before. Never heard of someone from a jury coming to visit. You ever heard of that, Sergeant Jones?"

"No I haven't, Mervin," Jones answered.

"What about the other one? The man named Zimmer."

"I remember him too. He was very tall. Taller than me. That's why I remember him. Nobody around here taller than me," Mervin proudly announced. "I told him what happened to Johanson, and he just left. Didn't say nothing."

"Thank you, Mervin. You have been very helpful. My boss will appreciate your help and let your superiors know. Thanks again."

Mervin went back to work.

"Sergeant, is that believable? Can he possibly remember that from almost a year ago?"

"He's not as dumb as he looks, or sounds. You can take it as fact. That's exactly what happened."

"Well then, let me thank you, Sergeant Jones, for your help. If there is anything I can ever do for you, or if you ever get to the city, give me a call."

"Maybe I will."

Willie began the long drive back to the city. It was not as pleasant as the drive up. The scenery was the same, but Willie had a very bad feeling. Brian would not like this turn of events. They had to talk to Peter Delaney and Thomas Zimmer. Maybe they were both on the jury.

What Willie, Sergeant Jones, and Mervin did not know was that Peter Delaney would never be talking to anyone again. In fact, he hadn't spoken in some time. But the last time he did speak, he said enough to change the lives of many, many people.

* * * * * * * * * *

Peter Delaney left Attica that day almost one year previously and drove back to Manhattan. He was a shoe salesman and could not afford to miss much work. He was married but had no children. He and his wife were just getting by on his meager salary. Why his wife wouldn't work was beyond him. She just sat around, watched TV all day, and bitched about being poor. She told him not to go to visit that pervert, but Delaney had to confront him. Delaney was convinced that Johanson was innocent, but he was no match for the others on the jury. He had to go along with them. He just wanted to tell Johanson he was sorry. Now that could never happen. By the time he reached Manhattan he was so upset he couldn't go to work, even though this was his late night at the store. He went directly home.

"He's dead," he shouted at his wife.

"Who's dead?"

"Johanson. He hung himself in jail."

"So what? Who cares? The world is a better place without him."

"Don't you get it, you stupid lazy bitch? He was innocent!"

Delaney stormed out of the apartment and went directly to The Beer Blast, a local bar he had been visiting with alarming frequency since the Johanson trial ended. He sat at the bar and began to drink. When the tall man with the blue eyes walked in several hours later, Delaney was quite drunk. The man sat beside Delaney at the bar and began to drink slowly. A conversation started, and the man bought Delaney a drink. Into the drink the man with the blue eyes put some powder, which went unnoticed by Delaney and the bartender. Five minutes later the blue-eyed man excused himself to go to the men's room and casually walked out of the bar. He waited outside, in the hallway of a small shop, where he had a clear view of the entrance to The Beer Blast. The powder began to work, and Delaney started to vomit uncontrollably. The bartender, who had to clean up the mess, became enraged and threw Delaney out onto the street. He was rescued by the tall man, who began to walk with him. They got into Delaney's car and began another trip to Attica.

At least that was the only reason Delaney's widow could give the state police when they called the next day with the news of the terrible crash that took Mr. Delaney's life and completely destroyed his car in an inferno seen for miles around in upstate New York. What no one could know was that, before the crash that took what was left of his life, Peter Delaney was questioned unmercifully, and very physically when necessary, for almost two hours until the man with the blue eyes knew everything he needed to know. Delaney's car was then appropriately fitted with the necessary explosives, and the very intoxicated Peter Delaney was blown into oblivion.

The police report and autopsy of what was left of Delaney would confirm what Mrs. Delaney told the police, and which was confirmed by the bartender at The Beer Blast. The poor man was distraught over the death of Johanson, drank himself into a stupor, and for some inexplicable reason headed back to Attica. While en route he lost control of his six year old Mercury, skidded down a steep embankment on the thruway, and died in the fiery crash. No one's fault but his own. Thank God he didn't kill anyone else. In reality, God had nothing to do with it.

The tall man with the blue eyes returned to Manhattan. He had gathered crucial information from Delaney, but he would have to cross-check everything before he began his mission. He had to be sure; he would leave nothing to chance. He was trained to be sure; trained to be careful. It would take months to be certain, but Delaney did not lie. No one could lie to the blue-eyed man without him knowing. And Delaney was not trained; he was just a shoe salesman. He told the truth, and now they would all pay. Every last one would pay with their life. And no one would know; no one but the blue-eyed man would ever know what happened. At least that is what he hoped. But the blue-eyed man had never met Detective Brian Michael Walsh.

Chapter 12

Tuesday morning's meeting brought both good and bad news. Brian now had the jury list, but the fact that Johanson was dead was very troubling. Brian had spent Monday afternoon looking at the police reports on Johanson.

"What do we know about Robert Johanson? Not much," Brian began. "He apparently was born in Chicago in 1936. His parents died early. He moved to New York with his new wife in 1958. He had trouble finding a job, but eventually started work in a sign painting factory on the West Side. They had a son in 1960, but unfortunately his wife died from some complication of childbirth—placenta praevia, whatever that is. He raised his son all by himself and continued to work in the sign factory. He did well, was taught the trade, and eventually became a painter, which apparently is a big step up in salary. He and his son lived in a modest apartment a few blocks from the factory. His son did well in school and he went away to college, graduating in 1981. He studied political science at Northwestern in Chicago. He started graduate school at Northwestern, and on a trip home to visit his father in 1982 was killed on the Ohio turnpike when an eighteen-wheeler crushed his car. Johanson was distraught but continued to work and go on with his life, even though he had nothing left. There is no family. He had no close friends. His life was very routine until February 1995, when he was arrested for molesting and raping a five-year-old black girl named Nancy Tailor. He is convicted at the end of a ridiculous trial, and is sent to Attica, where he hangs himself. The man has no previous police record. There has never been a complaint made against him for anything, much less child molestation. And you all have read the transcript of the trial and know that he certainly did not molest Nancy Tailor. We need to know much more. There is a patrolman, Leroy Phillips, coming in to be interviewed today. Willie and Paulie, I want you to grill this guy. He made the arrest and was one of the star witnesses at the trial. He supposedly saw Johanson talking to the Tailor child just a few hours before she was discovered in the alley. He isn't coming down because he wants to, so go softly at first but get everything. There's a rumor that he's dirty. Willie, don't shoot him."

"Now for the good news," Brian shouted as he hung a large cardboard sign in, thankfully, Betty's printing on the bulletin board. It listed twelve names. Twelve jurors. At least two dead citizens of New York.

Juror # 1	Rose Mason
Juror # 2	Susan Champion
Juror # 3	Peter Delaney
Juror # 4	Mable Johnson
Juror # 5	Herman Charles
Juror # 6	Michael Thomas
Juror # 7	Hui Chang
Juror # 8	Elizabeth Anderson
Juror # 9	Raul Sanchez
Juror # 10	Thomas Knox
Juror # 11	Lawrence Carson
Juror # 12	Harold Stanton

Everyone looked at the list, but no one said a word. They each wondered who was killing who. Were they looking at the name of a murderer? What did Chang and Anderson do to piss someone off? Certainly, it couldn't be one of the woman jurors. Or could it? Maybe all the jurors were going to die.

"It's a pretty well-formulated jury," Brian interrupted. "Six white. Four black. One Asian. One Puerto Rican. Four women and eight men. That's a little unusual, but not bizarre. We have their addresses, at least where they lived at the time of the trial. Betty and her girls will start making calls today to set up interviews, while Willie and Paulie interview Phillips. Tommy, I have something special for you. I want you to find out everything about the idiot attorney who defended Johanson. Your new girlfriend could have done a better job. His name is Irving Horowitz. I've never heard of him.

* * * * * * * * *

Irving Horowitz graduated from Brooklyn College in 1987. He was closer to the bottom of his class than the top. He didn't do much for the next year, and then decided, as do so many others who have nothing to contribute in life, to go to law school. It took him four-and-one-half years to graduate, but graduate he did in January of 1993. He then got a job working for Solomon and Solomon, two ambulance-chasing attorneys who had a storefront office down in Greenwich Village. They never once set foot in a courtroom to try a case. After a year of working for Solomon and Solomon, Irving Horowitz, unbelievably, passed the bar exam. He took the big plunge and opened his own law office. He had only a few clients but he did manage to actually win a case when he got a small-time punk named Billy Thorton off on a drug charge. Billy worked, when he did work, at the same sign painting factory as Robert Johanson. When Johanson was arrested, Billy sent Horowitz to visit with him, and Horowitz became Johanson's attorney. Mr. Johanson was a nice man who never questioned anything. He didn't know it at the time, but he was putting his life in the hands of someone who was just using him for practice.

After the trial was over, Johanson went to Attica and Horowitz went on with his life as if nothing had happened. He had taken the $36,545 that was Johanson's life savings and told him he would have to hire another lawyer for the appeal. Irving Horowitz did not do appeals. He shouldn't do trials either.

In late September of 1995, a new client visited Horowitz. The gentleman, who gave his name as James P. Clark, needed legal help. He was afraid he was about to be accused of rape, but felt that the lady in question could be talked out of it, if the price was right. He admitted that he actually did rape her, and he and Horowitz laughed as he described every sorted detail.

"Didn't you ever fuck her before?"

"Many times, and she always seemed to like it. This time she said no, but I said yes."

"Sometimes they don't know what they want. What do you want me to do?" Horowitz asked.

"I think if I give her five grand she will forget all about it. But she won't see me. You can make a quick two grand if you go and talk to her and get her to take the money. Get her to sign something. You know what to write. I want to get this behind me as soon as possible. Can you see her tonight?"

"For two grand I can see her anytime."

"She lives in this dive in the Bronx. Here's the address. There's seven grand in this envelope. Remember, two for you and five for her. Don't fuck with me on that, Mr. Horowitz."

Horowitz looked directly into the deep blue eyes of the tall man and something told him loud and clear that he was not someone to fuck with.

"Don't worry, Mr. Clark, it will be done properly. I'll make sure she takes the money. Call me tomorrow and we'll talk."

Irving Horowitz could not know that for him tomorrow would never come.

Two weeks prior to his meeting with Horowitz, Mr. Clark ran into a Miss Rose Mason in a nightspot she frequented on the Upper East Side. To say he swept her off her feet would be an understatement. She was twenty-eight years old and was getting to that stage in her life that she thought she would never meet Mr. Right. Then James P. Clark walked right into her life. He was very private, but very good to her. She found him quite handsome. James was a much better catch than she thought she would ever find. He was smart and seemed to have a pretty good job, although she had no idea what a systems analyst did. Her mother in St. Louis would be very proud. He respected her. In two weeks he never made an improper advance—not like those other animals she would always meet in the clubs. Finally, someone who wanted more than a blow job out of her. And tonight he was taking her to meet his father who lived in the Bronx.

"Rose, honey, I have a slight problem with tonight," the blue-eyed man spoke over the phone.

"Oh no, I was looking forward to tonight."

"We are still going, but I have to work late. I want you to meet me at my father's place. We'll go out after and have a great time. I got a big promotion at work today and I want to celebrate. Can you be there at ten?"

"Whatever you say, James. I'll see you then. Where does he

live?"

The blue-eyed man gave her the address in the Bronx and cautioned her about the appearance of the apartment house. It was old but clean. A lot of older folks lived there for a long time, and they didn't want to move even though the neighborhood was going downhill.

"James, would you do something special for me tonight? It makes me feel funny saying it."

"What?"

"Will you make love to me tonight?"

The tall man with the blue eyes paused, and then said in a very affirmative voice, "Rose, you definitely will be fucked tonight."

They both smiled, for very different reasons, as they each hung up the phone.

Mr. Clark then called Horowitz.

"Mr. Horowitz, I forgot to tell you one thing. In case she's not home, there is a key under a cracked brick by the front steps of the building. It's on the right side. You can't miss it. Let yourself in and go to apartment 402 and wait for her inside. And be careful; she's a hothead. She usually gets home at about 9:30 P.M." Clark hung up.

"A hothead?" Horowitz said out loud. "What did he mean by that?"

Horowitz reached into his desk drawer and pulled out his gun, which he placed in his jacket pocket. He started to think about what Clark said, and became apprehensive. He needed the two grand, though, and quickly dismissed all thoughts he had about not going. Mr. Clark did not look like a man who would take disappointment well. It was almost five o'clock. He would have dinner, alone again, and drive to the Bronx.

At 8:45 Rose finished putting on her best outfit, the pretty red and white dress she was wearing the night she first met James. She removed her diaphragm from its container and placed it in her purse. She would need it later that night, and she couldn't wait to use it. Her excitement grew by the minute. It had been some time since she made love with someone she really cared about. She finally completed her grooming and began her journey to the Bronx. She arrived at 169th street at 9:45. She wanted to be early and make a good impression on James' father. She had never been brought home to meet a boyfriend's parents before. Of course, James' mother was dead, so this would be easy. She glanced at her watch as she rode up to the fourth-floor apartment in the elevator. She didn't want to be too early. It read 9:51. She smiled to her-self that this would probably be the greatest night of her life, at least so far. She was partially right. She would remember it for the rest of her life, but that would require remembering something for only fourteen min-utes.

Rose Mason adjusted her dress, checked her face in her compact, and rang the doorbell to apartment 402. She had just begun her best smile when the door opened much sooner than she expected. Irving Horowitz stood before her, the sweat of anxiety beading up on his forehead. Rose froze, expecting to see a much older man. *Wrong apartment*, she thought to herself. Horowitz was not quick enough to realize that Rose should not have had to ring the doorbell to her own apartment. He grabbed her and threw her down on an old dirty couch. His adrenaline level was sky-high as he made her the offer.

"Listen, you fucking bitch. Here's three grand to dummy up on this rape thing. You better take it or I'll blow your fucking head off!"

The tall man with the blue eyes was listening. He shook his head in disgust when he heard Horowitz utter "three grand." *What a real dirt bag*, he thought. Horowitz wouldn't have the guts to shoot anybody.

Rose looked at Horowitz with disbelief. She had no idea what he was talking about. She said as much to him, and he hit her in the mouth with his gun, much harder than he intended. He cut her lip severely, and she bled profusely on her pretty dress and his pants.

"Stop it, you madman!" Rose screamed. "What are you talking about? What rape? Stop it, you animal!"

Rose was now curled up in a ball on the couch trying to cover her face and head. Horowitz had just started to back away from her when she mustered all the strength she had and kicked out at him. She missed his testicles, which were her target, but did manage to kick him in the stomach. The blow would have been more effective if he hadn't already started moving backward. As it was, it merely knocked him back a few feet. Horowitz paused for a few seconds as he looked down at Rose, a puzzled look dominating his face. At that moment the same thought passed through both their minds—each thought they had seen the other somewhere before— but in the heat of the battle no words were uttered.

Rose looked up at Horowitz and saw a look of terror suddenly appear on his face. He was no longer looking at her, but rather was trans-fixed at something behind her and to her left. Before she could turn around she heard three small pops, and Horowitz was hurled backward into the spot where the wall meets the floor, where he quickly formed a grotesque motionless pile. He was dead. His gun rested by his feet. Rose looked around and saw James running to Horowitz.

"Thank God, James. Who is this madman?" she yelled, while trying to hold her bleeding lip.

James picked up Horowitz's gun, turned, and to Rose's surprise, pulled the trigger once, ending Rose's perfect evening and not-so-perfect life. The blue-eyed man placed six thousand dollars of additional money into Horowitz's jacket and searched each pocket. When he found the document Horowitz had prepared he placed it in his own jacket pocket. He opened Rose's purse with his gloved hands and inserted the cocaine he obtained earlier in the day. He placed Horowitz's gun by his body, and took the gun he shot Horowitz with and put it by Rose's right hand. He took a small amount of powder from a sandwich bag he had in his jacket pocket and rubbed the powder on both Rose's and Horowitz's right hand. With his work completed, he left the apartment unnoticed, walked a few blocks to a phone, and dialed 911. He then boarded the subway to Manhattan.

The 911 call was answered quickly by the uniforms, who immediately called the homicide detectives to the scene. The crime unit was very meticulous. The investigation was begun quickly, and to no one's surprise was closed just as quickly and listed as a solved double homicide. The evidence was overwhelming, even though surprising. No one knew why attorney Irving Horowitz was buying such a large volume of cocaine, and no one could imagine Rose Mason as a dealer, but the evidence didn't lie.

The report concluded that Horowitz came to the home of a Julio Rodriguez, a known drug dealer currently at Rikers Island awaiting trial on another drug matter, to purchase 5.5 kilos of cocaine. He obviously did not bring enough money, or intended to rob the seller, Ms. Rose Mason, who had no known police record. A struggle ensued during which Horowitz fought with Mason. Her blood was all over his pants. She managed to pull out her gun and got off three shots. Two missed entirely, but one lucky shot got him right between the eyes. It was probably the third shot. While she was shooting at Horowitz, he was able to get off one shot, which struck her in the left ventricle of the heart, killing her almost instantly. Lab tests confirmed that both perpetrators did in fact fire guns and all money and drugs were found at the scene, thus eliminating any third party. Case closed.

No, Rose Mason's mother in St. Louis would not be proud of her.

Chapter 13

Tommy found the last known address of Irving Horowitz, where the current tenants said they knew nothing about him. Tommy traced him to Solomon and Solomon, and they relayed the story of the adventures of the late Mr. Horowitz, who they were clear to point out had long since left their prestigious firm before he got into all that drug trouble.

"Why did he leave your firm? Did you throw him out because he was mixed up in drugs?" Tommy asked the senior Walter Solomon.

"No. We never knew. Officer, you must believe me. We never knew he was mixed up in drugs. He seemed poor. I mean, not poor, but not like he had a lot of money. You know, the kind of money that the drug lawyers have."

Tommy thought to himself that if this was the senior partner in this firm, he wouldn't waste his time talking to anyone else.

"I'm sure you are not connected with this matter in any way, Mr. Solomon. Thank you for your help."

Tommy drove to the South Bronx, where he spoke to Detective Louis Dega and Detective Tony Romano, who investigated the murders of Horowitz and Mason. Tommy knew Romano from a few years back. They talked for a while.

"Tommy, it was just as the report said. These two assholes had a shoot-out and were just unlucky enough to shoot each other in the right places. There were 5.5 kilos of cocaine and thirteen thousand in cash right in the middle of the room. No one would have walked away leaving that around. We never found any other clue. No one in the building heard anything, which is not surprising. If a resident reported anything to us, they'd have about an hour to live. The building is a real cesspool. There are drug dealers everywhere. Rose Mason must have been working for Julio Rodriguez and using his apartment for a score while he was in Rikers."

"Did Rodriguez admit to knowing her?"

"No. But he wouldn't admit to knowing his own mother if a cop asked him. No Tommy, it's just what it looks like, nothing more."

"Thanks, Tony. Be careful up here."

"I will."

* * * * * * * * * *

Tommy got back to the squad at 2:30. Brian was stunned but not entirely surprised by the news.

"That's the third dead juror," Brian said glumly as he drew a thin line through the name of Rose Mason to join the lines through the names of Hui Chang and Elizabeth Anderson.

"And now you tell me Johanson's attorney is dead. And, of course, Johanson is dead."

Brian looked at the board for some time. He then looked at Tommy and said, "Betty hasn't been able to reach any of the other jurors yet. Maybe they are all fucking dead."

While Tommy was tracking down Horowitz, Willie and Paulie questioned patrolman Leroy Phillips. Paulie had his turn, so now Willie hammered this poor excuse for a cop.

"Tell me again, Leroy. I'm having some trouble understanding some of this," Willie continued. "When did you first see Johanson?"

"In the store. Right by the door."

"Was he completely inside the store or half inside the door?"

"What the fuck difference does it make? I saw him by the door!"

"The difference is simple. Look at the picture of the doorway. If he was inside you couldn't possibly see enough of him to identify him. And if he was even halfway outside the doorway, how could you see him talking to the little girl? You see my problem?"

"I saw him talking to the girl and giving her the candy. I know he was the one."

"How come no one inside the fucking store saw him talk to the girl, but you saw him from almost twenty feet away? You ever see Johanson before?"

"Just around the neighborhood."

"You have a hard-on for this guy Johanson?"

"No. I told you I didn't know him. Why would I try to fuck him up?"

"I don't know, but if I find out you are not being straight with us I'm going to fuck you up big time. You won't be able to go out at night without your mother. I would never shoot anyone in front of his mother. Is your mother alive?"

"Yes."

"Lucky for you. Tell me what you did later in the day when you found little Nancy."

"A lady came running out from behind the alley screaming something I couldn't understand. She was hysterical. I ran into the alley."

"Did you have your gun drawn?" Willie interrupted.

"No."

"So you want me to believe you ran into an alley, out of which just came a screaming woman, without your gun out?"

"Yes."

"Go on," Willie said, shaking his head in disbelief.

"I ran over and saw this little girl, this little black girl, beaten and bleeding, with her clothes half torn off. She wasn't crying. She was just scared."

"What then?"

"I called for an ambulance, and they came and took the girl away."

"You never found the lady who came screaming out of the alley?"

"No."

"Doesn't that strike you as strange. Why didn't she wait around? What did she see? She was black, right?"

"Yes."

"No one but you saw this screaming, howling woman at 2:26 in the afternoon on a busy street, is that right? That's your story?"

"I saw her. I don't know what anyone else saw."

"But no other cops who canvassed the area found anyone else who saw her, is that right?"

"Right."

"Are you beginning to see my problem, Leroy? I mean it was

pretty fortunate for that little girl that you happened along when you did. She might have died. She did live, right?"

"Yes."

"And you were a hero. You got a Mayor's Citation and all that."

"I was just doing my job."

"So what happened next?"

"What do you mean?"

"Within one hour of the arrival of the ambulance you arrested Robert Johanson. Share this brilliant police work with us, please," Willie added sarcastically.

"I remembered seeing little Nancy go into the store with her mother earlier and remembered seeing the man talk to her and give her some candy."

"And this makes him a child molester?"

"The D.A. thought he was guilty, and the jury convicted him. That's all I know. It's not my fucking job to do that. I just arrested him, and the detectives did the rest."

"You can't be that fucking stupid. You were the arresting officer, you testified at the trial, there was no one to refute your account of what happened. And, to make it worse, Johanson had a moron as an attorney and an imbecile as a trial judge. You set something in motion that could only have been stopped by you. It was the nature of the crime that convicted Johanson, not the evidence."

"I don't have to sit here and take this," Phillips shouted as he got up to leave.

Willie pushed his face right up to Phillips' face and said in a tone only Willie could project, "Sit down, you sleazy sack of shit! Sit down now! You leave when I say you leave!"

Willie sounded so scary that Paulie checked to be sure he was sitting.

"I don't know exactly what happened out on that street that day, but I know it didn't go down the way you say it did. If you think I'm that fucking stupid, you are making a big mistake. If you have second thoughts and want to do the right thing, call me. I will tell you this, Leroy. I will eventually find out what happened, and if you come down on the wrong side of this I'll be coming for you. Now get the fuck out of my sight!"

Patrolman Leroy Phillips left in a hurry. He would never call

Detective Hayes. If he told anyone what really happened in that alley his whole family, including his mother, would die a terrible death.

Brian had watched the interview through the one-way mirror. He loved watching Willie work. He was the best Brian ever saw. Phillips was lying like a rug. But why? Did he do it? Not likely, but not entirely impossible. Willie would eventually find out. Brian was sure of that.

Betty had some luck tracing a few of the jurors. The next day Brian would send Tommy out to visit with Herman Charles, juror #5.

Chapter 14

Tommy walked to 232 East 14th Street to visit Herman Charles. According to the record, he was a fifty-nine-year-old black male who lived with his wife. They had no telephone, so he could not call ahead. He hoped that Mr. Charles would be at home. He knew nothing else about him. When he arrived, he rang the bell from below and a woman answered.

"Mrs. Charles?"

"Yes."

"My name is Detective O'Neal. I would like to speak to your husband if I could."

"So would I. He's dead."

Tommy's heart began to race, and he could actually hear his pulse pounding in his ear. "Another dead juror," he mumbled. He then collected himself.

"Could I please come up to talk to you Mrs. Charles? It's very important."

Mrs. Charles pressed the buzzer and invited Detective O'Neal up.

Tommy rode the elevator to the third floor, walked down the dimly lit hallway to apartment 304, and anxiously pushed the bell. The door opened a few inches until it was restrained by its chain. Mrs. Charles asked to see some identification. Tommy showed her his shield, and she was kind enough to invite him into the apartment.

"What happened to your husband, Mrs. Charles?"

"He died last February. He had a heart attack right over there." She pointed to a small room off the living room. "It was on a Wednesday. It used to be his day off. He worked at the newspaper and had to work on Saturday, so he had Wednesday off. I used to work at the department store during the day, so he was alone when he had the heart attack, with no one to call for help. Now I work the 2:00 P.M. to 10:00 P.M. shift. I don't like it, but I have no choice; I have to work."

Mrs. Charles glanced at a picture on the fake fireplace. "That was my Herman."

Tommy walked over to the picture. *No wonder he had a heart attack.*

"My Herman was too big. His doctor kept trying to get him to lose weight but he wouldn't try. He loved to eat, and he had high blood pressure. A lot of black people do."

"I've heard that."

"I even bought him one of those treadmill machines when the store had them on sale. They let me make payments. But Herman would never use it. He never even got on it, until that day anyway. Imagine, the first time he uses it he has a heart attack."

"Didn't he check with his doctor before using it?"

"Yes. The doctor said he could use it slowly, but I never saw him use it. I came home from work that day, and he was dead on the floor. I ran next door to borrow the telephone and called 911, but there was nothing the paramedics could do. They said he had been dead for hours. The store wouldn't take the treadmill back, so I sold it to some nice young lady."

Mrs. Charles offered Tommy coffee, and he consented. He hated coffee, but he wanted to think for a few minutes. Surely this was a natural death. The guy had to weigh over three hundred pounds. Combined with high blood pressure and lack of exercise, it was a perfect set up for a heart attack.

Mrs. Charles brought the coffee.

"Mrs. Charles, was an autopsy done on your husband?"

"Yes. They said he died of a massive heart attack. Our doctor called me and told me that."

"Would you be so kind to give me your doctor's name. I would like to speak to him, with your permission."

"Certainly. I have his card inside."

She returned in a minute with a card that read Martin O. Davis, M.D., Cardiology. His office was only a few blocks away.

"Thank you very much for your hospitality, Mrs. Charles. I am very sorry about your husband's death, and I wish you good luck. One final question, if I might."

"Certainly, Detective O'Neal."

"Did your husband serve on a jury in May of 1995?"

"He most certainly did. He helped to put a real demon in jail. I was very proud of him. There is no room for people like that on our streets. We talked about it every night. We put that evil monster away. I like to think I helped."

"Thank you again," Tommy answered. *So much for jury instruction about outside discussion,* he laughed to himself.

Tommy walked directly to Dr. Davis' office, who was at first reluctant to talk about Mr. Charles. Tommy was able to convince Dr. Davis to speak to him, or they would have to go back to Mrs. Charles' place to get her permission. The patient's right to confidentially quickly diminished when the doctor thought about the havoc that the trip to Mrs. Charles apartment would cause in his waiting room.

"Yes, detective, Mr. Charles died of a massive heart attack, probably precipitated by an overexuberant use of his treadmill. Absolutely no question about it. It was confirmed by autopsy. It had to happen sooner or latter. I wish he had listened to me. He was such a nice man."

* * * * * * * * *

Mr. Charles listened to someone. He listened to the tall man with the blue eyes. He had no choice. On the morning of Wednesday February 7th, Mrs. Charles awoke at 6:45, made herself a cup of instant coffee, dressed quickly, and consumed her daily bowl of hot oatmeal. She slipped into her old but warm coat, wrapped a scarf around her neck, and began the cold walk to her job at the department store, leaving Herman sleeping peacefully in bed. He planned to sleep until noon, as he usually did on Wednesdays. The loud ring of his doorbell altered his plan at 10:15. It wasn't the downstairs buzzer, but to his surprise the doorbell right outside his door. It had to be someone already in the building, or maybe a fellow tenant, he reasoned. He slowly got out of bed, threw on his robe, walked to the door, looked through the peephole, and found himself starring at a blue eye.

"Good morning, Mr. Charles. I am Officer Campbell. Do you have a few minutes to talk to me about the burglary that occurred in apartment 307 on Monday night? I'm speaking to all the tenants."

The police officer stepped back so Mr. Charles could see his uniform.

"Sure, officer," Herman said as he released the chain.

Officer Campbell walked in. Herman was surprised at his height.

"Mr. Charles, as I am sure you know, there was a burglary Monday night in apartment 307 sometime after midnight. Fortunately, no one was home so there was no injury. Some valuable jewelry was taken; about two thousand dollars worth. Most of the value was in an old ring that was in the family for years. The lady, Dorothy Malone, who I believe is a friend of your wife, is distraught. Did you hear anything unusual on Monday night?"

"No, sir. We went to bed around eleven, and we didn't hear anything. I hope she gets it back. I know Dorothy is very upset about losing her ring."

Officer Campbell walked over to the small room off the living room.

"That's a nice looking treadmill. Do you use it much?" The tall man knew better.

"Look at me. Does it look like I use it?"

They both laughed. One for real, the other because he had to.

"I've been meaning to get one of these. Could you show me how it works?"

"Sure, if I can remember. I should sell you this one."

Mr. Charles, who had a tremendous respect for the police, was anxious to please Officer Campbell. In this neighborhood you want the police on your side. Herman took off his robe and started the machine at its slowest setting. He got on the treadmill and began his demonstration for Officer Campbell. Mr. Charles was in his boxer shorts, a tee shirt, and slippers. He would die that way.

The tall man pulled out his gun and pressed the barrel to Herman's forehead. At the same time, the man greatly increased the speed of the treadmill. Herman was shocked and terrified. The man told Herman he was playing a game. He resisted an impulse to tell Herman he was from the Fat Police. He told Herman that his only chance to live was to stay on the treadmill for ten minutes. If he made it that far, he would let him live. If he didn't make it, he would shoot him. To get Herman to take him seriously, the man showed Herman the empty chambers in his revolver. There was only one bullet. He spun the chambers and then fired at Herman's head. Click. An empty chamber. *Thank God*, Herman thought. The blue-eyed man knew God had nothing to do with it.

Herman focused on the moving treadmill with an intensity he had never devoted to anything or anyone. He had never used the machine to any great extent before, but he learned fast—he had a very demanding teacher. He worked very hard and sweated profusely. He lasted seven minutes and twelve seconds, and was able to work off 187 calories before he hit the moving tread with a thud. It was louder that the blue-eyed man expected. The treadmill kept running and Herman shot off the back. He didn't completely make it, however, and his head bounced for what seemed like minutes on the back end of the treadmill, until it finally was thrown onto the floor. The right side of his face was severely abraded by the tread. The blue-eyed man left him lying on the spot the treadmill selected and left apartment 304. As he walked past apartment 307, he reminded himself to send Dorothy's ring back. Officer Campbell disappeared in the elevator, and when its doors opened on the ground floor, a rather ordinary looking man, except for his unusual height, walked out.

Chapter 15

Tommy returned to the station house and walked slowly up the steps to the office to report the bad news to Brian.

"Boss, you're not going to believe it, but Herman Charles is dead. He died of a heart attack this past February."

"He may be dead, but he didn't die of a heart attack," Brian answered.

"No, really, he did. I checked with his doctor, a cardiologist named Davis. He had an autopsy that confirmed it. I saw pictures of Charles, boss. He had to weigh three hundred pounds or more, and he had high blood pressure. No way it wasn't natural."

Brian put a line through Herman Charles' name on the board.

It was then that Tommy noticed a line through juror #9's name.

"What happened to Sanchez?"

"He was killed in a holdup in a grocery store in his neighborhood. The report is on the table."

Tommy read the report of patrolman Juan Cortez. He read it twice more before he said anything.

"Someone is killing, or already has killed, them all. Oh my God. Who was this guy Johanson?" Tommy thought out loud.

"Tommy, I don't know. It doesn't make any sense. He appears to have been a nice man, but he was a nobody. He just painted signs. He painted fucking signs, went home, and came back the next day to paint fucking signs again. Nothing else. He never did anything else."

Tommy knew Brian was frustrated. The chief was coming over later, and Brian had nothing but bad news for him. Five dead jurors, out of five they could locate, did not bode well for the others. There was also a dead attorney and a dead convict.

Just then Betty walked in with more bad news.

"Boss, we found Peter Delaney, juror #3. Actually we located his wife, who moved back to Harrisburg after her husband's death."

"After his death?" Brian interrupted. "He's dead too?"

"He was killed in a terrible car accident in July of '95. He was DWI and killed himself in a crash on the thruway. I talked to his wife for a long time. I'm getting the report from the state troopers who handled the accident."

"Any more good news?" was Brian's sarcastic reply.

"Yes. We found Thomas Knox, juror #10."

"What do you mean you found him? You actually spoke to him?"

"Yes, just an hour ago. He's a truck driver, and he lives out in Queens. He moved there a few months ago. He used to live in Manhattan on Ave. D."

"What do you know, boss, a live juror," Tommy said.

Just then Paulie walked in. He looked at the board, saw the lines through Herman Charles and Raul Sanchez, and just shook his head.

"Paulie, you're going home early today. In fact, you're going home now," Brian announced.

"What?"

"You heard me. But on your way home, stop by the address Betty gives you in Queens and talk to Mr. Thomas Knox, who has the dubious, and hopefully not temporary, distinction of being the only live juror we can find. Find out everything about him and bring him to me tomorrow. Get some uniforms to guard him like their jobs depended on it, because they do. I want him kept alive!"

"Will do, boss. Thanks for the rest of the day off."

Brian smiled. He knew that Paulie would be talking to Mr. Knox well into the night.

Paulie left for Queens.

"Where's Willie?" Brian asked Betty.

"He's trying to find Mable Johnson. We traced her to an address in Harlem. We sent some uniforms to check it out, but she no longer lives there. Willie wanted to go himself."

"Come on, Tommy. Let's go to the Crocket Sign Works and find out more about Robert Johanson," said Brian. "We're all missing something. Someone this insignificant cannot be connected to at least seven deaths without more going on than we know. Betty, keep working. Find the other jurors, and find them fast."

Brian and Tommy arrived at Crocket Sign Works at about 3:30. They were greeted by a somewhat resistant secretary, who promptly brought them to Matthew Crocket's office when they showed her their gold shields.

"Sorry to keep you waiting, gentleman, the place is very busy today. My son is away and I have to watch everything. I'm Matthew Crocket."

"I am Detective Walsh and this is Detective O'Neal. We would like to ask you a few questions about a former employee, Robert Johanson."

Mr. Crocket sat at his desk and shook his head. Crocket was an older man. Brian guessed he was close to seventy.

Crocket began, "I am still distraught by everything that happened to Robert. I never believed, and still don't believe, that he was the one who hurt that little girl."

Brian thought Crocket was going to cry.

"It should make you feel better, Mr. Crocket, that Detective O'Neal and I don't believe he harmed her either. That's why we are here."

"Can you get him out? If you believe that, you can get him out, right? I'll pay for the attorney. Can you get him out?"

Brian and Tommy looked at each other incredulously.

"Mr. Crocket," Brian began, "Robert Johanson is dead. He hanged himself last July in prison." *How could Crocket not know?* Brian wondered.

The look on Matthew Crocket's face told both Brian and Tommy that he was in fact receiving this information for the first time. There could be no doubt about it. Crocket now began to cry. When he composed himself he said, "I wanted to do more. I wanted to testify at the trial and tell everybody he couldn't have done that. But my son and my attorney said I had to distance myself from him, for the business, you know. It couldn't look like we had those kind of people working here. We have been in business for a long time. My grandfather started the business in 1926. They said if he was innocent he would go free."

"It doesn't always work that way," Brian said. "Can you help us? Tell us everything you know about Johanson."

Crocket had Robert Johanson's employee record brought in.

"I know most of this, but at my age I sometimes forget things. I hired Robert in 1959. I remember him begging for a job. He said he would do anything. He had just been married and moved here from Chicago. He never even finished high school. But I'll tell you this, Detective Walsh, that man did more work than any three other men in this factory. He was the first one here in the morning and the last one to leave at night. He would watch the painters—you know, the ones who actually compose and draw the signs—and would practice every night. Those are the highest paying jobs in the factory. He eventually became my best painter, and my most loyal employee. His work became well-known in our business, and he could have gone elsewhere for more money. He never even thought about it. He never once asked me for a raise. I gave them to him voluntarily. He was so proud of his son. His son went to a big college in the Midwest. I forget the name."

"Northwestern," Brian added.

"Yes, that's it. Graduated summa cum laude, first in his class. I remember when Robert Jr. died in that accident. Robert was beside himself. He went out to Chicago for the funeral and came back a changed man. He was depressed. He threw himself into his work as never before. Can you imagine that? He worked three times harder than anyone before. I had to come back at night and throw him out. Sometimes he would even sleep here. I don't think he wanted to go home, knowing his son would never return. I got depressed just watching him. I tried to get him to see a psychiatrist, but he wouldn't go."

"During this period after his son's death, did his behavior change any?" Brian asked.

"I just told you. He became depressed."

"No, I know that. That was his mood. Did his behavior change? Did he argue with coworkers, become violent, drink, use drugs, anything like that?"

"No. He got along with everyone. He was never a problem."

"What about girlfriends? His wife died at an early age. He was, what, twenty-four when she died? There must have been women."

"None that I know of. He had pictures of his wife and son all over his work station. His apartment was the same way. I went home with him one night, and there were pictures of his wife and Robert Jr. all over the place; not the kind you could easily take down when a girlfriend came over either. No, there were no women in his life. His son was his whole life."

"Mr. Crocket, I hesitate to ask this, but I must. Any chance there were men in his life?"

"What do you mean?"

"Any chance he was gay? A homosexual?"

"Absolutely not."

"What about pornography? Did you ever see him or hear anyone else say he could have been involved with pornography?"

"No sir! Not Robert! He was a good man. I told you that," Mr. Crocket answered angrily.

"I'm sorry, Mr. Crocket, but the nature of the crime he was convicted of, although unjustly, requires that I ask these type of questions, if for no other reason than to set the record straight."

"I understand, Detective Walsh."

"Robert Johanson Jr. was killed in 1982, as I remember. Was Johanson depressed until his arrest? Maybe he was so depressed he snapped."

"No, no. It lasted until 1986. I remember it well. I finally made him go away. I paid for him to go on a vacation to the Bahamas in, I think it was April, yes April. He wouldn't go but I threatened to fire him if he did not go. He knew I wouldn't but he went, probably just to please me. He was gone three weeks. He went to a place called Paradise Island, in Nassau. I never went there myself, but a man from my club who I hardly knew said Robert would enjoy it, so I set everything up. First class. The whole works."

"What happened?" Brian continued.

"What happened? I'll tell you what happened. Nothing short of a miracle happened. It was as if he erased his past. His depression was gone. He came back to work a new man. It was unbelievable. He took all the old pictures of his wife and son out of his work station and, as I saw on a later visit, out of his home."

"Did he meet a woman down there?"

"I have no idea."

"He never mentioned what happened?" Brian asked, with a puzzled look on his face.

"The only thing he ever said to me about the trip occurred about two weeks after his return. He came into my office after work, hugged me, and thanked me for making him go. That's all he ever said."

"That is strange, Mr. Crocket. But you should feel good that you were able to help him change his life around."

"I did, until this trial thing. He never let me pay again either. He insisted."

"Pay for what?"

"The other trips."

"What other trips?"

"I'm sorry, I didn't tell you. He went back to the Bahamas every year in April, like clockwork, the same three weeks every year. It was the only thing he seemed to care about."

Brian sat stunned. He was okay with everything Crocket had said, until this last statement. It just didn't fit with everything else. Johanson must have met a woman in the Bahamas. That would explain everything. She was a married woman. That was it. Brian's head was spinning. Nothing made sense anymore.

Tommy could see that Brian had entered one of his thinking trances, so he took over the questioning.

"Did Johanson have any close friends working in the factory? Anyone who might know more about his trips to the Bahamas?"

"Scott Sellers worked in the work station next to Robert. He might know something. Shall I get him?"

"Yes, please do."

While Mr. Crocket went to get Scott Sellers, Brian turned to Tommy and said, "Maybe Johanson was a fucking drug dealer. Three weeks in the Bahamas every April. Just enough to bring enough drugs home for the next year."

"Boss, I know you don't believe that."

"I don't know what I believe any more, Tommy. I do know this: every time something begins to look one way in this case it winds up looking another. I don't think we have any idea what the fuck is going on, and I'm beginning to think we may never know."

Mr. Crocket came back with Scott Sellers. Fifteen minutes later Brian was convinced that *he* knew more about Robert Johanson than Scott Sellers did. Brian and Tommy thanked Mr. Crocket as they left.

Brian called Paulie from the car phone on the way home and was glad to hear that William Knox was still alive, and sitting right in front of Paulie. The uniforms were all over the house, but Mr. Knox was not happy. *Maybe tomorrow would be a better day*, Brian thought as he gunned the Jaguar towards Bayside and the one thing that still made sense to him.

* * * * * * * * * *

Thursday July 18 began on an up note. Betty had located two more jurors and they were alive. Lawrence Carson and Harold Stanton, jurors 11 and 12, were both alive.

"Thank Christ. Thank you, Betty. Thank you," Brian cheered. "Send some uniforms out to get them. Bring them to me. Handcuff them if necessary, but bring them to me. Now!"

Brian was euphoric. Three live jurors. In any other case they counted the dead, not the living. But this was certainly not like any other case.

Willie walked in with bad news. He could not find out anything about Mable Johnson. She left to visit a sick aunt and never returned. No one knows where the aunt lives.

Brian began to summarize out loud. "We have six dead jurors, three missing jurors, and three alive jurors. But for how long? My gut tells me that Susan Champion, Mable Johnson, and Michael Thomas are also dead. What are the odds of all three of them just disappearing over a period of a year? Virtually nil. They were made to disappear."

Brian was right again.

Chapter 16

Susan Champion, age thirty-three, worked as a hairdresser in Manhattan. She was also juror #2 in the Robert Johanson trial. She still lived with her mother, Mrs. Rudnick, who took her maiden name after her husband left twenty years previously. Susan never told anyone she still lived with her mother. It was too depressing for her to even think about it. Susan resigned herself to the fact that she probably would never marry. Her one and only passion was snow skiing. Sharing the rent with her mother enabled her to save enough money each year to go on a nice skiing vacation out West. She joined the East Manhattan Ski Club and had been taking these trips for five years. Her skiing improved with each trip, and she would occasionally have a short fling with someone she met on the slopes, but nothing lasting ever developed. It was early January, and she looked forward to her trip to Snowmass, Colorado.

Susan and the other members of her ski club boarded the plane at JFK Airport at eight o'clock in the morning on Saturday the 6th. She had a seat in coach, crammed in like everyone else. She would return on Saturday the 13th. For her return flight she had somewhat more spacious accommodations. Unfortunately for her, they would be in the baggage compartment.

Susan arrived at Snowmass in the early afternoon and was anxious to take a few runs before the ski slopes closed. With the time difference she figured she would have no problem. She checked into her modest condo, which she was to share with three other single girls. She did not know any of them but that did not bother her. It was frequently the case that she would room with strangers on these trips. She was here to ski, not socialize. If she met some nice people, fine. If she didn't, that was fine also. She walked over to the ski hut where a handsome but very disinterested employee, with the telltale raccoon eyes of a ski bum, measured her for her boots and skis. She always rented. Purchasing boots and skis was not possible on her modest income. She carried her skis to the beginner's chair lift, struggled temporarily with the boot buckles, and started the ride up Fanny Hill. Susan could feel the excitement building. She would start off slow, since it was almost a full year since her last trip. It was a beautiful day with the sun shining and the air cold, but not too cold. *It was just right.* She made several runs down the mountain and was pleased that her skills were returning so quickly. Susan was not a great skier, but she felt she was quickly becoming a solid intermediate.

She completed three runs and then took the Burlingham Chair further up the mountain. She planned to take an intermediate run down and call it a day, for it would be a long week. She had a fabulous run. The slopes were groomed perfectly for her type of skiing. She skied a run she particularly liked last year, named Coney Glade, and made it down after falling only once. She was pleased that she seemed to be progressing faster than she had hoped.

Susan returned to the condo, and one of the girls, who was also on the trip alone, invited her to dinner. The other two roommates were friends and they stayed to themselves the whole trip. Susan and the other single girl, Linda Turner, who was twenty-seven-years-old and on the trip for the sole purpose of meeting a man, had dinner at a quaint restaurant at the foot of the mountain. After dinner, Linda decided to begin her quest for a man in a bar across from the restaurant. Susan, who did not want to play that game, returned to the condo and turned in early, anxious to get an early start the next morning. She planned to ride the chairlift to Elk Camp and ski there all day. She fell asleep just before ten, and dreamed about the mountain.

The next day Susan woke up at seven, dressed, stopped at a shop to breakfast on coffee and a donut, and headed for Elk Camp. She thought she looked pretty neat in her new shocking pink ski jacket, and did not entirely dismiss the possibility that she could meet someone who loved skiing as much as she did. She skied all morning and broke for lunch. She was having a wonderful day. Her first run in the afternoon was down Bull Run, which was slightly more difficult than the runs she skied in the morning. When she had skied halfway down the mountain, she was passed by a man she had seen at the open-air restaurant at lunchtime. He was a tall man with deep blue eyes. *He's way out of my reach*, she remembered saying to herself. She watched him ski flawlessly down the mountain. He looked like those professional skiers she saw on TV; maybe he was a professional. He was a professional; but, unfortunately for Susan, not a professional skier.

The next three days were wonderful for Susan. She did not meet anyone exciting, but the skiing was the best she could ever remember. The weather was simply perfect. She improved her technique with each passing day and decided to try a black slope, which was supposedly only for expert skiers. She would do it; she would try a black slope. How bad could it be? She figured the worst that could happen was that she would have to traverse the mountain very slowly, but eventually she would get down. She would find a short run, just in case. She just had to give it a shot.

Wednesday night Susan and Linda had dinner together again. They hardly saw the other two girls in the second bedroom. Linda had met someone and was with him most of the week. Linda was just a beginning skier and didn't like it that much. She tolerated it more than liked it. Susan did not want to hang out with Linda since she had only two days of skiing left and she wanted to ski every minute. After dinner Susan walked back to the condo alone, started a fire in the old stone fireplace, opened her trail map, and began her search for the perfect black slope. The next day she would ski the Sam's Knob Chair. That would enable her to warm up on some intermediate slopes and then ski one of the short black runs also serviced by that chair. It would be her crowning achievement in skiing. She was ready.

Thursday morning came very quickly. Susan was amazed at how soundly she slept while away skiing; at home she could never fall asleep. The crisp bright day brought a few more inches of new powder, and she could hear the snow tractors out grooming the slopes. She felt the goose bumps run up the back of her neck as she looked through her bedroom window at the majestic mountain. *Perfect. Absolutely perfect.* She quickly dressed, threw her skis over her shoulder, and walked down to the small shop where she had breakfast every day. The tall man with the blue eyes watched from outside, pretending to idly wax his skis. *This will be the day*, he thought. Time was running out. The weatherman said there was a storm coming that night and that skiing on Friday may be suspended. He had to be out of Colorado that night. Susan Champion had already taken too much time, and there was much work to be done elsewhere.

Susan skied all morning off the Sam's Knob Chair. She noticed that really great tall skier a few times. After lunch she headed for Bear Claw. The man with the blue eyes could not believe his good fortune. It wasn't crowded at all on Bear Claw; in fact, it was empty. It was the only black slope on this section of the mountain that was not completely groomed. The top was groomed, but not the bottom. Everyone knew that. Apparently, everyone but Susan Champion. The man had seen her ski all week, and she had no business on this part of the mountain.

Susan paused at the top of the run. Her heart was pounding, pushed by her sky-high adrenaline level. She started down the mountain very slowly. The blue-eyed man watched. No one else was around. Susan fell almost immediately. She thought about walking up the mountain but resisted.

The blue-eyed man was concerned that his plan might not work; she was such a bad skier. He was glad to see her get up unharmed and again head down the mountain. Susan took off again, and a peculiar thing happened: she fell into a rhythm skiers sometimes get, and she began to ski way above her ability.

The blue-eyed man started down Bear Claw. *What an appropriate name*, he thought to himself.

Susan was skiing better and faster than at any time in her life. She was floating from ski edge to ski edge. She felt like one with the mountain. Unfortunately for her, her feelings were about to come true. She was headed for the left side of the run and had just started to put her weight on her left ski to turn when she felt the bump. *What's happening? I didn't fall.* She was still skiing, but her skis were off the ground. *I must have hit a mogul.* She couldn't turn and was headed for the trees. *Wait. I'm being carried*! Someone was indeed carrying her toward the trees. She tried to scream as she flew into the tree-dense area, but nothing came out. Susan's neck was broken by the man with the blue eyes. As her head rotated to the left, the last thing she saw was the face of that tall great skier with the gorgeous blue eyes. She was dead. The man, whose strength was incredible, held her away from him with his right arm and skied her directly into a tree. He left her in a pile at the base of a tall pine tree, gathered up her ski poles and placed them where they should be after a fall, messed up his tracks, and skied down the mountain. It was just starting to snow. With luck she wouldn't be found until he was long out of Colorado.

Linda came back to the condo after dinner with her new boyfriend and was surprised, but not disappointed, to find Susan gone. *Maybe she finally found someone*, Linda thought. Linda and her new friend Alan took advantage of the situation. They had been unable to get any privacy at Alan's place, and Linda wouldn't do anything with his roommates around. She would do it in front of Susan, who she knew she would never see again. It was a pleasant surprise not to find her there. Alan started right away. He was all over Linda, but Linda didn't mind. He was inside her in no time and they were both enjoying the moment. Linda was as excited as she had ever been, but as she inadvertently turned her head towards Susan's bed she realized for the first time that something might have happened to Susan. The moment of passion for Linda died as quickly as Susan did.

At approximately 10:25 A.M. Friday, after a two-hour search, Susan's frozen body was found in the trees off the Bear Claw run, partially covered with three inches of crystal-clear new powder. The ski patrol, alerted by her concerned roommate, Linda Turner, found the body. She was brought down the mountain by sled and taken to the local hospital where she was officially pronounced dead. X-rays were taken for the record, and it was determined that Susan Champion was killed by accident when she skied off the side of an expert slope into the trees. She unfortunately hit a tree with enough force to fracture her skull and suffer a fracture-dislocation of her upper cervical spine, which killed her instantly. Thank God for that. God had nothing to do with it.

The police called Susan's mother, who made arrangements to have her body flown home for burial. Ironically, she rode back to New York on Saturday with the other members of her ski club, most of whom did not notice she was missing, and none of whom really cared.

Chapter 17

Mable Johnson received the call from Reverend Robinson on Friday January 19th.

"Hello. Mrs. Johnson. My name is Reverend Robinson. I am calling about your aunt, Molly Richardson."

"Yes, Reverend. Is anything the matter with Aunt Molly?"

"Not today, but yesterday she was not feeling that well. She has had a touch of the flu, and when I visited her yesterday she mentioned that you were her only living relative. She said—and please don't be alarmed by what I am about to say—she said that she would like to see you before anything happened."

"But, Reverend, you said she was fine."

"She is fine today. God willing, she will continue to be fine, but my experience has taught me that sometimes elderly people get a feeling when things are going to go bad. After all, Molly is eighty-three years old."

"I'm fifty-nine, so she would be closer to eighty-four. My oh my, where does the time go?"

Mable thought to herself that Aunt Molly was always sick. She was always recovering from one thing or another, but she always recovered. Maybe this time would be different.

"We will all be with Jesus someday," the Reverend added.

"Yes, Reverend, we will. I would love to come and visit with Aunt Molly. Please tell her I will take the bus to Utica tomorrow or Sunday. Thank you for calling, Reverend."

"I will call on Molly daily until you arrive."

"Thank you again, Reverend."

Mable called the Greyhound Bus Company and was able to get a reservation on a bus going to Albany, Utica, and Syracuse on Saturday. Mable was a deeply religious woman, and to receive a call from Reverend Robinson might as well be a call from God Himself. She was excited about seeing Aunt Molly. She hadn't seen her for years, although she would occasionally call to check up on her. Molly wasn't actually her aunt, but she loved her just as if she were. When Mable's husband Leroy died six years ago, Molly wrote Mable a beautiful letter. Molly was Leroy's aunt, but as Molly said in the letter, she and Mable were the only two family members left. *Soon there would be only one*, Mable thought. Yes, that was true—Aunt Molly would live many more years.

Mable packed a small suitcase and went to bed early. She was going on her first trip in six years but there was no one to tell. That saddened her. She never worked. Her husband would never hear of it, and after he died, with his pension, she didn't have to work. She spent most of her time at the church doing volunteer work with the poor. They wouldn't miss her for a week or so. There were many other volunteers at the mission.

Mable boarded the Greyhound bus at 9:45 A.M. Saturday. It seemed to stop at every rest stop on the New York Thruway, but she arrived in Utica at 6:30 P.M., after a problem with the bus in Albany. She took a taxi to Aunt Molly's small but very well-kept home in a mostly black section of Utica. Aunt Molly was very happy to see her, but quite surprised that she had come. When Mable told her about the call from Reverend Robinson, Molly understood.

"For the past few days a new minister at the church has come to visit with me. He's very nice and spends a lot of time talking with me. That old Reverend Simpson hasn't been around in years."

Mable was surprised to see how feeble Molly had become. The past several years had not been kind to her. Molly looked as though she was having a hard time seeing, and her hearing was obviously deteriorating.

Mable and Aunt Molly talked until very late in the evening, and then they prayed together. After prayers they retired for the night, Aunt Molly to her room upstairs and Mable to the small bedroom off the kitchen on the first floor. Mable noticed that, even with her help, it was a major effort for Aunt Molly to climb the stairs, and Mable suggested that Aunt Molly should consider moving to the small bedroom downstairs. Aunt Molly would not hear of it. She would die in the same room as her husband did thirteen years previously.

The next morning Mable awoke early and prepared a wonderful breakfast for Aunt Molly, which she brought to her room upstairs. The thought of Aunt Molly going down the stairs was too much for Mable to imagine. After breakfast, Aunt Molly dozed off. Mable was sure Aunt Molly hadn't been up past nine in years, and last evening she was up until 11:30. Mable would let Aunt Molly sleep.

There was a knock on the door, and when Mable looked out she saw a man dressed in the clothes of a minister. She opened the door and met Reverend Robinson. She was astonished by his appearance. She was not ready for a tall white minister with deep blue eyes. She had nothing against a white minister, but had never had one at any of her churches. Things were obviously very different in Utica, New York.

"Good morning. I'm Reverend Robinson. Are you Mable Johnson?"

"Yes. It is so nice to meet you, Reverend Robinson. Aunt Molly has told me how concerned you have been about her. Please come in."

"How is Molly?" the Reverend asked as he looked out through the circular, multicolored, glass opening in the door he was closing. He put his briefcase down.

"She is upstairs sleeping. We stayed up very late catching up on old times. It's been six years since I last saw Aunt Molly. Would you like a cup of coffee, Reverend?"

"Yes, thank you. That would be nice."

Reverend Robinson followed Mable into the kitchen. He slowly looked around. From his previous visits, he knew no one could see into the house from the outside. He did not want a nosy neighbor screwing things up. He waited several minutes, drank some coffee, and made small talk with the very religious Mable Johnson. At the right moment, Reverend Robinson stood up, brought his cup over to the sink, and turned on the faucet. Mable jumped up to stop him. She would do it.

"Reverends do the Lord's work, not dishes," she protested.

Just then the Reverend dropped the cup on the floor and watched as it landed by Mable's feet. She made a motion to bend over to get it, but the Reverend politely stopped her as he reached down for the cup, which was touching her left foot. With every bit of strength the blue-eyed man had, he grabbed Mable's ankles, one in each hand, and pulled up as hard and as quickly as possible. He wanted her head to hit the floor with tremendous force. As she flew through the air, Mable had no comprehension of what was happening. When her head hit the flood with a dull thud, the blue-eyed man released her ankles, and she fell into a heap. When her right hip hit the floor, he thought he heard it break. He checked her pulse, and she still had a good one, but she was unconscious. She obviously fractured her skull, and probably fractured her hip, but she was still alive. He reached for his briefcase, put on a pair of powderless surgical gloves, very carefully lifted up Mable's dress, and partially pulled down her panties. He felt for the femoral pulse in her left groin and easily found it. That was good news and bad news. It would be easy to insert the needle, but her heart was still pumping strongly. He introduced a 22-gauge needle into her left femoral vein, which he knew was just medial to the artery, taking great care not to spill a drop of blood. He then injected her with enough insulin to drop her blood glucose to virtually zero. Twenty minutes later Mable Johnson's heart was faintly pumping but she was brain dead. The blue-eyed man then took an intravenous bottle of glucose out of his briefcase and connected it to the needle in Mable's left groin. As the glucose slowly ran into her femoral vein, her heart continued to beat faintly. Her blood sugar was rising to normal, but it wouldn't do her brain any good. When the infusion was completed, the man removed the needle and applied pressure. There was no bleeding.

He looked for the puncture wound where he knew it to be, lost in her pubic hair, and he could not see it. *No one will even look, much less find it,* he thought to himself. He pulled her panties up and pulled her dress down, but left it in disarray. He washed his cup, dried it, and placed it in the back of the cupboard. He carefully spilled some water on the floor, removed Mable's shoe, ran it through the spilled water to spread it appropriately, and replaced her shoe. He looked down at Mable, whose pupils were fixed and dilated. *Her heart may be pumping*, he thought, *but she's as good as dead*. He very carefully surveyed the room, looked at his watch, which read 10:16 A.M., picked up his briefcase, and quickly changed from a minister to an appliance repairman. He looked out the front door, saw no one, glanced back at Mable lying on the kitchen floor, slowly walked out to the car he had previously stolen, and drove away cautiously.

Aunt Molly found Mable at 11:32 A.M. and was able to make it to the phone to call the police. When the police came, Aunt Molly could not tell them anything about what happened. She was sound asleep when the accident occurred. Aunt Molly, who was known to most of the people in her neighborhood, was visibly upset and questioned as little as necessary.

Mable was brought to the local hospital by ambulance and treated in the emergency room. Her heart was faintly beating on arrival and an attempt was made to revive her, but when the emergency room physician thought better of it, the lady with the fixed and dilated pupils was pronounced dead at 12:24 P.M.

The coroner's office was notified, and a few days later the coroner's report related the unfortunate death of Mable Johnson, a dear niece of Molly Richardson, who came to Utica to visit and who slipped on some water on the kitchen floor. She had a terrible fall, which fractured her skull and caused a subdural hematoma. She died in the emergency room after a valiant effort to save her. The report indicated that there were no other abnormalities to explain her fall and that her death was an unfortunate accident. Mable Johnson would be buried in Utica, close to her last surviving relative.

By the time the coroner's report was issued, the blue-eyed man was back in Manhattan and Mr. Anthony Picciano's stolen car had been recovered. Judging from the amount of marijuana left in the car, it had been taken for a joy ride by teenagers. Mr. Picciano was happy to get his car back in one piece.

Chapter 18

Friday July 19th was a pivotal day. Brian was convinced they had to find out more about Robert Johanson. He wasn't sure how it was done, but he doubted that his death was a suicide.

"People, listen up. We need to be more aggressive with Robert Johanson. We have simply got to know more about him. Willie, I want you to go to Chicago and see what you can dig up. Go to Northwestern and find out everything about Robert Jr. Interview his friends, his teachers, anyone who knew him. Find girlfriends, boyfriends, pets, whatever, but find me something."

"Okay, Brian, I'll leave tonight. I'm going to drive so I can stop by that place in Ohio where Robert Jr. was killed."

"All right. If you need anything call Captain Polanski; he's John's Captain. And listen to this, everyone. My son John is no longer doing undercover. He's in homicide."

Everybody cheered.

"Finally one good detective in the Walsh family," Tommy couldn't resist.

Brian was very proud. In fact, he was beaming with pride.

"Paulie, you will continue to work with the three live jurors, and I'll help you with them. They must know something. Tommy, you too are taking a trip. I hate to do this, but I know you'll forgive me eventually."

"Oh fuck," was all Tommy could think to say. "Where do I go? Jersey, or someplace worse?"

"There is no place worse than Jersey," Paulie said.

"You get to go to Nassau. Nassau in the Bahamas, not the one on Long Island. Johanson spent three weeks there every year. There must have been something very special there. Find it, her, or him. But find it."

"Do I have to go alone, boss?"

"What a surprise question," Betty interjected.

Everyone was taken aback. As far as anyone could remember, this was Betty's first attempt at humor.

"No. You must go as a couple enjoying the sights. You will be less noticeable that way. Take Margaret. You are still with her, aren't you?"

"Yes, boss, I'll be with her forever."

"Yeah, right. We'll see," Brian answered. "Just remember why you're going to the Bahamas—I want information, and a lot of it!"

* * * * * * * * *

Paulie continued to keep the three live jurors as happy as anyone could be whose time on earth was probably limited, despite what Paulie assured them. All three had uniform police watching them around the clock in a very obvious display of power. Brian wanted time.

The tall man with the blue eyes took notice of all the activity, and came to the rather obvious conclusion that the other jurors' deaths were discovered. He was furious with himself. Every death was carefully planned and executed perfectly. But somewhere he slipped up. It could only have been Elizabeth Anderson. That is the only one he couldn't completely remember. The plan was perfect. It should have looked like a savage rape by four psychopaths. If only he could remember. He had never had a lapse like that before. He remembered stalking her and knocking her down in the alley, but was certain of little else. He was pretty sure he remembered injecting the semen into her vagina and rectum, but the next thing he remembered was looking down at her in the dumpster. He must have forgotten to do something. In his rage to kill the bitch, he forgot to do something. It was too late to second-guess himself now. The next three would take all his skills, all his training. The victims were now warned and protected. In a strange way, the blue-eyed felt serene. He no longer had to find ways to make the deaths look natural. He could do the spectacular. He could be the incredible killing machine he always was. It would be hell to pay for anyone who stood in his way. Thomas

Knox, Lawrence Carson, and Harold Stanton would all die. It would just take more time, more planning, and a little luck. He had heard of Detective Brian Walsh, and he would be a formidable opponent. But Detective Walsh would lose also. Everyone who had faced the blue-eyed man in the past had done so. But the blue-eyed man had a very different feeling in the pit of his stomach. He had already made one mistake, and that had never happened before.

* * * * * * * * *

Brian decided to spend the weekend at home with the transcript of Johanson's trial. He would take Maureen out to dinner and then disappear into the den with the transcript. *Surely there must be more to this than meets the eye,* he kept telling himself. Willie would be on his way to Chicago, Tommy on his way to the Bahamas, and Paulie and a mass of uniforms were all over the remaining jurors. What could go wrong?

Brian arrived home about seven, and he and Maureen drove to a small Spanish Restaurant they liked in Valley Stream. They had a wonderful dinner and renewed their acquaintance.

"Brian, I hate to bring this up, but you look exhausted. You need to spend more time in bed."

"Is that an invitation?"

"Yes. It's an invitation to sleep. Since Sal dumped this case on you in May you haven't gotten one good night's sleep. You can't continue like this. My God, Brian, you are fifty-four years old."

"I know honey. Everyone is working hard on this. We have seven dead people connected to this one trial. I can't let go until either we win, or he wins, or she wins, or they win, whatever. I can't go out like this Maureen. I just can't!"

"I understand, as long as this is the last one. I hope it is."

"It is, Maureen. There could never be a case like this again. Bear with me. I'll make it up to you when it's over. I sent Tommy to the Bahamas today. It looks like a place we should go."

"Good. Let's leave tomorrow."

"I mean when it's over."

"I know. Just trying," she teased.

They finished their meal and returned home. Brian had a little too much Sangria, and the combination of the wine and sleep deprivation put him into a deep sleep at 10:15. Maureen tucked him in and she began to read. Brian slept for twelve hours.

Chapter 19

Brian finally made it to the den with the transcript on Saturday afternoon and began reading. Jury selection took four days, May 8-11. *That was a little too long*, Brian thought, but certainly nothing strange could have happened. The A.D.A. was very methodical and got the jury he wanted. The trial began on Friday May 12. A.D.A. Joseph Hudson began his introduction: "Ladies and gentleman of the jury. My name is Joseph Hudson. I am an Assistant District Attorney, and I have been given the privilege of representing the good people of the Borough of Manhattan in their quest for justice for one of their smallest constituents, five-year-old Nancy Tailor. Nancy is too small to obtain justice for herself, so you and I will get it for her."

He made this opening remark with a picture of Nancy Tailor in his hands, and he continually showed it to the jurors. The picture was of Nancy sitting on her church steps in her best Sunday go-to-church outfit. She looked very pretty and very happy. Pictures would be shown later that would sharply contrast with these. *Nice move, counselor*, Brian thought. A.D.A. Hudson continued: "I will present irrefutable evidence that Robert Johanson was the perpetrator of this crime. Witnesses will testify that he was seen talking to the victim, little Nancy Tailor, just a few hours prior to the brutal attack. A patrolman in the area, Leroy Phillips, saw Robert Johanson give Nancy candy just a few hours prior to the attack. We all know what that means. This is the same patrolman who received a Mayor's Citation for saving little Nancy's life."

Jesus Christ, Horowitz. Object, you fool, Brian thought. No one could be this bad on purpose. It seemed to Brian that Horowitz was letting Johanson go upstate. Maybe he was set up. But why?

Hudson continued: "There will be other witnesses who will place Robert Johanson at the store. The storekeeper and other shoppers will testify. They will all say the same thing—that Robert Johanson offered little Nancy Tailor candy, and later that day he savagely raped and mutilated her just a few blocks from the store where he offered her candy. Just a few blocks from her home. Just a few blocks from her church. I will be asking you to convict Robert Johanson of attempted murder and rape. Attempted murder and rape of a five-year-old child, who could never have done anything to Robert Johanson to precipitate such an event. We are not talking of a provocative woman here—my God, she was a five-year-old child."

With that, A.D.A. Hudson walked in front of each juror and held up the picture of Nancy Tailor's smiling face. He then sat down.

Brian could not see the faces of the jury by reading the transcript but he imagined that it would be an impossible act for Horowitz to follow. He was right. Horowitz was in way over his head.

Irving Horowitz began his second trial, and, in reality, his first real test. Unfortunately for Robert Johanson, he would fail miserably.

"Ladies and gentleman of the jury," he stole from Hudson, "all the evidence you will see presented by Mr. Hudson is circumstantial. There will not be one solid piece of evidence Assistant District Attorney Hudson presents that will actually tie my client to the crime. Not one witness will testify that they actually saw Robert Johanson rape Nancy Tailor. Not one! In the end you will have to let him go because of reasonable doubt. Thank you."

Brian could not believe his eyes. He had read the transcript many times before, and each time he found it more unbelievable. Horowitz never said once that Robert Johanson was innocent. Not once. How fucking stupid was this guy? He basically said that Johanson was guilty, but that there was no direct proof.

Judge Morton Levy then asked A.D.A. Hudson to call his first witness.

"I call Juan Garcia to the stand, Your Honor."

Juan Garcia raised his hand and swore to God.

"Please state your name for the record," Hudson began.

"My name is Juan Garcia."

"Where do you work, Mr. Garcia?"

"I work at, I mean I own a grocery store on 23rd street. I work there."

"How long have you owned the store?"

"Since 1987."

"Do you work there a lot?"

"Every day. I open the store at six in the morning and I stay until eight at night. I sometimes go home for a few minutes during the day, but mostly I am there."

"Do other people work for you?"

"Yes. I have six other people who work at my store. They come at different times and on different days."

"Were you there on Tuesday March 7th of this year?"

"I'm there every day."

"Do you remember the day little Nancy Tailor was attacked?"

"Yes, I was at the store that day."

"What do you remember about that day?"

"I remember her being found by Patrolman Phillips, who is always in our neighborhood. Everyone was talking about it. It was terrible."

"Did you know Nancy?"

"Yes. Her mother would always bring her into the store. I would give her candy."

"Did you see her that day at about 10:00 A.M.?"

"I saw her and her mother in the store."

"Do you know the defendant, Robert Johanson?"

"I don't know him personally, but he comes into my store."

"You recognize him?"

"Yes, he comes into my store."

"Does he shop in your store? Does he buy a lot of food from your store?"

"Yes."

"Did you see him talking to Nancy that day?"

"No."

"You didn't see him talking to Nancy?"

"No."

"Were they there at the same time?"

"I think so."

"So they could have been talking, and you may not have seen them?"

My God, Brian thought. *Jump up, Horowitz. Object. Come on, Judge Levy. Even you see the absurdity in this. Apparently not. No objections.*

"It's possible," was Mr. Garcia's reply. "I work very hard and do not always see everything."

"How many other people were in the store at the same time as Nancy and Johanson?"

"You mean customers or workers?"

"Both."

"There were about fifteen customers and four workers."

"How long was Robert Johanson in your store that day?"

"I don't know."

"Was he still in the store when Patrolman Phillips found Nancy?"

"No."

And neither was any of the other fourteen ten o'clock shoppers, thought Brian. Who the hell shops at a little grocery store for four hours?

"Who is Patrolman Phillips, Mr. Garcia?" Hudson continued.

"He's the policeman who walks the streets in our neighborhood."

"How long have you known him?"

"Four or five years."

"What do you think of him?"

"What do you mean?"

"Is he a nice man?"

"Yes."

"Is he helpful? Is he a good cop?"

"Yes."

"Does he give you a sense of security? Does he keep undesirable elements away from your store and neighborhood?"

"Yes."

What else could this poor man say? Brian thought. Brian knew there was something rotten about Patrolman Phillips, but so far Willie was not able to find out what it was.

"Would you believe Patrolman Phillips if he told you something?" Hudson asked.

"Objection," Horowitz called out. "He's asking for an opinion, Your Honor."

"Overruled," was Levy's reply.

At least Horowitz knew he could object, Brian smiled.

"Would you believe Patrolman Phillips, Mr. Garcia?"

"Yes I would," Mr. Garcia answered sheepishly. If he didn't answer that way, he knew he would receive another beating at the hands of the good patrolman.

"Thank you, Mr. Garcia. That will be all."

"Please begin your cross-examination, Mr. Horowitz," Levy said.

"You did not see Mr. Johanson talking to the girl, isn't that what I heard you say?"

Horowitz realized that he had to at least look like he was trying to get this scumbag Johanson off. Others would read the trial record. He had already made up his mind that Johanson was guilty. What kind of a nut would rape a five-year-old? Horowitz could understand raping a twenty-five-year-old, but not a five-year-old.

"No I did not."

"Did you see him rape her?"

"No."

"Did you see him mutilate her?"

"No."

"Did you see him harm her in any way at all?"

"No."

"Until today did you ever see Mr. Johanson after he left your store on the morning of the crime?"

"No."

"Did you ever see Mr. Johanson harm anyone?"

"Objection," Hudson yelled. "That has nothing to do with this case, Your Honor."

"Sustained," Levy quickly answered. "Don't answer that question, Mr. Garcia."

"No more questions, Your Honor," Horowitz said as he sat down, quite pleased with himself.

"Next witness," Levy shouted.

"The people call Laquesha Washington, Your Honor."

Laquesha also raised her hand to God. She was a thirty-four-year-old mother of four girls, and was shopping at Mr. Garcia's store on March 7th.

"Please state your name," Hudson began.

"Laquesha Washington."

"Do you know Mr. Juan Garcia?"

"Yes. I have been shopping at his store for the past few years, ever since I moved into the neighborhood."

"Do you know Nancy Tailor?"

"Yes, I know Nancy and her mother."

"Do you consider them to be friends of yours?"

"More like acquaintances. I see them around the neighborhood."

"Do you know Patrolman Phillips?"

"Yes I do."

"From where?"

"From the neighborhood. He walks a beat in the neighborhood." Laquesha failed to mention to anyone that when he walks his beat he often stops by to give Laquesha a lot more than a friendly hello.

"Do you trust Patrolman Phillips?"

"Yes I do. I trust him with my life." No truer statement was ever made.

Brian could not believe what he was reading. The whole plan was to set Phillips up as some type of god and then bring him in to testify. Everyone was supposed to believe that whatever he said happened did happen. How could the jury not see this? What Brian did not know, and neither did any of the other participants in the trial, was that Phillips and several other cops were extorting money from several of the storekeepers in the neighborhood. They were also thought to be connected to Wild Clyde, a prominent drug dealer in the area who would stop at nothing to keep people in line. Laquesha was not fucking Phillips out of love, but rather out of fear for her life. She would love to scream it all out in the courtroom, but she had four girls to raise all by herself, and she had to play along. Phillips said that Johanson did it, and that, right or wrong, had to be enough for her. Surely the jury would not find Mr. Johanson guilty. He was always so nice to her and her little girls. He could never do this terrible thing. Thank God the jury would save him.

"On March 7th did you see little Nancy Tailor in Mr. Garcia's store?" Hudson asked.

"Yes I did."

"Did you see Mr. Johanson?"

"Yes."

"By the way, do you know Mr. Johanson?"

"I have seen him in Mr. Garcia's store at times."

"Do you have any children?"

"I have four daughters."

"How old are they?"

"Two, four, five-and-a-half, and eight."

"Did Robert Johanson ever talk to any of your daughters?"

"Yes, he sometimes would, when I was there with them."

"Did he ever give them candy?"

"Yes, but with my permission." Laquesha seemed to be the only one in the room that saw where Hudson was heading. Certainly Horowitz didn't.

"Did you see Robert Johanson talking with Nancy that day, March 7th, the day Nancy was raped?"

"No."

"But you saw them in the store at the same time, didn't you?"

"Yes. But not talking."

"Did you see him looking at her?"

"No."

"No further questions, Your Honor."

"Do you have questions, Mr. Horowitz?" Levy asked.

"Yes, judge."

"Mrs. Washington, did you see Robert Johanson rape or attack Nancy Tailor?"

"No I did not."

"Did you see Mr. Johanson later in the day covered with blood, or all messed up?"

"No I did not."

"So you did not see Mr. Johanson talk to the little girl, rape her, beat her up, or harm her in any way, did you?"

"No, I certainly did not."

"No further questions, Your Honor." Horowitz sat down.

You could not tell it from the transcript, but Horowitz became a trial lawyer at this very moment. Certainly not a very good one, but he realized one very important fact that any trial lawyer must eventually grasp—it is all a big game. It doesn't matter what is right or wrong, or what is just or unjust. Whether Johanson did it or not didn't matter. It was a game; one side against the other. He began to think that if he got this low-life Johanson off he could make a fortune defending others like him.

The thought actually got Horowitz to pay attention to the trial. Even so, Johanson was doomed to the apathy of others.

There were two other witnesses called by Hudson on Friday afternoon: Mrs. Thelma White and Mrs. Willa Jones. Their testimony mirrored that of Mr. Garcia and Mrs. Washington. Both were elderly black ladies who saw both Nancy Tailor and Robert Johanson in Mr. Garcia's grocery on March 7th. Neither one saw Johanson speaking to Nancy, and neither one saw him giving her candy. They both had seen Robert Johanson before, but did not know him other than to say hello to while shopping. Yes, they both knew Patrolman Phillips, and he seemed to be a very good and very caring policeman. They would both believe anything that he told them. Their answer to the only two questions Horowitz seemed to know was the same as the others: no they did not see Robert Johanson rape and mutilate Nancy Tailor, and they did not see him covered with blood later on in the day.

Judge Levy had enough for the day. He spent a significant amount of time in instructing the jury. They were sequestered but he was going to allow family members to visit. There could be no discussion of the trial, and no discussion of anything their visitors saw or heard about the trial in the newspapers or on TV. The press covered the trial, but for some reason, for which the judge was quite thankful, there was no media circus. In actual fact, no one cared that much about Robert Johanson, and little Nancy had made a complete recovery, at least physically. It was now old news.

Brian continued reading the transcript. He would love to have known what happened over the weekend in the hotel. He never heard of a jury that could completely follow the judge's instructions. As much as he hated to admit it, the judge's instructions were quite correct and to the point.

Monday began with a bang.

"Please call your next witness, Mr. Hudson," Levy began.

"The people call Raymond Sampson to the stand."

Mr. Sampson was sworn in.

Brian had heard about Mr. Raymond Sampson from some other detectives on the West Side.

"Please state your name for the record," Hudson began.

"Raymond Sampson, but everyone calls me Ray-Ray."

"Mr. Sampson, where do you live?"

"I live at 426 23rd Street. Right across the street from Garcia's grocery."

"How old are you, sir?"

"Twenty-eight."

"Do you wear glasses?"

"You don't see any on me, do you?"

"So you don't wear glasses?"

"No."

"Do you wear contact lenses?"

"No."

"You have normal vision?"

"Yes, 20/20."

"Where were you on March 7th at approximately 10:00 A.M.?"

"I was home doing my morning workout."

He was home all right, Brian thought, *but the only morning workout he ever did was collecting money from the string of hookers he had out on the street. How could Hudson use a lowlife like this?*

"And where do you do your morning workout?"

"Right in my living room. It faces the street. I open the shades because I like to see the sun come in while I'm working out."

"You do this every day?"

"Yes. I start at 9:30 and go for an hour or so."

"Why do you keep so fit?"

"My job. I work as a bouncer."

Brian laughed to himself. Any half-assed attorney could make this guy look like a fool. But Horowitz wasn't even a half-assed attorney.

"Where do you work?"

"A club over on eighty-seventh, The Night Owl."

"Do you shop in Mr. Garcia's store?"

"All the time. It's the only good one in the neighborhood. He does a good job."

"Were you shopping there on March 7th?"

"I stopped in around 2:30. I was there for only a few minutes. I just stopped to pick up some milk. I drink a fresh quart every day."

"Did you see anything unusual?"

"I heard a lot of commotion over by this alley, and then I saw someone running west past my apartment building. It was the same guy I saw from my window earlier that day when I was doing my workout."

"You saw someone from your window earlier in the day?"

"I saw that guy talking with a little girl in Garcia's store, by the door. I thought it was no big deal."

"When did you think it was a big deal?"

"When I heard all the commotion after the guy ran by. I went over to the alley. That cop Phillips found the same little girl in the alley, and I told him about the man running."

"You keep talking about the guy and the man. Who do you mean?"

"Robert Johanson, the guy sitting over there," Ray-Ray said, pointing to Johanson.

"What happened next?"

"The cop called for an ambulance, and one came and took the girl away. Then the cop went looking for the guy."

"What guy?"

"That guy. Johanson."

"And you are absolutely certain that the man you saw talking to Nancy Tailor and the man you saw running past your apartment are one and the same?"

"Yes. It was Johanson, that guy there," Ray-Ray said emphatically, pointing at Robert Johanson again.

"No further questions, Your Honor."

"Mr. Horowitz, any questions?" Levy said.

Horowitz was deathly afraid of this witness. He might very well say he saw Johanson rape the girl. He was obviously lying and was therefore capable of saying anything.

"How far is your apartment from Mr. Garcia's store?" Horowitz began.

"It's across the street."

"I know that. But 23rd street is pretty wide. What floor is your apartment on?"

"The third."

"So you must have been at least, what, 125 to 150 feet from the doorway of Garcia's store when you saw Johanson talk to the girl, and almost as far in the afternoon when you saw him running away?"

"So?"

"So, you expect me to believe you can positively identify him on both occasions?"

"I don't give a fuck what you believe."

"Hold it, mister," Judge Levy interrupted. "Don't ever speak language like that in my courtroom again, do you hear me? If you do, I'll lock you up and you'll spend a month in jail. Do you understand me?"

"Yes, judge. It was that guy, Johanson, who did that little girl. I'm positive."

Horowitz quit while he was ahead.

Hudson next called the emergency room physician who treated Nancy Tailor. The doctor gave a very factual, unemotional account of his findings. He obviously had seen the worse mankind had to offer.

"My name is Walter P. Keller, M.D."

"And where do you work, Dr. Keller?"

"I work in the emergency room of Belleview Hospital."

"I bet you see a lot there."

"Too much."

"On March 7th of this year, did you have an occasion to treat young Nancy Tailor?"

"Yes. She was brought in by ambulance."

"Your Honor, before I go on I want to let you know that Dr. Keller will be showing some rather graphic pictures of Nancy's injuries. There is no other way to do this other than to just show them, but I wanted to warn everyone."

"May I see the pictures, doctor?" Levy asked.

The clerk brought the pictures to Judge Levy. If Brian were in the courtroom, he would have seen the look of horror on Levy's face. It was a look the jury easily interpreted.

"I don't know of another way to present this information, so you may show them when asked by counsel, doctor," Levy continued. "Ladies and gentleman of the jury, I have looked at the pictures and they are quite shocking. If anyone feels they will not be able to look at the pictures without undue stress, feel free not to look. I will ask Dr. Keller to describe the pictures using his discretion when they are shown to the jurors who are comfortable looking at them. If you don't look at the pictures, pay close attention to the doctor's description. Please continue, Mr. Hudson."

"Your Honor," Horowitz interrupted, "may I look at the pictures also?"

"Haven't you seen them before?"

"Yes, Your Honor. I want to be sure these are the same pictures."

"Mr. Hudson, please show the pictures to Mr. Horowitz," Levy instructed.

Horowitz looked at the pictures and, with his new concern for the rights of the accused, objected to the pictures being introduced into evidence as they would be inflammatory and very prejudicial. Levy overruled his objection.

"Let us continue, Dr. Keller. Please tell us what you found on your initial examination of little Nancy Tailor."

"Nancy was brought to the emergency room by ambulance. She was nearly dead. Her blood pressure was 50 over 0."

"Doctor," Hudson interjected. "I am going to interrupt you when I feel the jury may benefit from an explanation of exactly what you are saying. Remember we are laymen, and what is simple to you may not be simple to us. What does a blood pressure of 50 over 0 mean? What is normal?"

"Normal is around 100 to 120 over 60 to 80, so 50 over 0 means the patient is in shock. She had a high pulse rate. She had an IV running and her hemaglobin was low. It was 7.2."

"What does that mean?"

"It means she lost a lot of blood."

"That would go along with the first set of pictures, wouldn't it?"

Hudson handed the pictures to the first juror who then passed them to her left. Mable Johnson did not look at the pictures at all. Elizabeth Anderson studied them. Raul Sanchez began to gag and was given a glass of water. Even the inexperienced Irving Horowitz knew that was a bad sign.

"Yes it would," Dr. Keller continued.

"Please describe the pictures, Dr. Keller," Hudson said as he took the pictures from Harold Stanton and handed them back to the doctor.

"As the pictures show, Nancy's clothing is covered with blood and she has several facial lacerations. Her face is swollen and her right eye is almost closed from the swelling. The next pictures were taken after her clothes were removed."

"Doctor, just so the jury understands. These pictures are taken by a photographer specially trained for this purpose, and he does not in any way interfere with, or slow down, your treatment of an injured victim, is that not so?"

"Yes. We don't even sense that he's there. He works in the emergency room and is familiar with everything we do. His sole purpose, and the sole purpose of the pictures, is to document the victim's appearance for legal reasons, so we can go full speed ahead with treatment. This procedure was initiated about four years ago and has been very effective. Before this procedure was initiated the nurses were responsible for documentation, and it was hard for them to do it properly in a crisis situation. My total concentration is on the patient."

The next set of pictures was passed around. This time fewer jurors looked. Elizabeth Anderson seemed to study them even longer than the first pictures.

"As you can see," Dr. Keller began, "the next few pictures were taken after her clothes were completely removed, to allow for more complete evaluation of her injuries. By this time a sample of her blood had been rushed to the lab for a T&C. T&C means a type and cross match, which enables us to give her a blood transfusion with blood that is compatible with hers, to combat the shock caused by blood loss," Dr. Keller simplified.

This doctor is good, Hudson thought. Hudson turned the doctor loose, knowing that the heinous nature of the crime, coupled with the doctor's ability to make the jury understand, would make conviction likely; unless, of course, Horowitz had some vague idea about how to practice trial law. Unfortunately for Johanson, all Horowitz had was a vague idea.

Keller continued: "Note the bruising around the neck. This is where the patient was held while she was raped and sodomized. The pictures of the patient's genital area show the tearing of the vagina and rectum, which is common in the rape of a sexually immature victim. In this case, massive hemorrhaging occurred."

"Please continue, doctor. What did you do next?"

"We immediately consulted with the general surgeons and the gynecologists. They evaluated the patient, and she was quickly taken to the operating room where she underwent four hours of surgery."

"Four hours of surgery," Hudson repeated. "Isn't that a lot of surgery? What was done?"

"I was not at the surgery, but the operating surgeons presented the case at the emergency room conference the following day and they reported what happened. The patient had a perforation of her rectum and her lower colon, causing contamination of her abdominal cavity with fecal material. The perforations were all repaired and her abdomen washed out. She also had extensive tearing of her vagina, which had to be repaired. She had extensive plastic surgery involving her face and her right ear. She had a fracture of her right orbit, which is the bone underneath the eye. This required surgery as well."

"That is amazing, Dr. Keller. And little Nancy Tailor made it, didn't she? She lived despite all that brutality."

"Yes, she did."

"Doctor, it's amazing what you doctors do. We all owe you a debt of gratitude, which we can never repay. How long was Nancy in the hospital?"

"About three weeks."

"Dr. Keller, is there any doubt in your mind that Nancy was raped?"

"None."

"Please explain."

"The injuries were consistent with rape, and semen was found in the vagina and rectum. There is no question that she was raped and sodomized."

"Was the semen analyzed?"

"Yes it was. It came from someone with type O positive blood. No DNA testing could be done, unfortunately, as the sample was inadvertently destroyed in the lab."

"How was it destroyed?"

"I don't know. The lab could never find the sample again, so they assumed it was destroyed."

"Do you know that a court-ordered blood sample was taken from Robert Johanson and that he has type O positive blood?"

"I do now."

"What does that mean to you?"

"Only that he could possibly be the rapist. But you could not be sure on the basis of only that information."

"Thank you, doctor. No more questions, Your Honor."

Horowitz was no match for this doctor, Brian thought as he continued to read.

"Dr. Keller," Horowitz began, "what is the most common blood type?"

"O positive."

"What percent of the population is O positive?"

"About forty-six percent."

"Forty-six percent? Are you sure?"

"Yes, forty-six percent."

"Doctor, we know that there are approximately eight million people in New York City. Assume that half are women. That leaves four million men. By my calculation, forty-six percent of four million is 1,840,000. Does that not mean that, using this blood type test alone, any one of these 1,840,000 men could have raped Nancy Tailor?"

"You could eliminate many other people—for example, people in surgery, people on airplanes, people in jail, et cetera, so the actual number would be much, much lower. But I agree with your point. This blood test alone can not identify a rapist."

"And you are as sure of that as your are that Nancy Tailor was raped?"

"Yes. Both statements are a hundred percent accurate, although your equating them is ridiculous."

"Please let me determine what is and what is not ridiculous, Dr. Keller," Horowitz said angrily.

"On the contrary, Mr. Horowitz. It is the jury's job to determine what, and who, is ridiculous," Dr. Keller spit back at Horowitz.

"Thank you, Dr. Keller. No more questions, Judge." Horowitz sat down.

Brian leaned back in his chair and tried to imagine the expression on Horowitz's face after Keller's comment. Brian was sure that Horowitz had seen enough of Dr. Keller, and was sure that he was glad to see the doctor leave.

The examination of Dr. Keller had taken all that was left of Monday. Brian glanced at the next few paragraphs of the transcript, remembering their content from his previous reading. Here Levy again admonished the jury, reminding them of the rules. It was important that no one speak about the trial yet, and Levy made this very clear. Levy told the jury that Tuesday might be the last day of testimony, since there were only a few more witnesses. He told the jury that he might be able to get the case to them late Tuesday, or certainly early Wednesday. Unfortunately, Judge Levy could not foresee the events of Monday night.

* * * * * * * * * *

Judge Morton Levy looked forward to Monday evening with great anticipation—Lucille Manero was coming to his apartment. The judge loved Monday nights. He had an early dinner after he finished some paperwork, and headed to his apartment on the Upper West Side. The apartment had been in the family for years, and he used it for preparing the week's work. Over the past few years, however, the apartment had a new purpose. His wife had become a pain in the ass and her sexual appetite had decreased significantly. Amazingly, his was increasing. First he started seeing his assistant, Rita Diaz. He still saw her occasionally, but since she moved to Brooklyn it was becoming less frequent. Then young Lucille stepped into his life. She was a waitress in a small restaurant he sometimes frequented. One Monday night they had dinner together, and later that night found themselves in bed at his apartment. He couldn't believe her body. She had the biggest breasts he had ever seen, even bigger than those in the girlie magazines he read as a youth. And, my God, what she could do with them. He couldn't wait for her to arrive. She rang the entry button at a quarter past eight, and he buzzed her up. They hadn't seen each other in three weeks, and she looked better than ever to the judge. After a few drinks they got right to the main event. Judge Levy entered Lucille at 8:46. He entered the emergency room of Columbia Hospital at 9:26 as a "rule out myocardial infarction." Lucille got on top of him shortly after they started screwing, and apparently the sensation that accompanied Lucille's huge breasts bouncing on his face was too much for him to take. Lucille confused shortness of breath with excitement and almost suffocated the judge, who was gasping for air while experiencing pressing chest pain. He was able to push her off, and she became horrified when she realized he was having a heart attack. He did not want her to be caught in the apartment, so she called 911 and left.

On admission to the emergency room at Columbia Hospital the appropriate bloodwork and EKGs were performed on Judge Levy. By Tuesday morning the doctors had determined that the judge did not have a myocardial infarction, but rather a bout of indigestion, or perhaps an anxiety attack, although there was no reasonable explanation for an anxiety attack in a man as secure and mature as Judge Morton Levy. The doctors who came to that conclusion had obviously never seen Lucille Manero in action.

Court was canceled for the day. That did not make the jurors happy. It was more bad news for Robert Johanson. Brian of course did not have the benefit of this information. The transcript simply stated that court was canceled on Tuesday May 16 due to the temporary illness of Judge Levy.

Wednesday began with the judge apologizing to the jury and other members of the court for his unavoidable illness. Everyone was thankful that he was well.

"Call your next witness, Mr. Hudson," Judge Levy stated. He was anxious to finish the trial. He hoped his illness wouldn't get Horowitz thinking about a mistrial, although there were certainly no proper legal grounds for one.

"I call Mrs. Gladys Tailor to the stand."

Brian read Mrs. Tailor's testimony again. You had to feel for the woman. Shortly after Hudson showed her the first picture of Nancy she became hysterical and was barely able to answer the simplest questions. She stated through her tears and screams that she let Nancy go out to play for a short period of time on the afternoon in question, and the next thing she heard was the ambulance siren. She ran outside and got to Nancy just in time to ride with her to the hospital, leaving her other daughter with her neighbor. She further stated that, although she saw Robert Johanson in the store earlier on March 7th, she did not see him talking with her daughter, and she was very surprised that he would do something so terrible. She then became completely hysterical, and even Horowitz was not stupid enough to ask her any questions, particularly the ones he had asked everyone else. Mrs. Tailor was escorted off the witness stand and out of the courtroom.

Another nail in Johanson's coffin, Brian thought.

After a short recess the trial continued.

"I call Patrolman Leroy Phillips to the stand," Hudson began.

Here it is, Brian thought as he read the transcript. The whole trial boiled down to this one witness. A pillar of the community. The honest, concerned, community-minded protector of the neighborhood, who Detective Willie Hayes knew was dirty. Johanson was convicted on the basis of this man's testimony, and the inability of the jury to see the truth.

If the people in Nancy Tailor's neighborhood knew who was protecting their streets they would never leave their homes, was Brian's final thought before he began reading again.

"Please state your name," Hudson began.

"My name is Leroy Phillips."

"And you are obviously a policeman, is that correct?"

"Yes, sir," Leroy smiled as everyone looked at his uniform.

"How long have you been with the police?"

"Eleven years."

"How long have you been walking your current beat around 23rd street?"

"About five-and-a-half years."

"Have you gotten to know the community well during this period?"

"Yes, I know most of the residents, at least by sight."

"Did you know little Nancy Tailor before you met her on March 7th in the alley?"

"Yes, I knew Nancy and her mother. I would always see them around the block. I saw them at Mr. Garcia's store. Everybody in the neighborhood shopped at Mr. Garcia's store."

"Did you ever talk to Nancy?"

"Many times. I talk to all the kids. I want them to feel they can come to me at any time, to help with anything."

"Is there a drug problem in the neighborhood?"

"There's a drug problem in every neighborhood in the city, Mr. Hudson, but I think ours is less than most."

"Why is that?"

"I keep the dealers out. I walk the streets, and I'm around for everyone to see."

"You're a pretty big man, Patrolman Phillips. How big are you?"

"I am six-foot-one and weigh 230 pounds."

"It looks like all muscle to me," Hudson smiled. "Do you keep yourself in good shape?"

"Yes, I workout at least three times a week in the weight room at the station house."

"So your appearance and presence adds a sense of security to the neighborhood, is that right?"

"I hope so. I think it does."

"Did you know Robert Johanson before you arrested him that day in March?"

"I didn't know him, but I saw him around the store."

"By the store, do you mean Mr. Garcia's store?"

"Yes."

"Did you see Robert Johanson at Mr. Garcia's store on March 7th, the day you saved Nancy Tailor in the alley?"

"Yes. I saw him that morning at about ten."

"What was he doing when you saw him?"

"He was bending over talking to Nancy, and he was giving her something. It looked like candy."

"Was he touching her?"

"He was handing the candy to her."

"What was she doing?"

"She was smiling."

"She was smiling at him, is that right?"

"Yes."

"Where exactly was Robert Johanson standing? Would you please show the jury on the large blowup where you were, where Nancy was, and where Robert Johanson was?"

Patrolman Phillips stood up and used a pointer to demonstrate to the jury.

"I was here," Phillips said, pointing to a spot east of Mr. Garcia's store, but on the same side of the street. "Johanson was here," he said, pointing to the doorway, "and Nancy was here," he said, pointing just inside the doorway.

"How far were you from the doorway?"

"About twenty feet."

"Patrolman Phillips, you don't wear glasses do you?"

"No. My vision is perfect."

"Then what happened?"

"I continued to walk around the neighborhood."

"For how long?"

"For another two hours. I stopped for lunch at about 12:15."

"Where did you eat?"

"At the deli on 25th street. Murray's Deli. I stayed there about forty-five minutes and then continued walking around. I like to keep moving."

"Where did you go?"

"I continued to make my rounds and check on everything, and then, at about 2:30 I was back on 23rd street."

"What happened then?"

"I heard these terrible screams coming from the alley between the second-hand clothes shop and the bar. A lady came running out screaming and ran away from me. I went into the alley to see what the problem was, and I found Nancy. She was hurt real bad. I called for an ambulance, and they took her to the hospital. She looked terrible. I thought she was going to die."

"Who was the lady who came running out of the alley?"

"I don't know. It happened so fast. She was in a big hurry to get away from that alley."

"What did she look like?"

"It was hard to see her. She was black, and she was wearing old clothes. She looked like a bag lady, but she didn't have a bag, or at least she wasn't carrying it when I saw her."

"Did you ever find out who she was?"

"No. Everybody tried, but no one found her."

"Who tried?"

"Me, the other uniforms, and the detectives who worked the case."

"How did you come to arrest Robert Johanson, Patrolman Phillips?"

"There was a witness who saw him running on the north side of 23rd street shortly after the lady came out of the alley screaming."

"Who was the witness?"

"They call him Ray-Ray."

"Yes, we heard his testimony. What did you do then?"

"I went to Robert Johanson's apartment to talk to him, and I found Nancy's shoe in his kitchen. I arrested him, and the detectives did the rest."

Phillips failed to mention that he brought the shoe with him, which made it infinitely easier to find.

"Did he confess to you? Did he tell you he raped Nancy?"

"Not in so many words. He said he was sorry."

"Sorry for what?"

"He just said he was sorry, over and over again."

Brian paused and wondered what poor Johanson was thinking during this testimony. The man probably thought he was having a nightmare. Unfortunately he was, but it was the kind you never wake up from.

Hudson continued: "Is there any doubt in your mind, Patrolman Phillips, that Robert Johanson was the man who raped, sodomized, and brutally beat little Nancy Tailor almost to death?"

"Objection," called out Horowitz. "It calls for an opinion."

"Exactly, Your Honor. I want his expert opinion as a policeman," Hudson replied.

"Overruled. You may answer, Officer Phillips," Levy allowed.

"There is no doubt in my mind."

"That's all I have Your Honor," Hudson concluded.

"Your turn Mr. Horowitz," Judge Levy announced.

Horowitz questioned Officer Phillips briefly, and got him to admit that he did not see Mr. Johanson in the alley with little Nancy. The second question in his repertoire—the one about seeing Mr. Johanson with blood on him later in the day—was answered with a deafening yes. Horowitz had nowhere else to go, and ended the cross-examination of Officer Phillips abruptly.

"Redirect, Mr. Hudson?" Levy Asked.

"No Judge." Hudson paused and then proudly announced, confident of victory, "Your Honor, the people rest their case."

"Mr. Horowitz, are you ready with your defense?" Levy asked.

Defense? What fucking defense? Horowitz thought to himself. *The son-of-a-bitch did it. I don't have a fucking defense.* "Yes, Your Honor. We are ready to begin after lunch," Horowitz said to the judge.

"We will recess until 2:00 P.M.," Levy stated. "Is it true you only will be calling two witnesses, Mr. Horowitz?"

"Actually, just one, Your Honor. Mr. Crocket could not make it."

The afternoon session began with Irving Horowitz putting Robert Johanson on the stand. It was pathetic. Brian could not bear to read it again. Johanson said he was innocent on direct examination, but the cross-examination was brutal. He was unable to account for his time after 10:00 A.M. on March 7th, other than to say he was home alone, reading. He did give candy to Nancy, but he did that for all the little children. He had no idea how her bloody shoe got into his apartment. *That was the final nail,* Brian thought, realizing that the shoe had to have been planted by someone.

Brian read Levy's instructions to the jury, which were quite proper. The jury got the case Wednesday afternoon and came back bright and early Friday morning with a unanimous guilty verdict. Robert Johanson was later sentenced by Levy to twenty-five years to life, with the added stipulation that he must serve at least twenty years before consideration for parole. Since Johanson was fifty-nine years old he was essentially given a life sentence.

This had to be the stupidest jury ever put together, Brian thought to himself. A complete moron could see Robert Johanson was innocent. He threw the transcript across the room, and for a brief second thought that maybe people this stupid should not be allowed to live. Obviously, someone else had the same thought.

Chapter 20

Willie stopped in the small town in Ohio where Robert Johanson Jr. was killed in the accident in 1982. He arrived on Saturday, and the police in Fremont were very cooperative. They were able to pull the police report up on microfilm. It was just another of the many high-speed crashes they see every week on the turnpike. Robert Johanson Jr. apparently was going over eighty miles per hour, and either he, or the eighteen-wheeler he was passing, lost control, and that was it for both of them. Both bodies were unrecognizable. Identification was made from dental records, and helped in Johanson's case by an old healed tibia fracture, compliments of a motorcycle which ran him down as he was crossing 23rd street in 1974. Johanson's mangled body was sent back to Chicago, where he was buried in a cemetery close to Northwestern University. There was simply nothing more to be learned in Fremont.

Willie stayed in Fremont Saturday night and got a well-needed solid night's sleep. He drove to Chicago Sunday, where he spent some time with Homicide Detective John Walsh. Willie had watched John grow up, and was almost as proud of him as was Brian. They had dinner together, and Willie asked John to help him with a small problem. John said he would give it his best shot, but it wouldn't be easy.

Monday, Willie went back to college for the first time in over twenty years. He spent the next two days trying to find anyone who knew Robert Johanson Jr. He did not realize that there was such a high turnover rate among college faculty. He finally followed a lead to Professor Emil Hoffmeister, who was Johanson's mentor while Johanson was in graduate school. The professor was a little bit up in years, and Willie doubted that he was still teaching. Professor Hoffmeister was delighted to talk about Robert Johanson Jr.; in fact, he literally went on for close to three hours about him. It was obvious that the professor had a genuine love for young Johanson, but he did not have a picture of Robert. Willie learned that Robert Jr. graduated summa cum laude and was first in his class. He completed college in three years, and he got a perfect 4.0 in every single course he took. He was, to use the professor's words, "The brightest and smartest individual it was my privilege to know." The professor took some time explaining to Willie the difference between being bright and being smart. Willie did not truly grasp the difference, but was smart enough not to admit that to the professor. Robert was on his way to a brilliant future in political science when his life ended on that turnpike. The professor was visibly shaken when talking about the accident.

Willie also learned that Johanson did not have a steady girlfriend, although there was no shortage of women in his life.

"Robert had his pick of the campus," the old gray-haired professor chuckled, "but he was more interested in political science."

Willie thanked the professor, and decided that no one could tell him any more than the professor did about young Johanson. Willie then called Detective John Walsh.

"Did you solve my problem John?"

"Yes and no."

"You are beginning to sound like your father. What does that mean, yes and no?"

"I got it, but it's a forgery. It should work though. Meet me there at a quarter to five this afternoon. The day people who run the place will be gone, and we can bullshit the others."

"You do sound like your father."

Willie pulled into Holy Angles Cemetery at 4:35 and asked to see the grave of Robert Johanson Jr., who was buried in 1982. An old caretaker showed Willie to the grave. John Walsh and his friend, Dr. William Grantham, arrived shortly thereafter, and John presented a very official document, which the gentleman in charge knew to be a court order for the exhumation of a body. He didn't know what they expected to find after fourteen years, but a court order was a court order. He summoned the gravediggers, and they began to wake Robert Johanson Jr. from his place of eternal rest.

"Why the forgery?" Willie whispered to John as the gravediggers worked.

"I assumed you wanted it this year. Do you have any idea how hard it is to exhume a body after fourteen years with absolutely no valid reason other than a New York City homicide detective's curiosity. Even dad couldn't talk a judge into that."

"Thanks, John," Willie smiled. "The doctor won't say a word?"

"Not if he wants to keep taking my money in poker every Thursday night."

Robert Johanson Jr. saw daylight for the first time in fourteen years. He was not much to look at. The only thing remaining was his skeleton—no smell, no flesh, just a partially burned skeleton. From what Willie could remember from the police report in Fremont, not much more went into the ground in 1982.

Dr. Grantham, who was a forensic pathologist John got to know on the job, and who became a close friend, took some measurements, closely examined the remains, and concluded that this definitely was the body of a male approximately six-foot-three to six-foot-six and approximately twenty-two to twenty-five years old. There was an obvious healed fracture of the right tibia, which was used to help identify Robert Jr. in Ohio. Dr. Grantham felt certain about his conclusion—they were definitely looking at the remains of Robert Johanson Jr.

They all watched as Robert Jr. was lowered into the ground, nevermore to be disturbed.

Willie had dinner with John and Dr. Grantham. The doctor was the only one who could finish his meal. Willie then headed east to New York to give Brian the news that, for the first time in this case, things are exactly as they seem. The history they had on Robert Johanson Jr. was accurate. What a waste of a brilliant mind. No wonder old man Johanson became so depressed.

While Willie was in Chicago, and Tommy in the Bahamas, more bad news came to Brian. Monica Berk, who Brian was only half kiddingly thinking of promoting to detective, traced Mable Johnson to Utica, New York. Brian spoke to the police in Utica, reviewed the faxed coroner's report, and agreed with them that it was an unfortunate accident. At least that is what he said to them on the phone. He knew that, as much as the report made good sense, Mable was murdered just as sure as the sun would rise tomorrow. *How the fuck do you convict a murderer of committing murders that were not even reported as murders?* he thought to himself as he hung up the phone. "That's making the somewhat arrogant assumption that anyone smart enough to murder everyone that way will be careless enough to be caught by a stupid fuck like me," he mumbled as he rifled the coroners report against the cork board in disgust. He then put a line through Mable Johnson's name. He wouldn't send anyone to Utica. It would just be a waste of time. "Slipped on water in the kitchen, my ass!" he yelled loud enough to startle Betty in the next room. She knew enough not to ask what was wrong.

Chapter 21

Paulie arranged for the three live jurors that they knew about to come to the station house on Monday July 22nd to be interviewed by Brian. Thomas Knox, Lawrence Carson, and Harold Stanton were three very nervous individuals. This was understandable, since they were surrounded by police twenty-four hours a day. Paulie noticed that Knox in particular was starting to fall apart. He was a truckdriver who moved to Queens shortly after the trial. He made a decent living as a long haul trucker, but did not appear to be a decent person. Paulie could not prove it, but he thought Knox was abusing his wife. Janet Knox seemed very happy to have the police constantly around. The bruises Paulie noticed on her face and arms the first time he visited with the Knoxes had not been replaced by others. He doubted that she really had slipped in the shower. Paulie felt that this had to be the longest Mrs. Knox had been bruise-free in many years. Thomas Knox was thirty-eight years old. The Knoxes had two children—an eleven-year-old girl and a nine-year-old boy. Mrs. Knox did not work. Her job was to take care of the house and the children. Thomas Knox made sure she was constantly reminded of this fact. Knox drank more than he should. Paulie was able to get a lot of information by just speaking to Janet. Thomas Knox did not say much to the police.

Lawrence Carson was an insurance agent. He was thirty-two years old, divorced, and considered himself quite an athlete. He told everyone he could that he was limping because he tore the anterior cruciate ligament in his right knee in the final game of his club's racquetball championship, which he was still able to win despite this severe disability. "Pure guts," seemed to be Carson's favorite phrase.

Harold Stanton was a forty-six-year-old assistant vice president at a bank. He, too, was single, and Paulie thought that fact showed great judgment on the part of the women of New York. Paulie thought he was a typical banker asshole, with a title and no money to accompany it. It seemed to Paulie that every bank employee he ever met was an assistant vice president of something. Stanton's goal in life was to make everyone with whom he came in contact as miserable as he was. Paulie began to think the money and manpower being used to protect these three gentlemen was a total waste of taxpayer funds.

"Gentlemen," Brian began, "I want to thank you for coming today. I know things have been very hard for you lately. I know you have questions, and I will be happy to answer them in due time, but first I would like you to just listen to me for a few minutes. What I say to you today is not to be repeated to any other individual—not your family, not your coworkers, not your friends, and especially not the press or media of any kind."

These assholes couldn't possibly have any friends, Paulie thought to himself.

"If you share the information I am about to give you with anyone, it could seriously hamper our investigation and, more importantly, put your life in grave danger."

Paulie, acting on Brian's instructions, had told each man the same bogus story—that detectives had received an anonymous warning from a very reliable source that threats had been made on each man's life, and that it was the department's policy to investigate any threat made in this manner. He did not tell either man about the other two, and did not tell any of the three that it concerned the Johanson trial. Brian would do that all now, when they were together for the first time since the trial.

"What Detective Lucero told you has not been the whole truth. The actual truth is that seven, and very probably nine, of the people who served as jurors with you on Robert Johanson's trial in 1995 are now dead. We believe someone is systematically murdering every member of the jury."

"Oh holy fuck," Knox yelled as he jumped up. "Holy fucking shit!"

Stanton and Carson said nothing, but Stanton began to sweat profusely and asked for water. Brian brought him a glass. Knox continued to pace. Brian and Paulie watched, listened, and waited. The three jurors were brought in so Brian could collect information, not distribute it.

Finally, Carson asked, "Who's doing it? Do you know?"

"No, we don't," Brian truthfully answered.

"Why is he doing this?" Carson continued.

"Because he's fucking pissed off, you asshole," Knox interrupted.

"Who's pissed off?" Brian asked Knox.

"Whoever is killing everyone," was Knox's answer.

"Do any of you have any idea who this could be? Is there anything, or anyone, you can remember that would help us figure out who could be doing this?" Brian asked.

Dead silence. No one had anything to say. They looked like they were trying to think of something, but no words came out.

Stanton finally said, "It's not my fault. I thought he was innocent."

"You fucking pussy," Knox yelled, now visibly upset. "Don't start with that fucking bullshit. I listened to enough of that from Carson during the trial. I don't have to listen here."

"Gentlemen, please," Brian interrupted. "Keep your cool. We want to hear what you each have to say, but we will not have outbursts like that again Mr. Knox. Do I make myself perfectly clear?"

"Yes, sir," Knox answered. Brian thought Knox had probably been questioned in a police station before.

"I want you all to work together here to tell me everything that went on in the jury room, and I mean everything. I read the transcript of the trial and, quite frankly, I do not see how you could have possibly come to the conclusion that Johanson was guilty. Others have read it as well, and they agree with me. These are trained police detectives, and they all concur, so something must have impressed all of you that we couldn't read in the transcript. I understand how that can happen. We could not see what you saw during the trial—the looks, the gestures, et cetera. I know that some people can even look guilty. I have even brought people in for questioning on the basis of looks alone. The highway patrol pulls people over all the time on the basis of looks. I tell you this because I want absolute complete honesty from you. I want to know every single thing that was said in that jury deliberation room by everyone. One other thing before you begin: you did not in any way do anything that could put you in jeopardy with the police, or the courts, so you may be comfortable and tell us everything."

"Suppose Johanson turns out to be innocent, and he gets out. Can't he sue us?" Carson asked.

"Absolutely not. A jury cannot be held libel for its verdict. I should tell you, however, that Johanson will not be getting out. He hung himself in prison last July."

"See, that proves we were right. He was guilty," Knox yelled.

"It was that bitch Anderson's fault," Carson said.

"What do you mean?" Brian returned.

"She was a psycho or something. She would have hung Johanson herself. She was a real bitch," Carson said.

It was obvious to Brian and Paulie that Knox was not going to be much help. He was too excitable, and would continue to argue with the others. They would probably not speak candidly in front of him. Stanton seemed the direct opposite. He was almost in a stupor, and wasn't the talkative type. They decided to speak to each one individually and would start with Carson.

"Gentlemen, we are going to do this one at a time. It will be easier for the stenographer, and probably all of us as well. Mr. Knox and Mr. Stanton, you may go. Sergeant O'Leary will have a squad car drive you home. We will call you later to let you know when we will need you. Thanks for your time. We will still keep men around you all the time for your own personal safety."

"How long will this last?" Knox asked. "I have to get back to work. I have bills to pay."

"Hopefully not too much longer," Brian lied.

Mr. Knox and Mr. Stanton left. Brian turned to Lawrence Carson and startled him when he said in a very firm voice, "Listen, Carson. You are elected. You will begin right now to tell me everything that happened, everything that was said, every argument that occurred, every gesture made in that jury deliberation room. If you do not, the cops stop watching you, and my guess is that you will be stone dead within two days. If you help, we may get this son-of-a-bitch, and you might live to play racquetball again. Begin now!"

Carson realized that this was a command, not a request, and it hit him, probably for the first time, just how high the stakes were. His expression changed and he began to talk. His memory was either very good, or he was very adept at spontaneous thought. Brian knew it had to be the former.

"On the first night of the trial she started," Carson began. "The judge told us not to discuss the case, but that didn't stop Elizabeth Anderson."

"What do you mean?" Brian asked.

"She started saying things like, 'If it were a black man who raped a little white girl, the cops would have shot him already,' you know, things like that. She wasn't even black. There were only four blacks on the jury—me, that guy Thomas, the old fat man Charles, and Mrs. Johnson. We weren't saying anything like that, but Anderson was. At first no one paid attention to her, but she wouldn't shut up. Delaney, I think his first name was Peter...yes, Peter Delaney. He finally told her to shut up or he would tell the judge about her. That slowed her down, but she kept talking to Thomas. The next day was Saturday. At the meal on Saturday night Thomas started in. He said just what you said before. He said that Johanson looked guilty to him. What an asshole. Then Anderson started in again. The whole weekend everyone tried to stay away from those two. Everyone stayed in their room except for their meals. We were all afraid of getting in trouble with the judge. Delaney swore that if he heard one more word, he was going to tell the judge. I don't know if anyone spoke to them the rest of the weekend because I stayed in my room. Some of the jurors had visitors, but I didn't. I knew something bad was going to happen."

"Why?"

"Everyone was very nervous. By Monday night Knox was complaining about being cooped up. He said he was going crazy. You've seen him. He can really get nuts. Today was nothing. He's a very violent man. When the judge got sick Tuesday, everyone was pissed, including me. We all wanted to go home. When the judge gave us his instructions on Wednesday I thought we would all be home Thursday night. I figured that, despite Anderson, Johanson would never be convicted."

"Who was elected foreman?" Brian asked.

"Delaney. Some of us liked the way he stood up to Anderson."

"Go on. Leave nothing out," Brian instructed.

"Delaney was elected foreman, and he decided to take a vote right away to see where everyone stood. He made it a secret ballot. The first vote was six to six. I couldn't believe it. I thought he was obviously innocent, and the others would see it too. When Delaney announced the vote Anderson went out of her mind. She jumped up and asked who could possibly be so stupid as to vote not guilty. She wanted to know who was going to let this rapist go free to rape other little black girls. I mean she went completely fucking crazy. She talked for over an hour. I don't think Delaney knew how to shut her up. She finally stopped and demanded another vote. I was sitting next to Susan Champion, and she whispered to me that Anderson must have been raped or something as a child. I remember that the lawyers asked that question during jury selection, and nobody answered yes. I just thought she was a head case.

"Rose Mason said she voted not guilty, and she did not appreciate Anderson calling her stupid. Rose tried to explain why she thought he was innocent, but Anderson kept interrupting her. I thought Anderson was going to hit Rose. Finally Chang said he also voted not guilty, and wanted to listen to Rose's explanation. Rose was very good. She made a good case. Rose said that she could not understand why someone who had never been in trouble before would do something so terrible. She said that if every person who gave candy to a five-year-old was arrested, the jails would all be full. She also said that she would never believe that someone planning to hurt the little girl would be foolish enough to talk to her and give her candy in front of so many people, including the child's mother and a policeman. I agreed. I was one of the ones who also voted not guilty."

"Why do you think Anderson was so hell-bent to convict Johanson?" Brian asked.

"I don't know. Delaney thought she hated all men. Maybe she was a lesbian or something. I mean, she turned on Chang when he said he voted not guilty."

"What did she say?"

"She said if it were a little Chinese girl he would think differently. He said she needed psychiatric help. It got nasty, and people began to be afraid of her. Some of the jurors never said a word. I don't think Mable Johnson said a word the whole time. I knew who four of the not guilty votes definitely were—Delaney, Mason, Chang, and me. I felt pretty sure Champion voted not guilty, but I couldn't figure out who the other not guilty was. I tried to figure it out in my mind while all the screaming was going on. Anderson started again, and began to describe the pictures of the little girl. Knox then let us all have his opinion when he was kind enough to let us all know 'that the fucker did it and we should just get on with it so we could all get home by Thursday night.' I knew then that the guilty voters were Anderson, Thomas, and Knox. I assumed that Charles and Johnson voted guilty because they were older, and old folks think the cops always get everything right. Also, they were shaking their heads yes when that asshole cop Phillips was testifying. They were also black. That made it five to five in my book. Sanchez and Stanton were the only two I couldn't figure out. One had to be guilty and the other not guilty, unless I was completely wrong on Charles and Johnson."

"Did you ever find out who the other not guilty was?" Brian asked.

"Not until today. I think it was probably Stanton. Didn't he say here before that Johanson wasn't guilty?"

"That may be his conclusion now. What happened next?"

"Anderson wanted another vote, but she wanted a verbal vote. It was getting to be late Wednesday night, and the guard said we had to stop deliberating by ten. Delaney called for a vote, but he kept it secret. This time it was seven guilty and five not guilty. The bitch Anderson was winning. We adjourned and went to our rooms. I had no idea who had turned, and I thought about it all night until I fell asleep. I was starting to think Johanson was in trouble."

"What time did you start on Thursday?" Brian asked.

"Right after breakfast. There seemed to be some urgency to get it over with. Anderson had the pictures of Nancy brought into the room, and she asked to have a copy of Patrolman Phillips' testimony to read. She read his testimony out loud to everyone, while we looked at the pictures. She said we had to believe Phillips, and if we did we had to vote guilty. Knox started in and was getting very, very, jumpy. He wanted to know who voted not guilty. He threatened Chang, who was slowly becoming a basket case, and then Knox had some comments about Delaney. He knew Delaney, Mason, and Chang voted not guilty, but he did not know who else. Thomas joined in and started accusing everyone of being willing to let Johanson off because he was white and the girl was black. I hated him for that. I told them all that I voted not guilty, and that was my final vote, and if my vote hung the jury, too bad. Knox stood right in front of me like he was threatening me, but I stood up and looked down at him, and all of a sudden he had very little to say. Thomas called me a traitor to my people. I called him an asshole, and all was quiet for a while. I remember thinking that my being black and voting not guilty threw them a curve. I thought it would be a hung jury. I think some others felt the same way.

"Then a surprising thing took place. Herman Charles, who up to this point hadn't said a word, stood up, walked over to the pictures of the little girl, turned to everyone, and started to speak. He spent the next thirty minutes telling us how it would be a terrible mistake not to convict Robert Johanson. He described him as a demon possessed by the devil. He told everyone that he discussed things with his wife, and that she had helped him come to the conclusion that Johanson obviously lost his mind, and that it would happen again if he were set free. Did we all want to be responsible for that? We couldn't take a chance, he said. What kind of person could do this to a five-year-old? The blacks in the community would be furious with us all if he were let free. What would happen to us if he were let free and he did it again? Could we live with that? Believe me, Detective Walsh, he was very persuasive. Anderson and Thomas cheered him when he stopped. Anderson and Knox demanded another vote, and again wanted it verbal. Delaney refused, and Knox went to strike him, but Thomas restrained Knox. The secret vote was now 10-to-2 for conviction. It was me and someone else, and I was pretty sure that it was Delaney.

"By this time it was late afternoon, and the pressure was mounting. No one wanted to stay in that crummy hotel another weekend. Stanton announced that he had a fishing trip planned and wanted to be home by Friday night. It was the first thing he said. How inconsiderate, I thought, for Johanson to screw up Stanton's fishing trip. 'How many fishing trips would Johanson go on if he was sent to Attica?' I asked that asshole. He said that Johanson could always appeal anyway, and if we made a mistake he would still go free. The debate continued and Delaney gave in and had a verbal vote just before dinner. It was still 10-to-2 guilty, and it was Delaney and me.

"I figured Johanson was still okay because I would hang the jury myself. Delaney and I talked during dinner and realized the night would be tough, but we felt it was important to do the right thing. After dinner Thomas demanded that Delaney get permission from the judge to go as long as necessary into the night with deliberations. Delaney agreed, and the judge granted permission. There was much debate and much yelling and screaming but the vote held. At 1:30 A.M. Friday morning Knox followed Delaney to the men's room and something happened, because Delaney caved in and the next vote was 11-to-1 guilty.

"It was an all-out war for the next hour. Delaney never said another word. It wouldn't surprise me if Knox threatened to kill him, but, truthfully, I don't know why Delaney changed his vote. It was Anderson, Knox, and Thomas against me. The others never said a word. I finally gave in at about 3:30 A.M., when Thomas said he would let every black member of the community know that I was the one who allowed the man who butchered little Nancy Tailor to go free. I gave up. I'm not proud of it, but I gave up. I was too tired to fight any longer. I started to rationalize that maybe I was missing something everybody else was seeing. But that was not true. I simply gave in out of fear. The rest is history. Friday morning Robert Johanson was convicted by a jury of his peers, most of whom never said a word one way or the other about the man, and most of whom couldn't give a damn if he lived or died. 'It was better to err on the side of conviction in a case like this,' were the final words spoken by Susan Champion. That probably summed up the whole thought process for most of the jurors."

"There probably would have been a much different outcome if Elizabeth Anderson was not on that jury. Did you read anything about her death, Mr. Carson?" Brian questioned.

"No, I didn't."

"She was a teacher, and she was a lesbian," Brian told Carson.

"I knew she hated men. Was that the reason she was so vocal?"

"We don't know. She was very passionate about all her interests. Why do you think she was so determined?"

"I don't know, Detective Walsh. I just don't know. I wish I knew back then; I might have been able to battle her more effectively."

"And you don't have any idea who could have killed all these people?"

"No, I don't. I wish I did. Is he going in order?"

"What do you mean?"

"You know, did he start with juror #1, Rose Mason, and go in order? The three of us left are numbers 10, 11, and 12. Is Knox next?"

"I hope so," Paulie injected.

"Me too," Carson said. "For several reasons."

"We cannot assume there has been any order. Michael Thomas and Susan Champion have not been located. They may still be alive," Brian said.

"What do you think the chances are of getting him before he gets us?"

"We don't know if it's a him, a her, or a them. We have absolutely no leads. I tell you that not to scare you, but to stress that you must do what we tell you when we tell you. You must not question us. Do you understand, Mr. Carson?"

"Yes, sir," Carson said very subdued.

Brian had gained some respect for Carson. If his version of the story was true, and Brian was sure it was, he at least made an effort to do the right thing. It had to be very difficult for him in that jury room. Unfortunately for Robert Johanson, it was too difficult. Carson was sent on his way.

Brian and Paulie interviewed Knox and Stanton individually the following day. Their stories were slightly different but, in the end, what Carson had said was as close to the truth as could be expected .

"It sure looks like Anderson had something against Johanson, boss," Paulie said after Stanton's interview.

"Or maybe just against men," Brian replied. "Or maybe she was raped as a child and this was payback. Who knows, Paulie? Who the fuck knows?"

Chapter 22

Even the tall man with the blue eyes did not know. The story that he was told by Peter Delaney in July of 1995 was not that much different from Carson's version. It was clear that Anderson was the spearhead of the attack on Johanson, but no one knew the motive, if, in fact, one existed. The tall man eventually came to the conclusion that the motive didn't matter. They would all be held accountable, from the most vociferous to the most meek. He would show them all what real justice was. He felt relieved when he listened to Carson's version of the story. It confirmed that they were all equally guilty of Robert Johanson's conviction and subsequent death. He was also happy that the bug was working.

Several days before, the blue-eyed man began planning the assassination of Knox, Carson, and Stanton. The preliminary work had been done during his original evaluation of all the jurors, but with the recent discovery by Detective Brian Walsh's squad, those initial plans had to be modified. Those plans, although quite creative, were based on the assumption that the victims were unaware they were targets, and the assumption there would be no police. Obviously, this was no longer true. The blue-eyed man enlisted the help of some organization men, and over the weekend, a short, Latin-looking man dressed in dirty work clothes did a very meticulous job cleaning all the windows in the station house where Brian's squad worked. The windows hadn't been that clean in years. Of course, he was not allowed into the squad's office. He hardly spoke any English, but he understood what the desk sergeant told him. The desk sergeant left the small Latin man to do his work, and walked away mumbling something about foreigners taking over the city. In fact, the Latin man was born in Philadelphia, graduated from Princeton University second in his class, and spoke seven languages. He was also the best electronics expert in the organization, and a personal friend of the tall man with the blue eyes. The lock on the squad's office took all of four seconds to penetrate. When the Latin man left the squad's office twelve minutes and eight seconds later, a small microphone was buried in the back of the wooden frame of the bulletin board hanging on the wall. It was covered over with wood putty, and it would probably never be found. He also had time to take pictures of everything in the room, including the items that were hanging on the bulletin board. The range of the transmitter was an astonishing two thousand feet. It easily reached the run-down, but relatively safe, apartment building across the street, on the third floor of which, in room 309, another man sat and waited. This man would tape everything the microphone sent. The blue-eyed man would now know every step Detective Walsh planned.

Chapter 23

Detective Tommy O'Neal and the recently fired Margaret Brennan landed in Nassau on Monday July 22 for what Tommy hoped would be more pleasure than work. They took a rather exciting taxi ride from the airport to Paradise Island. Tommy thought to himself that the cab driver would do very well in New York. They checked into their hotel as the O'Neal newlyweds. The hotel was breathtaking, and their room overlooked the ocean. The beaches were unlike anything Tommy had ever seen. The sand was clean and white, and the water was a crystal-clear blue-green. This would be the best time he ever had; he was sure of it. They had not made love yet, and Tommy had not pushed it because he felt Margaret was surely the one, and he would wait until she felt the time was right. There had been too many women in the past, and it was time to do the honorable thing.

Tommy and Margaret changed into their bathing suits, walked onto the balcony of their eighth-floor room, and stood hand-in-hand, mesmerized by the view. Soon they were walking on the beach and frolicking in the ocean. It was the off season, so the hotel was not crowded. Tommy looked forward to going to the casino in the evening, just a short walk from their hotel. Maybe he would strike it rich. Stranger things have happened in the Bahamas—much stranger things.

Tommy and Margaret had a lovely dinner at a restaurant named The Boathouse. *Thank God the department was paying for all this*, Tommy said to himself as he gave the waiter his credit card. He also showed the waiter a picture of Robert Johanson, just as he did everyone he met on the hotel staff earlier in the day; again no recognition. After dinner they strolled to the casino, where they rambled from table to table studying the players. Tommy had been to Atlantic City once with some of the guys, but it wasn't like this; this was a class act. Everyone was dressed nicely, and there were no seedy-looking characters around. They worked their way to a craps table, where Tommy showed Margaret how to play. Tommy loved the action of craps and had reviewed all the secrets of play in a book he read on the plane on the way to Nassau. They played for two hours. Tommy lost $200 playing according to the book, and Margaret won $150 playing the field whenever she felt good about how the shooter looked. "So much for the scientific study of craps," Tommy said to Margaret as they left. He had a lengthy conversation with one of the pit bosses and showed him Johanson's picture but, again, no recognition.

They walked back to the hotel, and rather than go up to their room, walked on the beach for a while. As they walked under the moonlight, with the warm ocean breeze blowing them into another world, they talked about many things, and Tommy found himself falling in love like a schoolboy. At the ocean bar they had a few drinks and slowly made their way back to the room, where they slept in separate beds, as Margaret made it very clear, in a very loving way, that she was not ready yet. She told Tommy he would know when she was ready, and it would be worth waiting for. Tommy had no doubt about that. In the morning they would go into Nassau, and Tommy would show the picture to every shopkeeper, if necessary. Someone had to know Johanson. Christ, he spent at least twenty-seven weeks of his life in Nassau.

The following morning Margaret was the first one up, and after she showered and dressed she woke Tommy. It was 9:30 by the time he finished dressing. They were ready to do their tourist act and go shopping in Nassau. They spoke to the concierge, who told them to walk over the bridge and take one of the small boats to the Straw Market. When they got to the dock there was a small boat just ready to leave, and they climbed up the crudely built stepladder and boarded. Joey, who was the local expert on who owned which mansion, and who did what to whom in Paradise, made the tour of Nassau Harbor more colorful. The boat stopped at the Straw Market, where Tommy and Margaret said goodbye to Joey while he collected his tips for his short but entertaining act. They walked around for some time, and Tommy purchased a hat that said, "It's better in the Bahamas."

"What's better?" Margaret asked.

"According to these folks, everything," Tommy answered.

"They might be right. Isn't it beautiful, Tommy?" Margaret also liked every previous trip she made to Nassau, carefully keeping this secret from Tommy.

"It's a poor second to you."

"Please," Margaret laughed.

"Let's go, honey. I'm sure Johanson didn't hang out at the Straw Market. I want to go to the shops along the main street and go into a few banks to see if anyone knows anything about Johanson. With the money the department is spending on this trip they want some results."

"Let's shop away."

They started at the west end of West Bay Street, which was the main shopping area in Nassau, and literally went into every store, both on the north and south side of the street. It took until late afternoon for them to cover half the length of the street. No one recognized Johanson. The litany of noes quickly frustrated Tommy, and Margaret could see his mood changing.

"Maybe he came here only once. Maybe he met someone that first time and he stayed in a private house on the other side of the island all the other years. This is going to be a waste of time. Brian is going to be pissed," Tommy mumbled out loud.

"We'll keep trying, Tommy. Besides, I'm having fun. Aren't you?"

"I'm having fun now. However, it will not be fun telling Brian that I didn't find out a thing. Believe me, that won't be fun."

They walked to Prince George Wharf and boarded a small boat back to Paradise Island, where they went for a short swim in the ocean and returned to their room for a short nap, again in separate beds.

They woke up in two hours, showered, dressed, and took a cab ride to the casino at Cable Beach. The cab ride was again exciting. Just then, Tommy realized that they drove on the opposite side of the road in the Bahamas. He couldn't believe he just noticed that very obvious fact. He was too embarrassed to tell Margaret, and chastised himself for being such a great detective that he could miss something so simple. Maybe he was too much in love. He had better concentrate more or Brian would have his ass. This trip had to be costing the department five grand.

They ate dinner at a fabulous steak house and arrived at the casino at ten o'clock in the evening. *This isn't such a bad life,* Tommy thought—*staying up late gambling, sleeping late, eating like a king, swimming in the ocean with a beautiful woman, and all on somebody else's dime.*

Tommy and Margaret began to play craps again. Tommy stuck to his guns and played according to the book, and Margaret played according to her feelings. By eleven Tommy had lost another $150, and Margaret won $275. Tommy was miserable. Margaret began to tease him and he loosened up. Big deal; he was down $350. He'd dropped that much at the track on one horse. But again, no one knew Johanson. He showed each of the dealers and the boxman the picture of Johanson as they rotated into the game, but no one recognized him. Maybe they knew him, but wouldn't tell a stranger. Tommy knew the casinos were very protective of their customers. It was Johanson that was really upsetting him, he realized, not losing the money. They kept playing and finally Tommy's luck turned. By 12:15 A.M. he was up $650 for the night. An elderly lady wearing a bright blue dress, with almost matching blue-gray hair, had a long hot roll, and Tommy did very well. Margaret also did nicely playing the field, and they both laughed while the whole table cheered loudly for the lady, who was having the time of her life. The lady finally threw a seven at the wrong time. After the initial groans died down, the players all gave her a big hand. She smiled appreciably. Tommy was now $1,560 ahead, and Margaret was up $875.

"Tomorrow we will shop for real," Margaret laughed.

"Sounds good to me," Tommy answered and gave her a big kiss. She kissed back, as best she could in the center of the Cable Beach Casino.

"I want to play some roulette," Margaret said. "I watched someone yesterday, and it looked like fun."

Tommy knew very little about roulette. They walked over and watched for a few minutes. There were openings at the table, and as they sat down to play the dealer explained all the options. They each bought in for $100 and were given different colored chips. They vowed that when they lost that amount they would go home. They made some bets on the numbers and lost several times.

"The money goes quickly here, doesn't it?" Tommy said to the dealer. The dealer just smiled.

Margaret bet four chips on the black eight and the ball landed on the eight. She screamed and wasn't sure how much she won. The dealer pushed seven stacks of pink chips in front of her—$140. It was more than she started with.

"The money can come back even quicker," the dealer said to Tommy, and again smiled.

Tommy showed the picture of Johanson to the dealer.

"No, sir, I don't know the gentleman," was his answer. "But I'm new here. Sorry."

They continued to play. Tommy lost, and Margaret continued to win. Tommy noticed that the green zero and the green double zero had not come up since they sat down almost an hour before, and he thought that was strange. He was into his second $100, which he justified because of his previous winnings, and bet ten chips on zero and ten on double zero. The ball landed on twenty. A new dealer came in and Tommy made the same bet, ten on zero and ten on double zero. The ball landed on twenty-eight. Tommy was not happy. He looked and saw ten pink chips on twenty-eight. Margaret won another $350 in one roll. Roulette wasn't his game. He reached for the picture and showed it to the dealer, a lady whose name tag said Irene.

"Oh, that's Mr. Johanson," was her answer.

Tommy's mouth dropped open. He did not expect that answer. Irene spun the wheel and Tommy looked at her, thinking what to ask next. He did not want to seem too anxious for fear Irene might be reluctant to talk about a friend. He did not make a bet.

"Double zero," Irene called out as she went to put the marker on double zero, but she had trouble finding room. She placed the marker high on a stack of pink chips.

Tommy was still dazed by her answer, and then he realized he forgot to make a bet. Just at that very second, before he looked at the number, he heard Margaret scream. He looked and saw the stack.

"Jesus Christ, Margaret. How many chips are on there?"

"Thirty."

"Thirty? I thought you hated that number."

"I had a feeling."

Margaret was beside herself as Irene gave her ten black chips and two green ones—$1,050 for one spin of the wheel. Tommy was happy for her, and very happy about what Irene had told him just before the spin.

"Irene, do you know Robert Johanson very well? He was a close friend of my father's, and my father lost track of him a few years ago when Mr. Johanson's son died. Mr. Johanson became pretty depressed."

"It must be a different man then," Irene said. "Mr. Johanson is one of the happiest men I have ever seen. He doesn't care if he wins or loses. He never bets more than a few hundred dollars a night, but he loves coming here. He's a fishing nut."

"A fishing nut? What do you mean?"

"He fishes all day and comes here at night. He only plays roulette, nothing else."

"Does he come alone?"

"I really can't talk to you while I'm dealing," Irene said in her British accent.

Margaret was counting her chips when she realized she had not made a bet.

"No more bets," Irene said as she waved her hand over the table.

Margaret watched in utter astonishment as Irene called double zero again and placed the marker on top of her pink chips, which the dealer never removes after you win.

"You win again, madam," Irene said.

Tommy could not believe Margaret's good luck, and his good luck as well to have found someone who actually knew Robert Johanson.

Margaret took her $1,050, and this time knew enough to remove her thirty chips.

"It couldn't come up again, could it?" she asked as she looked at Tommy.

"Why ask me?" he answered, "You're the one with all the money."

Margaret cashed in all her pink chips at the table and put $5 on double zero, just in case.

"Nine," was Irene's call.

"Good," said Margaret. "Let's go back to the hotel. I'm exhausted."

"Irene," Tommy started, "could you possibly meet my wife and I for lunch or dinner? I would like to talk to you some more about Mr. Johanson. My father would love to track him down. It's very important."

"I can meet you for lunch tomorrow, if you like."

"I like. Where?"

"Tomorrow I work from 1:30 in the afternoon until 9:30 at night. I'll meet you right here before my shift begins, at about noon."

"We'll be here. Thank you. You have been very lucky for us both."

Tommy and Margaret rode in a taxi to their hotel. Thoughts that this might be his lucky night evaporated when Margaret kissed him goodnight and climbed into what was now clearly her own bed.

Tommy lay in bed thinking about Robert Johanson. He was a fishing nut, the dealer said. Maybe this whole Paradise Island thing was just a big fishing trip every year. A lot of people do the same thing at the same time each year. That's probably all it was, nothing more. Brian would not like this. It was close to 4:00 A.M. when Tommy finally fell asleep.

Margaret was up first again and Tommy followed reluctantly at about ten. They dressed and headed for their meeting with Irene, who arrived promptly at noon. She took them to a very nice coffee shop in the casino, where they were treated like VIPs.

"Irene," Tommy began, "you said that Mr. Johanson was always alone. You never saw him with anyone at all. No lady friend?"

"Not that I can remember. He liked to talk to me. I know his wife and son were dead. I remember him telling me that."

"Where did he stay?"

"I don't remember him ever mentioning where he stayed. I know it wasn't here."

"Why do you say that?"

"He always had to leave by cab. He wouldn't stay too late because it would sometimes take quite a while to get a taxi."

"We found that out last night," Tommy agreed. "Does he fish with the same people every year?"

"I don't know."

"And he comes back every year at the same time?"

"I think he comes every April. But he didn't come this year."

And he wouldn't be coming next April either, Tommy thought to himself, *or any April thereafter.*

"Is there any chance he stayed at someone's home while he vacationed here?"

"It certainly is possible, although he never mentioned it."

"Did he ever make a pass at you?"

"No. He was not that type. He was a gentleman."

"What did you talk about?"

"Nothing special really. He liked fishing and talked a lot about what he caught each day. But it was really small talk. There are a lot of people, both men and woman, who I speak to and have gotten to know over the years by sight or name, but I never see them anywhere but at the roulette table. I never dated him, if that's what you're asking."

"No, I'm just trying to figure out where to look next to find him."

"Why don't you check with the fishing boats? They might remember him."

Tommy had already decided that the fishing boats would be his next step. Tommy and Margaret thanked Irene and took a cab downtown. They visited the shops along West Bay Street again, but this time Margaret spent some of the money she won at roulette the previous evening. No one else could, or would, identify Johanson. They stopped at several banks, and even went to police headquarters, but no one recognized the pictures of Johanson. They even tried the American Express office thinking that he might have needed money at one time, but again Tommy hit a dead end.

They boarded the small ferry that ran between Prince George Wharf and Paradise Island and arrived at the pier just in time to catch some of the charter boats coming back from their afternoon trips. Tommy showed Johanson's picture to everyone on the dock, but no one recognized him. One of the charter boat mates told Tommy that the charter boats come and go, and that there were so many tourists that go fishing that no captain or mate would remember a customer unless he was truly special. When asked what would require a customer to be special the mate replied that it would take a very big tip, or a very big fish. Tommy did not see Johanson as a very big tipper. *Anyone could catch a very big fish*, he thought. Tommy wrote the phone number for each boat that did not go out that afternoon on a small pad, and then he and Margaret walked slowly back to the hotel, stopping for an ice cream cone on the way. Margaret went for a swim in the pool while Tommy called each charter boat pretending to be Johanson, hoping for some recognition.

After calling every boat on his list and getting nowhere, Tommy decided to call New York and talk to Brian. Betty answered the call and warned Tommy that Brian was in a foul mood. Tommy instantly decided that he had nothing to report, and told Betty he would call again in a few days.

Margaret returned from her swim. Tommy lay on the bed thinking. It was now Wednesday evening, and he knew nothing other than the fact that Robert Johanson did come to Nassau every April to fish during the day and play roulette at night. Tommy didn't know who, if anyone, he came with, or who he met on the island. He didn't know where he stayed. He didn't know with whom, if anyone, he fished. He didn't know on what boat he fished. He really didn't know much more than he did prior to coming to Nassau. Tommy was upset, and he feared Brian would be furious. He would give it one more day and then return to New York to disappoint his boss.

"You don't look that happy, honey," Margaret began.

"I'm not happy at all. This looks like a wasted trip. Not for us," he quickly added. "But certainly for the department. Where do you think Johanson stayed?"

"Well, he wasn't rich, so I bet he stayed at some low-budget motel. He sure couldn't afford a place like this. And maybe he went on a small fishing boat, not one of the big ones we looked at today. They cost about four hundred dollars for a half-day. If he was here for three weeks, I can't see him spending close to eight thousand for fishing trips. I bet he had a friend who took him fishing."

"You may be right, Margaret. But where would he find a friend with that kind of money? He was a simple sign painter from New York. He came here the first time depressed and went home a new man. What would do that?"

"A woman."

"A woman?" Tommy answered. He looked over at Margaret, who had just taken off her bathing suit and was standing before him nude for the first time.

"Yes, a woman," she answered as she walked over to his bed and sat down facing him.

Tommy reached out and kissed her like he had never kissed a woman before. Margaret melted in his arms. They made love for the next forty minutes and then fell exhausted into each other's arms.

My God, it was worth waiting for, Tommy thought to himself as he looked at this beautiful creature half-asleep on his right arm. She definitely is the one. He would marry her tonight, if it wouldn't look so foolish. Actually, he didn't care how it would look, but he knew she was not ready for that type of commitment. He thought that Margaret might be right. Johanson found a woman in Paradise and came to visit her every year. But why the mystery? Why hadn't anyone seen her? She was married. That's it. He met a very rich married woman, and they met here on her yacht every April. Yeah right, and pigs fly. No fucking way, he smiled. Not Robert Johanson. He would call Brian tomorrow and go back to New York on Friday. He joined Margaret in sleep, and was awakened at 10:30 by the gentle tug of her arm. They were both hungry but did not feel like going out for dinner. They called room service, and ordered a small snack and a bottle of wine to celebrate the new level in their relationship. Tommy was in another world. He wanted to stand on the balcony and scream to the whole world that he had found heaven. After the bottle of wine was finished, Margaret took him to a level of happiness rarely experienced by any man. They both slept until noon the next day.

* * * * * * * * *

Tommy sent Margaret to the beach and called Brian. It was unfortunate timing. Betty had just told Brian that they located Susan Champion's mother, a Mrs. Rudnick, who moved to Cincinnati to live with her sister after the tragic death of her daughter.

"How did she die?" Brian asked Betty.

"She had a skiing accident in Colorado."

Brian started to laugh. "And let me guess," he continued. "She fell off a ski lift in front of fifty people, or fell while skiing over a mogul and fractured her skull, or skied into a fucking tree and broke her neck, and every fucking witness, including the cops and doctors, and even God Himself, has signed an affidavit that it was an accident."

"You're close, boss. She skied into a tree and broke her neck. She was found the next day. It was ruled an accident. Here's the police report, which they faxed. She died January 12th of this year."

Brian read the report. Nothing in it surprised him.

"Another murder that's a non-murder. Christ, Betty, this guy is good. How do you get someone to ski into a tree?"

"I don't ski, boss."

"Don't start. You might be next."

"Thanks a lot," Betty said as she left the room.

Brian knew all along Susan Champion was dead, just as he was sure Michael Thomas was also dead. Brian wondered what type of accident Thomas had. He was sure that the murder/accident was convincing, just like the others. He wondered how the deaths of Knox, Carson, and Stanton would occur. He seriously doubted that the other three deaths could be prevented, and he was going to tell Sal that at their lunch meeting the following day.

Betty came in announcing that Tommy was on the phone.

"Hi, boss, anything new?" Tommy asked.

"Nothing unexpected," Brian answered as he put a line through Susan Champion's name. I hope you have some good news for me, Tommy."

"Not really, boss," Tommy said as he winced, waiting for Brian's outburst.

No reply from Brian. Tommy continued quickly. "Johanson definitely came here every April. A roulette dealer recognized him without a doubt, but I can't find where he stayed or anyone else who saw him. Apparently he likes to fish, and maybe he just came here on a fishing trip every April. It may be that simple. He fished all day and played roulette all night. I know that doesn't fit his profile, but, and believe me when I tell you it hurts me to say this, I think I'm just wasting the department's money down here. I'll look around one more day and leave for New York on Friday, if you have no objections."

"It's your call, Tommy. Have some fun tomorrow. It won't be fun when you get home. How's Margaret?"

"She's great, Brian. She's really great."

"See you Friday," Brian smiled as he hung up.

"See you Friday, boss."

Tommy and Margaret enjoyed themselves the remainder of Wednesday. They rode jet skis in the ocean, frolicked in the pool, had a great dinner, and gave some money back to the casino on Cable Beach. Irene was not as lucky for them Wednesday night. She did mention to Tommy that she remembered one other thing about Robert Johanson. It probably wasn't much, but she did remember seeing him talking to a tall, very handsome man with deep blue eyes on more that one occasion. She didn't know his name, and he never played roulette with her. She would have remembered if he did, she assured Tommy. Tommy filed the information and enjoyed the rest of the night.

Thursday was another beautiful day, and Tommy and Margaret rested on the beach. They were happy just being together, but there was a subliminal uncertainty in Tommy's mind about whether things would change once they returned to New York. They had taken a major step forward, and he hoped it would lead to even better things.

* * * * * * * * *

Thursday was not that great for Brian. He had a luncheon meeting with Sal at Ryan's. The mayor was not pleased with the progress of the investigation. Brian had managed to keep most of the details of the investigation into the death of Elizabeth Anderson away from Sal and the mayor's office, for obvious reasons. Sal was perfectly okay with that, but the mayor's staff was not.

"Brian, what's going on? There are all kinds of rumors going around that you are sitting on a shitload of information. The mayor is breaking my balls."

"Sal, do you want the truth?"

"I don't know. Do I?"

"What will you do with it if I give it to you?"

"What the fuck do you mean 'if you give it to me?' You better give it to me. I'm the fucking chief of detectives, don't forget that. I'm your friend, but don't bullshit me. What's going on?"

"Here it is, but you won't like it. If you tell the mayor, he won't like it. And if it gets into the press, they will love it. We have a serial killer."

"Please, Brian, I told you before, anything but that."

"No, it's definite. We have a serial killer. But it is a special type of serial killer. He's the best I've ever seen. He makes the murders look like accidents, not all the time, but whenever he wants. But that's not even what makes him so special."

"I'm afraid to ask. What makes him special, Brian?"

"He's going to stop. He will stop after three more victims."

"How do you know that? They never stop. They only stop when they are caught. They always slip up. You'll catch him."

"I doubt he'll slip up. But you ask how I know he'll stop after the next three? Well, it gets even better. I even know who the three victims will be."

"No way."

"Yes. But I doubt I can stop the deaths."

"Lock them up. For their own protection, lock them up."

"You haven't asked how I know who will be next."

"Tell me."

"He's killing every member of the Johanson jury. Every fucking one of them."

"They're all dead? I knew you needed their names for questioning, but... what do you mean? Are they all dead? Are you serious?"

"Jurors one through nine are dead. We have located all but juror #6 and, without a doubt, eight of nine are dead. We have found jurors ten, eleven, and twelve, and they are alive, but for how long I don't know."

"What's the motive?"

"I have no idea what the motive is, except the obvious: that he wants them all dead. I don't know why, and I don't know who. By the way, Robert Johanson is also dead; and so is the attorney who defended him, Irving Horowitz."

"Jesus Christ, Brian. What's going on?"

"I have looked at every angle and can't figure it out. Robert Johanson was a nobody—a simple man with no family and no ties to any crime family or anyone sophisticated enough to carry this out. For all I know, it might not even be because of him. Maybe it's because of someone on the jury; I really have no idea."

"This is incredible. If the press gets this...If they find out we know three people are going to be murdered and we can't stop it...God! A jury, no less. A whole jury wiped out. No one will serve on a jury again if they think it's a death sentence," Sal rambled.

"Exactly, Sal. Exactly. What do you think the mayor's chance of reelection would be under that scenario?"

"Zero."

"Right again. That's why I'm sitting on everything. One of my detectives suggested we just let him kill the three remaining jurors and get it over with. Then he would go away."

"Brian, you can't be serious."

"I'm not, but it may end up that way no matter what I do."

"I'm going to leave you alone on this. You do whatever you want, Brian, but get this fucking guy. Use the jurors as bait, or whatever you want, but get this serial killer. And get him before the papers find out about him or we're all fucked. I told you before: I like this job. I'll tell the mayor you're close, and we have to sit on things for a while longer. How's Maureen?"

"Fine."

"We haven't seen you two since your birthday. Don't work yourself to death, Brian."

"I'm thinking of retiring, Sal."

"Don't even joke around, Brian. I know you. There is no way you will let this prick get away with eight or whatever murders. You'd rather be dead. You'll get him sooner or later, but you'll get him."

"I hope you're right, Sal, for everybody's sake, especially Thomas Knox, Lawrence Carson, and Harold Stanton."

"The three jurors?"

"Yes. God help them," Brian said as he got up to leave. "God help them all."

It would not be up to God.

* * * * * * * * *

Willie got back early Friday and went directly to the office. He told Brian everything he observed in Chicago. Brian was proud John was able to help Willie.

"You looked in the grave yourself?" Brian asked.

"Yes. He was there. The doctor, who's a close friend of John's, said the body definitely fit everything we know about Robert Johanson Jr. It was him, Brian."

"It was just a hunch. Willie, I want you to get on Michael Thomas. He's the only juror unaccounted for. I know he's dead, but find out when and where. Nobody else can."

Willie looked at the board and saw the line through Mable Johnson and Susan Champion.

"How did they die?" he asked.

"Accidental deaths," Brian smiled, and related the stories of each to Willie.

"He's good, Brian. Either that or these really are accidents."

"What do you think the odds are on the first nine jurors of any jury dying from any cause within one year of a trial? Trust me, Willie, don't ever book that bet."

Chapter 24

Willie began his search for Thomas. He would never find him. Michael Thomas had been dead since February. He died during a trip to the Florida Keys. He made the mistake of telling everyone at the gym where he worked about his upcoming trip. The tall man with the blue eyes heard the details during a workout. Thomas was trying to impress a young girl who he jokingly invited to go with him on the trip, since he was going alone. He had to get away from the gloom of the winter, he told her. She declined his invitation. *Lucky for her*, the blue-eyed man thought.

* * * * * * * * *

Michael Thomas arrived at Miami International Airport on Monday February 12th. He picked up his rental car and drove south to Islamorada, a quaint little town located one-third down the Florida Keys. He wanted to get away to just rest and sit in the sun for a few days. He planned to return to New York the following Saturday and wanted to spend every moment possible in the Florida sunshine. He loved the beach and thought he might do a little fishing. At least that is what he told the young lady, and inadvertently the blue-eyed man.

The first three days of the vacation were very restful. The weather was perfect, and Thomas enjoyed himself immensely. He looked at the charter boats Thursday morning and crossed fishing off the list of things he could afford. He sailed on a large schooner, with a bunch of other tourists, for a few hours Thursday afternoon, and was pleasantly surprised. He had never been sailing before. *Sailing wasn't one of the sports inner city black kids did much of,* he chuckled to himself, but he would definitely like to go sailing again.

Thursday evening, while drinking at a bar and listening to reggae music, Thomas struck up a conversation with a black man from the Bahamas. It turned out that the man from the Bahamas was a mate on a charter boat, which recently came over from the Bahamas to try fishing in the keys. They were going out the next day and the mate said he could get Thomas on board for only fifty dollars—since the boat was only being chartered by one man—and there would be plenty of room. Thomas realized the mate would be pocketing the fifty dollars but Thomas didn't care; he would get to go on his fishing trip. The mate gave him the name of the boat and told him to be at the dock ready to go at 7:30 A.M. sharp. Thomas had a few more rum punches and walked back to his modest motel. He turned in, wanting to get a good night's sleep. He looked forward to his first, and, as it would turn out, last fishing trip.

The following morning Thomas awoke at six, showered, dressed, and had a cup of free coffee in the motel lobby. He was at the dock at 7:15, looking for a boat named *Island Girl*. He found it without difficulty. It was an older boat, and she looked very beat-up when compared with the newer, well-maintained fishing boats that surrounded her at the dock. He greeted the mate who introduced him to the captain, and they made preparations to depart.

"Where's the man who chartered the boat?" Thomas asked.

"We'll pick him up at the dock of the house where he is staying," the mate answered. "It's only a few minutes away."

They cast off and headed along the shore for a few minutes. Thomas saw a dock protruding into the clear blue water and saw a man obviously waiting for them. The boat slowed, and a tall, blue-eyed man jumped aboard without the boat having to come to a stop. The captain then turned the boat east and gunned the engines as he headed for the fish-rich waters of the Gulf Stream. The mate introduced Michael Thomas from New York to Peter Matte from Switzerland. Mr. Matte climbed the narrow ladder to the flybridge to ride with the captain, while Thomas sat below in one of the fighting chairs and talked with the mate.

"What kind of fish will we catch?" he asked the mate.

"Mr. Matte wants to get some sailfish. It's a good time of year for them. We will go out into the Gulf Stream and try to get a big one for you."

Thomas was excited. They reached what the mate called the Gulf Stream in a relatively short time. It looked the same as the rest of the ocean to Thomas. They started trolling slowly with some live bait, and within fifteen minutes Mr. Matte hooked a large sailfish. Thomas had never seen anything like it. The fish jumped several times, and as Matte brought it close to the boat the mate reached over, grabbed the leader, pulled the majestic fish to the side of the boat, and grasped its bill. The mate removed the hook and gently pulled the fish along the side of the boat as the captain slowly pushed the throttle forward. The fish became more active, and when the mate was sure he had revived the sailfish, he let it go, happy to see it swim away. The mate explained why this was done to Thomas, who couldn't understand why they let the fish go.

They fished for several more hours and released four more sailfish. Thomas brought in two himself. This was rapidly becoming the vacation of a lifetime for him. No truer words were ever imagined. The mate then told Thomas that Mr. Matte wanted to catch a shark.

"A shark?" Thomas asked.

"Yes. They put up a good fight," the mate answered.

The mate began to throw some bloody chum off the back of the boat, explaining its purpose to Thomas. He did this for several minutes, and then the mate placed a large hook in a bonito and let it drift behind in the thick chum line. Thomas was both apprehensive and exhilarated. He had never seen a shark in the water, much less tried to catch one.

The captain reported from his vantage point on the flying bridge that several sharks were following the bait, which was floating in the chum line. The captain also noted to himself that there were no other boats in sight. Thomas stood by the transom looking back for the sharks when the tall, blue-eyed man sprang into action. The man struck Thomas on the back of the head with just enough measured force to stun him. The man did not want him dead yet. The mate and captain quickly striped Thomas naked and tied a rope to his right ankle. Thomas started to come around, and woke up quite suddenly when he was thrown overboard. He began to frantically swim to the boat, having no idea what had happened. He didn't have time to notice he was naked. He thought they must have hit something that caused him to be knocked overboard. As he swam to the boat, the boat slowly pulled away, just fast enough to keep Thomas about forty feet from the transom. Thomas regained his senses and saw Mr. Matte looking at him from the back of the boat. But, unbelievably, Mr. Matte was not making any effort to pull him back to the boat.

"Stay where you are, Mr. Thomas," Mr. Matte yelled. "The more you thrash about, the faster the sharks will get you. Tell me about Robert Johanson, and we will pull you back aboard safely."

"Who?"

"Robert Johanson. The man you were quick to send to Attica last summer. Tell me about him and you may live," the blue-eyed man lied.

"I was just on the jury. He raped a little girl. Nothing else. I don't know anything else, I swear. What's going on here? Who are you people?"

"He was innocent. I am now your judge and jury. The sharks are your executioners."

"Please! I beg you! Don't do this! Please! Don't do this!" Thomas begged as he tried to swim to the moving boat.

The blue-eyed man and the mate stood and watched. The first shark must have torn Thomas' right foot off. The yell was unbelievably loud, and then the rope was free. The mate slowly pulled the rope into the boat. The end that was tied around Thomas's foot was missing. Thomas was on his own now. Neither the blue-eyed man nor the mate moved. They stood and watched. They had done this before. They knew exactly what would happen, and it did. Within minutes a feeding frenzy began, and Michael Thomas was gone. The small pieces of Thomas that headed to the bottom would never get there. The smaller fish would make sure of that.

Just then a large shark hit the bait the *Island Girl* was trolling.

"Just cut it lose," the blue-eyed man said. "We don't want to see any more of Mr. Thomas."

The mate did what he was told.

The blue-eyed man looked around. There were no other boats in sight. He told the mate to put all of Thomas' possessions in the metal trash container and to burn them. The mate knew the routine. The ashes of Michael Thomas' possessions joined their owner in the dark blue, very deep, Gulf Stream waters, never to be seen again.

The following morning a man who looked amazingly like

Michael Thomas checked out of Thomas's room and thanked the clerk profusely for a wonderful stay, making enough noise to be sure he'd be remembered. He then drove to the Miami airport, again made himself noticeable while returning Thomas' rental car, and boarded Thomas' flight to New York. When he landed at LaGuardia Airport, he took a cab to Thomas' apartment, got out and overtipped the driver, telling him he had a spectacular time in the Florida Keys. As the cab pulled away, the man who was now Michael Thomas looked around, adjusted his hat in an obvious manner, and climbed into the nondescript brown Chevy that pulled up in front of Thomas' apartment. Michael Thomas would never be heard from again.

Chapter 25

William Knox grew weary of the constant surveillance by the police. By Monday August 5th, enough was enough. He could not live cooped up in his house any longer. He had to get back to work. It had been two weeks since his meeting with Detective Walsh, and the cops still hadn't found the murderer. It could take forever. They did not say he couldn't work, just that they couldn't protect him outside of New York. Knox thought he would be much safer outside of New York anyway. He told his wife he was going back to work, and as she thought about it, she was surprised that she had mixed feelings. She knew money was getting short, and when that happened her husband drank more and became more violent. She did not want him to be killed, however. At first she thought she wouldn't mind if he was killed, but she eventually realized that she still did love him, despite his shortcomings. The fact that he was unable to beat her during this period of police protection no doubt contributed to her change of heart.

Knox called his boss and announced he was coming back to work. His boss was ecstatic, for whatever Knox lacked in the social graces, he offset with his driving ability. Simply put, he made a lot of money for the trucking company. Knox was always on time with his deliveries, he was never hijacked, and everything arrived in one piece.

The uniformed officer watching Knox's house alerted Paulie, who was now the official babysitter for the three live jurors. Paulie made it clear to Knox that he was to notify the officer outside of any movement he planned. Paulie was upset as he called Knox.

"Mr. Knox," Paulie began, "Officer Wood tells me you are going back to work. I don't think that's wise, do you?"

"Whether it's wise or not, I'm going. I have about four hundred dollars left to my name and I have bills to pay. I'm going and you can't stop me."

"We don't plan to stop you, Mr. Knox. Remember, we're on the same side. We're just protecting your life. There are nine dead jurors, don't forget that."

"How the fuck could I forget that? Every place I look there are cops. Look, I appreciate what you're doing, but the simple fact is that I have to go back to work. I don't have the money Carson and Stanton have. They don't have families to support. Even they will eventually have to go back to work if you don't find the killer."

"I understand," Paulie answered.

"Are you any closer to finding the killer?"

"No, we're not."

"See what I mean? This could take months. I can't last any longer. I have to take a chance."

"Don't tell anyone where you're going. That is very important. No one at all. Just keep it between you and your boss, do you understand? It could mean your life."

"I think I'm safer out of New York anyway."

"Maybe you are, but don't assume that. Mr. Knox, be very, very careful. Don't make your wife a widow and your children fatherless."

"Believe me, Detective Lucero, I don't want to die."

Paulie stopped by the office to tell Brian, and the tall blue-eyed man, personally. Brian knew it would eventually come to this.

"There is nothing you can do, Paulie. The man has to make a living. The city certainly won't pay his way."

"I know, boss, but he has such a nice family. He's a jerk, but his kids deserve a father."

"Send some people to follow him on his first trip. That's the least we can do. But don't tell Knox. Let's see what happens. Send some really good people, people who you trust."

"I'll get right on it. He will be leaving Wednesday morning. I'll get his itinerary from his boss."

Paulie drove over to talk to Knox's boss at the offices of Baker and Sons, Long Haul Trucking. Mr. Baker was very cooperative. He did not want anything to happen to Thomas Knox, who was one of his better drivers. Paulie found that difficult to believe, but it was apparently true. Paulie did not tell Mr. Baker anything more than he needed to know, just that someone had made a threat on Knox's life, and the department took all threats of this nature seriously; after all, it was better to be too cautious rather than the opposite, wasn't it? Mr. Baker agreed with Detective Lucero and outlined Knox's trip for the concerned detective.

"That's quite a trip. When does he sleep?"

"He sleeps whenever he wants, in the back of the truck. There's a sleeper on all our trucks. It is really quite comfortable. Some of the drivers bring their wives. We don't encourage that, but some do. These truckers have a pretty good life."

"How much will Knox make on this trip?"

"About two thousand dollars, if he's on time at all his stops. There's bonus money involved for being on time, and Knox is always on time."

"Tell him to be careful. He wouldn't pick anyone up, would he?"

"Not if he wants to keep his job. That's rule number one in my company—no rides for anyone; and they all know I mean anyone."

"Do the drivers stop at the same place all the time? I mean, I know there are ... what do you call them? Truck stops? Do they always go to the same ones?"

"Not always. Why?"

"It might be a good idea for Knox to vary his routine, just in case someone is following him."

"I will suggest that. Knox doesn't stop much, though. He just drives and sleeps. He eats on the go. At least that's what he's told me. That's why he's always on time."

"How long will the whole trip take?"

"Round trip, about six days. He should be back Monday night. He can drive it much faster than that, but a lot of time will be spent loading and unloading. The drivers don't do that, and they have no control over the speed with which it's done. The drivers always blame the loaders when they're late."

"What time will he pull out of here Wednesday?"

"About 7:00 A.M."

"And his first stop is Richmond, Virginia, is that right?"

"You've got it all there, detective. He won't deviate from the route at all."

"Thank you, Mr. Baker, for all your help."

"Not at all. Thank you for keeping Thomas alive. I hope you're able to continue to do so."

"So do I," Paulie said as he left. "So do I."

* * * * * * * * *

On Wednesday August 7th at 7:09 A.M. Thomas Knox eased his fully loaded eighteen-wheeler out of its birth at Baker and Sons in Queens and headed west on the Long Island Expressway to the Brooklyn Queens Expressway, over the Verrazano Bridge, through Staten Island, and onto the Jersey Turnpike. He then turned south and pointed his truck for Virginia. Thomas Knox loved being on the open road. He had a feeling of freedom that he just couldn't get anywhere else, and he loved his job. It was the actual driving he loved, not the money he could earn. He was happy again. He was actually a nice guy out on the road, and his fellow truckers liked him. It was a far cry from the man who lived with Janet Knox.

He did not notice the two men following him in the Pontiac, and their skill at avoiding detection would keep it that way. Their instructions from Paulie were very simple: make sure nothing happens to Knox, or else. Paulie cautioned them that if they came in contact with the man who was trying to kill Knox, they should assume they were outmatched and should be extremely cautious.

Knox made it to Virginia without incident and pulled into the loading platform of an enormous warehouse at about 3:00 P.M. He walked into the office and shortly thereafter came out to open the back doors of his truck. Several workers emerged from the warehouse and began to unload the crates. The two officers were amazed at how many crates there were in the truck. The unloading and reloading process took two hours. Knox got back in the driver's seat and headed back to I95. He took I95 to I85 and headed for Asheville, North Carolina, just as his itinerary showed. Knox drove for two hours, stopped at a truck stop, and got out to eat at the small restaurant. One of the officers followed him into the truck stop and picked up some food. Knox sat with another man who looked like a typical trucker—sloppy jeans, an old baseball cap, and a torn T-shirt. The officer walked outside with his hands full of hamburgers and cokes, and thanked a tall, blue-eyed man for holding the door open for him. He went to his car and sat to eat with the other officer. Knox left the restaurant after forty-five minutes, climbed into his sleeper, and went to sleep. The officers were surprised by this turn of events. They assumed that Knox would drive to Asheville, and that they would get a room at some hotel and be able to get some sleep in shifts. They were disappointed that they would be sleeping in the car.

At 2:00 A.M. Knox jumped down from his sleeper and walked into the bathroom at the truck stop. He emerged a few minutes later, climbed up to his cab and started for Asheville.

The two officers in the Pontiac reluctantly followed.

The blue-eyed man watched as the Pontiac pulled away, and then he went back to sleep. He was not ready. He knew Knox's itinerary, and knew even more than Mr. Baker did about Thomas Knox's road trips. The blue-eyed man had followed Knox months ago, and now wanted to see if Knox had changed his routine. So far it appeared that he did not. The man would drive to Maryland and meet Knox and his officer convoy there on Sunday night. If Knox was true to form, he would spend all Sunday night in Maryland.

For the next few days, Knox drove all over the lower eastern portion of the Midwest and upper Southeast—from Asheville to Atlanta, from Atlanta to Nashville, from Nashville to Louisville, from Louisville to Knoxville, from Knoxville to Asheville, and finally from Asheville back to Richmond. Everyone in the closely knit trucking family seemed to know Thomas Knox and, surprisingly, everyone seemed to like him. He picked up a full load at Richmond late Saturday, parked in the warehouse parking lot, and slept in his sleeper the entire night.

Knox awoke early Sunday morning and headed up I95. He stopped at the first truck stop, where he showered and shaved. To the best of the officers' knowledge, this was the first time he showered on the trip. It put Knox one up on them. They had already decided to tell Paulie that this was the last favor they would ever do for him. They thought they would be sleeping in a motel every night, and that the trip would be a minor inconvenience. It was in fact a total disaster as far as they were concerned. They could not wait for Monday. They hoped that Knox would drive straight through to New York Sunday night. They calculated he should be able to do it without any problem, and were getting downright giddy about the possibility of sleeping in their own beds after four nights of sleeping in shifts in the back seat of a Pontiac. But, unknown to the officers, Knox had other plans. He had already made the call. Darlene would be ready. No one knew about Darlene, unless of course you count the blue-eyed man. He had seen Mr. Knox and Darlene in action a few months before.

Knox pulled out of the truck stop—showered, shaved, and wearing fresh clothes—at about noon. The traffic was terrible, and Knox finally pulled into another truck stop just north of Baltimore at 6:35 P.M. The two police officers could not believe their eyes when he pulled in. They could be home in five hours. They were furious.

Knox walked into the restaurant, sat down in a booth, and waited for Darlene. The blue-eyed man was already having dinner. He was pleased to see that Knox continued to be his punctual self. Darlene joined Knox, and they enjoyed a slow dinner. They talked for a while, and at about 8:30 walked out to Knox's truck, where, to the amazement of police officers Robert Whitehead and Elmer Oldbrick, they climbed into the sleeper. The officers would not be home until Monday. They resigned themselves to that fact and decided to go into the restaurant and have a good dinner. Knox wouldn't be going anywhere in the immediate future. Besides, they reasoned, they could see the truck easily from the restaurant.

The blue-eyed man also watched the truck. When he saw the two police officers coming towards the restaurant, he quickly finished his meal, paid the check, and headed for his car. It was just beginning to get dark. The blue-eyed man got into his car and thought for a while. He could do it here but there would be some risk. He may have to kill the two officers, and he did not want to do that. Judging from their appearance, they would not likely follow Knox again. Knox would die on another trip, not tonight.

The blue-eyed man pulled out of the truck stop and drove back to New York. For the first time in five days the two officers ate a meal while sitting at a table.

Thomas Knox and Darlene spent the rest of the night doing everything that Janet Knox would not do. *After all, what are hundred-dollar-a-night hookers for anyway?* Knox thought to himself as he lay back enjoying Darlene's increasingly energetic attention.

Darlene climbed down from the sleeper at 5:15 A.M., walked to her car, and drove away. Knox followed a few minutes later. He walked briskly to the restaurant, purchased some coffee and donuts, and quickly returned to the cab of his truck. He slowly pulled out of the truck stop and began his trip to New York. The very grubby, angry, and tired officers followed Knox back to Baker's yard in Queens. It was 11:45 A.M. Monday morning when they called Paulie and told him briefly about the trip. The main thing was that Thomas Knox was still alive. Paulie was pleased to hear that, and he immediately relayed the news to Brian, who was standing next to him in the squad room. Paulie told them to wait for the uniformed officers to arrive, and then they could go home. Officer Wood was there in a matter of minutes, and Whitehead and Oldbrick left in a hurry. Knox pulled out in his car a few minutes later and drove home to Janet. He kissed her hello and climbed into bed, where he slept until Tuesday.

Chapter 26

On Tuesday morning, as Brian and Paulie discussed Knox's next trip, Lawrence Carson hobbled into the room. It took him several minutes to negotiate the single flight of stairs to the squad's office after he was announced on the intercom by the desk sergeant downstairs. When Carson came into the room, the explanation for the delay was obvious—he was on crutches.

"What happened to you?" Paulie asked.

"Nothing new. My knee is giving me fits. I had an MRI yesterday, and my anterior cruciate ligament is completely ruptured. I knew it was torn, but I was hoping it was only partially torn. It isn't. The whole thing is gone, and I also tore my cartilage. The medial meniscus, I think they call it. I'm hurting."

"Shouldn't you be home in bed or something?" Paulie asked.

"Probably. But I wanted to talk to you guys. The officers brought me in to see you. Have you gotten any further with who killed the other jurors?"

"No," Brian answered.

"Is Knox still alive?"

"Yes he is," Brian reassured him. "Don't be sure he's going in order Mr. Carson. Don't let your guard down."

"There are so many of your men all over me, I feel pretty safe. How long can this go on?"

"What do you mean by 'this'?" Brian asked.

"The around-the-clock protection."

"Indefinitely."

"My doctor says I need an operation on my knee if I ever want it to be close to normal again. I'm going to have it done now, since I'm not working. What do you think?"

Brian looked pensive and then said, "That should be all right. We can just as easily watch you in the hospital as in your home. What do you think, Paulie?"

Paulie knew that Brian would never actually ask one of his detectives for an honest opinion in front of an outsider. He obligingly answered, "That should be no problem, boss."

Carson seemed pleased with the response he was getting from the two detectives.

"Where will you be having the surgery?" Paulie asked.

"I don't know. I'm seeing my doctor later today to go over things. His office is in Brooklyn where I work, so I guess the surgery will be in Brooklyn."

"Be sure you let us know," Paulie continued. "We want to be sure we have the hospital covered."

"Are you kidding?" Carson proclaimed. "He would never try anything in a hospital. There are too many people around."

"You're probably right," Brian answered. "Paulie just wants to be careful. You understand that, don't you, Mr. Carson?"

"Sure, I understand. I'll call you tomorrow."

With that, Carson slowly struggled out of the room.

"What are you thinking, boss? We hate watching people in a hospital. There are too many different faces."

"I'm thinking of something Sal said to me the other day. I don't think he meant it, but it sounds good now."

"What?"

"We will use Mr. Carson as bait. We will catch the son-of-a-bitch in the act of trying to kill Lawrence Carson."

"Not likely, Detective Walsh," the tall man with the blue eyes said when he listened to the tape Tuesday night. "Not likely."

* * * * * * * * *

Lawrence Carson had an appointment with his orthopaedic surgeon, Dr. Jeffrey Schwartz, at 3:30 on Tuesday. Dr. Schwartz went into more detail about the upcoming surgery than Carson really needed to hear. He was beginning to have second thoughts, but realized that he had to proceed with the surgery if he ever wanted to get back to sports. This was as good a time as any, he reasoned. It would help him pass the time until the killer was caught. He also thought that Detective Lucero would never be able to stop protecting a helpless man. The surgery was scheduled for Tuesday September 3rd. It couldn't be any sooner as Dr. Schwartz planned to leave on Saturday for a much-needed two-week vacation with his family. The surgery would be at Kings County Hospital in Brooklyn, where Dr. Schwartz was an Assistant Professor of Orthopaedic Surgery, and Chief of the Division of Sports Medicine. Dr. Schwartz's fellow, Dr. Tokes, would make all the necessary arrangements for the surgery and handle any problems while Dr. Schwartz was away. Carson left Dr. Schwartz's office feeling he was in good hands. He would win the club racquetball championship again.

On Wednesday morning Carson called Paulie and told him of his plans. Paulie and Brian discussed how they would deal with Carson's surgery and decided to go visit Kings County Hospital personally the following day.

* * * * * * * * *

Willie got back to the office at 10:00 A.M., and Tommy strolled in a few minutes later. It was the first time the squad was together in over three weeks. Willie gave everyone the bad news.

"I traced Michael Thomas through an acquaintance of his at work. It seems he went on a trip to the Florida Keys in February."

"And never returned," Tommy added.

"No, he returned. He took his flight back on time, and we even traced a cab that picked him up at LaGuardia and drove him to his apartment. But then he appears to have disappeared off the face of the earth. No one ever saw him again. He never went back to any of the gyms where he worked. He had a number of part-time jobs at different gyms, so nobody missed him that much. I found his apartment, and his belongings were removed after he didn't pay the rent for three months. They were in storage in the basement of the building. They didn't amount to much, and I didn't find anything unusual in them. He just disappeared. Simple as that."

"It sounds like he ran away from someone, or something," Paulie added.

"He didn't run from anything," Brian said. "He's dead. You can bet your last dollar on that. Don't waste any more time on Michael Thomas," Brian added as he put a line through Thomas's name. "Forget about him. Let's try to keep these last three alive."

Brian continued to speak. "We have got to get the edge on this killer. There are only three jurors left. We know that, and he knows that. I'm sure that he knows we know who his remaining targets are. That was part of our plan. We wanted a show of force. So far it may have worked. I say that only because Knox, Carson, and Stanton are still alive. We've thrown a fly into the ointment, but it's only temporary. He'll be very careful now, and he won't allow any slip-ups. He'll wait for the right time. Gentlemen, today we were given a gift by Lawrence Carson. He is going to have some kind of knee surgery. He will be in the hospital overnight, and I plan to use him as bait for our murderer. I want to protect Carson, but I don't want it to be obvious. I want it to look like it's the right time to strike. I want Carson to look like a sitting duck, and when the killer tries to strike I want that son-of-a-bitch!"

"Where's Carson having his surgery, boss?" Tommy asked.

"Kings County Hospital, in Brooklyn."

"Christ, Brian. I've been there. That place is huge. There is no way we can cover it. No fucking way," Tommy answered.

"Exactly," Brian said. "It's so big we can hide an army there and no one would know. Paulie and I are going there tomorrow. We'll check out the orthopaedic floor and the operating room. It may work, people. I hope it does, because I can't think of anything else. If anyone has a better idea, I'm listening."

No one ever had a better idea than Brian. There was silence.

"What's Stanton up to, Paulie?" Brian asked.

"He just sits around his apartment. He doesn't do much. The only time he left for any length of time was to go fishing on one of those drift boats out of Sheepshead Bay. It wasn't a problem. I had no problem finding uniforms who wanted to go with him. It appears to be the only diversion he has."

"And Knox?" Brian continued.

"Knox made it through his first trip without any incident. He got back Monday and slept until Tuesday. He seems a lot nicer to his wife now. Its amazing what a blow job will do."

"What do you mean?" Brian asked.

"It seems that the last night of his trip he spends shacked up with some girl in the back of his truck. The officers said it definitely was planned. He began getting ready for it in Virginia. She is either an old girlfriend or a hooker. My guess, as well as Oldbrick's, is that she's a hooker. They frequent the truck stops and apparently make good money keeping the truckers company. I mean, some of these guys have been away for weeks. My real problem, though, is that the trip was a disaster for the cops. Knox slept in this huge sleeper in the back of the truck, and the cops slept in the back of a Pontiac. Those two told me they wouldn't do it again, no matter how much overtime the city paid."

"Get them a van," Tommy said. "I had one of them in my younger days. You can sleep very nicely in a van."

"That's a good idea. Paulie, get one for the next time," Brian ordered. "I was going to drop the surveillance after one trip, but let's not. Let's not lose Knox while we're setting our trap with Carson. When does he go out again?"

"He's home for four days and then does the same trip again. He'll leave Friday morning."

"Get the van. Put Betty on it. People, forget about jurors one to nine; they're history. Concentrate all your efforts on ten, eleven, and twelve. Paulie, spend the rest of the day briefing Willie and Tommy on the three of them. I'm going home early to see if I still have a wife."

The blue-eyed man listened to the Wednesday tape meticulously. Not a word was missed. He would take the challenge. His teachers would say go away, wait, be careful, the police will lose interest. Strike then, but not now. No, he would take the challenge. He had to; it was his nature. Brian knew that too. The man could not turn Brian down. Brian realized that when he found the bug in the bulletin board on Monday. Brian would tell no one about the bug. Activity in the squad room had to be perfectly normal. He would get this butcher; this genius who killed people naturally; this man who could make people ski into trees, slip on floors, shoot attorneys, make people die of heart attacks, make people crash their cars, make people completely disappear, and who could savagely beat a woman to death. He would answer to Detective Brian Michael Walsh. And he would answer with his life. The man would never be glorified in the press like the Son of Sam, or Bernard Goetz. He would die quickly and disappear as fast as some of his victims. Brian himself would see to that. He would do it even if it meant losing his shield.

The blue-eyed man knew he had two weeks to set things up. That would be plenty of time for him. Tonight he would plan the deaths of Knox, Carson, and Stanton in his mind. The preliminary work on Knox and Stanton had been done, but he would be very busy the next few weeks. He would kill Knox, and then Carson, right under Walsh's nose, and that would be his answer to Walsh's challenge. It would be eleven down and one to go. That would drive them insane. He would have killed Carson, and defeated the best New York had to offer. Unless, of course, Walsh got him. The man with the blue eyes thought that was a real possibility.

Chapter 27

On Thursday August 15th, Brian and Paulie left for Kings County Hospital immediately after the morning briefing. They thought that nothing bad happened overnight. They were wrong. The blue-eyed man went to bed at 6:38 A.M.; it took him that long to plan the deaths of Knox, Carson, and Stanton.

Brian and Paulie arrived at Kings County Hospital at 9:15 A.M. and immediately observed a hospital full of activity. Betty had arranged for one of the hospital administrators to show them around. He was not told why, but was told that it was the mayor's request that he show Detectives Walsh and Lucero every courtesy. Mr. Anthony Scalici did just that. They first toured the orthopaedic floor, where there was a large open ward and several double rooms. They looked at the access stairs, and Brian visualized where he would put Carson. Clearly the double room would be best, and Carson would be the only patient in the room. The second bed would be occupied by a detective. There was only one staircase at the end of the floor.

"Where does that staircase go, Mr. Scalici?" Brian asked.

"It connects all eight floors. We're on the fourth, as you know, so it goes up to nine and down to the basement."

"Which floor is the operating room on?"

"It's on the second floor."

"Please take us through every step a patient takes from the time they come into your hospital for surgery until they get to their room on this floor. And I mean every step. Leave nothing out."

"Well first the patient goes ..."

"I'm sorry," Brian interrupted. "I mean literally take us through each step. Make believe I am a patient. Let's go."

"What is this all about?" Scalici asked. "That will take some time."

"If I tell you, you must keep it quiet. You must tell no one."

All of a sudden, Scalici wasn't sure he wanted to know, but he said, "I will tell no one."

"Of all the hospitals in New York City, the mayor has chosen your hospital to have some elective orthopaedic surgery done this September. It is our responsibility to care for his safety, and we must begin now to formulate a plan. I am personally responsible for his safety, and I take my job very seriously, so I must walk the path he will take."

Scalici was stunned. "What an honor," he said. "We'll lay out the red carpet for him."

"That is exactly what we do not want. You were selected as the contact person by his office, and you will not tell another soul. By the way, do you know the mayor?" Brian continued.

"No."

"Well, someone in his office must know you. Do you fully understand what I am saying to you?"

"Yes, Detective Walsh. I just realized who you are. I will tell no one."

"Good. Let's begin. Please leave nothing out. If you don't know what happens in a certain area, don't be embarrassed. I often have no idea what procedures my detectives follow," Brian lied. "Just ask someone who knows so I can make an accurate assessment of what is going to happen to the mayor. Do you understand?"

"Yes, sir."

It was obvious to Mr. Scalici that Detective Walsh was a serious person, and one on whose good side he would do best. He began the tour by taking the detectives to the preadmitting area down on the first floor.

"The patient comes here about one hour before his surgery. Blood is drawn, and if ordered by his surgeon, a chest x-ray and EKG are performed. That usually depends on the patient's health and age. Sometimes these tests are done a few days before by the patient's physician. I would strongly recommend that these tests be done beforehand for the patient we are discussing. The patient is then taken to the pre-op holding area on the second floor."

"How do they get there?" Brian asked Scalici.

"They're brought in a wheelchair by an aide. They go through that door and use this elevator," to which Scalici led Brian and Paulie.

They rode up in the elevator with Scalici.

"I notice that this elevator says it is restricted to pre-op use. Is that so?" Brian asked.

"Yes. There are usually twelve eight o'clock cases, and they must start on time or the OR schedule for the day becomes a nightmare. There's a security guard that makes sure this is so. He's only here until 9:30 in the morning, however; then he has other assignments."

Good, Brian thought to himself, as he pictured Willie in a security guard's uniform.

"Please continue," Brian directed.

"In the pre-op area the patient undresses and is given a hospital gown. The patients are then evaluated by a nurse and seen by an anesthesiologist. If the patient has any medical problems, they will have been seen by an anesthesiologist a few days prior to surgery, but if they are healthy, as most of the elective orthopaedic patients are, they meet anesthesia for the first time here. But quite frankly, each surgeon does it differently.

"An IV is started and any pre-op medications are given. While this is going on, the patient's operating room is being made ready by the surgical team. The circulating nurse then comes out and brings the patient to the operating room. We obviously can't go in there," Scalici said as he brought Brian and Paulie up to an electric door that controlled entry into the operating room.

"Is there any other way into the operating room?"

"No."

"No back stairs? No fire stairs?"

"No. This is the only way in or out."

"What next?" Brian asked.

"After surgery, the patient is brought to the recovery room where the patient does just that—recovers from anesthesia. He will be monitored very closely until he is completely awake. He will be given pain medication and all preparations will be made for sending the patient to his room. The recovery room nurse will call the nurse on the orthopaedic floor and sign the patient over to that nurse's care. He will be transported by aides through this door to this elevator and then up to the orthopaedic floor, where we were earlier today. Some patients have a private-duty nurse, and your patient will probably have one."

Another possible spot for a detective, Brian thought.

"I noticed, Mr. Scalici, that all the nurses and aides have picture identification tags. Is that true of everyone?"

"Yes, Detective Walsh. Everyone, including the doctors, is supposed to wear one. Sometimes the doctors don't. Doctors do pretty much what they want around here."

The tour took two hours. Brian and Paulie did not miss a thing. Brian himself saw at least seven locations where an experienced assassin could do his work, but not one where he would go unnoticed. One thing was certain: there were always a lot of people around. At no time did Brian see a patient left alone. To use any of these points of attack, the assassin would have to kill others, but he had not done that before. Brian doubted that this was the kind of man who would just come in and blast away. No, he was precise. The killing would be attempted here, but where, and how? Brian now had less than nineteen days to figure it out. The blue-eyed man had already figured most of it out.

Chapter 28

On Friday August 16, Dr. Jeffrey Schwartz worked hard to keep his office schedule on time. He did not have any surgery scheduled for that day, as he felt uncomfortable performing surgery just before going out of town. His fellow, Dr. Tokes, would take excellent care of the patients, but the patients wanted his attention, not the fellow's. It was close to four o'clock and he was just seeing his three o'clock patient. Things were not going well. He had promised his wife he would be home by seven, and that now looked impossible. This was not the way to start the only two-week vacation he had taken in three years. He resigned himself to the fact that he would shortly be calling his wife to give her the bad news. It was a call he did not look forward to making. He could hear the conversation on the other end of the phone as if it were happening at that moment. He decided he would wait, hoping that some of the patients would not show up. His 3:15 patient was brought into the consultation room at 4:25.

Mr. Kevin Rivers told his story of woe. It was the thirty-second patient Dr. Schwartz saw that day, and the stories and patients began to merge into one giant headache. Mr. Rivers had twisted his knee two months previously while playing in a pickup basketball game with some of the guys from work.

"I know it was stupid to play at my age, doc, but you know how it is. One minute you're fooling around, and the next it's a war on the court," the tall, blue-eyed Mr. Rivers said.

"I know," Dr. Schwartz said, smiling.

"I saw my family doctor after about a month or so of pain. I was hoping that it would get better on its own. How many times have you heard that one, doc? He's a nice guy, but I don't think he knows a knee from an elbow, if you know what I mean. He sent me for an MRI of my knee, and here I am, torn cartilage and all. It's killing me, doc. We've got to do something."

Dr. Schwartz examined Mr. Rivers, and then the fellow examined Mr. Rivers. They both came to the same conclusion, confirmed by the MRI, that Mr. Rivers had sustained a large tear in the medial meniscus in his right knee.

"It is obvious what your problem is, Mr. Rivers. You have a large tear in your medial meniscus. The MRI shows the tear right here," Dr. Schwartz said, pointing to the tear.

The blue-eyed man looked at the tear, just as he did the previous evening when he broke into the private office of Dr. Charles Mann's radiology center on Kings Highway in Brooklyn. In less than one hour, copies were made of a positive MRI, the name changed, and then copies made again with the name Kevin Rivers.

"You will need arthroscopic surgery to remove the torn portion of your medial meniscus," Dr. Schwartz continued. "That's the structure we call a torn cartilage in layman's terms. Do you know anything about arthroscopic surgery?"

"I sure do, doc," answered Mr. Rivers, who proudly pulled up his left pants leg and showed Dr. Schwartz the scars from previous arthroscopic surgery. "I was scoped four years ago in Texas. My left knee works great now. That's why I feel stupid for putting this off. I know arthroscopic surgery is no big deal. I want it done as soon as possible. Monday would be fine for me," the blue-eyed man answered.

"Unfortunately, actually fortunately when I think about it, I am going away on vacation for the next two weeks. We will do the surgery when I return, if that's okay with you. That will give us time to get permission from your managed care plan anyway," Dr. Schwartz said as he rang for his nurse to schedule the surgery.

"When will you be back, doc?" the man asked.

"Tuesday September 3rd will be my first day back," Dr. Schwartz said as his nurse came in to take the information.

"Let's do it then. I would like it the first thing in the morning. I don't do well without breakfast. And forget about insurance; I don't have any."

Dr. Schwartz and the nurse paused. Patients without insurance were always a problem, both for them and the hospital. Kings County Hospital was a city hospital but there was now a large private service as well at the hospital. A patient on the private service of Dr. Schwartz had to pay, otherwise the residents had to take care of him and he was wasting Schwartz's time.

"Don't worry, doc," the blue-eyed man answered, sensing their concern. "I don't have insurance because I don't believe in that managed care garbage. I will be paying you your full fee today for the surgery, and if your nurse would be so kind to tell me the hospital cost, I will pay that in advance as well. I bet you don't see that too often, do you doc?"

"That's an understatement," Dr. Schwartz laughed.

"One other thing, doc. I want a local anesthetic. No general anesthesia or spinal. Any problem with that?"

"No problem. Local it is."

Dr. Schwartz left and his nurse scheduled Mr. Rivers for surgery on Tuesday September 3rd for approximately 11:00 A.M. It would have to be the second case, she explained, because Dr. Schwartz already had an anterior cruciate ligament reconstruction scheduled for eight o'clock, and that could not be changed.

"That will be fine," Mr. Rivers said, not hearing that information for the first time.

"Dr. Schwartz's fellow, Dr. Tokes, will be calling you to arrange your preoperative screening and to set up an appointment for you to meet the anesthesiologist at the hospital. That is usually done a few days before surgery. Here is a patient information sheet for you to fill out. Please take it with you and bring it to your pre-op appointment. Any questions, Mr. Rivers?"

"No, you've been very through. One thing, though. I travel a lot and you will never get me at this number, so I will call Dr. Tokes next week, if that's okay with you."

"Sure. That will be fine."

The blue-eyed man walked out to the front office, asked the amount of Dr. Schwartz's fee, and paid in cash. He left the office, leaving Dr. Schwartz's receptionist in a near state of shock.

The blue-eyed man still had much to do. Knox left on his road trip earlier in the day, and that would put him in Maryland on Tuesday the 20th. *That was as good a time as any*, the blue-eyed man thought. A dirty, dark blue van was now following Thomas Knox's eighteen-wheeler down I95.

The blue-eyed man drove from Dr. Schwartz's office to Ocean Avenue, which he followed to Sheepshead Bay. He would be fishing in the near future and he wanted to familiarize himself with what was available. He parked his car and carefully surveyed the area. He had never been there before. It was a small, quaint section of Brooklyn, and probably had not changed for many years. He walked up and down the pier and casually looked at the large fishing boats. His photographic mind painted an indelible picture of every minute detail; nothing would be missed. His life could depend on the most insignificant item. He noted the names of the boats and the times they fished. Some took half-day trips and some full day trips; several went out at night. He was able to limit his selection to the two boats that fished at night. They both made trips on Tuesday, Thursday, and Friday nights. He made arrangements to fish one boat, *Tight Lines*, Thursday night, and the other boat, *Widow Maker*, on Friday night. On Tuesday night, the tall man with the blue eyes had a previous engagement with Thomas Knox.

The blue-eyed man drove to the organization's compound in Manhattan and began to work on a small mechanical device. He would be driving out to Long Island early Saturday and needed to begin work on it that night. It would be tricky, but the blue-eyed man felt it would work. He had arranged for one of his subordinates to steal one of the devices from a local hospital, and he was now sitting and looking at it in the workshop below the living quarters in the compound. The device would have to be modified, but if the changes were subtle no one would notice them until it was too late. He worked later into the night than he planned, and was disappointed with the results. It would be more difficult than he first thought. It was, however, beginning to look like it was at least possible. It had to be improved significantly to satisfy the blue-eyed man. He finally gave up and turned in for the night. He couldn't sleep. Walsh had issued a challenge. The blue-eyed man was sure Walsh had discovered the bug and would now be feeding him carefully selected information. Some information would be true, other information false. Determining which was which would be the problem, and the challenge.

The blue-eyed man woke up at 6:00 A.M. and planned to use an organization car to drive to Long Island. He was now using organization resources and manpower. It was not approved, but the blue-eyed man did pretty much what he wanted. Everyone knew enough not to question him or discuss him with superiors. Besides, most had a genuine regard, if not love, for the man. They knew he would do anything for them, and they reciprocated. The organization compound was actually a series of five four-story townhouses on the west side of Manhattan. The houses looked normal enough on the outside, but nothing anyone could imagine, would prepare one for what was behind those innocent-looking doors—electronic devices, explosives, weapons of all types, surveillance equipment, experimental medications. The experts who worked with this material were also available for consultation. The compound was impregnable, and if by some chance there was a successful invasion, the explosion that would follow would leave no trace of the compound or, unfortunately for the other residents of West 67th Street, the remainder of the block.

The blue-eyed man arrived in Freeport, on the south shore of Long Island at 7:45 A.M., just in time to see the fishing boats load up and leave on their Saturday trip. The weather was beautiful, and the man half thought about going on the trip himself, but he had other work to do. He spent the next several hours looking at much smaller boats than the fishing fleet. He walked up and down both sides of the canal looking very carefully, but he could find nothing satisfactory. The area was too crowded and much too busy. At 11:30 he got back into his car and headed further east to Merrick. He did not want to go too far east or the trip to Jones Inlet would be too long. *The longer the time spent inside the inlet, the greater the chance of detection*, he thought.

As he looked at the waterfront in Merrick, he realized he would have a better chance of locating what he needed. There were no large commercial fishing boats here, just pleasure craft of all sizes. He parked and went into a small restaurant overlooking the bay and the marina. He had a short lunch and, playing the tourist role, walked around on the docks. It was not unusual to see people just walking, looking at the boats and the water. Perhaps he was just dreaming of the day when he too could afford the pleasures of owning a boat. Water seemed to attract everyone. The number of boats was surprisingly large. He saw several possibilities and decided he would return the following day to fish in one of the small boats that were rented out each day. He would be able to see more from the water. He reserved a boat for 7:00 A.M. Sunday and purchased charts of the south shore area from Merrick to Rockaway Inlet, which included the route he would travel from Merrick to Sheepshead Bay. He then returned to Manhattan, had an early dinner, and sat down again to work on the device. This time he was not alone. A small Latin man began to work with him, and soon the device was beginning to function as he planned. *It will work*, the blue-eyed man said to himself as he put his head on his pillow for the night while the Latin man continued to work.

The following day was a beautiful August day, warm, but with a nice breeze from the southeast. The blue-eyed man arrived in Merrick at 6:30 A.M. and purchased sandwiches from a small restaurant. He rented a fishing pole with all the necessary equipment, got his bait, loaded up his boat, started the small outboard motor, and headed into the large fishing fleet far out in the bay. The main thing that set him apart from the other fishermen was the high-tech camera and binoculars that would enable him to see and photograph virtually anything. The other thing that set him apart was the fact that he couldn't have cared less about the number of fish he caught. He anchored his small rental boat far enough from the restaurant and docks so that no one could see him, even with ordinary binoculars, but close enough so he could see every boat leaving the marina with his binoculars. He would photograph whichever boats looked like possibilities and then have their ownership checked. He wanted to pick one that day, for time was getting short. He had to be in Maryland Tuesday night, and his surgery was two weeks to the day after that. He was on schedule, but there was no room for error. *There's never any room for error in this business*, he thought to himself, *especially with Walsh on my trail*. He began to get that feeling in his stomach again. His teachers would say he was trying to do too much. "Take your time," they would say. "Time is your ally. Wait and strike when you're ready." They were right, he agreed, but he was ready. The deaths of Carson and Stanton would be unbelievable. To his knowledge, no one had ever assassinated a target using the methods he was now planning.

The blue-eyed man continued to fish and continued to photograph boats. By 11:45 he hadn't seen one boat that would serve his purpose. At 12:45 it appeared. He saw it from a distance. The hull was a classic, and it had the required twin engines. And most important of all, it was made of wood. He took as many photographs as he could of the boat as it passed within thirty feet of him while it was heading west. He had no trouble reading the numbers. He would phone them in to the organization, and by the time he returned to Manhattan a full dossier on the owner of *Yellow Tail* would be available. He fished for another hour and actually caught three fluke. He headed back to the marina, and then back to Manhattan, but he was wrong; the dossier on the owner of *Yellow Tail* would not be ready until Monday. The fresh sea air always relaxed the blue-eyed man, and he retired early. The next week would require much nighttime activity and he needed to be sharp. He fell asleep reviewing all three plans. He knew Knox would be the easiest. Stanton's would be the most difficult physically, but Carson's, with Walsh expecting him, would be the most risky. For that single reason, he could not wait to kill Lawrence Carson.

* * * * * * * * *

On Monday August 19th Brian assembled the staff for the morning meeting. He still had not told anyone about the bug. He needed everything to sound natural. While the blue-eyed man listened to the tapes of Saturday and Sunday early Monday morning, he began to question whether Brian had found the bug. The conversation of Willie and Tommy, who were in the office on Saturday, had some material in it there was absolutely no benefit to passing on to the man with the blue eyes. Why would they tell him about the dark blue van that was following Knox on his trip? It made no sense to the blue-eyed man. Now he would be extra careful. Walsh had to know that two police officers posing as husband and wife could not possibly stop him. Maybe there were more and they were not saying anything about them. *Thanks for the warning, Tommy*, the man smiled to himself.

Brian and the staff talked for about an hour. They discussed the whereabouts of Knox and the upcoming surgery of Carson. Stanton was doing reasonably well, and essentially put himself on house arrest, never leaving his apartment except for food, and his now weekly nighttime fishing trip. Brian felt that Stanton was the safest of the three, even when he went fishing. *There were more cops on the boat than fish*, he laughed to himself. Brian spent a great deal of time outlining the trap for the killer, and the various locations that Carson would be exposed to an assassin of this skill during his hospital stay.

"Thank you for the compliment, Detective Walsh," the blue-eyed man would say when he heard the tape Monday night.

"At this very moment there are uniform police in Kings County Hospital familiarizing themselves with the layout. The hospital administrator is being very helpful, although he has no idea what is really going on," Brian continued. "We will all be there. Tommy, you will be a patient in the bed next to Carson, and Paulie, you will be the uniform standing right next to him. No way this son-of-a-bitch will get Carson," he said to the blue-eyed man. "No fucking way!"

The blue-eyed man sat incredulously listening to the tape Monday night. Walsh either did not find the bug or was smarter than the man thought. The blue-eyed man had analyzed every aspect of the path that Carson would take and had come to the same exact conclusions as Walsh. Well, almost the same. Walsh did not mention the path that the blue-eyed man would take. How could Walsh figure all the others but leave this one out? *Is that the trap?* he asked himself. The man concluded that the path was so original that no one would figure it out. *Time would tell*, he thought.

The blue-eyed man returned to the lab, pleased that the modified electronic device was working well. One part was approximately the size of a silver dollar and about 5mm thick. It was magnetized and would easily stick to the second piece of equipment that would be used. The small Latin man helped. It was imperative that the small electronic device and the larger box work together as a unit, or Carson would live. They tried the two over and over. Twelve times in a row the two devices worked together perfectly. The men were both very satisfied with their work. The modified large device would be undetectable to all but the sharpest of eyes.

They turned to another device that would be needed for Stanton's death. It was much longer, approximately forty-six inches in length. It took several minutes to assemble all the parts, and only then could one recognize its true purpose. The large bulbous piece on the end made it look ridiculous, but the blue-eyed man had used something similar before, and it worked; there was a dead general in Central America who, if he could, would testify to that. He would practice with the device over the next few weeks, whenever he could. The Latin man worked further into the night, while the blue-eyed man slept.

Chapter 29

Tuesday morning started well for Thomas Knox. His trip was going nicely and he made all his stops on time. There would be another $2,000 check waiting for him at Baker's the following morning. He had made the call to Darlene and was on his way, oblivious to the dark blue van that was following him. Unlike the last time, the occupants of the van were well rested. Tommy was right; you could sleep very well in a van. Nevertheless, the two police officers were anxious to get home to their respective mates. They knew about Darlene, and that made officer Mary Patronie particularly angry. She did not tolerate infidelity in any man, and was quick to come to a boil when her Italian temper got the best of her.

Officer Patronie and her partner of six years, Richard Albury, followed Knox to the truck stop in Maryland. It was just as officers Whitehead and Oldbrick described. Knox had prepared for his meeting with Darlene as before and walked into the restaurant. Darlene was already sitting at a table. She liked Knox, but the real attraction was the hundred dollars. Knox sat down and they began to eat dinner. In a booth on the other side of the restaurant the tall man with the blue eyes finished his dinner. A couple in their late thirties entered the restaurant and sat relatively close to the blue-eyed man. He had watched them emerge from the blue van several minutes after Knox sat down with Darlene. The blue-eyed man paid the waitress and left. He saw no other activity; it appeared that the two officers were the only escort. The man was not sure why Tommy wanted him to know this information, if in fact the bug was found. The man realized that he was spending too much time and, what was worse, too much thought, on this question. *Forget it, just be careful,* he concluded.

Knox and Darlene spent a long time at dinner. The two police officers finished their meal and walked out to their van long before Knox and Darlene emerged from the restaurant. It was dark at 9:05 P.M., when Knox and Darlene climbed into the sleeper of Knox's truck. It took only a few minutes for them to get very busy. Officer Albury climbed into the back of the van to get some sleep, giving officer Patronie the first watch. The blue-eyed man stationed his car on the opposite side of the truck from the van. He wore old jeans, a windbreaker jacket, a two day old beard, and an old New York Yankees baseball cap. When he figured Knox was too involved with Darlene to care about anything else, and after checking the surrounding area carefully, he slid out of the driver's side of his car. The truck stop was active, but it was too early for most of the drivers to be in the sleeping section for the night, unless of course they had plans similar to Thomas Knox.

The blue-eyed man carried a package in a brown paper bag, and looked no different than any other trucker carrying part of a meal from home. The man approached Knox's truck and quite skillfully dropped out of site. No one noticed his disappearing act. He began his deadly business under the cab of the truck. He could hear Knox and Darlene in the sleeper above him, but they were much too busy to hear him. He carefully removed the explosive device from the bag. He had done this before, and he was no stranger to the underside of a truck cab. He tied the bomb to the structure of the cab with a strong and special yarn that would incinerate instantly. The bomb itself would leave no trace. It was made out of as little metal as possible, and what metal was used was made out of the same material as the structure of the truck's gasoline tank. *Sure,* he thought, *everyone will think it was a bomb, maybe even be sure it was a bomb, but just let them try to figure out what type of bomb, or who planted it.* That would be the test; no one had ever figured it out in the past, and no one would now.

Just as the blue-eyed man was completing the final attachments, he was startled by a banging on the door of Knox's sleeper. Knox and Darlene were startled as well. A woman began to yell at Knox.

"Knox, you low-life dirt bag," was the first thing that the blue-eyed man, Knox, and Darlene heard from the woman's mouth. "Get away from that whore!"

Officer Albury heard the screaming, looked up quickly, wiped the sleep from his eyes, and stared out of the van window. What he saw entered his mind under the category of being "un-fucking believable."

His partner, officer Patronie, was banging on Knox's door, with her gun drawn. Albury jumped out of the van and ran for the truck. Knox looked out and saw a woman, who he definitely did not know, standing in the dark parking lot, and she was holding ... "She's got a fucking gun!" Knox yelled.

"Who?" Darlene yelled at Knox. "Your wife?"

"No. I don't know who the fuck she is. But I'm not getting out. Quick, get down!"

The blue-eyed man froze. If he had to move, or if someone looked under the truck, a lot of people would die at the truck stop. He slowly pulled out his weapon.

"Come out, you worthless piece of shit!" Patronie yelled just as her partner got to the truck.

More footsteps, the blue-eyed man noted. Things did not look good. He hated to kill cops. To the best of his knowledge he never had.

Two other cops watched the circus unfold. Brian had Paulie send another car, a fact unknown both to the occupants of the van and the blue-eyed man. They looked at each other in disbelief before slowly moving out of their car and cautiously heading for the truck.

"Mary, what the fuck are you doing?" Albury yelled at his partner as he reached Knox's truck. "Put your gun away. Paulie will have our asses for this. What are you going to do, shoot the guy the whole NYPD is protecting just because he's banging a whore? You better get some help. You need a shrink or something. Get the fuck back to the van! Now! Move!"

Mary Patronie put her gun away and headed back to the van. Knox looked out of the window, and Albury pulled out his badge to show Knox, who jumped out of the sleeper as Darlene buried herself under the covers, terrified. The blue-eyed man continued to be as immobile as a stick ... but a very dangerous stick—a stick with a gun; a special gun that would allow the man to take the lives of Knox, Darlene, and two of New York's finest in seconds. The blue-eyed man truly hoped it would not be necessary.

"Listen, Mr. Knox. We were sent by Detective Lucero to keep a close watch on you, for your own safety. My partner must have flipped out when she saw what you were doing. You know how women sometimes get about this fidelity thing. I think her first husband cheated on her or something. Just forget about everything."

"Forget about everything? Flipped out? You must be as fucking nuts as she is if you think I'll forget about this. If that's what she does when she flips out I'd hate to see her go completely fucking nuts. What does she do then, shoot little kids? I thought she was going to shoot Darlene and me. I almost had a heart attack or something."

"Calm down, Mr. Knox. Here's the deal. It's real simple, but listen good. You tell no one about this incident and we don't tell your wife about Darlene. Nobody gets burned then. And you can bang your friend here forever, for all I care. Is it a deal? Remember, we have pictures of you climbing into the sleeper with her," Albury lied.

Knox calmed down.

"Okay, okay. But keep that nut job under control!"

Just then Detective Jack Daly and his partner William Boyle stepped silently around the truck with their guns drawn. The only one who heard them coming was the blue-eyed man, who was now seriously considering a very violent option—a lot of people were about to die in Maryland. Both Albury and Knox were startled when Daly and Boyle jumped out and threw them both against the truck.

"Don't make a fucking move," Daly spoke. "Walsh sent us to keep an eye on the three of you. What was that bullshit with your partner about?" Daly asked Albury.

Albury knew Daly by reputation, and he knew he was one of Walsh's hand-picked insiders, so Albury wasn't about to give him any shit; he also knew that Daly wouldn't take any.

"My partner flipped out, that's all. No harm done. She's back in the van. Everything is okay."

"Everything is not okay! It looked like a fucking zoo out here! If anything happens to Knox my ass is in a sling. I don't need some fucked-up lady cop fucking up my career. You got that? Keep that bitch in the van! If I see her again I'll blow her fucking head off, and Boyle here will do the same to you. Believe me, Walsh won't miss you two assholes."

Albury looked at the two detectives, turned, and walked gloomily back to the van. Daly and Boyle walked back to their car, fuming. The blue-eyed man waited. He heard Knox climb back into the sleeper, and he and Darlene began to laugh the nervous laugh of those who just escaped a disaster. One of them was correct.

Darlene was excited by the events of the previous fifteen minutes, and she brought a new enthusiasm to their activity. The blue-eyed man finished his work and slowly slid out from under the cab. He was not certain where the second group of cops went, but he saw nothing alarming and calculated that the two new cops had to be on the same side of the truck as the van since they saw everything so clearly. Fortunately for everyone at the truck stop that night, he was correct. The blue-eyed man walked into the restaurant and ordered some coffee. His gun was ready, but no one approached him. *That whole event could not have been planned*, he thought. It accomplished nothing, other than to upset Knox. He wondered what kind of idiot the lady cop was to completely lose it over something as simple as Knox getting laid.

The blue-eyed man returned to his car, waited, and watched. There would be no sleep tonight, not with that crazy lady cop around.

Everyone made it through the night without further incident. Albury let Patronie sleep the whole night. He would have to get a new partner, he concluded. She was getting too weird for him lately. He realized that his career would be over if she shot Knox, and even though she said she was just trying to scare Knox, he did not believe it for a minute.

Darlene and Knox climbed out of the cab at 7:15 A.M., still hugging, and walked to the restaurant. Knox cleaned up, walked back to his cab, climbed up the steps to the driving platform, started his big diesel engine, and pulled his eighteen-wheeler out onto I95 at 7:43 A.M. *What a night*, he thought, a big grin still planted on his face. Darlene was clearly at her best when frightened. He definitely decided he would tell Detective Lucero that he did not want any more protection on his trips. "Some protection," he laughed out loud. "A fucking cop almost killed me!"

The van followed, with officer Patronie driving.

"Try to resist running him off the fucking road, Mary," Albury said sarcastically as she pulled out. Their relationship was obviously very strained. Patronie said nothing.

Daly and Boyle followed.

The blue-eyed man watched the little caravan leave, and when he was sure there were no stragglers, he followed. A few miles down the road, Knox was back in his element and happy. He took no notice of the car that passed him approximately twenty miles into his trip. The blue-eyed man, driving a dirty, white, four-year-old Chrysler, stationed himself about four-hundred feet in front of Knox. The man did not wish to harm anyone else, so he waited. Just before the Delaware border, as the truck entered an open area on I95, the blue-eyed man pushed a button, and Mr. Thomas Knox, fresh from the greatest sexual experience of his life, was no more. The blue-eyed man didn't look back or speed up; rather, he continued calmly on his trip to New York.

"Jesus Christ!" Albury yelled as he saw the cab of Knox's truck literally disintegrate. The cab lifted what seemed to be thirty feet into the air and exploded into an infinitesimal number of minute pieces. The trailer skidded to a halt on the right shoulder of the road, and, just as it was coming to a complete stop, flipped on its side in a slow-motion dance of death. Officers Patronie and Albury jumped out of their van and ran to where the cab of the truck should have been; it was gone, and Knox was gone.

"We are fucked, Mary. That's it. He died under our very noses. Someone blew up his fucking truck under our very noses!" Albury said in a monotone.

"We better call Lucero," was all Mary said.

Daly and Boyle pulled up to the disaster, and, after calling Albury and Petronie every name he could think of, Daly led Boyle back to their car and back to New York. They had seen enough of Albury and Petronie. They had seen the last of Thomas Knox as well.

The Maryland Highway Patrol arrived and Albury explained what had happened. The supervisor followed and made sure Albury understood his opinion of the events, saying something about keeping their murders in New York where they belonged.

At 8:53 A.M. police officer Richard Albury called Detective Lucero to give him the bad news. It took some time for him to get up the courage to make the call. He liked being a cop, and he was sure that was about to come to an end.

"What do you mean he blew up?" Paulie shouted.

"We were following him home on I95. The whole trip was routine up to that point," Albury lied, "and the truck just blew up. Obviously some type of bomb. No accident or anything; it just blew up."

"Was anyone else hurt?"

"No one else."

"Thank God for that," Paulie answered. Again, God had nothing to do with who died and who did not.

"Stay in Maryland. Find out everything about what happened. Get the local police to call the FBI in. I want to know everything about the bomb that was used. Maybe we can trace it to someone."

"Detective Lucero, we are way out of our league here. You better send some heavyweights. I sense that the locals are already pissed at us."

"Okay, I'll send some people. Stay there and help out."

Paulie told Brian as soon as Brian returned from an early meeting with the mayor and Sal. Brian took the news better than Paulie thought he would. In reality, he was surprised that Knox lasted as long as he did. You can't protect someone who is as exposed as he was. It simply can't be done. He would, however, protect Carson and Stanton. They would not die. The trap would work. The man who killed Knox would be caught and killed himself.

Paulie had already drawn a line through the name Thomas Knox.

Chapter 30

On the afternoon of Wednesday August 21st, the blue-eyed man called Dr. Schwartz's office to speak to Dr. Tokes. The man hoped Dr. Schwartz was having a restful vacation and wanted to make his appointment to get his pre-op testing done as soon as possible. The man told Dr. Tokes that he had an important business trip that just came up, and he would have to get the tests done sometime in the next two days. Dr. Tokes did not think that would be a problem, and after a few phone calls, Mr. Rivers had an appointment to visit with the anesthesiologist at 9:30 A.M. Thursday at Kings County Hospital.

The blue-eyed man arrived promptly at the hospital at 9:00 A.M. Thursday morning. He was escorted into a reception area in the business office, where he answered questions put to him by a polite but obviously inexperienced clerk. The man astounded the young lady by insisting on paying his hospital bill in full, with nice new hundred dollar bills. The man was next sent to the lab to have some routine blood work drawn, leaving the business office with the unique problem of trying to figure out where to safely store the first cash payment ever made to Kings County Hospital since the private service was started.

The blue-eyed man was brought to the pre-op area where he met an anesthesiologist, Dr. Walter Mack. The place was incredibly busy. The anesthesiologist briefly examined Mr. Rivers and took a detailed medical history. Dr. Mack did not feel there would be any problem with the surgery, as the man was a healthy specimen and obviously in great shape.

"Mr. Rivers, I see you are having your arthroscopic surgery done under local anesthesia, is that correct?"

"Yes, Dr. Mack. I had one done like that a few years ago in Texas and everything went fine."

"What we usually do with the patients who have local is give them a little intravenous sedation just to take the edge off. Sometimes there is some pain when just local is used," Dr. Mack continued.

"I won't need any sedation," Mr. Rivers said firmly. But go ahead and start an IV, but no sedation unless I ask for it, okay?" The man knew the request for sedation would never be made.

"Okay," Dr. Mack said, thinking to himself that Mr. Rivers would be asking for the sedation shortly after the surgery began, just like everyone else.

"Will you be in the room, Dr. Mack?" Mr. Rivers asked.

"Yes, I will."

"Good. I'll see you on Tuesday the 3rd then," the blue-eyed man said as he got up to leave. As he shook hands with Dr. Mack, the man "inadvertently" bumped into the doctor and was able to remove Dr. Mack's nametag from his lab coat without Dr. Mack noticing a thing.

The man asked to see the postoperative area where he would recover from surgery. The nurse said that was usually not done, but the man was able to convince her that he was extremely nervous and just wanted to look at the room for a few seconds. A few seconds would be all he would need to imprint even the smallest detail in his brain forever. She obliged him, and he left the postoperative area after a quick look around. He walked out towards the preadmitting area, where he first entered the hospital, but abruptly turned into a small men's room he noticed previously. He removed Dr. Mack's ID tag from his pocket and placed his picture over Dr. Mack's. It did not look perfect, but no one seemed to look at the name tags anyway. There were simply too many people in the place to keep a tight control over who did what and who went where. There were too many anesthesiologists, and anesthesia residents, to keep track of everyone. The man rightly supposed that half the nurses couldn't remember the names of more than a few of the anesthesiologists at best.

He then removed a white lab coat from the small sack he was carrying, smoothed out a few wrinkles, applied Dr. Mack's name tag with the altered picture, and walked calmly out of the men's room. The blue-eyed man spent the next three hours roaming the hallways, floors, and, most importantly, the tunnels under the hospital, which connected one building with the next. He knew about the tunnels from old architectural drawings he was able to find in the city records, and they would be his escape route if anything went askew. The hospital itself was huge, built during a time when money meant very little. There were rooms on every floor that showed signs of little, if any, current use. At the end of the long hallway that led away from the recovery room, he found a small room. *This might suit my needs*, he thought. He unlocked the door with a small pick and entered the room unnoticed. Judging from the dust on the floor, the room had not been used for some time. The small light bulb hanging from a frayed wire in the center of the low ceiling was burnt out. A narrow beam of light entered the room through a hole in an old cracked yellow shade covering a small dirty window, allowing just enough illumination for him to survey the room. *Perfect.* He would have to chance it. Next week the place would be crawling with cops getting ready for him, so it had to be done now. He opened the small sack he had carried around all day. It did not attract attention since it looked like a small backpack that half the world carried. He took a medical device out of the sack and again examined it; it was shaped like a small box. Everything was in place. It would take only a moment to attach it to the IV pole and make the switch. The less time it took, the less the chance of detection. No adjustments could be made once it was up. He placed the device into an old paper bag that was also in the backpack, and hid the bag in the back of the small room behind some old papers. He left the room, and this time did walk out of the hospital.

The blue-eyed man left the hospital at about 1:15 P.M. He drove back to Manhattan and spent a few hours practicing with the equipment with the bulbous end. He again reviewed the information he had on the owner of the boat named *Yellow Tail*. The boat itself was over thirty years old, but its owner, Aaron Richardson, obviously kept it in pristine condition. Mr. Richardson was a forty-six-year-old lawyer who had a love for old boats. Judging from his credit card statements from the marina, he did not have much time to use *Yellow Tail*; nevertheless, he kept her well maintained, at considerable expense. The boat itself was twenty-six feet in length and equipped with twin 75-horsepower outboard engines. *Not exactly a rocket*, the man thought, but it would get him where he needed to be in ample time; having a second engine was a necessary pre-caution. After reviewing the records, the man dressed in his fishing clothes and drove to Sheepshead Bay. He arrived in time for his night-time fishing experience on the boat *Tight Lines*.

The trip itself was uneventful. The man fished a little and, using a handheld global satellite positioning device, was able to chart the loca-tion of each spot at which the boat stopped. He did this charting in the boat's head, for he knew that fishing spots were a closely guarded secret among most captains. With the new equipment, however, any novice could track the commercial vessels with little effort, so secrecy was more of a courtesy than anything else. The trip lasted from 7:00 P.M. until 1:00 A.M., as advertised, and the boat caught a fair amount of fish. There were twenty-three men on board, most of whom were diehard fishermen.

The boat itself was lit up like a Christmas tree, more a conces-sion to the insurance company than the fishermen. One slip in the dark and another liability suit would begin, even though anyone with half a brain should understand that fishing at night—on the wavy ocean, on a wet, slimy floor—was dangerous in its own right. Any slip would of course have to be the boat owner's fault, not the fisherman's, who, no doubt, was on his sixth beer before he fell.

The blue-eyed man tipped the mate well and had him clean his fish while he pumped him for information. "Yes, the boat is usually this crowded. Yes, they go pretty much to the same spots, unless the fish stop biting. Yes, they always leave at 7:00 P.M. and return at 1:00 A.M. Yes, the other boat, *Widow Maker*, is owned by the same company, and usu-ally the two stick pretty close together," a fact that somewhat concerned the blue-eyed man. As the two boats pushed their way back to Sheepshead Bay, the blue-eyed man studied every feature of *Widow Maker* from the deck of *Tight Lines*.

The following night, while he was fishing *Widow Maker*, he studied *Tight Lines* from the deck of *Widow Maker*. At the end of two nights he was ready for the main event, assuming it would ever occur. First he had to kill Carson and get out of Walsh's trap.

Chapter 31

Saturday, August 24th, Brian got up early. Friday night he had a late dinner with Maureen and Maryann. His daughter set up the dinner to tell them that things were getting pretty serious with Dennis. Maureen was pleased that Brian seemed to be tolerating Dennis. No one would be good enough for his daughter; that was a given. They talked about many things, including Brian's eventual retirement. He was calm and listened. He was not having fun on the job at this time, and that was obvious to everyone. The death of Thomas Knox brought a lot of heat from the mayor, and everyone knew that once someone from the press got hold of what was really going on Brian might be happy to retire. He knew his only chance was to get the killer, using Carson as bait. He did not share that with Maureen or Maryann. He would tell Maryann very little from here on in about his cases. He loved her very much, and trusted her more than anyone, but he knew that with a lover and probable future husband in the D.A.'s office, he had to be careful.

Brian spent most of Saturday going over plans in his head. He went through every scenario he could imagine concerning the upcoming surgery of Lawrence Carson. Ironically, the blue-eyed man did the same exact thing.

* * * * * * * * * *

Paulie, Willie, and Tommy spent all day Saturday at Kings County Hospital where they coordinated every detail of what was expected from each individual on the task force. They had no idea what the assassin or assassins looked like. They did not know where or when he would strike, or even if he would strike.

"Maybe he'll just blow the whole fucking place up," was Tommy's answer to what he thought was a stupid question from one of the uniforms. Tensions were mounting.

* * * * * * * * * *

The next week was just more of the same. The blue-eyed man practiced with his equipment, confident he would get to use it. He stopped listening to the tapes coming from the squad room because he could not tell fact from fiction. He was spending too much time trying to figure out Detective Brian Walsh, rather than on what was important—execution. His teachers taught him over and over the importance of proper planning and proper execution. The average man will have two or maybe three plans at most; have six or seven or eight, they would say—whatever it takes to get the job done and, most importantly, to get away. A blown assignment can always be rectified later. Death could not be rectified.

By Sunday morning September 1st, the blue-eyed man could not absorb another fact, or think another thought, about Lawrence Carson. He had had enough. He was the athlete who was ready for the big game two days early. He had to wind down. He knew it, and the Latin man knew it. He hadn't been with a woman in over a year, ever since the whole mess started. The string of ladies he had left behind seemed endless, but he was so consumed by his need to complete this job that he had forgotten about his real two passions, women and horses. He would make a call and drive to Saratoga that night. The horses were still racing and she would still be there. He made the call and was able to get through to her on her cellular phone.

"Brenda, it's Kevin. How are you?" The blue-eyed man began.

"Where have you been?"

"I was away on assignment. You know what that means."

"Where are you now?"

"I can't tell you that, but I will be in Saratoga this evening. Any chance of us getting together for dinner?"

"When are you going to stop this cloak-and-dagger crap and tell me who you really are and what you really do? Then we might have a normal relationship, or at least give it a chance."

"How are the horses doing?" Kevin asked, changing the subject quickly.

"Not that well. Thank God I have a rich owner who is patient with me."

"It helps that he's your father, don't you think?"

"Come on up, Kevin. We'll have dinner. But that's it. Dinner only. You understand. Dinner only!"

"I understand. I'll meet you at seven. Are you still at the same house?"

"Yes. My father wouldn't sell it for anything. He rolls out of bed in the morning and walks two blocks to the track."

"See you later."

"It's good to hear your voice, Kevin."

"Yours as well," the blue-eyed man said truthfully as he hung up the phone.

Kevin arrived at Brenda's father's house at 7:05 P.M. Her father was back in New York City. Kevin and Brenda ate dinner at a local restaurant, populated mostly by horsemen, and talked for hours. There was an affection between them that even long separations could not tarnish. It was disturbing to Brenda that she really had no idea who this man really was, or what he did for a living. What he did was not that important to her, but the fact that she did not know was unsettling. After all these years, she was just starting to learn to let things be. Every time she pressed him on the issue, he disappeared. She would just accept him for whatever, and whoever, he was.

After dinner they drove to her barn at Saratoga Race Course to see the horses. The night was cool and crisp, and they spent some time talking while walking hand in hand. They returned to Brenda's father's house and started a fire in the old stone fireplace. Brenda opened a bottle of wine. They had been there many times before, and within a short time, were duplicating past times as they lay on the thick rug in front of the fire making love as if there was no tomorrow.

But tomorrow did come. They slept in front of the fire, and Brenda awoke at five in the morning. A horse trainer needs no alarm clock. She walked the few blocks to her barn to supervise the daily care of the horses, two of which were entered in races that day and required special preparation. She was anxious to get back to Kevin. *Maybe this time will be different*, she allowed herself to foolishly think. When she arrived back at the house at 11:15 A.M., Kevin was gone, but there was a note. *That's a first,* she thought as she began to read. She read the short note a second time, and tears began to run down her cheeks. They were, however, tears of happiness, not sorrow. She smiled as she folded the note and put it away for safekeeping. Yes, this time would be different.

By the time Brenda had folded the note he left her, the blue-eyed man was halfway to Manhattan. He spent the rest of Monday relaxing, had an early dinner at the compound, and climbed into bed at eight o'clock, planning to arise at four the next morning. Sleep did not come quickly, as he lay thinking of Brenda and what a good life they could have if he were someone else. But he wasn't someone else, and Lawrence Carson and the whole NYPD would find this out over the next thirty-six hours. Either that, or he would die in Detective Brian Walsh's trap.

Chapter 32

Lawrence Carson also rested on Sunday and Monday. Brian, Willie, Tommy, and Paulie did not. Carson awoke at 4:00 A.M. Tuesday September 3rd, dressed, and was driven to the hospital under the direct supervision of Detective Brian Walsh, who slept on Carson's couch. Carson was due at the hospital at 6:45 for his 8:00 surgery. Brian and his two-car escort had Carson at the hospital on time, and they watched closely as Carson hobbled on his crutches into the preadmitting area on the first floor. He was greeted by his assigned nurse, given a hospital gown, blood was drawn for a CBC, and a urine analysis was performed. After an EKG, Carson was placed into a wheelchair and brought to the elevator by an aide. Brian was still by his side. Willie, dressed as a security guard, stood by the elevator.

"Nothing strange, boss," Willie said.

"So far so good," Brian answered.

"Keep it that way," Carson added, smiling.

The aide had no idea what they were talking about. Another patient with his own aide was brought to the elevator. Then a third, and then a fourth. The door opened and a uniform, who Brian knew, looked sternly out at him.

"All clear, Detective Walsh," the uniform said to Brian.

The four patients were wheeled into the elevator and brought up to the second floor to the preoperative anesthesia area. Paulie, dressed as an anesthesiologist, winked at Brian, who thought Paulie looked ridiculous. Carson was placed on a stretcher, and a nurse, who had previously been checked out and specifically selected for the job, started an intravenous line on him. The anesthesiologist walked over and again explained the plan for anesthesia to Mr. Carson. The doctor's name was Herb Snell, and he had met Carson and Brian before.

"Are you all set, Mr. Carson?" Dr. Snell asked.

"As ready as I will ever be," was Carson's response.

"Good. Dr. Schwartz wants you to have some antibiotics prior to your surgery, so we will be running them through the IV in your arm. You won't feel any pain. In fact, all your medications will now go through the IV, so that little stick you felt to start your IV was the last pain you will feel."

"Until I wake up from surgery, you mean. Dr. Schwartz told me this operation hurts a lot afterwards because he has to drill tunnels in my bones, and take out a bone graft to make my new ligament."

"That's true, but we will be giving you pain medicine to help you with that. Don't worry, Mr. Carson. You will get through it fine."

Brian hoped the doctor was right.

Dr. Schwartz walked into the pre-op area at 7:45 and greeted Mr. Carson. Dr. Schwartz was never told anything about Brian, or the fact that Carson was a target. Brian reasoned that even the best surgeon could not function properly under that stress.

The circulating nurse wheeled Lawrence Carson into the operating room at 7:50, and Dr. Schwartz and his fellow, Dr. Tokes, watched as Dr. Snell administered general anesthesia. Carson went to sleep, and Drs. Schwartz and Tokes performed a faultless anterior cruciate ligament reconstruction. The operation took two hours and fifteen minutes. Mr. Carson was brought to the recovery room, where Paulie waited anxiously, at 10:15. Carson was in obvious discomfort, and Paulie had trouble looking at him. The man in cubical six had just vomited, and that did not sit well with Paulie, who clearly was a better detective than he would be a surgeon. Still, he watched Carson like a hawk. The room filled up quickly, with many of the eight o'clock cases finishing within ten minutes of each other. Carson was moaning louder than most. Paulie couldn't help but remember Carson's words when he initially described his injury—"pure guts." *Where are your guts now Carson*? Paulie thought to himself.

In actuality, Carson was behaving better than most of the other patients. He did have a very painful operation. The nurse read Dr. Schwartz's post-op orders and called anesthesia over to start a patient-controlled anesthesia morphine pump to decrease Carson's pain. The PCA pump was a great device that allowed the patient to push a button and self-administer pain medication whenever it was needed. Of course, the machine was set so that only a certain amount could be given at any one time, and only a certain amount over a specified period of time. In short, it was impossible for the patient to overdose himself. The PCA pump was always attached to an IV pole by the patient's bedside. It looked like a small box with a syringe on one side. The IV tubing ran through the box, and the morphine was injected by an automatic syringe into the IV tubing and then into the patient's vein. It worked very well, and most patients liked it. The nurses loved it—they got less calls for pain medication. Dr. Schwartz used a PCA pump on all his ACL reconstructions.

* * * * * * * * * *

The blue-eyed man, unshaven but clean, arrived for his surgery at 9:45 A.M., as directed. He entered the preadmitting area, and his previously drawn blood tests were placed on the chart. He was given a gown and was shown to a cubicle to change. His clothes were placed in a small overnight bag that he brought with him, and an aide appeared with a wheelchair and brought him to the elevator. He was pushed right past Willie, along with two other patients, and brought to the preoperative holding area. He arrived at 10:18. A nurse came over to start his IV, but before she could begin he asked her, "How is Larry Carson doing?"

"Who?"

"Larry Carson, Dr. Schwartz's eight o'clock ACL reconstruction. I'm following him. How did he do? He's a close friend. Could you check?"

"Sure, post-op is right across the hall," nurse Melissa Corum answered.

The nurse turned to check on Mr. Carson, not sensing the blue-eyed man following her into the post-op area. Dr. Schwartz was standing at the foot of Carson's bed writing in the chart when the nurse walked up and asked how Carson was doing.

"Fine," was Dr. Schwartz's answer. "Do you know him?"

"No. Your next patient knows him. I was just checking him in and he asked me to find out how Mr. Carson did. Mr. Rivers seemed a little bit nervous, so I'll tell him Carson's doing great."

"Hi, doc," came a voice from behind Dr. Schwartz. "How is Larry?" the voice continued as it walked right up to the head of Carson's bed.

"He's fine, Mr. Rivers," Dr. Schwartz said. "He's still groggy, as you can see, but he'll be okay. You better get back to pre-op. You're next."

"Mr. Rivers, please come with me," Nurse Corum said rather firmly, surprised to see him out of his bed.

"Sure. I want to get this over with. I hope you're ready, doc," the blue-eyed man said as he walked back to the pre-op area with the nurse.

"Funny, I didn't think he would be the nervous type," Dr. Schwartz said to Carson's nurse.

What nobody saw was the subtle movement of the blue-eyed man's left hand during the nervous chatter, when he placed a small magnetic device about the size of a silver dollar on the back of Mr. Carson's PCA pump.

Mr. Rivers returned to the pre-op area, and his nurse started an IV without difficulty. Mr. Rivers was much calmer now, and he was shortly wheeled into the operating room for his surgery. Dr. Mack, the anesthesiologist Mr. Rivers met the previous week, helped to wheel him into the room.

"Do you want any sedation, Mr. Rivers?" Dr. Mack asked.

"No way. I want to watch."

"Okay," Dr. Mack answered.

Dr. Schwartz placed the MRI film up on the x-ray view box while Dr. Tokes helped to prep the patient. Dr. Schwartz and Dr. Tokes left the operating room to scrub their hands and eight minutes later returned to begin the procedure. Mr. Rivers was still wide-awake.

"I guess you really want to watch," Dr. Schwartz said.

"I watched the last time I had this done, doc. I want to see who's a better surgeon," Rivers joked.

Before Dr. Schwartz began the surgery, he injected Mr. Rivers' knee with Marcaine, a local anesthetic. He also injected the skin in three areas where he would cut three small openings into his knee. Dr. Schwartz began the arthroscopic surgery.

Lets see how honest Dr. Schwartz is, the blue-eyed man said to himself.

Dr. Schwartz made three small incisions: one on the medial side of the patella tendon at the joint line, one on the lateral side at the same level, and one in the medial side of the knee up by the patella. He then inserted a cannula into the patella incision, and a second cannula into the lateral incision. The inflow of fluid was started, and the arthroscope, which was attached to a TV camera, was inserted through the lateral cannula. The inside of Mr. Rivers' knee was now on TV for everyone, including Mr. Rivers, to see. Dr. Schwartz looked under Mr. Rivers' patella first.

"All normal there, Mr. Rivers. See that, where I'm pointing with the metal probe? That's your patella, your kneecap. Now for your tear," he said as he passed the arthroscope into the medial compartment of the blue-eyed man's knee to look at the medial meniscus. When Dr. Schwartz looked at the medial meniscus he could not see a tear. He took his probe and felt all over the meniscus. No tear. Dr. Tokes was also surprised. Schwartz handed the scope to Tokes and walked over to the x-ray viewbox. There was a huge flap tear in the posterior portion of the medial meniscus. No doubt about it. Schwartz then got a terrible feeling in the pit of his stomach, started to sweat profusely, and became light-headed. He operated on the wrong knee! The most dreaded thing an orthopaedic surgeon could do. No, wait. The MRI says right knee. The consent says right knee. "Yes" was written on the right knee. The patient is awake. No, thank God almighty; it was something else. The wrong MRI. The idiot radiologist gave Rivers the wrong MRI. No, there's his name, Kevin Rivers. What the hell is going on here?

Dr. Schwartz regained his composure and returned to the OR table. He looked at the lateral meniscus, and there was no tear there either. He looked back at the medial meniscus, and looked at every structure for a third time. It seemed like an eternity to Schwartz, but it only took fifteen minutes by the clock. Everything in Mr. Rivers' knee was completely normal.

"Mr. Rivers," Dr. Schwartz began, "I don't know how this could be, but your knee exam is perfectly normal. There is no tear in your medial meniscus. The only thing I can think of that could cause an event like this—and, quite frankly, I have never seen it—would be a mix up at your radiologist's office, where the wrong name was put on the films. This MRI must be someone else's, and they must have been given yours. It's the only explanation I can think of. I'll call Dr. Mann's office tomorrow and see who else had an MRI of the right knee on the same day as you. Maybe we can straighten this out that way."

"Whatever you say, doc," Rivers answered. "I'm just glad my knee is normal. I want to keep as much cartilage as possible."

Dr. Schwartz looked at his friend, Dr. Mack, and their eyes said it all. With any other patient this would be a huge malpractice suit.

"Of course, Mr. Rivers, my secretary will be giving you a complete refund tomorrow, when you come in for your post-op visit."

"Forget it, doc. Keep the money. You did an honest thing here today. Some other asshole would have taken out half my meniscus just to cover his ass. We've got to keep honest docs like him in business, don't we, Dr. Mack?"

"Yes we do, Mr. Rivers," Dr. Mack said. "Yes we do."

Dr. Mack was fifty-eight-years-old, and he had been administering anesthesia for exactly thirty years last month. He thought he had seen it all, but he had never seen the likes of Kevin Rivers before, and probably never would again. In fact, after that day, no one in the room would ever see Kevin Rivers again. When Dr. Schwartz called Dr. Mann's radiology office the following day, he was once again surprised by Mr. Rivers. His friend, Charlie Mann, told him that he was fucking nuts—that they never did an MRI on a Kevin Rivers on that day in July, or, for that matter, on any other fucking day. And that his MRI technicians would never make a stupid mistake like putting the wrong name on all nine films of a standard knee MRI. "No one, except maybe an orthopaedist operating on a normal knee, could be that fucking stupid," he added as he slammed down the receiver in Dr. Schwartz's ear.

Mr. Rivers was brought into the post-op area at 11:45. Torn meniscus or not, he still had arthroscopic surgery and had to recover. He had no pain. Dr. Schwartz had injected his small incisions with more Marcaine, and he would not feel any pain for hours. He would be going home in about an hour.

Lawrence Carson left the recovery room at 11:05, and was escorted to his room by Paulie and Willie, who was no longer needed at his post by the elevator. Brian was already on the orthopaedic floor, and

Tommy was tucked away in the other bed in Carson's room. It was the first time a patient at Kings County Hospital had a submachine gun hiding under his bed sheet; well, maybe not the first time.

Carson made it to his room uneventfully. Brian knew that the attack would probably occur here; all the rest was just for show. If Carson was to die at Kings County Hospital it would be in his room, and they were ready for anything.

Time passed slowly. Carson was restless, and would wake up in pain, press the button on the PCA morphine pump, and then dose off again. Paulie looked at Carson and decided he would never have that operation, no matter what happened to his knee. If he were Carson, he would have just given up racquetball. He seemed to be in agony; at least he looked that way in the recovery room. The only thing that kept him from screaming was the morphine. Carson was in a brace and had at least six months of painful rehabilitation ahead of him. For what? To play racquetball. *No way*, Paulie concluded.

"Just be sure you don't shoot me with that gun, Tommy," Paulie said.

"I won't shoot anybody today. And neither will you. I can't believe Brian believes our guy will hit Carson here. A blind man could see all the cops. This is a total waste of time, Paulie. He'll shoot Carson somewhere else, or blow him up in his car, not in a hospital with at least a hundred cops all over the fucking place. Not a chance."

"How are things with Margaret?" Paulie asked.

"What things?"

"What do you mean what things? I thought she was going to be Mrs. O'Neal."

"So did I, Paulie. So did I."

"What happened? If I might ask."

"She said we were going too fast for her. She needed some time."

"So, you'll give her some time."

"Paulie, never go to Paradise Island. It's heaven."

"Maybe I'll take my wife. Things are getting a little stale, if you know what I mean."

"Why don't you try being home sometimes. That might help," Tommy jabbed.

"I think we'll all have a lot of time off soon. Two dead guys from now." They both laughed.

At 12:35 P.M. Kevin Rivers was able to stand without any pain. He would be heading home shortly. A friend was coming to pick him up, he told his nurse. She sent for an aide, who would take him to the discharge area in a wheelchair.

"That won't be necessary," Mr. Rivers answered. "I feel fine. I'm great with crutches."

"Hospital policy," she answered.

The blue-eyed man backed into the chair holding his crutches and thanked everyone for what they had done for him. The nurse placed his small overnight bag on his lap, and the aide wheeled him to the elevator. They rode down to the first floor, and Mr. Rivers had the aide stop by a small bathroom.

"I have to visit the men's room. I might be awhile, so you don't have to wait."

"I have to wheel you out. Hospital policy," she replied.

The blue-eyed man knew he wasn't the first to try and walk out of the hospital. Everyone knew the standard answer: "hospital policy."

He went into the men's room and was furious with himself. How could he have missed this simple little detail. Every hospital movie he ever saw made a joke about it, but this wasn't funny. This aide was going to push him out to the pickup area no matter what he said. Getting back in would probably be easy, but would increase the risk of being noticed tremendously. He would just wait in the men's room. She would no doubt get tired of waiting and send someone in to check on him. Maybe that person would be more reasonable. He hoped so.

The aide began to talk to another worker who was interested in more than conversation; he had been hitting on her for weeks. After fifteen minutes, she asked her friend to check on Mr. Rivers. The man opened the door to the men's room and found Rivers sitting inside a stall.

"I'm fine. Tell her to go. I might be some time, if you know what I mean."

"He's fine," the aide's friend said as he exited the men's room. "He said he'll be awhile and you should go. He'll get out fine by himself."

The aide reluctantly pushed the empty wheelchair back to the recovery room area upstairs. The aide's friend stuck his head into the bathroom and reported her departure to Mr. Rivers.

"Thank you, my friend. Sorry for any inconvenience," the blue-eyed man answered.

Mr. Rivers waited a few more minutes and emerged as Dr. David Fisher, a member of the anesthesiology department. He didn't look like David Fisher. Or maybe he did; he didn't know. He had never seen Dr. Fisher. In any case, it didn't matter since Dr. Fisher was on vacation, visiting his parents in Nebraska. At least that is what the blue-eyed man heard last week during his pre-op visit. With more time, and the help of an expert forger, the ID tag he wore on his white jacket looked a lot better than the one he wore two weeks previously.

The blue-eyed man, recently Mr. Rivers and now Dr. Fisher, climbed an out-of-the-way staircase to the second floor and briskly walked to the small room down the hallway from the recovery room, where he had stored his equipment of death on his previous visit. No one stopped him at any point along the way. He opened the door with the same pick he used the last time he was there, and was inside in a few seconds. He was glad to see no one had been in the room since his last visit. His paper bag was exactly where he left it the previous week. He would be in the room for many hours. It was now 1:30 P.M., and he would make his move sometime between three and four o'clock in the morning. He sat back and rested. It would be a long, boring wait, but he had waited longer.

* * * * * * * * *

By 10:00 P.M. Brian began to think he had misjudged the killer. He thought surely he would take the challenge. Carson would go home in the morning, sometime before eleven, barring any complications. The killer had to know that. Tommy dosed off in the bed next to Carson. Willie had relieved Paulie, who was across the street getting some pizza. Brian paced the hallway. Two pizzas and two quarts of coke later, it was midnight. Still no action.

At 1:00 A.M. the blue-eyed man made his first move. He removed a small transmitter from his overnight bag and pressed a button. The impulse went up two floors to the orthopaedic floor. It was received by a small electronic device, which was held by magnetic force to the back of Lawrence Carson's PCA morphine pump. The small device then did exactly what the Latin man programmed it to do—it shut off Carson's

PCA morphine pump. Carson could push the little joy button all he wanted, but no morphine would be injected into his bloodstream and he would get no pain relief.

The blue-eyed man waited until 2:00 A.M., when he carefully exited the small room carrying a large paper bag. He left his overnight bag in the room, noting that it probably would be found in about five years, judging from the dates on the newspapers in the room, which gave a detailed description of Operation Desert Storm.

The blue-eyed man alertly made his way to the recovery room. Just as he expected, it was empty. The elective surgeries were long finished. The only patients going through the recovery room at this hour would be emergencies, and most of them were routed directly to the Intensive Care Unit. He sat down and called the operator, told her he was Dr. Schwartz, and asked for the extension of the anesthesia call room. She gave him the extension, and he found a phone in the recovery room with a bank of extensions, one of which was 2108, the anesthesia on call room. He knew from speaking to Dr. Mack that an anesthesia resident would be taking calls at night. The attending physicians were all at home, but there were three residents in the hospital at all times. The chief resident ran the show, and could call in others, including attendings if necessary, but it was rarely done.

The blue-eyed man planned to wait in the recovery room and intercept the call. If that did not work he would go to plan B. There was a plan C, D, E, and F as well. After that things would get a little too risky, and he would bail out and try some other time. His knee was beginning to ache, but it was nothing he couldn't deal with. *Not like the pain Lawrence Carson will soon be having,* he thought.

The blue-eyed man used his time productively. He removed the bulky dressing from his knee and applied three Band-Aids over the small openings. He took a razor out of his paper bag and shaved his almost two days of growth. He would be ready when the call came.

Upstairs on the orthopaedic floor, Lawrence Carson was not doing well. His pain was getting stronger and stronger. Tommy sat listening to Carson's moans, and Paulie was more convinced than ever that Carson had done a stupid thing. The nurse came into Carson's room for the third time in an hour. Her name was Barbara.

"What's going on?" Tommy asked.

"The morphine's not holding him. They may have to increase the dose. He's getting a pretty strong dose, though. If it doesn't let up soon, I'll have to call the anesthesiologist on call."

By 3:15 A.M. Carson was screaming, and his nurse made the call to anesthesia.

Extension 2108 rang only once. Before the anesthesia resident who was soundly asleep in the on call room could even hear the ring, the blue-eyed man picked up the flashing extension in the recovery room.

"Yes," he answered very sleepily.

"Sorry to wake you, doctor. This is orthopaedics. We have a patient of Schwartz's who is on a PCA pump. It's not holding him at all. He's writhing in pain."

"Okay, I'll be up shortly," the blue-eyed man answered.

The blue-eyed man messed up his hair and threw some water on his face. He had already gone into the operating room dressing area and changed into a scrub shirt and scrub pants. He threw a white coat over the scrub suit and headed up to the orthopaedic floor. His ID was clipped to his white jacket. Dr. David Fisher would be happy to help the nurse on the orthopaedic floor.

Paulie did not like the fact that someone new, and unknown, was coming. Brian and Willie were in another part of the hospital, but Tommy was awake and ready with his weapon of destruction. Paulie again reminded him that it wouldn't be good to kill everyone in the room. Paulie was clearly nervous around machine guns. He called the nurse into the room.

"Barbara, who's the resident who's coming up?"

"I didn't ask."

"You should have."

"He was asleep in the on call room, whoever he was. You can ask him his name when he gets here," she returned caustically.

Paulie had a book listing all the house staff and all the attendings.

"Do you know all the residents by sight?" Paulie asked the nurse.

"Are you kidding? They rotate all over the place. I see the anesthesia resident maybe once or twice a month, and it's never the same one. I don't know any of them."

Just then Dr. David Fisher walked into Carson's room, yawning.

"Good morning," he mumbled.

"What's your name, doctor?" Paulie asked while showing the

blue-eyed man his shield.

"Fisher," was the response as he pointed to his hospital name tag somewhat sarcastically. "David Fisher. Who's this? A VIP or a criminal? Those are the only two who get you guys. What's the problem?" he asked the nurse, ignoring Paulie.

"The pump isn't holding him. He's all over the place, screaming and yelling. He needs something more, I think," the nurse answered.

Paulie came across the name David Fisher in the list of anesthesia residents and felt a little easier. Tommy's carefully concealed submachine gun was aimed at the doctor's head.

Dr. Fisher asked the nurse, "Was he getting relief earlier in the night?"

"Yes, he seemed to be fine until about 2:30; then things kept getting worse."

"The pump probably isn't working. We've had several of them go down lately. Before I switch his medication, I'll bring up a new pump," Dr. Fisher said as he walked slowly out of the room and down the hall to the elevator, unimpressed by the detectives.

The blue-eyed man took the elevator back to the second floor and carefully made his way back to the recovery room. He took the special PCA pump that he and the Latin man altered out of his paper bag and started back to the orthopaedic floor. He was soon in Carson's room again. He removed the old pump and placed the new one on the IV pole. He tightened the clamp in back and told the nurse to use the same medication orders but to get a new syringe full of morphine. The nurse, who already had decided she would do almost anything Dr. David Fisher asked, particularly after noticing the lack of a wedding ring on his fourth finger, dutifully went off to get a new syringe of morphine for Mr. Carson. Dr. Fisher stayed in the room talking to Paulie, and agreed with him that ACL surgery was too painful for him as well.

The nurse returned with a new syringe of morphine and inserted it in the holder in front of the PCA pump.

"Mr. Carson, try the button now," Dr. Fisher said.

He didn't have to tell Carson twice. He pressed it four times in a row.

Paulie jumped.

Dr. Fisher smiled and said, "Relax, detective. He can press it as much as he wants. He only gets the first dose. After a period of time, another dose will be available for administration. He can't possibly get too much. Well, back to sleep for me."

The tall man with the blue eyes made a lasting impression on Nurse Barbara Sutton. She would like to see him again. Carson calmed down quickly. The medication was working. Paulie sat back in his chair, much relieved.

The blue-eyed man stepped off the elevator on the second floor just as Brian Walsh walked into Carson's room. Paulie told Brian of the events of the past few minutes, and Brian became alarmed. Paulie reassured him that there was definitely a David Fisher, and the nurse was sure he was an anesthesia resident. Brian walked out to the nursing station, where Nurse Barbara Sutton was telling another nurse about the gorgeous Dr. David Fisher. Brian could not help overhearing, and wanted to speak to nurse Sutton. He was not the only one who overheard her excitement about Dr. Fisher.

"Stay away from him, Barbara. He's a real jerk," a third nurse said as she walked into the nurse's station. "I went out with him twice, and that was two times too many," she continued.

Brian looked carefully at the nurse who was speaking to nurse Sutton, and charitably decided that anyone who would go out with her twice would have to be very desperate, unless she was the best fuck that ever lived. A quick second look eliminated that possibility.

Brian turned to the nurse who just finished speaking and flashed his shield in her face. "Quickly, describe Dr. Fisher to me," he ordered.

The nurse was startled but quickly said, "Average-looking face, with dark brown hair and brown eyes. About 5-foot-eight or nine. Not that good-looking really."

Brian turned to nurse Sutton and asked the same question.

"Gorgeous. At least six-foot-five with deep-blue bedroom eyes. Brown hair ..."

Brian ran back to Carson's room before she got to the part about the deep-blue bedroom eyes. Beauty was in the eye of the beholder, Brian realized, but no one could be five-foot-eight to someone and six-foot-five to someone else. The killer had just walked past two of the best detectives in New York, and probably injected Carson with a lethal dose of something.

Brian ran into the room and pulled the IV out of Carson's arm. Nurse Sutton followed him into the room, and Brian ordered her to call a real doctor right away, someone she absolutely knew was a real doctor. Mr. Carson's life would depend on it.

Barbara ran out the door, called the emergency room, and convinced Dr. James Wagner to come to orthopaedics. She knew him very well, in every sense of the word. In the meantime, Brian called Willie on the walkie-talkie and had him spring the trap. The son-of-a-bitch was in Carson's room less than five minutes ago.

"We got him!" he screamed into Willie's ear. "We fucking got him!"

Brian told Paulie and Tommy to stay with Carson, and Brian took off running.

The blue-eyed man proceeded with plan A. He would simply walk out of the hospital in his scrub suit and walk east on Clarkson Ave., like so many other doctors and nurses did every hour of the day. When he got to the first floor he saw a level of activity that was highly unusual for 3:45 A.M. His internal alarm sounded. *Plan B*, he thought as he turned and walked slowly to a staircase that he knew would bring him to the first of several underground tunnels. He would follow the tunnel to the second building east, E-Building, and walk out. He entered the tunnel uneventfully.

Upstairs, every exit from the hospital was immediately sealed by the mass of uniform police carefully hidden in the hospital and disguised as security, orderlies, aides, nurses, and even doctors—all of whom now had a description of Dr. David Fisher. Brian and Willie raced down the stairs from the orthopaedic floor to the basement door, which opened into the tunnel system. Brian was sure that the tunnel would be the killer's path to freedom.

As he walked through the tunnel from the main building to E-Building, the blue-eyed man had his gun drawn but well hidden under his white coat. He would use it only as a last resort, but if he had to use it he wouldn't hesitate for a second. He cautiously walked past one of the many staircases that emptied into the tunnel and continued on his way. No one else was in the tunnel. In the winter the tunnels were used frequently, but there was no need today. The man heard the loud echo of a door being slammed against a tile wall; the door to the staircase he passed a few minutes before now hung on one hinge, compliments of Willie Hayes. The tunnel was a straight line at this section, and the man turned around. Detective Brian Walsh quickly joined Detective Willie

Hayes in the well-lit tunnel, and with their guns drawn, they looked in the direction of the tall blue-eyed man, who stared back at them. The man had his hand on his gun, but kept it hidden under his white coat. They were approximately two hundred feet apart. The blue-eyed man quickly calculated that the odds of either of the detectives hitting him from where they were standing with their police weapons was extremely small and would require pure luck. He further calculated that he could hit them both without any luck at all with his modified gun.

"Dr. Fisher?" Brian yelled.

"Just for today," was the man's smiling reply. The blue-eyed man knew that Detective Walsh did not come to speak to Dr. Fisher.

The man turned and ran east, away from the two detectives and deeper into the yellow tile-lined tunnel. Every footstep echoed from wall to wall; it sounded like the whole precinct was following the blue-eyed man. Willie and Brian continued after "Dr. Fisher."

It's going to end right here in the tunnel, Brian thought as he ran as fast as his fifty-four-year-old legs could carry him. Ordinarily, the race would be no contest, but the blue-eyed man's right knee slowed him down just enough to keep the detectives close. Still, he ran faster than anyone ever had less than one day after arthroscopic surgery.

The tunnel forked and Willie and Brian clearly saw the killer disappear to the right. They pursued him cautiously into the smaller tunnel. After about 150 feet, the tunnel emptied into two staircases—a staircase that went up to the right and a staircase that went down to the left.

"Willie, you go down and I'll go up," Brian said. "And, for God's sake, Willie, be careful. This guy's the real thing."

"You too, Brian."

Willie disappeared down the unlit staircase to the left, and Brian started up the dark staircase on the right. Brian could feel his heart pounding, but he couldn't see a thing. He hadn't been in a chase like this in years. There would be no back-up. He told Willie not to use the walkie-talkie unless absolutely necessary. The man would die tonight, and only Willie and Brian would ever know the details. Brian slowly worked his way up the steps in complete darkness. He reached a corridor after what seemed an eternity, but which was in fact only up a single flight of stairs. He hugged the right wall, which was slowly curving to the left. *What kind of place is this?* he thought. He progressed slowly, his heart pounding out of his chest as he searched unsuccessfully for a light switch. Sweat poured off his forehead into his eyes. He paused and wiped his face on his sleeve. At any second the man could step out, and that would be the end. Brian knew he would be no match for the man one-on-one. Maybe the man already had him in his sights and he would never hear the shot that killed him. He had flashbacks to Vietnam as he again began to slowly move along the peculiarly curved wall. If it came, at least it would probably be over quickly, he justified. At that moment, Brian was blinded by a light that seemed brighter than the sun. He could not see a thing. He would now die at the hands of the blue-eyed man. He was defeated. Brian fell to the left and stumbled into what felt like movie seats. He fell onto the floor and covered his eyes until he could slowly pull his hands away as his eyes adjusted to the blinding light. He stood up and was surprised that he was still alive. He saw where he was, but did not initially comprehend what it was he was looking at. He was standing adjacent to a triple row of theater seats, with the second row much higher than the first, and the third higher still. There was a large window that looked down into a large room from where the incredibly bright light was emanating, and he could see two men in the room. *My God*, Brian thought, *Willie has him*. Willie had his gun drawn and the man had his back to Willie with his hands up in the air. They were both standing in the middle of this huge room, with Willie about ten feet away from the man. Brian could see that Willie was in the crouched position with his gun extended, and looked ready to shoot the man if he moved at all.

Brian could not hear anything through the large thick window, but he could see Willie's mouth moving. He now realized where they were. He remembered the drawings of the hospital, which he reviewed all last week—the old surgical amphitheater. It was here that, many years ago, residents, interns, and medical students would come to watch their professors demonstrate their surgical skills. It was no longer used. Brian thought it ironic that the man would die in such a place; a place where others learned to save lives. He took a quick look below at Willie and the man, and saw that he was more than halfway around his half of the circular amphitheater. There was a door below, which was directly across the amphitheater from the door Willie and the man used. There was another staircase that led down to that door, and that would be the quick- est way to get to Willie. That entrance would place the man between Willie and himself, and the killer would be trapped with no chance of escape.

Just as Brian started to move, he watched the unbelievable happen and was powerless to do anything about it. Willie said something to the man, and Brian saw the man throw a gun to the other side of the room, obviously following Willie's command. The man started to walk slowly to the wall, with Willie following behind him at a safe distance. Then the man tripped and fell forward. It looked like a simple stumble to Brian, and to Willie as well, but it was a carefully calculated move the man taught to many of his associates. As he was falling forward, the natural reflex to extend his hands to cushion the fall was overcome, and the man, in a whip-like motion, which only Brian could see from his side angle, hurled something between his legs back at Willie. The man fell forward, taking the full force of the fall on his right shoulder after turning his head acutely to the left. It appeared to be happening in slow motion, but from Willie's point of view that was not so.

Willie's head was thrown forward as his body was thrown backward. He could not breathe. The man had struck him in the Adam's apple with something, and Willie began to bleed profusely, as he gasped for air. As he fell backward, instinctively grabbing his bleeding neck, all power he had to hold a gun rapidly dissipated, and the gun fell on the floor several feet from Willie. Brian could see Willie lying on the floor struggling to catch his breath. The whole event was over in less than ten seconds, and Brian ran down the staircase that led to the door of the amphitheater. The blue-eyed man ran to get his gun and then stood over Willie. He removed Willie's walkie-talkie from his jacket and looked down at his latest victim.

"You'll be okay," the blue-eyed man said. "It looks and feels worse than it really is. Try to breathe slowly, and don't try to talk. You'll feel better in a few minutes," the man added as he ran to the door—the same door that Detective Brian Walsh was running to with all possible speed.

The blue-eyed man and Brian reached the door at exactly the same moment. They froze and stared at each other through the upper half of the door, which was thick glass. They each had a gun in their hand, but the man, unknown to Brian, had the upper hand. The man could see that the door was bolted from the inside, and he was on the inside. They each calculated their next move. Brian quickly tried the locked door. He looked at the man and then at his best friend lying in a pool of blood on the floor. Brian thought Willie was dying. The blue-eyed man knew there was no way Walsh could run up the stairs, around the circumference of the amphitheater, and down the stairs to the opposite door faster than the man, bad knee and all, could run across the room. The blue-eyed man had also seen the plans of the hospital. Brian thought about shooting through the glass, but discarded that idea and began running up the stairs. *Fuck this guy*, he thought; he would save Willie. When Brian turned, the blue-eyed man turned and bolted for the opposite door. He reached it long before Brian and headed back into the tunnel, knowing full well that Brian would not follow. As he ran down the tunnel the man thought, *plan C*. He made it back to the main tunnel and turned towards the main part of the hospital where all the police were looking for him. He felt sure that plan C would work, but it would not be fun. He used Willie's walkie-talkie to announce to everyone listening, "Code red, code red, old surgical amphitheater," which meant, for this particular exercise, that a detective was down.

"Create turmoil," the blue-eyed man said out loud, smashing a fire alarm that he ran past. He made it to the second floor and was shortly inside the small room down the hallway from the recovery room. He did not expect to ever see that room again, but was very happy to be there.

Back in the amphitheater, Brian ripped off part of Willie's shirt and pressed it firmly against Willie's bleeding neck wound. *Pressure dressing*, he remembered from Vietnam. Willie seemed to be breathing much better. His pulse was regular and forceful, as best as Brian could tell. Brian was about to call a code red, when he, unbelievably, heard the man who almost killed Willie make the call.

"What happened?" Willie asked.

"He hit you in the neck with this," Brian answered as he showed him "this."

"What the fuck is that?"

"I don't know, Willie, but it looks like you probably don't want to get hit with it again."

Brian held up a small, rock-hard, round object with several pointed spikes protruding from each side.

"It looks like a handball with spikes," Brian exclaimed. "That's a new one on me. You ever see anything like this before, Willie?"

"No."

Brian and Willie both realized that Willie was going to make it.

"Brian, he could have easily killed me."

"It sure looks like he tried to."

"No, really. He stood right over me with his gun and told me I'd be okay and told me to breathe easily. One shot and I'd be dead. I don't get it. I was going to shoot him if this didn't happen."

"Jesus Christ, Willie. He's killed eleven people we know about, if you count Horowitz a person. Don't get soft on me. If you needed to die you would have, believe me."

Help arrived shortly, and Willie was brought to the emergency room where his neck was sutured and x-rays taken. They were negative.

"If you're going to be wounded, you might as well do it in a hospital," the ER physician told Willie. The ENT resident insisted on admitting Willie for observation because he wanted to watch for further swelling that could compromise Detective Hayes' breathing. Willie was admitted to the ENT service on Brian's orders. It was the first direct order Brian had given his close friend, and despite not wanting to follow it, Willie did so out of respect and love for his friend.

* * * * * * * * *

It was 5:15 A.M. and Mr. Carson now seemed to be resting comfortably. Dr. James Wagner, who Nurse Sutton definitely knew to be a real bona fide doctor, was a surgical resident rotating through the emergency room. He ran up to examine Carson immediately after Barbara Sutton called him on Detective Walsh's command at 3:42 A.M.. Dr. Wagner immediately called the anesthesia chief resident, who he knew personally, to come check on Lawrence Carson. Dr. Marco Gionetti was a top-notch anesthesia resident. He took charge on arrival and completely removed all the IV tubes and medication from the PCA pump. He took blood samples, which he sent stat to the lab, and restarted Mr. Carson's IV. He personally supervised and checked every bit of tubing as well as the new syringe of morphine that was inserted into the PCA pump. There was no reason to change the PCA pump as it was purely a mechanical device with no direct contact to the patient. He assured Paulie and Tommy that Carson appeared to be fine. All his vital signs—pulse, blood pressure, respirations—were normal. Whatever the man was going to inject, or whatever he put into the syringe with the morphine, simply did not have time to be injected before Detective Walsh pulled out the IV. Thank God for that. Everything will be analyzed—the IV, the fluid that dripped on the floor, the contents of the syringe, everything—Dr. Gionetti assured the detectives. All Paulie knew was that Carson was alive, and that no one other than Nurse Sutton and Dr. Gionetti would be allowed in the room again.

* * * * * * * * * *

The blue-eyed man looked at his watch at 5:20 A.M. It was almost time for the medical device that he and the Latin man worked so hard on to begin its work. He had hoped to be long gone by now, but now he would have to begin the unpleasant work required in plan C. As he thought about what was coming, he grimaced. He changed from his scrub pants and shirt to the outfit Kevin Rivers wore to the hospital for his surgery the day before. He rolled up the pants on his right leg, removed the Band-Aids, took out a small knife, and removed the only suture in the small opening on the inside of his knee. There was no bleeding, just as he expected. He grabbed his scrub pants and stuffed his mouth with as much of the pants as he could and bit down hard. He stuck the knife through the small opening on the inside of his knee. He cut just deep enough to get the soft tissues bleeding, and painfully continued with this procedure for fifteen minutes. As he moved the knife around the pain was significant, but he did not utter a word. The scrub pants were a precaution, but proved unnecessary. His knee swelled tremendously as it filled with blood, and would shortly be of such a size that the emergency room physician would be quite alarmed. The man hoped he would not get an infection.

At 5:43 A.M. Lawrence Carson joined Thomas Knox, with one major difference—he went out with a whimper, not a bang.

At 5:30 A.M. a timing device in the specially constructed PCA pump clicked on. The PCA pump looked like any other PCA pump to the naked eye; the blue-eyed man and the Latin man spent a substantial length of time working to achieve that very thing. It was the same color, almost the same weight, and had the exact same appearance from the front. The dials were the same, and the slot for the syringe, which was usually filled with morphine, was exactly the same. What was different about this PCA pump was the back, where it was enlarged to hold a small timing device and two 60cc syringes. When the timer went off at 5:30 A.M., several well-timed events occurred. First, an extra dose of morphine was administrated to Carson. The dose was carefully calculated not to be lethal, but rather to minimize the pain he would soon be having. Secondly, an eighteen-gauge needle slowly penetrated the IV tubing just below the morphine syringe. The two 60cc syringes in the back of the newly designed PCA pump rapidly injected their contents through the needle and into the tubing, sending the material into Carson's right arm. The needle then retreated to its hiding place in the back of the pump, never to be seen again. The 120cc bolus of material made its way through the deep veins of the right arm, to the superior vena cava, and to the right atrium of the heart, where it began its work. Try as it might, Carson's right atrium could not pump the 120cc of air that was injected by the PCA pump through his heart. The heart, realizing its dilemma, began to pump more rapidly. Bubbles of air danced around the atrium as the heart continued to speed up in a valiant attempt to find much-needed blood carrying its vital supply of oxygen. But a very effective air lock had been created. No oxygen would be getting to Carson's heart ever again. Carson became uncomfortable, but the morphine in his system dulled whatever chest pain he had. He did not move in the bed, and appeared to be sleeping comfortably. No blood was getting to the critical area of the heart through the coronary vessels, and soon an arrhythmia occurred. Shortly thereafter Lawrence Carson's heart stopped, and he died under the watchful eyes of Paulie and Tommy. Nurse Sutton would discover Carson was dead on her 6:00 A.M. rounds. Until then, he would sleep peacefully.

   At 5:45 A.M. the blue-eyed man, who was once again Kevin Rivers, limped down to the emergency room. He had rolled his pants leg up above his knee so everyone could see the blood gushing vigorously down his leg from the small wound. He left a trail of blood behind him, but he was careful not to begin the trail until he was just around the corner from the emergency room. There were police around, but the man guessed correctly that most of them were searching the buildings in the east section of the campus, where any sane man would make his escape.

"What happened to you?" a nurse asked as the tall man limped in, bleeding quite profusely from the wound on the inside of his knee. "Where did you come from?" she added, since he did not come through the usual emergency room entrance.

"I had surgery yesterday, and I went back to the outpatient area. The guard sent me over here," the man partially lied, in an excited voice loud enough for everyone, including any of the police listening, to hear. "My doctor is Dr. Schwartz. I had arthroscopic surgery yesterday and I was doing great. I had no pain and no swelling and I even went out to dinner last night. I went to bed early and had a large ice pack on my knee throughout the night, but at about four in the morning I woke up, and my knee was badly swollen. I put some more ice on it, but it continued to swell and became very painful. I had arthroscopic surgery on my other knee a few years ago and nothing like this happened. I was getting nervous so I took the dressing off and saw that the swelling popped the stitch, so I figured I'd better get my ass in here right away. It's not serious is it, nurse?"

"Let's get you into a bed and get you looked at by the ER physician," the nurse answered.

The nurse and an aide helped Mr. Rivers into a bed, and the nurse called the ER physician, Dr. James Wagner. The nurse, who was a strikingly beautiful dark-skinned girl with an Italian name the blue-eyed man could not make out because her name tag was stained with fresh blood, took the patient's vital signs and playfully asked him why none of the patients ever remove their hospital wrist bracelets.

"I don't know," he replied, thinking to himself that the tag would come into play if plan D was necessary.

Dr. Wagner came to examine Mr. Rivers, and his first words startled the beautiful Italian girl.

"Holy shit. What happened to your knee?" he said before he even introduced himself to the new patient.

"Is it that bad, doc?" the patient asked before repeating the story he just told to the nurse.

"You won't die from it, but it's the biggest effusion I've ever seen after an arthroscopy. We will have to put a needle in your knee and draw all the blood out. A small vessel must have just started bleeding and couldn't stop on its own, although it appears to have stopped now," the doctor said as he looked at the small wound on the inside of the patient's leg.

"Marie, set up an aspiration tray for me and get some Marcaine," the doctor ordered as he went on to other business.

The emergency room was not particularly crowded, but there was always a steady stream of patients. Many used the ER as their family physician, despite the fact that it was not encouraged. The nurse set up the aspiration and brought Mr. Rivers the blanket he asked for, saying to him that she hoped he wasn't coming down with an infection.

"No, I'm just a little cold," he answered as he wrapped the blanket around his head and shoulders, leaving only a small portion protruding in case someone came looking for Dr. Fisher. He was strangely relaxed, and hoped that Dr. Wagner would be busy for some time. *I could look at this nurse forever*, he smiled to himself. Dr. Wagner, as it turned out, would be very busy for quite some time.

Nurse Sutton entered Lawrence Carson's room at 6:09 A.M., starting her rounds with him. Her shift would be over at 7:00 A.M., but she rarely got out before 7:30. Today she would not leave until 9:00 A.M. It would take that long for Brian's questions.

When she reached out for Carson's left arm she knew something was wrong. He looked pale and was not moving at all. That fact was noticed by Paulie earlier, but he assumed it was the morphine doing its job. The nurse knew better, and she quickly felt for his pulse, first in his wrist and then in his neck. Both were absent. She knew he was dead, but took his blood pressure nevertheless; it was unobtainable. The nurse listened to Carson's heart and heard nothing. Carson was dead but she quickly ran outside and called a code blue on the orthopaedic floor.

People came from everywhere—nurses, doctors, a respiratory therapist, more nurses, medical students, Dr. Wagner from the ER, and Dr. Gionetti from anesthesia. They all tried to bring Mr. Carson back to this world but, as Dr. Gionetti said, he was too far gone.

Brian was visiting with Willie on the ENT floor when the code blue call was made by Nurse Sutton. He told Willie that they had not seen the man who injured him, and thought he was still somewhere on the east side of the campus, hiding in one of the buildings. They had every tunnel and exit sealed off, and unless he was Houdini, they would eventually get him, now that they knew what he looked like. Just as he completed his sentence, he heard the code blue call over and over, and instinctively knew what it meant and who it was for. Brian asked one of the nurses, already knowing the answer he would receive.

"Nurse, what is a code blue?"

"Cardiac arrest," she answered. "That one is on the orthopaedic floor."

Brian ran from the sixth floor, where the ENT service was, to orthopaedics. He shot down the stairs, thankful that orthopaedics was two floors down and not two floors up. He was too old for all the running he did tonight. He arrived in time to see the residents start the resuscitation attempt, and watched the whole painful ordeal as Dr. Gionetti made every attempt to bring Carson back. Brian knew they were wasting their time. The killer did not come this far to have his victim saved by medical science. Whatever he injected Carson with, would be so potent that nothing could be done. When it was over, he slowly walked over to Dr. Gionetti and spoke softly to him. Brian could see the pain in Gionetti's face.

"Dr. Gionetti, I want you to take personal charge of everything from this minute on, until you get further instructions. This man was murdered, make no mistake about it, and I don't want anyone but you touching anything in this room, no matter how insignificant it may seem. Call the head of pathology and get him down here as soon as possible. I want to know exactly what killed Mr. Carson, and I want to know exactly how and when it was done. Do you understand the urgency and seriousness of what I am telling you, Dr. Gionetti?"

Gionetti knew. No one had died on the elective service in a long time, and no one had ever been murdered on his service. He was as pissed as Detective Walsh, but for different reasons. He vowed to work with pathology and the medical examiner to determine exactly what happened to Lawrence Carson, no matter how long it took.

Dr. Wagner returned to the ER after helping on the code blue up in orthopaedics. He walked into Mr. Rivers' cubicle after checking on the status of the ER with the head nurse. Fortunately, nothing of any significance came in while he was with Mr. Carson.

"What was that about?" the pretty nurse, who the blue-eyed man had spent the last forty-five minutes with, and whose name he now knew to be Marie Romero, asked Dr. Wagner.

"Some guy up in orthopaedics boxed," he answered. "He must have flipped an embolus, or had an arrhythmia," he added.

The blue-eyed man thought Dr. Wagner would have to improve

his bedside manner if he were going into private practice, even though one was certainly not needed in the chaos of the emergency room at Kings County Hospital.

"Are you ready, Mr. Rivers?"

"Ready for what?"

"As you can see, your knee is very swollen. The pain is coming from the pressure inside your knee. I'm going to insert a needle into your knee and draw out all the blood."

"Won't that hurt?"

"I'll numb it for you, but it will still hurt somewhat. But we have to do it, otherwise you will continue to have pain and your recovery will take much longer. It won't hurt that much."

"It won't hurt you that much, is what you really mean," the blue-eyed man answered, trying to respond like a normal patient. "Go ahead, doc, stick me."

Just as Dr. Wagner was about to aspirate Mr. Rivers' knee, one of the detectives who was watching the emergency room looked inside the cubicle.

Dr. Wagner then inserted a sixteen-gauge needle into Mr. Rivers' knee and drew off 105cc of blood. The detective felt weak and left in a hurry. The blue-eyed man was relieved; he did not want any gunplay in the hospital ER.

"That's close to a new record," Dr. Wagner said.

"That's great, doc. I always wanted to be famous. What now?"

As he dressed the wounds and wrapped an ace bandage around Mr. Rivers' knee, Dr. Wagner explained that he wanted him to go home and keep his knee packed in ice for the remainder of the day. He wanted Mr. Rivers to call Dr. Schwartz later in the day to fill him in on the events of the night.

Not likely, the blue-eyed man said to himself.

"That feels a lot better, Dr. Wagner."

"It should. Once all that pressure is relieved the pain decreases significantly. Limit your activity. If it starts to swell again call Dr. Schwartz. Marie, please get him some crutches, and then he can go."

The blue-eyed man looked at his watch at 7:05 A.M. He looked around and saw several cops guarding the exit of the emergency room.

"Miss Romero, is there any way you could call me a cab? I didn't want to wake up any friends in the middle of the night so I took a cab here."

"Sure," Miss Romero answered. She walked over to the clerk and had her call a cab. Fifteen minutes later, Miss Romero herself, after giving the blue-eyed man her home phone number, personally placed the blanket-wrapped Mr. Rivers in the obligatory "hospital policy" wheelchair, and pushed him past the police guarding the exit to the emergency room. The detective who watched part of his aspiration stood at the exit and looked at the blue-eyed man as he passed.

"That must have really been painful," the detective said.

"It was," the blue-eyed man answered. "Don't let anyone ever do that to you unless you are unconscious or very drunk," he joked with the detective.

Nurse Romero then wheeled Mr. Rivers out to the ramp behind the ambulance entrance and to the waiting taxicab. She helped the blue-eyed man into the cab, and as the taxicab pulled away, watched him wave his final goodbye to Kings County Hospital.

* * * * * * * * *

By 11:00 A.M. Wednesday, Brian was convinced that the killer had somehow escaped from the hospital. He accepted the inevitable, and concluded that the man was incredibly brilliant, or incredibly lucky, or both. He walked back to ENT to check on Willie, and was pleased to find him doing well. There was no further swelling and the prognosis was good. Other than a scar approximately two inches in length, and his severely wounded pride, Willie would return to normal.

Brian left Willie and rounded up Paulie and Tommy. He left the two of them in the hospital supervising the questioning of everyone who had anything to do with Mr. Carson from the minute he entered the hospital until he left for the next world. Brian returned to Manhattan for a meeting with the mayor and the chief of detectives, both of whom insisted on hearing about the fiasco, as the mayor called it, in person.

With his best condescending voice, the mayor's aide began to speak. "Detective Walsh, please explain how something like this can happen. How the biggest and the best, and the most highly paid I might add, police department, cannot prevent the murder of one individual, when you know when and where he is going to be murdered."

"Mr. Mayor," Brian answered, looking directly at the mayor and totally ignoring his aide, who Brian, and Sal for that matter, thought was a complete asshole, "we are not sure how, but it is obvious that the man we are hunting was able to murder Mr. Carson and somehow escape our trap. We don't even know how Mr. Carson was murdered. We will have to await the results of the autopsy. As for how he escaped, we don't know that either."

The mayor's aide started to say something, but before he could get a word out, Brian looked directly at him, pointed his right index finger at his face, and threatened him between clenched teeth. "Don't say a fucking word; not one fucking word!"

The mayor's aide had completed his conversation for the day. The mayor was not foolish enough to go to his aide's rescue.

"What are you going to do now?" the mayor asked Brian.

"Keep doing the only thing we can—try and catch the son-of-a-bitch and try to keep the last juror alive."

"The press will get this now," Sal added. "It's too big an event to keep quiet. I hate to say it, mayor, but if the last juror dies the killing will stop. We must do everything to protect him, but every psychiatrist in the department says this guy is not a true serial killer. It ends either by us catching him or by him killing juror #12. Detective Walsh will continue to do his best, and he has my full support."

The mayor already knew that.

Brian and Sal left the mayor, who was mumbling something about the upcoming election.

"Brian, what really happened in that hospital?"

"Sal, I wish I knew. This guy's just too good. The chief anesthesia resident doesn't know what happened. One minute Carson is alive and then he's dead. Sal, I knew the guy was coming and I couldn't stop him. Paulie and Tommy were in the fucking room when he died. If I was Stanton I'd move to Alaska or something."

"Brian, if Stanton is killed, we need to consider catching someone, if you know what I mean. Find someone, some low-life drug dealer, shoot the prick and blame him for everything. What do you think?"

"What do I think? Are you losing your mind, Sal? No one would believe that. There isn't a drug dealer alive smart enough to pull off any of this stuff. The mayor will just have to live with it. No one from my squad is going to blow their career for him."

"You're right, it was a stupid idea. Just get the prick, Brian, please," were Sal's departing words.

Brian drove back to the squad's office, sat down, and reviewed the events of the day. He knew Stanton was a dead man, so he reasoned: why not use him as the ultimate bait? The only chance Stanton had to live out his life span was for Brian to get the killer before he got Stanton. It was that simple. No one could protect Stanton forever; not the whole New York City police force could protect the sniveling fool forever.

Brian drove out to Bayside. He was tired and needed a soft shoulder to cry on. He hated to end his career this way. He was actually starting to look forward to retirement. Maureen was very sympathetic and reassured him by reminding him that they did their best and that was all anyone could do. And thank God Willie was going to be okay. Brian could not bear to tell her that God had nothing to do with it.

Chapter 33

By Friday September 6th, the blue-eyed man was recovering nicely. The swelling in his knee was down considerably, and it appeared he would escape without an infection. He walked without crutches, but still had a slight limp. It looked like he would eventually be as good as new, and now he began the final touches on his plan to kill Harold Stanton.

He was taught by his teachers that once a job was over you erased it from your mind—no second guesses, no accolades—and moved on. Learn from your successes and failures yes, but move on. Today he would allow himself the small pleasure of reviewing the murder of Lawrence Carson in his mind. Someday he would share it with others, for the man knew there would be no way for the pathologists to figure out how Carson died. Even if they suspected it, their queries would come only after the more common causes of death had been ruled out, and then it would be too late. He sat back and congratulated himself on what was probably his finest moment. He took Detective Walsh's challenge and defeated him; he defeated the best New York had to offer. He would not let this go to his head, but he would enjoy the moment.

As he relaxed in his chair, Lawrence Carson's autopsy was in full progress; the blue-eyed man of course did not know this. The autopsy was started on Thursday under the watchful eyes of four pathologists—the chief medical examiner, an expert in forensic pathology from Cornell, the chief of pathology of Kings County Hospital, and Dr. Susan Blakely, who was there at Brian's insistence, as he respected her honesty.

The knowledgeable staff of four, and their assistants, spent all

Thursday and Friday dissecting every aspect of Lawrence Carson's being. Toxicology studies were begun immediately after his death, and more split samples were sent to several reliable labs throughout the country. Every vital organ of juror #11 was examined. As time went on, the pathology team became more and more apprehensive. The cause of death was not obvious. It must be some special toxin, they began to think, because gross and microscopic examination of every one of the victim's organs examined to that point were completely normal.

The forensic pathologist, Dr. Alan Murray, who was recognized as one of the leading experts in the field, was given the assignment of removing and examining the heart. While the others watched, he removed the heart by cutting the great vessels—the aorta, the right and left pulmonary arteries, the right and left pulmonary veins, the superior and inferior vena cava—and then placed the heart on a metal tray. The heart lay on the tray for several minutes while he palpated the vessels in the body cavity, noting that they were free of clots. He carefully opened the heart, and with that cut, any chance of ever finding what actually killed Lawrence Carson evaporated into thin air. None of the four ever entertained the possibility of an air embolus, which would require opening the heart under water. It was, after all, the rarest of all deaths. The microscopic sections would be inconclusive, revealing only slight anoxia, but no infarction. Two days of gross examination, and several more microscopic examinations by virtually everyone in the pathology department, revealed nothing significant.

Over the next week, the toxicology studies returned. Without a doubt, the only chemical in Carson's body was morphine, and the concentration was such that it could not possibly have had anything to do with his death. The results were confirmed by several independent labs, all using split samples. The final cause of death would have to be listed as unknown, but natural; most probably some type of cardiac arrhythmia.

The chief medical examiner called Detective Walsh on Friday September 13th with the bad news. That the call would come on Friday the 13th was not lost on Brian, who was angry.

Brian had never dealt with such a man before—a man who could bring death and destruction at will and not be detected. Who had this kind of power, and who, if anyone, could stop him? For the first time, Brian began to think that no one could. *Desperate times call for desperate measures*, he thought to himself as he began to formulate a plan. He knew it would be his last chance at the man, for there was only one juror left.

* * * * * * * * * *

It was Friday September 13th, and the blue-eyed man's knee had improved significantly. He had started exercises for his knee, and his strength was returning rapidly. His own estimate was that he was almost ninety percent normal. This could not be said of Dr. Jeffery Schwartz, however, who had heard about Mr. Rivers' visit to the emergency room and was now very distressed at not being able to contact Mr. Rivers. Every day the first question he asked his staff was whether anyone had heard from Mr. Rivers since his surgery. Dr. Schwartz had never seen a complication this severe from a simple arthroscopy, much less from one where he didn't have to do any actual surgery. He was concerned that maybe he had missed something, and poor Mr. Rivers had some disaster where he bled to death. *Maybe Rivers has a bleeding disorder*, he thought to himself. The relief Dr. Schwartz felt when he received the call from Mr. Rivers at 4:15 P.M. that day could not be measured by any method currently available.

"Hi, doc. Sorry I never made it back."

"I heard about the bleeding you had and the visit you made to the emergency room. Can you come right over now? I want to see your knee?"

"No need to, doc, everything is fine. The sutures are out, the swelling is completely gone, and I feel great. My pain is all gone. I don't know what you did, but the knee is as good as new."

"That's just it, you know I didn't do anything. I tried to call you at your number since last Wednesday. Where were you?"

"I had to go out of town on another business trip. I'm fine, doc; don't worry about it. Thanks again for everything," the man said as he hung up.

Dr. Schwartz hung up much relieved, but shaking his head, not having any idea as to how he helped Mr. Rivers. He would never know.

* * * * * * * * * *

When Harold Stanton was told of Carson's death by Paulie on Friday September 6th, he lapsed into a stupor, which even by his standards was quite severe. He did not leave his apartment for the following week. By September 13th Paulie had grown tired of Stanton's foolishness. Paulie knew that he could keep Stanton alive locked in a four-room apartment forever, but the cost would be prohibitive, and very boring. It appeared to Paulie that Stanton would be satisfied to have the NYPD wait on him hand and foot for the rest of his life, and Paulie had no intention of letting that happen. Brian worried that the killer would get impatient and try something desperate, risking the lives of some of his men. He knew the killer wouldn't stop at eleven jurors. Brian had discussed with Paulie getting Stanton to request another fishing trip. It would be another trap for the killer and their last chance to get him, and although it was a long shot, Brian knew that long shots occasionally do pay off. He once bet a hundred dollars on a long shot in the Breeders Cup Classic just because Jerry Bailey was riding the horse, and when it won at over a 100-to-1, he walked away with over ten thousand in cash. Maybe it would happen again. Brian hoped so, because he could not think of anything else to do. Stanton did not look like he was making a major contribution to society, but Brian Walsh was a police detective and he would not give up until every possibility was exhausted. He would put all his energy, and all the skills of his men, into this one last battle of his one last war.

Brian spent the weekend relaxing, as much as that was possible. He spoke to Brian Jr. in Florida, who told him that his daughter-in-law was doing well and was still pregnant. This information—that he would shortly be a grandfather—had a strangely calming effect on him. It gave new meaning to what he did. He was the one who made it possible for normal people to go on with their lives; he was the one who helped to remove the scum from the street so they couldn't hurt others again. He was perhaps the last line between sanity and chaos, and at times it was a very, very thin line.

Monday morning Brian had Paulie tell the officers guarding the apartment that Stanton wanted to go fishing again, even though Stanton did not know it yet. It was the information the blue eyed man may have wanted to hear, but he did not hear it the way Brian thought. The microphone in the bulletin board in the squad's office was transmitting, but no one was listening, as the blue-eyed man had his people abandon the apartment across the street just after the death of Carson. The blue-eyed man would hear it from Stanton himself, through a small transmitter in his kitchen that was installed by a Latin-looking, pizza deliveryman prior to the death of Knox, and prior to the almost live-in supervision of Stanton.

The blue-eyed man listened to the tape with amusement as Stanton told Paulie late Monday afternoon that he was afraid to go fishing, and that even though he loved fishing he didn't love it enough to die for.

"You couldn't protect Knox and Carson, so what makes you think you can protect me?"

"They wouldn't listen to us," Paulie partially lied. "Knox went out of town—remember, Harold, he died in Maryland—and Carson had surgery at the biggest hospital he could find. Keeping it small is the secret, Harold. I have no trouble finding cops who want to go fishing with you. We'll fill the boat with cops and go at night; you told me that you like night fishing better anyway. We'll decide on the night we're going at the last minute; no one but you and me will know. I would like to go also. I'm getting as bored as you are with this apartment. You must be going fucking nuts."

"I am. I'll go, but I want to decide when. It has to feel right. I know you don't think much of me or my life, Detective Lucero, but it's all I have."

"I understand, Harold. I really do," Paulie answered, with some true compassion for the man who he knew would probably never see another Thanksgiving or Christmas.

Brian hoped the killer would get on the boat with Stanton, but he knew he was too smart for that. No, the hit would come either just before Stanton boarded, or more likely, as he was leaving the boat at the end of the trip. The latter would probably be best, Brian thought, since the killer would assume that many of the fisherman would be drunk and tired and easily confused, but he prepared for both contingencies. Brian knew that the man expected the boat to be packed with police, but that would not stop him. If the display of force at the hospital did not stop him, twenty cops on a boat wouldn't either.

Brian outlined his plan at Thursday morning's staff meeting.

Prior to the meeting he had removed the microphone from the bulletin board and discarded it, planning to never tell anyone of its existence. He decided that the killer was smart enough to figure out when Stanton was going fishing without any help from him, and there were some aspects of the plan that he needed to keep secret.

"People, it is very simple. Perhaps the hospital plan was too complicated; we'll never know how he got away, but the past is the past. We're going fishing with Harold Stanton on Thursday September 26th, weather permitting. It looks to us like the hit can occur in only one general area, but at any of four times. The killer will not go on the fishing boat with us; that's a given. He'll therefore try to get Stanton either as he gets on the boat, as he gets off the boat when returning, or on the boat while it is either just leaving or returning to the pier. We have discussed this in detail with the best sharpshooters the department has, and they have been out at Sheepshead Bay over the past few days looking at the possibilities. Their conclusion is that, although a shot could be made to a target on the boat while it was leaving the harbor or returning, the shot would be quite difficult and very risky. For example, we doubt that the man would plan to make the shot as the boat was leaving, not having any control over where the victim would be standing. Stanton might go to the head to take a leak, and the short time for the shot would disappear. The killer would either have to wait several hours, hoping not to be discovered, or leave and try some other day. A similar problem would occur on the return trip, although that's more of a possibility since, if the shot was not possible, he could wait a few minutes and get Stanton as he walked off the pier. The lighting would be a problem at that time of the morning, however, according to the team who looked at the area at one o'clock this morning." He pointed to the end of the pier on an enlarged picture Betty had placed on the bulletin board. "The glare of the lights on the boat makes it a difficult shot, until he gets to this area here. As you can see, the pier narrows at this spot, just as he would get on or off the boat, and the lighting is perfect. The sharpshooter told me he could make that shot ten out of ten times from the roof of at least three of the buildings in range of the pier."

"Boss," Tommy interjected, "why are you so sure it would be a shot? He only used a gun once, on that guy Sanchez, and that was at close range. Maybe he will just blow up the boat."

"I don't think so, Tommy. He hasn't killed anyone who was not associated with the trial. Believe it or not, I don't think he wants to have any innocent victims," Brian answered.

"Tell Willie that," Tommy returned.

Willie said nothing.

Brian continued, "Obviously, Stanton could also be hit getting on the boat, and this must be considered a real possibility. The only downside for this, because the lighting is surely much better, is the high level of traffic in the area at that hour, both pedestrian and automobile, particularly if the weather continues to be nice and warm. His escape would be more difficult, but judging from his performance at the hospital, he may handle it easily, so this would be our second choice."

"Who will be on the boat?" Willie asked.

"Paulie and I will be on the boat, and Willie and Tommy will be on the pier. At least half, or possibly more, of the fishermen will be cops. There will be cops on every rooftop, except these three," he said, pointing to the ones to be left open for the killer. "And cops in every restaurant. There will be cops ready to block every street that could possibly be used as an escape route, and even those that can't. This will essentially be a dragnet once an attempt is made on Stanton."

"What does Stanton think of all this?" Willie asked.

"He thinks he's going fishing, which hopefully he is," Paulie added.

"The long-range weather looks good, so keep your fingers crossed. I doubt he would attempt a shot like this in the rain, so we would abort the trip," Brian said. "As to Stanton's safety, he'll be wearing a vest, and a helmet under his fishing hat."

"A helmet? What the fuck is that?" Tommy asked. "You mean like a football helmet?"

"No, the SWAT guys have this small helmet very similar to a baseball helmet that protects the back of the head and the sides. They say it's effective."

"Why don't we just put him in a steel box with his face sticking out?" Tommy joked. "Then, when he's shot, we can just close it like a coffin."

Nobody laughed, mostly because they all felt Stanton was a dead man. Tommy just had the balls, as usual, to say it. With that comment, the meeting ended.

* * * * * * * * * *

Brian and Paulie drove to Sheepshead Bay early Friday morning for an appointment with the captain of *Widow Maker*. They wanted to reserve several spots for a fishing party they were having for the Police Benevolent Association on Thursday September 26th. The captain was very helpful, and, as it turned out, he would be able to give them the whole boat. This time of year the number of fisherman decreased significantly, and they had a sistership that could handle any overflow. He would be happy to support New York's finest and would do his best to show everyone a good time.

"Just do everything as you ordinarily would," Brian told the captain. "Nothing different or special, please. And don't tell anyone about who your passengers will be; you never know whether some nut would want to wipe out twenty-five police officers," Brian continued as he watched the captain's smile acutely disappear.

On Saturday morning, September 21st, the blue-eyed man placed a tape in his recorder and listened to Paulie tell Stanton that the NYPD had chartered a fishing boat for the sole purpose of making Harold Stanton's life more pleasurable. They would be going night fishing next Thursday, September 26th, weather permitting. No one would be on the boat except the crew and police officers, including Detective Walsh himself.

"Harold, you will be safer on that boat than in this apartment. You will wear a bulletproof vest and a helmet under your hat. You will enjoy yourself. My God, how much TV can anyone watch?"

Harold smiled as he said, "If I'm going to die it might as well happen when I'm having fun."

"You won't die, Harold," Paulie answered uncertainly.

A helmet, the blue-eyed man said to himself. *That will be interesting.*

The blue-eyed man immediately sent for a car and headed to the Queens Midtown Tunnel and onto the Long Island Expressway. He turned onto the Van Wyck Expressway, which took him to Southern State Parkway and finally to Merrick, on the south shore of Long Island. He wanted to have a final look at the boat named *Yellow Tail*, owned by

Aaron Richardson. He drove to Merrick Bay and had lunch at the quaint restaurant overlooking the marina. It was a gorgeous day, and yet *Yellow Tail* was still in her birth. The blue-eyed man had previously discovered that Mr. Richardson was an attorney in the export business and very often traveled to Europe. His secretary told the IRS agent who called that Mr. Richardson would be away for the last three weeks in September. She was quick to add that Mr. Richardson's accountant would be happy to help the agent if necessary. The blue-eyed man assured her that it was not a significant matter, and it could wait until Mr. Richardson's return.

The blue-eyed man finished his broiled scallops, walked down the pier in the direction of *Yellow Tail*, and struck up a conversation with the only boat boy on duty.

"They have you working alone today, on a Saturday?" the man began.

"I'm the only one left. All the rest went back to college. I go to Hofstra, so I can work on the weekend."

"That's a gorgeous boat," the blue-eyed man said, glancing at *Yellow Tail.*"

"It sure is. There are only a few wooden boats still around, and that's the best one. Mr. Richardson once told me he'd sooner get rid of his wife than that boat," the boy laughed. "But he hardly ever uses it. He only takes it out when the weather is perfect, and usually only for a short run to keep the engines working. He pays me twenty dollars a week just to keep an eye on it."

The blue-eyed man did not like hearing this last piece of information.

"So you work every night then?" the man asked.

"No more. There's no one here at night anymore, since the season is ending and the boats don't go out that much during the week. It's pretty much a weekend crowd from here on, and that slows down very quickly this time of year. When the first cold weather comes the smaller boats will be pulled for the winter." The boy walked over to the gas pump to service a small fishing boat.

The blue-eyed man took one final look at *Yellow Tail*, casually strolled back to his car, and returned to Manhattan.

That night he practiced several hours with the bulbous-tipped device he knew he would soon be using and collected his scuba gear. There would be no time for a test run; it would have to be right the first time. The helmet he heard about this morning would cause him to change his plans slightly—he would need special bullets. With everything considered, he knew it would come down to the weather; the seas had to be calm.

Chapter 34

Brian woke up early on Thursday September 26th. He knew this would be either his finest hour, or his biggest failure, in a career that spanned over thirty years. He spoke to Sal the day before and got the impression that Sal wanted it over one way or the other. The fact that no one from the press put the murders together was unbelievable to both of them. In reality, though, there was only one definite high profile murder—Elizabeth Anderson—and the department was still actively working on that case, with an arrest imminent, according to the police liaison. The press had their suspicions, but they were only suspicions. There was never any clear-cut evidence of anything else. The press did not know of the accidental deaths, and certainly did not connect Chang and Anderson. Knox and Carson were ruled accidental and natural by the best physicians around. Nothing was ever published about a jury. There was still only one murder, and thankfully that was the way it was being treated by the press—a savage assault by four deranged animals.

Brian ate breakfast with Maureen, who knew what this day meant to him. She begged him to be careful and then they kissed good-bye. Brian headed for work in the red Jaguar.

* * * * * * * * * *

The blue-eyed man slept late on Thursday, resting for the night of his life. Carson was more intellectually challenging, but this would be more physically demanding. He was thankful his knee was back to normal.

Stanton was his usual bland self, and did not seem that excited about his upcoming fishing trip. Paulie arrived at Stanton's apartment about 11:00 A.M. and found him moping around.

"Harold, cheer up. It's a beautiful day. We'll have a great time tonight and you will be perfectly safe," Paulie reassured him.

"Do you think so, Detective Lucero? Do you really think so? Do you think I will be safe?" Harold Stanton asked, in a very serious, but almost childlike, fashion.

"Yes, Harold, you will be safe. I myself will be right beside you every step of the way."

"Then I will go, and I will enjoy the fishing."

Harold spent the rest of the day getting ready for the trip, although he didn't seem to be doing anything.

Brian and the rest of the squad orchestrated the disbursement of all the members of the team attached to Operation Fish Hook, as the plan to capture the assassin was named. Throughout the day, as inconspicuously as possible, members of the New York Police Department infiltrated the area around the docks of Sheepshead Bay. They were disguised in every manner possible, from sanitation workers, to Con Edison employees, to women walking with their baby carriages. Several police officers were even assigned the pleasant duty of fishing on the early boat trips so they would blend in nicely with the late-day crowd when they returned. The weather, to everyone's relief, was beautiful—seasonably warm with no significant wind.

At 5:45 P.M. Paulie turned to Harold Stanton and said, "Lets get ready, Harold," and he helped Harold into the vest and the helmet, which was actually quite comfortable, and which was well concealed by Harold's fishing hat. They left his apartment for Sheepshead Bay and the uniquely named fishing vessel, *Widow Maker*.

Paulie reached the pier at Sheepshead Bay at 6:45, after taking a very indirect route, and Stanton immediately walked from the dock onto the boat. Paulie winced when Stanton walked through the narrow area where the sharpshooter said the shot could easily be made. No shot. Good news for Stanton, bad news for the police. Brian was already on the boat, and he nodded to Willie, who, posing as a mate, cast off the line and stayed on the pier with Tommy.

Harold immediately got out of sight and stayed that way until the boat was long out of the harbor. He performed this disappearing act without any help from Paulie, who actually wanted Harold to stay on deck and act as a target. Of course Paulie never told Harold that, but it was Brian's plan. Now the hit had to occur as Stanton got off the boat at the end of the trip. With this knowledge, there was a wave of relief, which moved rapidly through the "fishermen" on the boat. They could relax for the next several hours and be ready for the assassination attempt, which would occur as Harold Stanton walked down the pier at 1:05 A.M.

Widow Maker pushed her way to open water. The seas were calm, and there was not a zephyr of wind.

"It'll be a great night," Harold said as he emerged from his hiding place. He was ready to fish.

The blue-eyed man and his driver left Manhattan at 5:00 P.M. The traffic on the Long Island Expressway was the usual crawl, and they arrived in Merrick at 6:38. The scuba gear was carefully packed in several bags, which disguised their contents nicely. The plan was for the two men to simply walk up to the boat and load the equipment. Then the blue-eyed man would take off alone, leaving the other man, of almost equal capability in all matters, to deal with any problems that arose.

The blue-eyed man was pleased to see that the boat boy was correct; there was no one there except the customers at the restaurant, who were of no concern. The plan unfolded exactly as designed. The blue-eyed man started the engines of *Yellow Tail* at exactly 6:52 and pointed the old, beautiful, elegant wooden boat out into Merrick Bay, taking great care to follow the speed limit so as not to call attention to himself. His partner watched from the pier, and when the boat began to speed up, raising a glistening wake behind it, the blue-eyed man's partner left Merrick and drove to the next rendezvous spot to begin his long wait.

The blue-eyed man gunned the engines of the boat as soon as he was past the five-mile-per-hour speed zone and set course for Jones Inlet. The first part of the trip would be quite enjoyable. The boat was an old wooden Lyman, a boat very popular in the 1960s. It had new twin 75-horsepower engines and could move along at a much better clip than the blue-eyed man expected. The man appreciated the work Mr. Richardson put into the boat to restore it to its original form, and the upgrades that were necessary to allow her to carry such power. He felt somewhat sad that this would be her last trip.

The warm fall air blew through his dark brown hair, and he thought of the night in Saratoga earlier in the month. *Life could be good with her*, he smiled, and that jolted him back into reality. In his line of work he could not think of the things that make normal people happy. If she knew what he was she would leave him in a second.

He piloted *Yellow Tail* under several bridges and soon had Jones Inlet in sight. Darkness had not yet come as he skillfully navigated through the inlet and pointed the old wooden boat directly out to sea. Her last voyage would be the longest one she had taken in many years. The man would eventually head west, but he had hours to kill and work to be done.

Approximately ten miles west of *Yellow Tail* the fishing vessel *Widow Maker* also headed out to sea. The blue-eyed man hoped the tracking device he installed during his trip on the *Widow Maker* would still function, but in the end it really didn't matter. He plotted every one of her stops and could easily find her with his handheld global positioning system. Even if that failed, he laughed, the two boats were lit up like Christmas trees, and a blind man could find them.

The blue-eyed man continued offshore, and then eventually turned *Yellow Tail* west. He was now traveling at a low rate of speed. He had assembled a fishing rod so it appeared that he was trolling, although the last thing he wanted to see was a fish.

Widow Maker drifted in her first of many fishing spots, and to the surprise of almost everyone on board, Harold Stanton hooked into a small blue shark, which fought dearly for its life. The fish lost, and Harold was elated. He asked permission to remove his helmet and vest and Brian agreed, knowing that he was safe out on the ocean. The fishing continued and Harold was soon ahead in both pools: the pool for the biggest fish and the pool for the most fish. He would, ironically, die a winner.

Stanton and his police bodyguards continued their assault on the fish of the Atlantic, but the catch was not bountiful. Those days were long gone in these over-fished waters. At least the weather held. They fished all the captain's favorite spots, including the secret ones, the captain assured Brian, where he only took special guests. At every stop they were tracked by the blue-eyed man in his boat.

It was getting late as the captain circled his last stop, the spot where fish were always caught. There was an old wreck that attracted the small fish, which attracted the big fish, and every captain knew he could keep his customers coming back with a few big fish at the end of the trip.

The blue-eyed man was ready. He had slipped into his wet suit and his scuba gear was assembled. His placed his clothes in a small waterproof bag, which he would tow behind him during his swim. He took out the metal tubes that to an ordinary citizen would look like useless pipes; but as he began to assemble them, the deadly shape gave away their use. It was a special type of rifle, with a strange bulbous tip and a tube hanging from the bulbous end. The rifle was wrapped in a waterproof bag to protect it during the long swim.

Yellow Tail was now drifting approximately one mile from *Widow Maker*, and she was invisible in the black night. Her lights had been out for some time, and her windshield with the huge volume of glass had been smashed and removed completely when she was far out in the ocean earlier in the evening. The blue-eyed man calculated the time he would need and removed a hand drill from one of his cases. He had already moved anything that could possibly float into the cuddy cabin and locked the door. He then began to drill several small holes in the bottom of the beautiful old boat, which began to immediately take on water. As the boat began to fill, the man continued to get ready, and when everything was set he slowly slid over the side of *Yellow Tail* and started his journey of death. He had calculated exactly how long she would take to sink, and made enough holes so that it would be quick but quiet. He swam on top of the water for a short distance until he was sure *Yellow Tail* had sunk, looked up at *Widow Maker* and *Tight Lines*, which was about two hundred yards to her east, and then swam underwater to the west side of *Widow Maker*. He swam slowly but deliberately. He towed two small pouches and pushed a much longer one, which he held out like a spear gun. He wanted to get within two hundred yards of the fishing boat before he took his first look. When he got to the estimated spot, he slowly came to the surface, knowing full well from his trip on the fishing boat that, because of the bright lights, no one would be able to see him. He reached for the two pouches he was towing and pushed away the soft one with his clothes. He opened the other one and removed a special monocular telescope, which put him the equivalent of twenty feet from the boat. *Perfect.* They were fishing on the ocean side of the boat, drifting towards shore. He knew that would be the case because of the tides, but he was glad to see things developing as he planned. He would need to get at least a hundred yards closer to attempt the shot. To the best of his knowledge, no one had ever made a shot like this—while floating on the ocean, aimed toward a boat one hundred yards in the distance. No one would expect it. No one would believe it.

The blue-eyed man slowly and quietly swam on the surface, closing the gap to *Widow Maker*. He could hear the laughter on the boat as another fish was landed. While he was swimming, he reached forward and began to slowly pump air into the bulbous device that was attached to the underside of the barrel of the rifle. He did this by using the small pump attached to the device, not unlike the pump used to inflate a blood pressure cuff. As he squeezed the small hand pump, more air was forced into the larger rubber support, and the tip of the rifle became more buoyant. The rifle had a very long barrel, enabling it to shoot accurately over a longer distance, but its end had to be supported by something since it was out of the man's reach. The bulbous cushion, when filled with air, would lend this support. The blue-eyed man would rest the rifle on the cushion of air, inflate it to the proper level, and then take the shot at Stanton. He stopped swimming, looked again through his telescope, and saw Harold Stanton, who was standing between Detective Walsh and Detective Lucero, both of whom the blue-eyed man easily recognized. He felt sorry for them both, but there was nothing he could do now. Stanton had to pay, just like the others. He would wait for the moment. He looked through the scope on the rifle and could easily see Stanton, who the blue-eyed man happily noted was not wearing a helmet. He adjusted the pump on the bulbous device and inserted the two exploding bullets into the special chamber. The flat seas made it easier than he anticipated; if they would hold for only a few minutes longer. He let the rifle barrel float in the water on the bag of air and allowed himself to float freely. He carefully looked into the riflescope, studied Stanton, and waited for the right moment.

Harold Stanton fished between Brian and Paulie, feeling very safe in that position. They were all having a good time, and the boat would be heading back to Sheepshead Bay shortly, so everyone was trying to catch the last fish, which was worth some big money in the pool.

"You were right, Detective Lucero. This was a great idea. Thanks for making me go."

"I'm glad you had fun, Harold, although I'm not happy you took all our money," Paulie joked.

"Did you have fun, Detective Walsh? You don't look like much of a fisherman," Stanton said to Brian.

"You mean you don't think I had fun catching those two puny sea robins?" Brian answered sarcastically.

Stanton laughed and replied, "Don't give up yet. This is the best spot. I always catch fish here."

"What do you mean the best spot? How do you know? You can't tell exactly where you are," Brian asked.

"That's not so. The captain comes to this same spot every night. The same exact spot. He does it with satellite navigation," Stanton countered.

Brian got a horrible feeling in the pit of his stomach. If Stanton knew that, then the killer knew that. He was just about to turn to speak to Stanton again when a warm liquid splashed onto the left side of his face. He wasn't sure what it was until he turned to his left and saw the right side of Paulie's face covered with blood and some gray material—and Stanton was gone. He looked back and saw Stanton's body sliding on its back across the slippery deck; most of his face was missing. Stanton's lifeless body slid to the opposite side of the boat with such force that it almost tumbled into the ocean. Brian looked out over the ocean and saw nothing through the bright lights of *Widow Maker*. He thought he heard what could have been a gunshot just after he felt the warm fluid on his face, but now he wasn't sure.

"Turn the lights off, captain!" Brian yelled.

The captain acted quickly, but the blue-eyed man was already five feet below the surface of the water and going deeper. He headed north to the beach. He would have at least a three mile swim, but he could do that easily. While he was swimming he pulled out his knife, punctured the bulbous device, and let it fall to the bottom of the ocean. He subsequently dissembled the rifle and dropped each piece as he swam along. Even with the remote chance that any one piece would be discovered, its identity would forever be a mystery. The only thing he kept was the small pouch with his clothes, his flashlight, his compass, his knife, and his portable global positioning system. As he continued his swim, his partner, who had driven him to Merrick earlier in the evening, waited at a prearranged location on Atlantic Beach.

Brian looked carefully out over the dark ocean and saw nothing but the lights of a few boats in the distance, certainly too far away to have anything to do with the shot that just killed Stanton.

"Jesus Christ, Brian. A shot from a boat. SWAT said no fucking way when you asked them that," Paulie yelled. "No fucking way."

"Tell that to Stanton," Brian said as he ran to the captain.

"Captain, how many inlets go out to the ocean around here, within, say, twenty miles of this spot?" Brian asked.

"Well, there's Rockaway Inlet, East Rockaway Inlet, Jones Inlet, and then Fire Island Inlet, but that's about thirty miles away. So you have three, and of course New York Harbor isn't that far away."

Brian called Willie on the phone and told him what happened.

"Willie, call the Coast Guard and have them stop every boat going back into every inlet from Rockaway Inlet to Fire Island Inlet, and I mean every fucking boat. And send every police boat we have in New York Harbor to the south part of the harbor and do the same thing."

Brian was barking orders more out of desperation than of any real expectation that the man would be caught. He knew his escape would be perfectly planned; if he could get out of the hospital he could certainly get off the open ocean.

As those thoughts passed through Brian's mind, the blue-eyed man continued to swim towards Atlantic Beach, unaware that he was now being tracked by something not human.

On *Widow Maker,* Paulie covered Harold Stanton with a blanket, but left him lying where he died on the deck of the boat. Brian and Paulie cleaned up, which included removing part of Stanton's brain from their hair. Paulie was particularly distraught; he had never seen a man with his face blown off before, much less one that he was standing next to and talking with. Brian had another flashback to Vietnam, where he had seen this all too often.

The fishing boat pushed on to Sheepshead Bay at full speed. Brian and Paulie sat watching over Stanton in death, just as they did in life. No one said a word. It was the end, but not the end they wanted.

The blue-eyed man was about to have the fight of his life. He continued to swim towards the beach, and was halfway there, when he made a necessary course correction after checking his compass and the specially built waterproof global positioning system. It was the correction that gave him a fighting chance. He had taken out his flashlight to better see the global positioning system, whose lighted dial had stopped working. It was then that he saw the shark. The shark made a quick pass and bumped his tank. The blue-eyed man's knife was out in an instant. This was no small blue shark that could be frightened away. It looked to be ten to twelve feet in length, and more than a match for the blue-eyed man. *It's a Mako, or maybe even a Tiger.* How ironic, he mused, to almost complete the task he worked on for over a year and die at the hands of a fish. No, he would not let that happen. Better and smarter had tried and failed; he would not succumb to the fish. He quickly swam to the surface and pulled off his air tank. He pushed the tank under him and tried to climb as high as possible. He wound up with only his chest and upper abdomen above the water. While partially draped over the tank, he outlined the tank from above with his flashlight, hoping that no one but the shark would see the light. He had to chance it, though, as the shark was the immediate threat. The fish looked up at the shadow and hit from below, lifting the tank and the blue-eyed man out of the water. The shark clamped down on the tank for just a moment, and, with all the strength he could manage, the man wrapped his stronger right arm partially around the shark, letting the beast pull him into the ocean. Using his left hand, he stuck his knife deep into the belly of the shark just forward of the pectoral fin, and used all the skills he had accumulated over the years fishing for the beasts to locate its heart, which he continued to cut at with a vigorous side to side motion, hoping desperately to hit it even once. The shark continued to fight but the blue-eyed man held on. He knew he would have to let go soon to try to get back to the surface for air, but he also knew that letting go would give the shark an even greater advantage than it now had. He cut faster and faster with the long knife, and, as the shark's flesh tore, the cuts became easier, and the man cut deeper. The shark slowed down its violent shaking ever so slightly. The blue-eyed man could hold on no longer. He pulled his knife out, let go with his right hand, and watched as the shark swam away.

The man reached the surface, gasping for air. He knew the battle was not over. He waited quietly and tried to catch his breath. His experience told him the shark was circling and would soon attack again. He could see the waves breaking on the shore but it was too far for him to swim with one spurt; the shark would surely attack if he tried. He waited for what seemed like an eternity, and then he saw the fish. The shark was obviously hurt, but it was slowly skimming the surface and heading for the blue-eyed man. Was instinct telling the fish it had finally met its match? The man hoped so. Unfortunately, that proved to be wishful thinking, as the shark speeded up and headed for the man. The shark's mouth opened and snapped shut on the man's left thigh, but there was no violent shaking. The shark was dying. The man, without regard for his leg, plunged the long knife into the shark's head, right through where the blue-eyed man knew its brain to be, and deep into his own thigh. This linked them in mortal combat, as the two killing machines would fight each other to the death. The only thing that was clear was that at least one, and very probably both, would die in the ocean, just a few hundred yards off Atlantic Beach, on this beautiful and peaceful evening.

The man was grateful that they were now floating on the surface, but he realized that other sharks would soon be attracted to the blood—both his and the shark's—that permeated the water. He pulled the knife out of the shark's head and realized that the beast was dead. He pried the fish's mouth open and carefully pulled his leg out of the fish's huge mouth. The leg was bleeding, but everything appeared to be functional. He shivered to think what would be left of his leg if the shark had that grip when it was not dying; his whole leg would have been ripped to pieces and probably torn completely off, and he would float on the ocean waiting to be eaten alive. *That could still happen*, he thought, and he began to swim as quietly as possible to the shore. The blue-eyed man was exhausted. Every movement of his arms was an effort. He did not even attempt to kick his legs. He made slow but steady progress towards the beach, being ever so grateful that the tide was carrying him to the beach faster than his feeble attempt at swimming. When he was thirty yards from the beach he heard loud splashing behind him, and when he turned he saw what he recognized to be a feeding frenzy. A school of smaller sharks had found his latest victim. He swam the last thirty yards as fast as he could, and landed on the beach with the help of a breaking wave. He collapsed into a pile, unable to move another inch. He rested for a few minutes and slowly removed his swim fins, which had miraculously stayed on during the battle. Everything else was gone now—the knife, the global positioning system, his flashlight, and his clothes. A quick assessment told him it would be better to be caught in a wet suit bleeding to death than nude bleeding to death, so he headed for the rendezvous spot wearing what was left of his wet suit.

His waiting partner was very concerned. The blue-eyed man had never been this late before. He was able to monitor the police radios and the Coast Guard channel with the special equipment in his car, and the level of activity told him that the hit had occurred. The escape should have been uneventful. He waited in the bushes just above a small dune, and soon saw the blue-eyed man struggling up the beach, walking, but falling every few steps. The blue-eyed man fell for the final time and lay motionless. His partner reached his side and recoiled at what he saw. The wet suit was shredded terribly, and the left leg of the suit was missing. Fortunately, a leg, although a very torn and bloody one, protruded from what was left of the suit.

"Kevin, what happened?" his friend began.

"A shark. Can you believe it? After all we've been through, a fucking shark almost kills me. I got Stanton, though. I got them all, David. I got every last one of them," he said as he passed out in David's arms.

David now had a big problem, for he could not go to any hospital. That was forbidden by the organization. He would have to kill Kevin and leave him if death was certain—standard organization policy. "No fucking way," David said to himself as he carried the blue-eyed man to the car as fast as he could and sped for Manhattan. Kevin was still alive, with a rapid but forceful pulse, but he had lost a lot of blood and was going into shock from the blood loss. David had placed a pressure dressing on his left leg, which controlled the bleeding, and was now on the organization phone barking orders. The necessary codes were used and the Latin-looking man who received the call sprang into action. Cars were sent to meet David and the blue-eyed man on the expressway, to act as blockers. The organization's physicians were called and were soon present at the compound. The nurses arrived, and the appropriate blood for the blue-eyed man, A positive, was obtained.

Within twenty minutes of David's call, the medical team was ready and waiting in the most modern treatment/operating room that an unlimited source of money could assemble. There wasn't a hospital in Manhattan that had better equipment, or for that matter, better trauma physicians. The organization did in fact stretch far and wide, and its members were truly dedicated. Nothing would be spared to save the blue-eyed man, the man who had done so much for so many, and at such great personal sacrifice.

The blockers led David from the Long Island Expressway through Manhattan to the compound in record time, and the blue-eyed man, who was now conscious, was rushed to the treatment/operating room where his wounds were assessed. An IV was immediately started and his hemoglobin checked. The result of 6.8 was startling, and blood was immediately hung. Lifesaving blood that had previously been matched to the patient and kept frozen at great expense was now flowing through a blood warmer and into the blue-eyed man's veins.

The trauma surgeon and the orthopaedic surgeon examined Kevin. The orthopaedic surgeon, who was a close friend of Kevin's, and who went through the program in the early stages with him, announced to everyone's relief, "False alarm. The pain-in-the-ass will live. Kevin, you must be the luckiest guy alive. The leg wounds will require a lot of my handiwork, but neurologically you are intact and there are no obvious fractures. Just a lot of small bleeders, but you missed all the big vessels. We'll get x-rays in a few minutes, after we get more of that blood in you. How do you feel?"

"Thanks for asking. Maybe we should have one of the nurses sew me up. I can't take my shirt off in public after the scar you put on my back the last time you worked on me," Kevin joked with his friend.

"And you still haven't figured out that the drug dealer with the chain saw might have had something to do with the size of your scar. David, I thought you told me Kevin here was one of our brightest people. Maybe he missed the part of the manual that says you shouldn't go swimming at night; you know, the part of the survival manual that says sharks feed at night. Have that section copied for him to read while he sits on his ass for the next few days."

The crew who worked on the blue-eyed man had no idea what he was doing in the ocean, and knew enough not to ask.

Kevin stabilized quickly and x-rays were taken. The orthopaedist was right; there were no fractures. The treatment area was converted to an operating room with the addition of certain instruments, the closure of certain doors, and the flick of a switch, which turned on the laminar flow ventilation. The anesthesiologist present gave Kevin some IV sedation. Kevin's wounds were washed with large amounts of antibiotic irrigation and he was given intravenous antibiotics. It took almost three hours to repair the lacerations on Kevin's left leg, chest, and arms, but in the end everything looked remarkably good. There was a large drain exiting the deep wound in his left thigh, and he had bandages everywhere, or so it seemed. No one had ever seen him injured so severely, certainly not by a human. The blue-eyed man was brought to a special area where nurses would care for him around the clock, even though he felt that it was overkill. But, just as he expected those under him to obey his orders without question, he knew that the doctor was in charge in this situation, and he obeyed.

Widow Maker pulled into her birth at Sheepshead Bay at 12:45 A.M., back earlier than usual for obvious reasons. The medical examiner was present and began his investigation immediately on the boat. After looking at the obvious, Stanton's body was removed. The cause of death would not be a mystery this time. "Very few people can survive without half a head," were the ME's parting words to Brian.

Brian didn't even hear him. Sal was on the pier, and pulled Brian aside.

"Listen, Brian, you did everything humanly possible to save them all. Now it's over. Do you hear me? It's over. This is going down as just another murder in Brooklyn, and I'm giving it to Brooklyn to investigate. Your man is gone and that's that. Leave it be. This will die down eventually. Even the death of Anderson is dying down. Everyone, including the radicals, realize that sometimes things just happen and you have to get on with your life. Go home. That's an order, detective. Go home to Maureen and meet me for lunch Monday. Now get out of here, and take Paulie, Tommy, and Willie with you. This fucking case is over, and thank God for that." Again, God had nothing to do with it.

Brian told Tommy and Willie to take the rest of Friday off, and that he would see them again on Monday. He got into Paulie's car and they drove back to Manhattan so Brian could get his car. The case would never be over in Brian's mind, as long as the man who killed thirteen people on his watch lived. Unfortunately, the blue-eyed man knew this as well and he could not have any loose ends. Detective Brian Walsh was a loose end.

Chapter 35

By Sunday night, three days after the attack, the blue-eyed man showed his usual amazing recuperative skills. The drain had been removed and there was no sign of infection. He walked with crutches and could put some weight on his left leg. He was still very sore, but there were no feats of strength planned in the immediate future. He would still have to deal with Detective Walsh, but that could wait for now; Walsh wasn't going anywhere. All that talk he heard on the tapes about his retirement may have fooled the others, but the blue-eyed man knew better—there would never be retirement for Detective Brian Walsh until he knew and dealt with whoever murdered the Robert Johanson jury. As the blue-eyed man recovered from his injury, he formulated a plan to solve his dilemma.

* * * * * * * * * *

The weekend was terrible for Brian. Nothing Maureen could do or say could get through to him. Brian did not take failure by others well, but he could not begin to tolerate failure in himself. Even calls from his children could not change his depressed mood.

"Maureen, I will never be happy again until I get this son-of-a-bitch. He blew Stanton's fucking head off right in front of me. He made a fool of the squad and me in front of the whole world. I know it sounds ridiculous, but I have got to get him. He's some kind of fucking monster."

Maureen let the F-word slide this time.

Brian sat around thinking about the man all weekend. He had concluded long ago that this was a specially trained assassin who probably got his training in the military. Brian had known men like that before, and for a short time in Vietnam, was not very unlike the man. Brian just did not have the stomach for the work. But this guy knew much, much more than even the best-trained soldiers Brian had ever seen. Who trains such a man, and for what? What else has he done? Are there others like him? And what the fuck does this all have to do with a simple sign maker named Robert Johanson? Why can't anyone figure this out?

Maureen's level of concern increased significantly at 7:30 P.M. Saturday night when she noticed that Brian, for the first time ever, could not finish his steak at Peter Lugers. When they returned home she called Sal, while Brian sat in the den in a stupor after emptying almost half a bottle of Scotch.

"Hi, Maureen, how's Brian?"

"Not well, Sal. And Sal, friend or not, you listen to me. Brian took this case to save your hide. You better figure out a way to get my old Brian back or I'm going to be one very unhappy wife who may just write a book about the whole mess. And I'm not kidding. Do you understand me, Mr. Chief of Detectives?"

Sal was speechless. He had never heard Maureen speak like this before and had no reply. He had always heard that you never piss off an Irish woman but he thought it was just a saying. It took a few seconds to find his voice. "Maureen, you know Brian is my best friend. We'll work something out, I promise you. We're having lunch Monday, and I'll get him to understand. He'll listen to me. Maureen, it should be over now. Stanton was the last one," Sal stumbled.

"Well it's not over for Brian. Just come over and look at him and you can see it's not over. You better make it be over, Sal, and I mean it. Brian told me everything about this case," she lied, "and I'll go to the press if I have to. How many publishers do you think would want a book written by Mrs. Brian Walsh? And believe me I'm not kidding."

Sal knew Maureen was not kidding.

"Relax, Maureen, everything will be okay, I promise. Make plans to go on a vacation and I will make him go. Take him to that place

Tommy's always talking about, and get him out of here."

"What place?"

"Paradise Island, in the Bahamas. He needs to get away."

"I'll do just that. But you make him go. Fire him if you have to."

"I can't do that, Maureen, but I'll make him go. Goodbye, and don't worry."

* * * * * * * * * *

Monday morning September 30th began with a gloomy Brian addressing a morose squad.

"People, as you know, with the death of Harold Stanton," Brian began as he placed a line through Stanton's name on the board, "the serial killer responsible for the death of thirteen people will probably disappear forever. The murders of Stanton, Sanchez, Anderson, and Chang will never be solved. The disappearance of Michael Thomas will never be solved, and the accidental or natural deaths of Champion, Delaney, Johnson, Herman, Knox, and, unbelievably, Carson will remain just that—accidental or natural deaths, whatever they choose to call them, although we all know differently. The only murders that were solved were Mason and Horowitz, who shot each other, but we all know that it did not happen that way either. I've thought about this all weekend, as I know you all have. I don't know what to say. We were beaten by a superior individual. We lost the Super Bowl 50 to 0, and that's that. It's over. My first thought was to spend the rest of my life looking for this guy, but I don't think I would ever find him, and if I did, he would probably win again. No, Sal is right. It's over. We will go back to what we usually do, perhaps a little more humble, and use this as a learning experience. I want no guilt feelings from any of you, no second-guessing, no looking back. We will look forward, and do the best we can. Maybe chance will bring the killer our way again, and we will do better, but we will not look for him. Would anyone like to say anything before we try to get back to normal?"

"I don't mind the prick getting away," Tommy started. "He wasn't the first and he won't be the last, and I can live with that. I just wish I knew why it all happened. Who was Robert Johanson anyway?"

"I wish I knew, Tommy. Every piece of information we have, from our files to the FBI's, says he is just a simple sign painter. Maybe he had nothing to do with anything. We will never know, and we will have to live with that," Brian answered.

There were no more questions.

* * * * * * * * *

Brian met Sal at Ryan's at 1:00 P.M.

"Brian, I got a call from a very pissed off detective's wife Saturday night," Sal cautiously began. "Any idea whose wife that could have been?"

Brian smiled and answered, "Maureen told me. I once told you never to piss her off. I wasn't kidding. Relax, I'm over it. I realized Sunday that there was nothing more we could have done."

"Thank Christ," Sal yelled loud enough for half the patrons in Ryan's to hear. "Thank Christ. It's over now, Brian. Forget about it. I want you on a vacation and that is a direct order from, if I might para- phrase Maureen from the other night, Mr. Chief of Detectives, not your friend Sal."

"I'll go. I'm actually looking forward to getting away. The past five months have been a nightmare, and I've neglected Maureen. We talked all last night and we're leaving for the Bahamas on October 12th for two weeks. I might even read a book."

"That would be much better than Maureen writing one," Sal laughed.

Brian began to laugh also, and Sal was relieved to see the old Brian coming back so quickly. Sal could not know that it was all an act. Brian had vowed to himself Saturday evening that he wound never rest, and that he would devote the rest of his life to finding the man who stood no more than six inches in front of him that night in the hospital. How different things would have been if that door was not locked, or the glass was not so thick, or if Willie was not injured. Brian would have battled the blue-eyed man until one of them was dead, and as far as Brian was concerned, it would have not mattered who it would have been.

* * * * * * * * * *

The blue-eyed man continued to improve and began his rehabilitation. By Saturday October 5th he was working out daily, not at his
usual pace but making steady progress. The sutures were still in his deep
leg wounds and they pulled on his skin as he did his exercises. The physical therapist was amazed at his pain tolerance, even though she had
worked with him before. He was one of the best-conditioned individuals
she had ever seen. His strength was incredible, but his muscle bulk was
much less than the weight lifters she worked with, and she had no reasonable explanation for his exceptional power. She did not understand
why this was so, but she kept her place and did just what was expected,
although she was dying to do much more, but he never asked.

The squad was almost back to its regular routine, except that
Tommy was quite unpleasant to be around. It seemed that Margaret
would not be Mrs. Tommy O'Neal, as he had thought. She literally disappeared out of his life a few weeks previously, without warning, and
without a trace. He thought things were going well, and although she did
ask for some time to think things through after their trip to the Bahamas,
he felt certain she would come around. Obviously, she felt otherwise. He
checked her apartment, but she had moved with no forwarding address.
She must have found a new job out of town. He would recover, but it
would take some time. He would probably be a strain on the rest of the
squad for a few months.

* * * * * * * * * *

Willie's wound healed nicely, but there was something slightly
different about him. Even Brian noticed the change. He was more docile
since the injury. Brian's experience in Vietnam taught him that staring
almost certain death in the face had different effects on different men.
Brian felt Willie would get over it with his first altercation.

Brian actually felt much better inwardly. Once he made the decision that he would continue to look for the man, he seemed at peace with
himself. Outwardly, he looked almost bubbly, telling everyone he was

looking forward to the trip to Paradise Island. In reality he was. He would go on the trip to make Maureen happy, and come back and spend the rest of his life hunting the tall man with the blue eyes.

Brian did not notice the man who shadowed him from morning to night. The man was given the assignment immediately after the injury to the blue-eyed man. The blue-eyed man wanted to know what would happen to the squad after Stanton's death, and targeted Brian as the obvious one to follow. The man who followed Brian was a master of disguises and would never be noticed. He even followed Brian into the police station on two occasions, but purposely avoided the squad room. It was in the station house that the man following Brian heard about the trip to Paradise Island. When he reported the information on Tuesday October 8th, the blue-eyed man sat and smiled. He would be ready to meet Detective Walsh in the Bahamas, ironically, on the blue-eyed man's turf. *How easy could it get*? the man thought. Walsh would be in the Bahamas for two weeks, and that would allow the blue-eyed man to tie up some other loose ends.

On Wednesday October 9th, after the blue-eyed man finished reading the transcript of the Robert Johanson trial again, a copy of which he had even before Brian, he called his team together for a meeting. There were others who had to pay as well. Patrolman Leroy Phillips was the key. Phillips would tell the man what happened in the alley. He will not want to, and he may resist for a while, but in the end the man knew he would tell all. Why would he be any different than any other man the blue-eyed man interrogated? They all eventually tell; some just take longer than others. The blue-eyed man guessed that Phillips would be faster than most.

"I want to be in the Bahamas two weeks from today. That will give me a few days to take care of Walsh, so I want to wrap up everything in New York by then," the blue-eyed man began. The group of five included the blue-eyed man, who was known as Kevin to the others; the Latin-looking man, named James; David, who saved Kevin's life; the man who followed Brian, named, ironically, Brian; and a man named Michael, who had listened to the tapes from the squad room for Kevin. What their real names were nobody really knew, and David had joked that his name was changed so many times he truly could not remember what his birth name was.

"Have the boat sent to Paradise Island and be sure it arrives before the 12th," the man said to the group. He did not have to tell who to do what; this was a finely tuned machine that had worked together for years, and everyone knew their roles.

"I want Phillips picked up and brought to the warehouse on the 16th. We will talk to him then. I want a tail on the moron they call Wild Clyde, who must be connected to this in some way. There's another sack of human waste called Ray-Ray. I want him dead before I leave for the Bahamas. Nothing fancy, just a typical street killing. Make no attempt to make it look like anything other than a drug deal gone bad. And farm it out to another department; you guys have better things to do. Any questions?"

There rarely were any questions.

David spoke to Kevin after the meeting and asked, "How's the leg doing?"

"Amazingly well, David. You know you saved my life that night. I won't forget that—ever."

"By my count that would make it Kevin four, David one," was David's smiling reply.

"Get to work," the blue-eyed man smiled.

Chapter 36

Brian and Maureen arrived at Nassau airport at 1:15 P.M. on October 12th. Maureen was amazed at the beautiful blue-green water she saw from the plane. It was nothing like New York. Tommy was right; this really looked like paradise. Unfortunately, he was also right about the cab drivers. Brian and Maureen held on for dear life during their ride to Atlantis. The Atlantis Hotel was breathtaking. They were given an oceanfront room with a view that seemed to go on forever. There were water slides and a giant aquarium, which housed all kinds of fish, including sharks.

Over the next few days they roamed the grounds of the hotel and became one again. The horror of the past five months was left behind, even in Brian's mind. He began to realize that the capture of Stanton's killer was just like any other case, and did not have to ruin his life. A few days after their arrival, the metamorphosis was complete when, on the night of October 16th, they made love for the first time in several weeks. *The old Brian is finally back*, Maureen thought as she dosed off in Brian's arms.

* * * * * * * * * *

Patrolman Leroy Phillips was not doing as well in New York. On October 16th he was picked up by a group of "detectives" and brought to an old warehouse, where he thought he was going to assist in an interrogation. It never occurred to him that he would be the one being interrogated. The detectives and Patrolman Phillips arrived at the warehouse at 9:45 P.M. Phillips was grabbed and tied into a chair. He did not resist. The chair had armrests, and Phillips' hands and wrists were taped to the armrest with duct tape. The blue-eyed man walked into the warehouse at 10:05. By then, Phillips was very nervous. He realized that these people were not police detectives, but he could not figure out exactly who they were. They didn't look like anyone from Wild Clyde's group, and certainly were not Mafia. He was either too smart or too afraid to ask. He thought he was relatively safe since it took a lot of balls to whack a cop in New York City. What he did not realize was that Mr. Balls himself was now walking straight towards him.

"Good evening, Patrolman Phillips. I hope you are as comfortable as possible under the circumstances. I want to ask you a few questions," the tall, blue-eyed man began.

"Who the fuck are you and what's this all about? I'm a cop, for God's sake. You can't do this," Phillips blurted out.

"I'm sorry, Patrolman Phillips, perhaps I did not make myself clear, and I will therefore forgive you your breach of etiquette this one time. I will be asking the questions, not you. Do you understand?"

"Fuck you. I'm not answering any questions until I know who you are and what this is about!"

As the blue-eyed man reached behind his back, David placed a small club in his hand, which the man raised above his head. With all the force he could manage, he swung the club down on Patrolman Phillips' right hand, literally smashing it into a pulp. Phillips' knuckles were flattened between the immovable armrest of the chair and the club, but one had to look quickly, for the swelling that began almost immediately was truly remarkable. The yell from Phillips was deafening. He tried to jump out of the chair but he couldn't.

"That, Patrolman Phillips, is what TV cop shows call an attention getter. Do I have your attention, Patrolman Phillips?"

Phillips could hardly speak, but the blue-eyed man had his absolute undivided attention.

The blue-eyed man was right; Phillips would cave easily. *He would probably admit to being pregnant*, the man laughed to himself.

"Patrolman Phillips, I am going to ask you some questions about the Robert Johanson case, where you rescued a girl named Nancy Tailor in an alley. Before you answer, I want you to know that I know exactly what happened in that alley," the man lied, "and I'm only asking you for corroboration. I tell you this because I want you to know that, if I even think you are lying, the pain you feel in your right hand will be nothing to what you will feel elsewhere. Do I make myself clear?"

"Yes, sir," the enlightened Patrolman Phillips answered.

"Go ahead and tell us exactly what you saw when you walked into the alley," the man continued.

"A black lady came screaming out of the alley, and I went running into... AWGH," Phillips screamed as the club came smashing down on his left hand.

The left hand now looked worse than the right, if that was possible.

After a few minutes of watching Phillips writhe in pain, David bent over to look at Phillips and said, "Listen, asshole. There was no lady in that alley—not black, white, purple, or green. My friend is being patient with you. Take a good look at what used to be your hands. Now imagine what your dick will look like, because that's next."

Patrolman Phillips began to speak so fast that they had to slow him down.

"Slow down, Patrolman Phillips. From the beginning, and leave no detail out," the blue-eyed man commanded.

"I heard some screaming in the alley and ran in, and I saw Wild Clyde's crazy brother Jerome raping the little girl. I mean she was only five, but Jerome is crazy; everybody knows that. He was raping one of his own kind. He's fucking crazy, I tell you, fucking crazy," Phillips cried out excitedly.

"What happened then?" the blue-eyed man continued.

"I pulled him off, and he recognized me. He knew I helped his brother sometimes, and he laughed and ran off. I was so mad I wanted to shoot him, but I let him go, thinking I could do myself some good with his brother, if you know what I mean. I called Wild Clyde on his cell, and he told me to find another guy to hang the rape on. That's it. That's the whole truth. I swear."

The blue-eyed man whispered something to David, who left to make a call and then returned. Two of the "detectives" then walked out of the room.

"What about Robert Johanson?" the man continued.

"He was just an old guy in the neighborhood, that's all. He didn't have a family or anything, so I decided to hang it on him. I figured no one would care. Besides, if I didn't do what Clyde said I was a dead man; it was that simple. It was Johanson or me."

"What did Wild Clyde give you for your help?" the man asked.

"Ten grand, and some coke to sell."

The questioning stopped, and Phillips began to breathe easier. He began to think he would live through the night. The men, who said they were detectives but obviously were not, were waiting for someone.

After sitting in his chair for thirty-six minutes, Phillips got his answer when Wild Clyde walked into the room escorted by the two men who left earlier. His crazy brother Jerome was dragged by the biggest man Phillips had ever seen and thrown into a pile on the floor. The blue-eyed man shook the hand of the giant, who then walked out of the room. Jerome was tied hand and foot and was going nowhere. Clyde was too smart to move.

The blue-eyed man introduced himself to Clyde and his brother as Detective Kevin O'Reilly. He said he belonged to a special force investigating crooked cops and that Phillips was suspected of being one of those.

"I don't know anything about anything," Clyde began. "I never saw this cop before. I want my lawyer here now. Right now. I'm not saying another thing. You kidnapped me, and I'll sue the city for that."

"What about you, Jerome? You ever seen this cop before?" Detective O'Reilly asked.

"No way. Fuck you, anyway. You cops are all dickless fucks anyway. Get my fucking lawyer here now!"

"What about in an alley, like, say, when you were raping little Nancy Tailor?" O'Reilly added.

"Fuck you, dickless!" was Jerome's reply.

The blue-eyed man reached down to the human pile of shit on the floor and grabbed Jerome with his powerful right hand. As he lifted Jerome to the standing position, he stealthily slid his gun between Jerome's legs with his left hand and pulled the trigger, letting Jerome fall to the floor in a bloody pile.

"Who's dickless now?" the man asked without any emotion.

The sight of dickless Jerome bleeding all over the floor, squirming in pain, and screaming like an animal immediately led both Clyde and Phillips to the conclusion that they would not live through the night. No cop does that to anybody and leaves witnesses. Clyde spoke first.

"I'll tell you anything you want to know. Phillips is a crooked as they come. He's on my payroll every fucking month. You'd be doing me a favor by shooting him right now. I can make you guys so rich you wouldn't believe it. How much fucking money do you make anyway?" Clyde asked Detective O'Reilly.

"I don't know," the blue-eyed man answered. "Maybe two or three in an average year."

Looking puzzled, Clyde asked, "Two or three what?"

"Million," the blue-eyed man answered truthfully as he used Patrolman Phillips' gun to shoot Wild Clyde right between the eyes. He then turned and shot Jerome twice, once in the heart and once in the brain. He turned to Phillips and said, "Nice shooting, Patrolman Phillips." David handed Kevin Wild Clyde's gun. Phillips knew he was a dead man and began to beg for his life. He volunteered to give up every crooked cop he knew. Kevin wrote down every name, and when he was finished said to Phillips, "I'm thinking of letting you go. If there is one innocent cop on this list I will come back and kill you and your whole family in the slowest way possible. Are you absolutely sure?"

"I swear on my mother," Phillips truthfully answered.

Kevin looked at him carefully, decided he was telling the truth, and then shot him six times with Wild Clyde's gun.

The blue-eyed man looked down at the lifeless bodies of Wild Clyde, Jerome, and Phillips, shook his head, and faintly mumbled, "For this he died?" He turned to David and said, "You know what to do. Follow the plan exactly."

The blue-eyed man walked out alone, without any remorse for what just happened, but with a tear forming in his right eye.

* * * * * * * * *

On Thursday October 17th the blue-eyed man walked to a courier service on the west side of Manhattan and sent two packages: one to Judge Morton R. Levy at his office, and the other to Mrs. Levy in

Scarsdale. The package being sent to Judge Levy was larger, and had a copy of the receipt for the package sent to his wife. The instructions were explicit to the courier service, and if carried out properly, both packages would arrive at the same time on Friday morning October 18th. *Time will tell*, the blue-eyed man said to himself as he handed the courier a hundred dollar tip.

The package arrived at Judge Morton R. Levy's chambers at exactly 10:00 A.M. Friday morning and was brought to him by his new executive assistant. Levy opened the package and found a videotape and a second very well-wrapped package. There was also a sealed envelope with instructions to "open first" on the outside. Thinking he received some sort of present, he opened the letter and began to read:

Dear Judge Levy:

You have been judged by a higher court, and have been found to be unworthy to sit on the bench. The final straw was your mishandling of the Robert Johanson trial, which resulted in the conviction of an innocent man. There is no dispute about the matter. The innocent man is now dead, and I hold you responsible. The only option you have is the following. In the red package is a gun, which I urge you use on yourself in the following fashion. First, completely destroy this letter and everything in the package. Then take the weapon, place it in the back of your mouth, and pull the trigger. It will be painless. You are probably laughing by now, but before you dismiss the idea please review the enclosed tape. As you can see from the receipt, a copy of the tape has arrived at your home in Scarsdale and is being viewed by your wife as you read this letter. If I read of your death in tomorrow's paper, then the original tape will be destroyed. If I do not read of your death in the paper, then a copy will be sent to your daughter and every newspaper and TV station in New York. Try to be a man and go out with some dignity.

Sincerely,

Your Judge

Levy put the tape in the VCR and watched as first Rita Diaz, and then Lucille Manero, performed every sex act imaginable with him. The clarity of the tapes was amazing, and the judge felt that, somehow, some-one must have been in the room with them, but he knew that could not be so. The Latin-looking man, James, would be proud that the judge was so impressed with his work.

The judge looked at the receipt for the delivery to his wife, watched Lucille Manero's huge breasts bounce on his face for the last time, pulled the tape out of the VCR, and placed everything but the gun into the package, which he personally carried to a garbage can on the street. He then walked back to his chambers and called his wife to see if a tape had arrived. The maid answered and said that Mrs. Levy was at that very moment watching a tape that had just arrived by special delivery. The judge hung up the phone slowly, collected his thoughts, put on his black robe, placed the gun in the back of his mouth, pulled the trigger, and became victim number eighteen of the blue-eyed man.

* * * * * * * * *

The blue-eyed man sat on the terrace Saturday morning drinking his coffee and enjoying the article on the death of the Honorable Morton R. Levy, who apparently took his life because of some health problems. It amazed the man how someone's life always improved by dying. Everyone knew Levy was a completely incompetent judge, and they were now writing about him like he was Oliver Wendell Holmes. His widow was particularly upset, the article continued. The blue-eyed man smiled and hoped Mrs. Levy enjoyed the tape of *The Lion King* he sent her.

The man sat on the terrace and reflected. The end was near. There was only one loose end to tie up, and that was Walsh, who ironically enough was having breakfast at the same time on a terrace over-looking the beautiful Atlantic Ocean almost fifteen hundred miles away. In one week it would all be over.

* * * * * * * * *

On Monday October 21st the squad was all abuzz over Levy's death. Tommy wanted to call Brian in the Bahamas, but Sal had told them not to call Brian under any circumstance. If they did, he threatened, they should then come to Sal with their resignation papers all filled out, and he would be happy to expedite them. No, the good news would wait until Brian's return.

The only other event since Brian left was the death of the low-life drug dealer Ray-Ray, which was being handled by the usual homicide rotation, and about which no one was particularly depressed.

On Tuesday the 22nd a private jet carrying the tall, blue-eyed man departed from an airport in New Jersey—its destination the Bahamas. It landed in Nassau and was met by a private car, which took the man to a spacious mansion overlooking Nassau Harbor. It was the private home of the blue-eyed man, and the place he loved more than anywhere in the world, at least until last year. His houseman greeted him like a lost son, and Mr. Kevin, as he was known here, walked down to the beach to again look at the beautiful clear water that first attracted him to the area years ago. He would stay at his home for a week, and then he was needed in Kentucky. He looked over the harbor and could just make out the Atlantis Hotel in the distance. He wondered what Detective and Mrs. Walsh were doing on this beautiful afternoon.

Mr. Kevin returned to the house and made a call. The boat was ready. The weather was to be the same for the next two days, and then might change Friday. Thursday would be the day, Mr. Kevin told the man on the other end of the line; Thursday afternoon.

Mr. Kevin dined at home Tuesday and Wednesday night, and enjoyed the sun during the day. Charles, the houseman, noticed the new scars on Mr. Kevin, but he too worked for the organization and knew not to concern himself with things other than his assigned duties.

Brian and Maureen fell in love again, not that there was ever any doubt in each other's mind about the other's love, but now the infatuation was back. They had made love more times in the past ten days than they had since May, when Brian was given the case by Sal. They shopped holding hands and laughed about the silly things that lovers laugh about. On Thursday morning at seven, there was a knock on the door to their hotel room. Brian looked through the peephole and saw a black male who was definitely not hotel staff but definitely Bahamian.

"Present for Mr. Walsh," the man said.

The man looked harmless enough, and Brian saw one of the maids down the hall, so he opened the door.

"Present for Mr. Walsh," the man repeated, his large white teeth gleaming through his ear-to-ear grin, a sharp contrast to his jet black face. A piece of paper he read from said: "Willie, Tommy, and Paulie, have bought a fishing trip for you today."

"A fishing trip?" Brian answered. "Today? Where?"

"On the boat by the bridge. The boat is called *Island Girl*. One o'clock today, by the pier. You must come. You can walk there. You don't have to bring anything, just sunscreen and a hat. And good fishing luck," the man laughed loudly as he gave Brian the piece of paper. "It is all paid for," he said as he walked away.

Brian looked at Maureen, who was smiling.

"Brian, they told me they were going to do something for you, so go and have a good time. It's by the pier where we took the small boat to the Straw Market. You can't hurt their feelings."

"I never wanted to go fishing again after Stanton."

"This will be different."

"What will you do?"

"I'll go shopping. No, I'm going to go to the spa and spend the whole afternoon getting pampered. You know tomorrow is our last full day in paradise."

"God, these two weeks went fast."

"We had a great time. Remember, we can do this anytime we want when you're retired. We should enjoy our lives now. I don't know how many more years we can do what we did last night, if you know what I mean," Maureen said, winking at Brian.

"That was great, wasn't it? Okay, I'll go fishing."

Maureen called and set up her afternoon at the spa, and they strolled down to the pool to relax for a while. They enjoyed an early lunch, and then walked back up to the room. Brian prepared for his fishing trip, and Maureen left for her spa appointment at noon. Brian applied sunscreen all over his already sunburned body, put his "It's Better in the Bahamas" hat on, and headed for the pier with the directions given him by the Bahamian man. He arrived at the pier in twelve minutes and easily found *Island Girl*. The Bahamian man was already on the boat. He explained to Brian that he was the mate and that the captain would be on board shortly. He also informed Brian of their itinerary: the boat was going to pick up one other fisherman at another dock, the fish were running, and they would have a good day because the dolphin were really big this week. The captain arrived at 12:45 P.M. and started the engines.

Brian couldn't help but notice that the boat was much older than the other fishing boats at the dock, but his confidence increased when he saw that the other captains stopped to ask the captain of Island Girl which waters to fish. *It's going to be a good fishing trip*, Brian thought. In reality, it would be the last fishing trip he ever took.

Island Girl pulled out of her berth and headed slowly into Nassau Harbor in the general direction of the Straw Market, where they would pick up the other fisherman who often fished with them. He was an expert, and to have him on board was a special honor for the captain. The mate did not tell Brian that the man owned the boat, and that both he and the captain worked for him. Michael Thomas found out this information too late for it to do him any good.

Just as the boat pulled up to the dock by the Straw Market the mate asked Brian to help him bring up some beverages from down below, and Brian obliged. At that moment, a tall, blue-eyed man with a large straw hat jumped on the boat and immediately climbed up to the flybridge to talk to the captain. The boat pointed west out of Nassau Harbor, passed the lighthouse, and headed into the Atlantic Ocean, where the captain put it on a heading of due north and pushed the throttles forward to the maximum. The old boat, with her twin turbocharged engines, jumped up and threw a huge wake at the Atlantic. The mate worked hard at keeping his balance as he fitted each of the fishing poles with the trolling bait. After a twenty-minute run, which was much further than necessary to catch fish, the captain slowed down to trolling speed. The mate let out four baits, two on each side of the boat, and directed Brian to the middle fighting chair. The captain had decided that Brian would get the first fish. Brian still had not met the other man, which he thought was somewhat strange, but the man and the captain seemed to be engaged in an ongoing conversation, so Brian sat in the fighting chair as directed and began to fish. After about fifteen minutes, a large bull dolphin hit the outward starboard line, and the mate handed Brian the pole. The fish fought dearly for its life and jumped twice, but in the end Brian landed the monster, with some timely help from the mate and his gaff. Brian finally got to see the fish in all its glory. It was magnificent, and he couldn't believe its size. The mate put it in the fish box and congratulated Brian, telling him the fish was close to forty-five pounds. Pictures would be taken later, the mate told Brian. Brian was smiling like a kid.

"Congratulations, Detective Walsh," the blue-eyed man said as he climbed down the steps from the bridge to the cockpit, "that's a nice fish."

"Thank you," Brian said as he turned around, suddenly hearing his name in his mind again. *Detective Walsh*. He didn't tell anyone he was a detective. *Oh, the squad must have said something when they scheduled the trip*, he concluded. He then watched the man take off his straw hat, which the wind tried to blow away, and Brian instinctively reached for his gun, which was in New York.

"Relax, Detective Walsh, you're in no danger here," the blue-eyed man said.

The man could see Brian looking around to assess his situation. He helped Brian come to the obvious conclusion.

"Detective Walsh, you are about eight miles from land, on my boat, with my crew, who, I might add, are as skilled as I am in certain matters. There's absolutely no one else in sight. You are in what we call a hopeless situation. But please take comfort in the fact that if I wanted you dead, you would already be at the bottom of the sea, if not eaten by the sharks on your way down. I only want to talk to you, and we'll do some fishing if you like."

"What I would like is to be taken back to Nassau as quickly as possible," Brian demanded.

"And waste this beautiful day on the ocean? You'll be brought back at the usual time the charter boats return. No fishing boat in the Bahamas goes in early, least of all the *Island Girl*," the blue-eyed man said smiling. "Come with me up to the bridge; I want to tell you a story. Believe me, you will want to hear this story. And detective, please don't try to be a hero. I don't want to make your beautiful wife a widow."

The blue-eyed man climbed up the ladder to the bridge and took over the controls of the vessel. The captain motioned to Brian to sit next to the man. The captain then climbed down to the cockpit and began to fish with the mate.

"If you hook a sailfish or a marlin let us know," the blue-eyed man yelled to the crew. "I want Detective Walsh to have a shot at it. Better the fish than me," he laughed.

Brian was not amused by any of this, but he knew his position was hopeless. He would listen to the story and hope to make it back to Nassau alive to fight another day. He remembered that the man could have easily killed Willie, but he didn't.

The blue-eyed man began, "First of all, my name is Kevin. May I call you Brian?"

"Whatever."

"I will take that as a yes. It will probably surprise you, but we are very similar, and we are actually on the same side."

"The same side of what?" Brian asked.

"The same side of the law. Don't you watch any TV. They always say that," the man joked, trying to get Brian to relax a little. "The only difference is that you have a much larger rule book for your game. And make no mistake about it, it is a game. In your line of work you have to follow the rules—which are made by a bunch of fools, I might add—and answer to the political whims of the times. What is good one year might be unacceptable the next, so you have this huge political machine, including the press, that pushes you along. You are essential, and you do your job well. You must keep order for our system to work. I also am essential, and I do my job well."

"What exactly is your job?" Brian asked.

"We'll get to that later. I know you feel let down by the rulebook and would like to change many, many of the rules, but that's not your job. Others make the rules, and you follow them the best way you can. Sure, you bend them now and then, but you essentially follow them. I know your frustration when someone you know is guilty gets off because of some asshole lawyer, or some asshole judge like Morton R. Levy. You are essential to society, and I know you know that. I am also essential. My first plan was to simply go away after the death of Stanton, but I got to know you during the past weeks and I heard some things I didn't like. I don't need some homicide detective, particularly one with your ability, looking for me for the rest of his life. If I was convinced that was your goal, I would have to eliminate you as well because you might interfere with my job at some time in the future. The stakes are too high for me to take that chance. I promise you, you can be candid today. You will not die today, no matter what you say."

"What stakes? What are you talking about? You just killed, or somehow caused to be killed, thirteen people, and I don't know why. What bullshit answer do you have for that?"

"It was eighteen, to be exact. And everyone of them deserved to die."

"Eighteen? Who else?'

"Levy is dead, Phillips is dead, Ray-Ray is dead. Wild Clyde and his fool brother are dead."

"Jesus Christ, you are fucking crazy. How could they all deserve to die? Eighteen deaths? It's unbelievable. Who the fuck are you? *What* are you?"

"It's simple. I'm the referee. When the game gets out of hand, I step in. I level the playing field again. I right what's wrong."

"Do you really believe this shit? You should hear yourself. You just killed eighteen people and you're the fucking referee. You belong in an asylum."

"Brian, what you need to understand is that I killed eighteen very evil people—people who had harmed, or were harming, other people, and one in particular, Robert Johanson."

"I would love to know who he was. We could never figure out why he triggered the execution of his jury. Who was he? You must know."

"He was my father."

"You're Robert Johanson Jr.?" Brian asked incredulously.

"I was, in what seems like another life."

"We dug your grave up. You were there, fractured leg and all. What's going on here?"

"It's really very simple, but quite unbelievable. When I was at Northwestern studying political science, I was approached by a certain organization. The organization is quite large for an organization almost no one knows about. Simply put, the organization runs The United States of America. Not officially, of course, but it definitely does from a purely practical point."

"Be serious. You are fucking crazy."

"I am serious. Do you think the government is really run by those fools in Washington? They may think they do, but they don't. Sure, they do the day-to-day stuff, but the real decisions are made by others, people who have no maniacal political affiliation but care deeply about America, and even more importantly, about what is right and wrong. The organization represents the people; the common man if you will.

"Brian, it's like this boat. The boat is on a certain course, and sometimes a wave pushes it a little bit one way, and then the next wave pushes it a little bit the other way. There is a direction the boat is heading, and as long as the boat is headed in the general direction of where I want to go I don't care about the minor changes. I just let it be. If one of the waves alters the course significantly then I have to make a radical correction. The organization lets the people in Washington, including the President, push the country forward by whatever honorable means necessary, as long as it continues to move forward in the proper direction. If that stops, decisions are made at the highest level of the organization—which, I might add, has members of all political parties—and the referees step in and make adjustments. That's what I do."

Brian listened intently but still had nothing to say.

"Well, back to my father. I elected to join the organization, but I had to start over. Robert Johanson Jr. had to disappear, and he did on that turnpike in Ohio. And before you ask, they did not kill any innocent people in the crash; they were already dead. It was the hardest thing I have ever done in my life because I had to make my father think I was dead, and I knew he would be hurt. He raised me all by himself, and I loved him more than anyone could imagine. I had served the organization well, and in 1986 they allowed me to reestablish contact with my father for a few weeks each year. He would spend every April here with me in the Bahamas. Those were my favorite weeks of the year. He was taken from me by the eighteen people who are now dead. Every one of them played a part in his death. I know you read the transcript of the trial, and you must have realized he was innocent. A child could see it. If you knew him, you would know how absurd the very thought of him raping a child was. Unfortunately, at the time of the arrest and trial, I was involved in an operation so secret that there was no way for me to know about what was happening to him. I would have stopped it."

"How could you have stopped it?"

"Be serious, Brian. I can stop almost anything."

"You are starting to make me very nervous. Is this all really true?"

"It is true. I took some time off and decided to find out exactly what happened to him, and the rest is history, as they say. They all contributed to his death—some directly and some indirectly—by just not doing the right thing. One person on that jury, any one, could have voted not guilty, and there would have been a hung jury. The next judge would have thrown the case out the window. Just one juror!"

"So they all had to pay?" Brian asked.

"They all paid with the same thing they took from my father."

"Who raped the little girl? Do you know?"

"Clyde's crazy brother, Jerome. Phillips told me before I shot him."

Brian did not like Phillips, but you don't shoot a cop, not even a bad one.

"You shot him? Why?"

"He set my father up. He was a crooked cop, Brian. Come on, you had to know that."

Brian knew but kept silent. He wasn't sure who he was talking to—a raving psychopath, or a new type of policeman; one who just stepped up and killed the bad guys; one like everyone in Brian's squad wanted to be; one like Willie sometimes was.

"So all this was for revenge. Why all the subterfuge? Why the natural deaths, the accidents?"

"I didn't want anyone to discover what was happening because it would be easier for me, and also because I didn't want to jeopardize the organization. The first nine jurors were quite easy and involved no risk at all. The last three, once you got on the Anderson case, were much more difficult, both in execution·and in the degree of risk. But I screwed up with Anderson. I became so infuriated with her that I blacked out and left her genital area untouched. I didn't realize that until I saw your squad all over Knox and had the bug planted. I heard Tommy and Paulie talking one day about the lack of injury to the genital area, a real rookie mistake. I don't know why she was so hateful towards my father. Do you?"

"No, we never found a connection," Brian truthfully answered.

"From then on the game changed," the blue-eyed man said.

"What happened to Thomas? He's the only one we never found. I assume he's dead."

"He's dead. He went fishing with us one day in the Florida Keys and was eaten by sharks."

Brian turned pale, and the blue-eyed man saw the change in his expression.

"Brian, I told you not to worry," Kevin said.

"How did you kill Carson?"

"Some things must remain a secret, Brian. This isn't show and tell."

"How did you get out of the hospital?"

"Same answer."

"You think you can justify killing all those people because they were bad, some more than others, but you really can't, and you know it. Whatever you call yourself, you're just a murderer, nothing more. You say you don't kill innocent people, but how guilty could someone like Mable Johnson be? She probably didn't even know what was going on during the trial."

"Stupidity is never an excuse. Just because I didn't mean to run you over with my car doesn't help you one bit while you are bleeding to death on the road, does it, Brian? The act speaks for itself. Mable Johnson could have said not guilty. Her vote would have been the equal of eleven others, and my father would be alive today, wouldn't he? Let me ask you this, Brian. How many innocent people did you kill in Vietnam?"

Brian got sick to his stomach and vomited over the side of the bridge. The captain and the mate thought he was seasick, but the blue-eyed man knew better. He knew everything about Brian's record in Vietnam, and that Brian was now vomiting into the ocean meant that Brian knew that he knew.

"You don't have to answer, Brian. I know the whole story. After you realized what was happening you decided to stop it, didn't you. The village was full of women and children, and when you discovered that fact you stopped the attack. Your orders were overridden, and the butchery continued until you blew your first lieutenant's head off. No one said a word, and that was that. You murdered a man, a fellow soldier, an American during a war, but you did the right thing. He was an evil psychopath who enjoyed butchering and raping women and children. The right thing is not always easy, but it must be done. Brian, do the right thing and forget about me. Go back to New York and let me make you a hero."

"How do you know about Vietnam?" Brian demanded.

"We have access to everything."

"There were no records of that event...anywhere. You could not know."

"Well, obviously I know. I couldn't have guessed it, could I? I'm not clairvoyant. And we both know I didn't make it up. Let it be enough that I know."

"You are really a sick fuck," was Brian's answer.

"I've been called worse, but not called worse by better. Brian, you could have been one hell of a referee."

"What's with the hero shit?"

"Oh yes, I almost forgot," the blue-eyed man lied. "Go home to New York tomorrow and go to this address. You will find something very interesting. Trust me, you must go."

By now *Island Girl* was on her way back to Nassau, and the crew had three more dolphins for display on the dock. *A very successful fishing trip*, the blue-eyed man thought as he looked at Brian sitting on the transom absorbing the day's conversation. Brian now believed every word the man said, and that terrified him more than the murder of eighteen citizens of New York City.

The boat entered Nassau harbor, and slowly made her way to the dock by the Straw Market. As the blue-eyed man climbed off the *Island Girl* he turned with some departing words for Brian.

"Come back to Nassau the same time next year and I will find you. Please don't make me have to find you before then," he concluded as he extended his hand to Brian, who took it, although somewhat hesitantly.

The man started to leave but turned around one more time. "I'm sorry that Margaret did not work out for Tommy. Tell him she really did like him."

"What did you do with her?" Brian shouted angrily.

"Nothing. She works for me," Kevin said as he jumped onto the dock.

The boat headed for the Paradise Island pier on the other side of the harbor, where the mate insisted on taking Brian's picture with the four dolphin.

The mate's parting words were, "Sir, this never happened. For your own good, and your family's, do as Mr. Kevin says."

Brian walked back to the hotel, stepped onto the terrace of his eighth-floor room, sat down, and began to stare at a large grouping of rocks several hundred yards off shore. He soon became mesmerized by the waves breaking over the rocks, sending their spray into the air in an ever-changing kaleidoscope of shapes and colors. He wasn't sure he could tell what was real anymore. Maureen, who fortunately was real, interrupted his trance.

"How do I look, Brian?"

"Fantastic, just fantastic, honey," Brian said unemotionally.

"How was the fishing?"

"Unbelievable, honey. Truly unbelievable."

"We should come here again, Brian, we really should."

"We will, honey. Same time next year."

Just at that moment room service arrived, bringing a gift of Champagne with a card from Willie, Paulie, and Tommy.

"Not another gift?" Maureen asked.

Brian just grunted on his way to the shower.

After his twenty minute shower Brian seemed to have his senses back. No, it was not a dream. Unfortunately for eighteen people—nineteen counting Johanson—it was all very real. He dressed, called the airlines, and discovered that his reservations had already been changed. He lied to Maureen, and told her that Sal had called and wanted him back as soon as possible. Brian took Maureen to the Boathouse Restaurant that Tommy had raved about. After an unbelievable dinner of steak and lobster, cooked by a master Bahamian chef right at their table, they gambled in the casino and had a wonderful last night in Paradise, which culminated in bed at 2:35 A.M.

* * * * * * * * *

When Brian and Maureen landed at LaGuardia Airport just before noon the next day, they were met by two cars; one brought Maureen to Bayside and the other rushed Brian to the squad's office. Willie, Tommy, and Paulie were anxiously waiting for Brian, who had called them from the Bahamas telling them to be ready, although ready for what was not explained.

Brian walked into the squad room and was immediately greeted by Tommy, who couldn't wait to tell Brian about Judge Levy.

"He blew his head off? God, I wonder how he got him to do that?" Brian answered.

"Who got who to do what, boss?"

"Forget it, Tommy. Just forget it."

"Did you and Maureen like Paradise Island? What did I tell you, boss? Is it paradise or what?"

"You were right, Tommy. It was the most exciting and beautiful place I have ever been," Brian truthfully answered. "Trust me when I tell you, I will never forget the experience." Brian turned to Willie.

"Willie, did you check the address? Who lives there?"

"Wild Clyde. What's going down?"

"I don't know, but I got a tip."

"You got a tip?" Paulie asked. "You got a tip in the Bahamas?"

"Don't ask. Let's go, people."

The four detectives drove to the address on the lower West Side and walked cautiously up to the third floor. The apartment was quiet. Willie opened the door with his special tool, and the four detectives ran into Wild Clyde's apartment with guns drawn. They would not need guns today. They could not believe their eyes. There were four bodies on the floor—what was left of Patrolman Phillips, Wild Clyde himself, and his younger brother Jerome. Brian had no idea who the fourth body was, but he had no doubt why he was there. Even more surprising were the numerous pictures of Elizabeth Anderson that were scattered all over the room—pictures of her very alive, pictures of her very dead. There was a book, which had been nicely fabricated by James, showing payoffs from Wild Clyde to a long list of crooked cops. Brian smiled. He knew Clyde's and his brother's fingerprints would be all over every piece of evidence.

"Brian, what the fuck is going on here?" Willie asked.

"I give you the four animals who butchered and raped Elizabeth Anderson," was his answer.

"No way. No fucking way," Tommy answered.

"Get the crime lab here, right now, and let's see," Brian ordered. "I guarantee you that when they search the rest of this place they will find enough evidence to prove that these four scumbags killed Elizabeth Anderson, and maybe twenty other unsolved murders," Brian added sarcastically.

Chapter 37

On Monday October 28th the lead article in all the New York newspapers was a story on the capture of the four men who brutally attacked, raped, and murdered Elizabeth Anderson, one of New York's finest teachers, in April of 1995. The description of the shootout between Detective Walsh's squad and the perpetrators was particularly exciting—especially for an event that never occurred. Each article had its own slant, but the Daily News tried to please everyone with, "Through the diligence and perseverance of an elite squad of detectives led by Detective Brian Walsh, and backed up every step of the way by Chief of Detectives Sal DeCicco, and with the total cooperation of the mayor's office, these animals were brought to justice." The mayor was quoted as saying, "This fine police work should be a warning to any other criminal that New York's finest will not rest when an injustice such as this is perpetuated on any citizen of this great city. The fact that a police officer was involved should further demonstrate our determination to apprehend, arrest, and convict any criminal, no matter who he might be."

Sal had no idea what happened, and really didn't care. He had his murderers, and the city didn't have to go through the emotional trauma and expense of a trial. Brian just wanted to be left out of the whole charade.

Everyone in the police department was relieved that the investigation had come to an end. The department's spin doctors were already at work putting a positive side on the capture of Patrolman Philips, telling anyone who would listen that the NYPD would not hesitate to shoot its own.

The blue-eyed man would never be relieved. The Bahamas would not be the same for him ever again. But it was time to get back to work; he had been sent for. The organization's jet left Nassau Airport on Tuesday October 29th with one passenger, and pointed northwest to Lexington, Kentucky. The jet landed at 10:15 A.M., and the man who used to be Robert Johanson Jr. was met by a blond woman driving a British Racing Green Jaguar. The blue-eyed man climbed into the driver's seat and drove through the horse country of Kentucky. He loved driving through the winding narrow roads bordered by the white fences over which one could see into the endless fields of bluegrass. Some of the foals had been weaned, and there were herds of future Kentucky Derby hopefuls running up and down the hills of each farm that he passed as he drove deeper into the bluegrass country. *Such a peaceful existence*, he thought to himself. He let his mind wander to thoughts of Brenda, who was now the closest thing to family that he had. He drove to a very special farm, which was the field headquarters of the organization he served, and where Kevin, as he was known here, received his orders. As he approached the farm he jolted himself back to reality. He was a referee, and that was all he could ever be. It was the life he chose many years ago, and it was a job he felt was necessary for the good of all. He truly believed every word he spoke to Detective Walsh that day on the boat. He would have no problem dying for those words; he knew that someday he would.

The farm itself was over four thousand acres, and to all outward appearances was a fully functioning horse farm with all the necessary equipment to masquerade as such, including a training track and a huge band of broodmares. The farm sold many of its yearlings at the sales. It was reported to belong to a very wealthy but reclusive man. No one would ever be able to trace the ownership of the farm, no matter how sophisticated the investigation, for the owner simply did not exist.

The farm, however, changed radically at its very center, where approximately one hundred acres were used as the operational base for a vast organization to which no one seemed to belong and of which no one seemed to know. The heart of the building was below ground, and was as secure as was humanly possible. The living quarters would make the manager of the most lavish resort jealous. People lived at the farm for months at a time, and were able to do so very comfortably.

The blue-eyed man was coming off an extended leave of absence, and was reporting to his controller, Johnathan Pierce, who had new orders for him. Mr. Pierce had been with Kevin from the very beginning, and there was a deep mutual respect between them, but that was all that was permitted. The organization worked on a need-to-know basis, and Mr. Pierce was really just a conduit from those above. Kevin and Mr. Pierce accepted their orders with blind obedience, as did every other successful member of the organization. The ones that did not—and they were few and far between because of the comprehensive screening method used—just disappeared. Kevin had been with the organization since 1982, and he was clearly the best at what he did. In fact, he was the best ever at what he did.

The green Jaguar stopped at the main gate of the horse farm where its occupants were thoroughly checked, and identified as Kevin and Tanya. The Jaguar itself was electronically scanned as it sat over a special grate. When cleared, Kevin guided the Jaguar through the winding roads of the farm to the control center where the car disappeared into an underground garage. Kevin and Tanya emerged from the car and were met by four members of security, who confirmed their identity. Tanya disappeared, and Kevin headed for Mr. Pierce's office.

"Kevin, my boy. Welcome back," greeted Mr. Pierce, who was at least twenty-five years Kevin's senior.

"Thank you, Mr. Pierce, it's good to be back."

"A cognac Kevin?"

"Yes, thank you, Sir. That would be nice."

"Did you have a fruitful leave of absence?"

"Yes, Sir. I accomplished everything I needed to."

"So I heard," Pierce replied, handing Kevin his cognac. After a significant pause Pierce continued, "I am so sorry about your father. By the time I heard it was too late."

"I know. It was unavoidable. Just an incredible series of bad events. If only I had not been so occupied with that Russian project. I was out of contact for so long."

"I heard you made the necessary corrections."

Kevin sat in silence sniffing his cognac.

"Kevin, what are your immediate plans?"

"I thought you sent for me for an assignment."

"I did. I was instructed to send for you. This morning I was given the reason. But before we get to that, I want you to take a few weeks off and rest. I know what you have been through. Get this all behind you, as best you can. Go to the races. I know you love Keeneland, and the horses are running there now, because of the construction at Churchill Downs.

"Yes, there's someone at Keeneland now that I should see. I owe her that."

"Go then, and I'll see you two weeks from today," Pierce said as he stood up.

"What's the assignment?" Kevin asked.

"It can wait until we talk in two weeks."

"I would prefer to know it now, Sir. You know how I like to think things out in my mind."

"Are you sure? It's a tough one."

"Yes, Sir."

"Very well," Pierce said as he handed Kevin a large envelope. "It's a straight assassination. They would like it to be an accident, if possible, but that's not mandatory. He must be dead by the date shown."

The blue-eyed man opened the envelope, whose seal was already broken by Pierce, and slowly pulled out the 8x11 photograph of his next victim. Kevin didn't move or say a word for several minutes. He just stared at the picture and listened to his heart pound. Time passed in slow motion, and finally the blue-eyed man looked up at Pierce.

"There must be some mistake. They can't be serious."

"There's no mistake. I checked it myself. I couldn't believe it either. They're always serious and they never make mistakes, you know that."

Kevin knew it was not a mistake. He suspected the organization had done it before. Kevin shook his head in saddened disbelief as he pushed the photograph of the President of the United States back into the envelope. As he slowly stood up and walked out of the room, a tear rolled down his right cheek.